JAW

## "Perhaps you don't know what love really is, Hope."

"I know what love is, Cotty, because I love *you*," she answered softly. "I've always loved you."

He could not take his eyes from her face, and without really knowing how it happened, he was on the bed and she was cradled in his arms. "I love you, too, Hope."

She raised a radiant face, and he felt that he had never seen anything so beautiful. He kissed her, first gently and then with a passion that he had never before known. Her arms went around him, urging him closer, and he could feel the supple firmness of her body yielding to him.

But that closeness jolted him back to reality. "I love you Hope, but I cannot, I *will not*, marry you."

---

"Patricia Matthews never disappoints her readers. She writes wonderful, sensual stories."

—Romantic Times

---

# Patricia Matthews

## The Dreaming Tree

**W🌐RLDWIDE.**

TORONTO • NEW YORK • LONDON • PARIS
AMSTERDAM • STOCKHOLM • HAMBURG
ATHENS • MILAN • TOKYO • SYDNEY

**THE DREAMING TREE**

A Worldwide Library Book/June 1989

ISBN 0-373-97103-6

This book is dedicated to my editor, Dianne Moggy,
whose excellent editorial skills and unfailing
good nature are much appreciated.

# PART ONE

## *July, 1791*

Come all you wild young native lads
Wherever you may be,
One moment pay attention
And listen to me.
I am a poor unhappy soul,
Within these walls I lay
My awful sentence is pronounced,
I am bound for Botany Bay.

# CHAPTER ONE

IT WAS A SPLENDID HARBOR, there was no gainsaying that. The bay itself was comprised of many small coves in which the water lay sheltered from the violent body of the sea. Rolling hills eased themselves from the shoreline toward the interior of this new frontier.

As the ship slowly approached the rocky headland of Sydney Cove, Faith Blackstock tightened her grip upon the sleeping form of her three-year-old daughter, Charity, whom she cradled in her arms. Hope, her five-year-old, pressed close to her side. The older child was trembling with excitement.

A brisk breeze carried the blessed smells of the land to Faith—earth; growing things; wood smoke. Despite her bone-deep weariness and depression, she felt her spirits lift. Whatever awaited them in New South Wales had to be better than life had been aboard the convict ship. And at least they would have solid ground beneath their feet once more.

Dropping her left hand to touch Hope's fair head, Faith studied the approaching cove, where a reach of what looked to be solid rock extended seaward like a beckoning finger. To the left of the rocky promontory, the mouth of a stream emptied into the bay. Behind the rock, a small cluster of odd-looking huts crouched. They seemed to be constructed of bark, leaves and mud. And behind the huts she could see a number of larger structures made of wood, brick and stone. Gum trees grew down to the water's edge, and Faith could see and hear bright-colored birds—parrots, they appeared to be—flying noisily among their branches.

"Momma?"

A small hand tugged at her skirt, and Faith gazed into the upturned face of her elder daughter. The girl's ash-blond hair, which grew in ringlets around her heart-shaped face, was matted and grimy now, and her pale skin was smudged with dirt. But the child's green eyes peered at Faith unflinchingly, and the woman felt her heart warm. Despite the lack of food and the squalid conditions of the ship, Hope's childish beauty still bloomed like some delicate but courageous flower. Hope had endured eight months of rough seas, inadequate and often spoiled food and miserable sleeping conditions. Scurvy had been prevalent on board; rats ran free in the passenger holds; and fresh water had always been scarce. Bathing had, of necessity, been done with seawater so salty that it burned like fire, and opportunities to wash their ragged clothing had been almost nonexistent. Many had died on the long voyage, and rumor had it that the shipmasters of the Third Fleet were actually pleased when this occurred; for then they could sell the food rations of the deceased to the people of Sydney Town at a nice profit.

While others, including Faith and Charity, had fallen victim to mal de mer and the other myriad and unpleasant illnesses that had raged through the population of the ship, Hope had remained healthy and good-tempered throughout the voyage.

"Momma?" the girl said again. "Is this where we are to live? Will we get to leave the ship now?"

Faith smiled, attempting to convey a confidence that she was far from feeling. "Yes, darling. This will be our new home. I know it will seem strange to you and Charity at first, but you will get used to it. Don't let the strangeness frighten you."

"I won't, Momma," the little girl said stoutly. "I'll be brave, just like you told us when we left home."

Faith moved even closer to Hope and then stood silent, staring at the approaching shoreline through eyes misted with tears. Being brave was not going to be enough, she well realized.

Charity stirred with a whimper, and Faith dipped her head to brush the child's cheek with her lips, crooning to her gently. Charity had been just two years old when they'd sailed from England, and Faith had feared that her younger daughter would not survive the arduous journey. Hope had been a great help, tending her sister when Faith was either too exhausted or sick to do it herself, and not complaining when Faith had given Charity the larger share of their pitiful ration of food.

And Charity had survived. They had all survived. Faith felt the burn of tears again. She loved the girls so; they were all she had. If only she could offer them something better than this; to be driven from their native land, transported to a convict settlement in a strange and far-off country; branded as the daughters of a convicted thief! Just where had this chain of events started? When Luther had abandoned them? Or when she had married Luther Blackstock?

Her father's angry warning echoed sharply in her mind, although it was difficult now for her to remember his face. "Mark my words well, girl! Marry that man and you will live to rue the day. The ones who come from the London slums always keep the stench! He only wants you so that he can better himself. He'll leave you with child, and penniless, and you needn't think you can come running home to me! I've warned you, and you won't listen. Let it then be on your head!"

Faith's mouth twisted in a wry smile. She had never known whether her father had just been a good judge of character, or whether his words had acted as a curse; for what he had predicted had come to pass.

As the daughter of a successful shopkeeper in Bath, Faith had been raised in a certain amount of comfort. Her mother—who had borne six children, only two of whom had survived—died when Faith was fifteen, killed by the pox. Faith had managed the house, for her father had shown no interest in marrying again. Her older brother, with whom she had never been close, had run away to sea. It had been a quiet life, but comfortable.

Marriage to Luther Blackstock had changed everything. Luther had dazzled her with his dark good looks and cozened her with his charm. But before he left her, with one babe in her arms and another in her belly and without two farthings in her pocket, he had admitted that he had counted upon the forgiveness of her father. He had been sure that the old man would come around in time and settle upon his daughter a suitable, if somewhat belated, dowry.

But Luther had incorrectly gauged the depth of her father's stubbornness; and when, after two years of marriage, Faith's father had died of the bloody flux, and it was obvious that neither forgiveness nor money was forthcoming, Luther had taken his leave without so much as a backward glance. He left his pregnant wife and child with no place to turn.

Faith shook her head, as if to shake away the memories of that time. But she knew they, and the shame, would always be with her: the filthy, demeaning work—when she could find it; the begging; and finally, the stealing of food just to stay alive.

She was still filled with a burning anger whenever she thought of the price she had to pay for her family's survival. She had stolen not for greed, not for gain, but to keep her babies alive. A loaf of bread— the price of which was next to nothing—had cost her her freedom. She would never forget the words of the scowling, red-faced magistrate: "I sentence you, Faith Blackstock, to transportation across the seas for fifteen years!"

A loaf of bread! Banishment from their homeland was the price they had paid for one miserable loaf of bread!

She still burned with the shame and anger of those hours spent on the docks waiting to board the convict ship. A group of sassy boys had capered around them, singing, "Thieves, robbers and villains, / We'll send them away, / To make a new people at Botany Bay!"

Charity gave a sharp cry and Faith, realizing that she had unconsciously tightened her grip upon the child, attempted to soothe her. Charity, unlike Faith and Hope, who shared the same fair hair and evenness of feature, was dark like her father. Her features were more like Faith's mother's—pretty, but rather weak and delicate. The child yawned, and Faith shifted her weight to the other arm. Although Charity was small for her age, Faith felt the weight of her and rested her arms against the railing as she turned her glance once more toward the approaching shore.

"Look, Momma!" Hope cried. "Look at the funny men!"

Faith looked in the direction of Hope's pointing finger and saw several men, with fishing lines in their hands, squatting upon the steep rocks around the harbor. They were as dark as the darkest blackamoor and, as far as Faith could ascertain, almost completely naked.

"Cor! Blimey!" exclaimed a red-faced, slatternly woman standing close to Faith along the rail. "I seen some blackamoors in me time, but I ain't never seen nothin' like those buggers! I 'ope they ain't as mean as they looks. I don't relish livin' amongst that lot, I can tell you that!"

The man standing next to her gave a hacking cough. "I've 'eard tell that they killed some of the blokes what came over with the First Fleet," he said in a raspy voice. "But I 'ear that they've mostly settled down now."

"Cor! Will you look at that! Hardly a stitch on 'em. Ain't they no shame?"

The man coughed again. "Well, wot do yer expect? They're bloomin' savages. They don't think like white men, now do they?"

Faith, tugging Hope's hand, moved farther down the railing, away from the pair, pushing the carpetbag that held their few belongings along with her foot. She did not wish to be drawn into the conversation.

Some of the convicts on board were not bad people; those who, like Faith, had been arrested for some small crime. However, most of them were a rough-talking, rowdy lot, and this certainly included the vast majority of the women. They smoked short tobacco pipes, dressed either in blatant finery or filthy, tattered garments, and were profane and quarrelsome. Faith had tried as much as possible to keep herself and her daughters separated from them, without arousing their anger or ill feeling.

She felt Hope tugging again at her skirts. "Look, Momma! There are funny women, too. In the boats."

Faith shifted Charity's weight and raised one hand to shade her eyes. Not too far from the ship were several small, slender boats constructed from tree bark. The small craft appeared to be very flimsy and unsteady, and Faith was surprised to see that they carried women who were as naked and black as the men fishing on the rocks. From what she could see, these people looked nothing like any blackamoor she had ever seen.

The women, too, seemed to be fishing, and Faith could see smoke rising from the small boats, floating in thin streamers over the heads of the passengers.

"Are their boats on fire, Momma?" Hope asked excitedly.

Faith shook her head. "I don't know, dear. I don't think so. Perhaps they are cooking the fish in the boat, as they catch them."

Hope grew still and quiet, pressing close against Faith's legs as the ship slowly passed near one of the canoes.

"That one has a funny face, Momma!" she cried, not able to contain her surprise any longer.

"Hush! She might hear you."

But the child was right, Faith thought. The woman's face was indeed different, with a protruding brow over deep-set eyes, and a heavy mouth and jaw. Her hair was wiry and black, and surrounded her head like a huge black hat. She was small of stature, with a rounded belly and thin, muscular legs. She seemed to be a young woman; her breasts were small and still high and proud. As the great ship moved past, the woman in the canoe stood and looked directly at Faith, the darkness of her face splitting in a wide, white and very charming smile. Faith, startled, smiled back. It was, she realized, the first really friendly gesture anyone had made to her since she had boarded the ship back in England.

The ship had drawn quite close to the shore now, and Faith could hear the sound of the anchor chain being dropped. There must be a sharp drop-off, she thought, for them to be able to anchor so close to shore. Charity was wide-awake, and squirming, so Faith set the child down upon the deck, holding her firmly by the hand.

A great bustle on deck began as boats were lowered and the British marines, who had been sent along to guard the convicts, started forming lines and began herding the new settlers toward the Jacob's ladder. Although it was winter in New South Wales, the weather was warm, and the soldiers looked hot in their thick, red jackets and white breeches.

Since Faith and her daughters were already at the rail, not far from the ladder, they were put on the second boat sent ashore. Charity, frightened by the steep descent down the ladder, was whining and crying, but Hope was wide-eyed with wonder and curiosity.

As the longboat was rowed toward the western shore of the cove, Faith glanced to her right, to the long finger of land jutting out into the harbor. Now she could see that there was a small structure perched upon it, like a gull on a whale's back. Built of brick, it was very small, no larger than a hut, and stood alone, the only building on the promontory. I wonder who lives there, she thought, as she pointed the little building out to Hope.

Then the boat nosed into the wharf, and they began the process of disembarking. After so many months at sea, Faith stumbled and swayed when she set her feet on solid ground; and yet standing on the earth felt good. She longed to bend down and touch it with her fingers, but the soldiers were pressing them forward toward a group of people in rough clothing who immediately surrounded them.

Voices battered them from every direction.

"Did you bring provisions? We're near starving here!"

"We be down to eating roots and bark and what fish we can catch."

"The cattle and sheep all be lost, or struck by lightning."

"Ants and field mice ate the seed grain almost as soon as we planted it!"

"Our stored provisions be ate by rats! And the storeship, *Guardian*, struck an iceberg off Cape Town and sank!"

Attacked by this barrage of complaints, the officer in charge stopped the band of convicts and at-

tempted to calm the settlers. Faith, with Charity back
in her arms and Hope clinging to her skirts, could
feel the fear and anger emanating from the crowd,
and her spirits sank even lower. Were they to starve
*here* instead of in London?

"Wait!" the officer shouted. "Listen to me, good
people. We have brought provisions. There is food
for you. As soon as we have unloaded the convicts,
we shall bring it ashore."

As his words finally penetrated the anxious crowd,
the clamor died down, and most of the demonstra-
tors dispersed. A few remained, clearly curious about
the new arrivals.

# CHAPTER TWO

HOPE, WHO WITH THE DISPERSAL of the crowd had released her mother's hand, stared at a lad of about twelve who had lingered behind. Thin and wiry, with inquisitive blue eyes and brown hair braided into a pigtail, he darted in and out among the new arrivals, asking a question here and there, then darting on.

Faith had found an empty crate to sit upon and now had Charity cradled in her lap. The carpetbag with their belongings rested at her feet. All her attention was directed to Charity, and Hope experienced a brief flash of resentment. During their time on the ship, Charity had received most of their mother's attention and more than her share of their scanty food ration. Usually, Hope had not given this a second thought. She knew that Charity was still a baby and that she was not strong; yet sometimes when Charity was whiny and fretful, or when her mother devoted too much time to her, Hope could not help but feel a brief flare of something hot and cross, something she could not put a name to.

Then, seeing how pale and drawn her mother looked, Hope felt guilty. She must be her mother's good little helper, because she was strong. Although she was only five, she knew this, for people had often told her so. But even as she thought that she must help her mother, her eyes were busy, taking in the scene around her.

A curious child by nature, born with boundless energy, Hope found anything new fascinating. True, the voyage had been tedious and long, yet she had always found something new to snag her attention. And now, here she was in a brand-new country with so many things to see that she hardly knew what to do first.

She noticed that all the male convicts were being herded off to one side, into a rough semicircle, surrounded by soldiers, their muskets at the ready. A soldier was going from one convict to another, pinning a number on the back of each.

Soon, the urge to explore overcame Hope's awareness that she should stay close to her mother. Seeing that Faith's attention was still devoted to the squirming Charity, Hope began moving among the people in the wharf area. She had never seen buildings that resembled the funny huts, and she could not resist peeking into several. They smelled something awful, and most were so dark that she could see very little inside; but they all seemed to be empty, so no one challenged her.

Growing braver, she stepped all the way inside one hut, her small nose crinkling at the odor. Her eyes were just becoming accustomed to the gloom when, without warning, what she had thought to be a bundle of rags in one corner stirred, and an unkempt head reared up. Angry eyes glared at her.

"Here now," a rough voice growled. "Can't a bloke catch a little rest without being bothered? Who are you, girl, and what are you doin' in my hut?"

Hope froze in fright.

The wild-haired apparition rose higher. "Now away with you!" He bared broken teeth like fangs. "Off with you, or I'll eat you for my supper."

Hope wheeled and fled. Outside, head down, running hard, she plowed head-on into a hard body and careened off, loosing her balance. She would have fallen had not hands caught her under the arms and held her upright. She looked up into bright blue eyes.

"Better watch where you're goin', girl." The lad, for a lad it was, began to grin. "Why, you're just a baby!"

Hope, embarrassed and angry, glared at him. "I am not! I'm five!"

"Five, is it?" He made a mocking bow. "Pardon my ignorance, milady."

It was the boy with the braid she had seen earlier. From Hope's perspective he seemed very tall, a grown man, yet she knew that he was not.

"I'm Cotty Starke by name," the boy said. "Did you come by the prison ships?"

Still embarrassed, but somewhat mollified by the boy's manner, Hope grew suddenly shy and hung her head.

Cotty squatted in front of her and lifted her chin with one thin, slightly dirty finger. "Come now. You needn't be afeard."

Slowly, Hope raised her eyes. He had a nice face, she decided. Still feeling unable to talk, she nodded, hoping that would be sufficient.

"Ah! So I figure. Convict, or settler?"

Hope was not quite certain what a convict was, but she did know that there was shame attached to it; and that her mother bore that shame. She hung her head again, and again he raised it.

"It's nothing to be shamed by, girl. Most of the people here came the same way. What's your name?"

His blue eyes were kind now, and Hope finally found her voice. "Hope."

"And do you have a family name?"

"Blackstock," she whispered.

"Well, Hope Blackstock, me own dad was a convict. We was among the first ones here, with the First Fleet. You should have seen the place then. Nothing here at all except the natives. It was hard scrabble, believe me. My dad's dead now. Died last year, leavin' me on my own."

Her interest captured and her shyness abating, Hope asked, "Where's your momma?"

"Me mum died back in London, afore we shipped out." A dark shadow seemed to slip over his face. Then he smiled again, taking her hand. "Mayhap we best be findin' *your* mum."

As Cotty led her back to the group of convicts, Hope caught sight of her mother, Charity still in her arms, looking around frantically. She was being restrained by one of the soldiers. Hope knew that it was because she had run off, and her feeling of excitement changed quickly to guilt. She loved her mother dearly and hated to see her hurt.

Quickly releasing Cotty's hand, she ran toward her mother. "Here I am, Momma!"

Faith looked relieved, then angry. "Where have you been, child! I thought something had happened to you! You stay close to me from now on, you hear?"

Hope buried her face in her mother's skirts, nodding mutely. She heard Cotty's voice: "She didn't come to any harm, mistress. She did get a little fright, nosin' into one of the convict huts." He laughed lightly. " 'Twas old Ben Cort's hut. One look at him is enough to frighten anyone. Old Ben is abed today with some ailment."

Faith looked the boy over intently. He seemed to be a likely enough lad, intelligent, by the look of him, and older than his years; but the London streets had taught her to be wary of boys, for they meant trouble more often than not.

"Who are you, boy?"

"Cotty Starke, Mistress Blackstock."

Faith drew Hope closer against her. "How did you know my name?"

"Your daughter here. She told me."

"Did you come with the Third Fleet?"

"No, mistress. My dad and me, we come with the First Fleet."

"Is it..." Faith hesitated, glancing around. "Is the life hard here? For the convicts, I mean?"

"Life is hard here, mistress, for convicts and free men alike. Food has been in short supply. Promises have been made for provisions from England, promises not kept. What ships were sent never arrived. People have starved to death, and many have died of the pox."

Faith eyed him doubtfully. "You appear to be healthy enough, young Cotty."

Cotty grinned, unabashed. "I've learned how to fend for myself. It takes a ferret's quickness, quick and sly enough to frisk the cly and fork the rag!"

Faith recoiled. "You're a pickpocket then!"

"Not so, Mistress Blackstock," he said, still grinning. "There are no pockets in Sydney Town fat enough to pick. But there are other ways, if a man is sharp enough."

"You call yourself a man then?"

Cotty stood a little taller. "In New South Wales, especially here on the Rocks, you become a man quick like."

"I suppose," Faith said, gazing off. "And I have no room to scorn you by calling you a thief. I'm a thief as well. That is why I am here."

"And so are most of us. Thieves or worse."

Faith was gazing across the narrow inlet to the eastern side. "Why is that brick building standing all by itself over there on the other side of the cove?"

"That's Bennelong's hut."

Faith frowned. "Who is Bennelong?"

Cotty looked toward the wharf, where another longboat was being loaded. "Well, it's not a short story by any means, mistress, but it appears they're still unloadin', so I reckon we have the time. Why don't you take a seat again? That wee one must be growin' heavy."

Faith seated herself again upon the crate, and Charity at once began to squirm. "Want down!" she said firmly, as her face began to pucker.

"Now, now," Cotty said, squatting and putting his face close to the child's. "Now, a pretty little lass like you don't want to make her face all ugly with cryin'. Just you listen now, and Cotty will tell you a story."

Charity stared at Cotty in fascination, forgetting to cry, and Hope pressed close, looking at Cotty with admiration. Faith heaved a sigh of relief. She was very tired and she had no idea what the rest of the day might bring. Anything that could give them a brief respite from fatigue and worry was more than welcome, and it seemed clear that young Cotty Starke had a way with small children.

"Tell us the story, Cotty," Hope said eagerly.

He smiled. "All right. It goes like this, you see. Bennelong is a black fella, one of the natives of this land. Governor Phillip tried to make friendly contact with these natives, but it didn't work out too well, so he finally ordered some captured. Two of them as was captured was Bennelong and Colbee, a native chief.

"They was locked up, with leg irons roped on, but this Colbee, he gnawed through the ropes and made good his escape. But Bennelong, who's a cheerful, smart fella, didn't try to escape. He wanted to stay and learn our ways. The governor became his friend, and Bennelong even ate at his table. 'Tis said he dearly loves food." Cotty grinned. "'Tis said he can eat enough for six men at one meal."

Faith looked down and saw that Hope's eyes were wide in wonder, and Charity was staring at Cotty, seemingly fascinated also.

"Now when food became scarce, people began to complain about Bennelong's eatin' so much, and Bennelong went away to Manly. Later, when Governor Phillip was speared by an unfriendly black fella, Bennelong came back to see how the governor was farin', and this time he stayed. The governor ordered that the brick hut over there be built for Bennelong and for his friends when they come to visit."

"But why build it over there, all by itself?" Faith asked.

Cotty rubbed his chin. "Well, you see, Bennelong is a black fella. White folks hereabouts don't much favor havin' them around underfoot . . ."

"Hey, now! On your feet. Move lively there!"

Faith glanced up to see soldiers moving through the crowd of convicts, which had now grown to considerable size.

"It looks as if all are ashore now," Cotty remarked. "The soldiers will be takin' your names, and assignin' you to your master. If you want, I'll take the wee one for you."

Carefully, Faith handed the squirming Charity to the boy and got to her feet. Now not only was she very weary, she also felt a bit faint. It had been some time since they had eaten, and apprehension had set her heart to hammering. What kind of a master would she get? But it would do no good to fret about it, for it was something over which she had no control. She pulled Hope close against her and put her hands upon the girl's shoulder.

"Do you have a good master, young Cotty?"

Cotty, bouncing the whimpering Charity in his thin arms, shook his head. "I have no master, Mistress Blackstock. I'm free. As free as anyone in this place can be."

Faith glanced at the soldiers, who were still some distance away. "You seem knowledgeable about the life here. Can you tell me something about what I can expect? For instance, do the convicts dwell with their masters?"

Cotty hesitated. "Not usually. Especially since there are three of you, I would think not. Most of the settlers live in small houses, some not much more than huts, with room only for themselves and their families.''

''But where shall we live then?'' Faith asked in dismay.

''Well, since many of the convicts have died of late, mayhap you can find an empty hut, although since I count a goodly number of new arrivals with this fleet—mostly men, I notice—they may grab all the empty ones first. Should that happen, you will need to build one for yourself.''

Faith felt as if she might collapse. Were they to have no place to live then? No roof to shelter them? It was simply too much!

''Build a hut? How can a lone woman and two babes build a hut? I know nothing of building.''

Cotty gave her a reassuring smile. ''It's not all that hard, mistress, and I will be most happy to help. Simple dwellin's they are, made of cabbage-palm logs and the joints plugged with clay and wattle, then whitened with pipe clay found along the Tank Stream at the head of the cove. The roofs are thatched with blackboy leaves or harbor rushes.''

Faith studied him closely. ''I would very much appreciate your help, Cotty. But tell me . . . why are you being so kind to utter strangers?''

Her question caught Cotty off guard. Why was he putting himself out this way? He had learned early on that, to survive in the Rocks, a man had to always think of himself first, and he readily admitted he had no one he could call a close friend. Could it be that he was lonely?

''You are much different from most women convicts, Mistress Blackstock,'' he said in reply. ''Most are a rough lot.'' He glanced down at Hope. ''And I guess I miss having a family, my own havin' passed on.''

''Poor lad.'' Faith touched his cheek gently. ''How old are you?''

''Twelve, mistress.''

Hope had been listening to her mother and the boy talk without understanding a great deal, but she knew she liked Cotty Starke. He seemed very much grown up. Hope had always wondered what it would be like to have a brother, especially an older one, a brother to protect her, to advise her. However, she somehow knew that what she felt toward Cotty was somewhat different from what she might feel toward a brother.

Without thinking, she reached out, her hand stealing into his.

Cotty glanced down in surprise, scowling. And then his face cleared as he smiled and closed his hand around Hope's much smaller one.

At that moment an officer approached them, making his way through the crowd of marines and convicts. Stopping in front of Faith, he looked down at a piece of paper in his hand. ''Name?'' he said brusquely, not even looking at her.

''Faith Blackstock,'' answered Faith, shooting a sideways glance at Cotty, who smiled at her reassuringly.

''You are to be assigned to Master Simon Marsh.'' The officer glanced up, still avoiding Faith's eyes. ''Come with me.''

Her heart again pounding, Faith took Hope's hand, and with Cotty carrying Charity, they followed the officer's broad, unfriendly back to the outskirts of the crowd to where a tall, stooped, dour-faced man was waiting.

"Master Simon Marsh. This woman is Faith Blackstock. She has been assigned to you to serve out her term of fifteen years."

The man looked Faith over disapprovingly and then ran his eye coldly over the children. "Does this lot belong to her?"

"The two girl children only," the officer said.

"She don't look too strong to me," Marsh said in a surly voice. "And the bairns will be a drain on her. They be too young! I pray to the good Lord that she don't die on me like the last."

"If she does, you can always get another from the next fleet," the officer said coldly. He turned to Faith and began to recite by rote, "You, Mistress Blackstock, are now bound over to Master Simon Marsh. I place you in his charge. I command you to work diligently in his service, and obey his orders in all matters. Disobedience and sloth are subject to severe penalties." Without further word, the officer turned smartly on his heel and marched away.

Faith viewed Simon Marsh warily. He was certainly not a young man, and time had inscribed his character on his face. The sight was far from reassuring. The coldness of his narrow, dark eyes and the bitter twist of his mouth told Faith that he would not be a generous or kind master. She had hoped for someone possessing a softer disposition.

"Well, don't just stand there agapin'," he said in his rusty, rather high voice. "Come along! The Lord does not approve of idlers!"

Without waiting for a response, he turned on his heel, apparently assuming that she would follow without question.

With a weary sigh, Faith reached out to take Charity, but Cotty shook his head. "I'll walk along with you to keep you company."

Faith managed a weak smile, grateful beyond words for the lad's kindness and his cheerful ways. She realized that if they were to stay alive in this foreign land they would need help, and this boy, for all his tender years, appeared to be the only ally they might find.

Although fatigue made her feel as if her limbs were wooden, Faith picked up her carpetbag and followed in the footsteps of her new master. She led Hope by the hand, and Cotty walked by her side, carrying Charity.

Fortunately, Simon Marsh's legs seemed to be as painful and weary as her own. He walked with a stiff, halting gait, and at a moderate pace, for which she was deeply grateful. As the group made their way along the rough street, Faith glanced from side to side, and her dismay deepened. The huts were ill-kempt and sorely in need of repair. The people they met evinced no curiosity concerning them and looked half starved and poorly clothed.

Seeing the direction of her gaze, Cotty said, "This here is Rock's Row. Most of the convicts live here."

Faith shook her head mutely, and looking back at the lad, saw his face register sympathy.

As if to distract her, he said, "You appear to be a lady of some learnin', mistress."

They had turned off Rock's Row and were now following a steep and narrow path. Faith had to catch her breath before she could answer. "I was raised the daughter of a merchant in Bath. He was an educated man in his way, and although he was a hard man, he was kind to me when I was a child and let me follow my fancy, which was bookish."

"Then you can read and write?"

Faith shifted the carpetbag to her other hand. "Yes, although much good it did me after I married."

"Will you be teaching your girls then? To read and write, that is?"

"I expect so. They must be taught, and I would seem to be the only one to do it."

Breathing heavily now, Faith hoped their trek would soon end. On a rise farther to the north she could see some finer buildings, and high on a hill, a windmill was turning slowly in the wind; but she suspected that convicts were seldom allowed in that area. That was surely where the officers and the more affluent settlers resided.

She realized that Cotty had resumed talking. She glanced over at him and saw that his gaze was fixed on his feet.

"I have no learnin'. I would much like to learn to read and write and cipher. I figure that a man's *got* to have some learnin', if he wants to make his way in the world. When you teach your girls, would you teach me, too? I would be most grateful, and I would be more than willin' to return your kindness in what ways I can." He added sourly, "Those here in the Rocks have no use for learnin', and those of quality, up on the hill, have no use for such as me."

Marsh seemed to be slowing down now, and Faith attempted to see past him, to get a glimpse of their destination.

"I would be more than happy to teach you what I can, young Cotty, but I have scarce few books." She raised the carpetbag to illustrate her point.

"There are books I can get," he said excitedly.

Faith, despite her fatigue and worry, found herself touched. "You help us find a place to live, and I will gladly include you when I tutor Hope and Charity. A bargain, young Cotty?"

Cotty grinned widely. "A bargain, mistress."

"Now as to this Simon Marsh..." Faith shot a glance at the man limping ahead of them, lowering her voice. "What is your estimate of the kind of master he will be?"

Cotty hesitated. "No worse than any other, I should think. One thing..." He leaned close to whisper in her ear. "You won't have to be worryin' about... about sharin' his bed."

Faith gave him a startled look. "Now why should I need to worry about that?"

"Like I said, with him you won't. But women out here are scarce, mistress. Most of the convict women become the mistresses of their masters right off."

"I had to fight off advances on the ship, but most of the men kept their distance because of the little ones. But I thought I would be safe once off the ship."

"With Master Marsh you will be." Cotty was clearly uncomfortable with the subject. "He is a strict man of God, doesn't believe in breakin' the commandments. *That* particular commandment, at any rate. By profession, Master Marsh is a weaver, although wool is in short supply in New South Wales. Most of it comes by ship from London. Most of the sheep brought over with the First Fleet have died.''

"Then why does he need my services?''

"I expect he has been promised wool from England. Mayhap a shipment came with this fleet. After all, what will you cost him? You'll likely be paid no wages, only supplied with food and clothing, and that is provided by the government to the masters you are assigned to.''

"No wages at all?'' she said in dismay.

He shook his head. "It's up to the masters whether to pay or not. Besides, there's very little money to be had.'' He smiled. "Rum is generally what we use for tradin' here in Sydney Town. Only those who are in the employ of His Majesty's Government have any real money to spend.''

Simon Marsh's steps had grown slower still, and Faith looked up to see a signpost on the street. Huge letters had been burned into the wood: China Does Not Lay Beyond The Blue Mountains.

"Cotty, what does that mean?'' Faith said, nodding toward the sign.

He laughed shortly. "It's in the nature of a warnin', Mistress Blackstock, put in a jokin' way. It's meant for the convicts. Many think they can escape if they get beyond the Blue Mountains to the west. They believe that China lies just beyond.''

Faith stopped for a moment to catch her breath, staring at the sign. "Do many escape?''

Cotty shook his head. "Though many have tried and keep tryin'. Most of them starve to death, or are killed by the natives in the bush.''

Faith could not take her gaze from the sign. "But *some* escape?"

"Aye. Yes, a rare one now and then. One such was a friend of my pa's. A good man, Peter Myers by name. Not long after we landed here, he took to the bush. Later explorin' parties brought back tales of a white man livin' with the blacks, just like one of them. They couldn't get close enough to see him good, but some said he was Peter Myers. How much truth there is to the tale I know not."

Faith jumped when she heard Simon Marsh's raspy voice: "Are ye goin' to stand there like a gowp all day? Move yer limbs, woman! The shop is just ahead."

# CHAPTER THREE

*EXCERPTS FROM THE JOURNAL OF
PETER MYERS*

*May, 1787*

I BEGIN THIS JOURNAL upon the bitterest day of my
life. At this moment, it is impossible for me to believe that anything of a positive nature will ever be
transcribed upon these pages. I write this solely in the
hope that by so doing I may protect my sanity during the weeks and months to come and, that if I do
survive, my family will have some record of what has
befallen me.

I am sitting in the belly of a ship bound for the
penal colony at New South Wales, to which place I
am being transported for life. My crime: the crime
of owing a debt I could not pay, to an utterly ruthless man. For this heinous crime I have been torn
from my home and loved ones and banished to a land
so new that little or nothing is known of it. Eleven
ships comprise our shameful armada, and they say
there are over one thousand souls aboard these ships:
men, women and a number of children and babies.
There are also horses, cattle, sheep, goats, pigs,
chickens, rabbits and ducks. It would seem that we
have all the things required to build an English settlement on that far-off primitive shore toward which
we are relentlessly heading.

Of these thousand or more souls, some three hundred are officers, crew, and the soldiers of good King George who have been sent to keep us under control. There are also a few freemen who are going voluntarily to settle this new land. The remainder are convicts: prisoners of His Majesty, King George III of England, 548 male and 188 female, some accompanied by their unfortunate children.

The convicts are, for the most part, an unsavory lot: thieves mostly; pickpockets and highwaymen, sheep stealers, shoplifters and burglars. Strangely enough, although there are few of them in relation to the number of men, many of the worst behaved, the most raucous and violent are the women; most of whom are whores and petty thieves. I am pleased to say that they are kept separate from the male convicts although, I gather from hearsay, not from the sailors or the soldiers, who freely avail themselves of the women's favors.

Thrown in among these hardened criminals there are a few like myself, more unfortunate than criminal. There is one old woman, Elizabeth Beckford, aged seventy, whom they say was transported for seven years for stealing twelve pounds of cheese; and another, a middle-aged man, whose crime was the poaching of a rabbit so that his hungry children might be fed. It is this that drives me to deep despair; that we live in times such as these, when our society punishes so cruelly a transgression that any decent, God-fearing man or woman would forgive. It is a terrible world that we live in, and I have almost lost my will to stay part of it.

*July, 1787*

We have now been over thirty days at sea, and I am beginning to have some idea of how I shall fare on this voyage. Examining myself and the situation with as much logic as my despair will permit, I am forced to grant that my chances of survival are only fair. Physically, I am in considerable discomfort. I am ill-equipped to deal with the sort of men I am forced to live with daily; for, like ill-natured children, they are quick to bully and pick upon anyone whom they consider different from themselves. I also find it very difficult to resign myself to my condition.

The worst feature by far is the lack of bathing facilities. Saltwater only can be used, and that on rare occasions. Alas, few of the convicts deplore this situation and, as a result, the foul stench belowdecks is beyond belief! What a blessed relief it is when we are allowed on deck, so we may breathe fresh salt air. Yet the stench never completely leaves, and I do believe that I shall carry it always, like the memory of a bad dream.

The redcoats, our keepers on this voyage, are on the whole not a bad lot, but there are a few who, in their boredom, enjoy abusing us. One in particular, a hulking brute named Wilburne, seems to have taken a particular dislike to me because I am an educated man. He makes life difficult for me at every opportunity. My one advantage is my mind. I have vowed to attempt to keep myself as unnoticeable as possible, for I believe this to be the best way to survive.

Still, in this journal, I have also vowed to be as honest as possible in my recording, and so I must also note that conditions aboard ship are not nearly as bad as they might be. Some care has been taken that we should arrive in New South Wales alive. Before leaving London we were given uniform clothing, of a coarse make, and allowed also to bring what we wished of our own. Much of the clothing for the female convicts was not finished before we sailed, and the women complain of this often.

In fairness, also, I must admit that our rations have been, considering the circumstances, adequate. Our daily fare includes, bread, salt pork, salt beef, peas, oatmeal, butter, cheese and vinegar. Whenever we reach a port, fresh meat and vegetables are obtained, if available. The sick are given special compensations. Many of the convicts who were starving at home think themselves well off. I understand that we owe this to Captain Arthur Phillip, who is in command of the First Fleet, and who is said to be a conscientious and humane man. I have seen him on board our ship, for he makes it a practice to check on the ships regularly during the voyage. He is a man of mature years, nearing fifty summers, I should guess, and not particularly prepossessing to look upon. He has a small, narrow face, a thin, aquiline nose, full lips and a sharp, powerful voice. Yet his men seem to respect and admire him.

It is a rough, cruel life. I miss my wife, my own dear Elizabeth, and my children, James and Kate, who have been left fatherless. It is a bitter thing that they will grow into manhood and womanhood without really knowing their own father. The only consolation I have is that Elizabeth's parents have taken in my family, and can be counted upon to care for them. My heart aches for the innocent children, who, by force of necessity, have had to come on this voyage, sharing their parents' punishment.

There is one man on board, a certain Henry Starke, who has with him his son, a boy of eight, called Cotty. The lad is quick and clever, and if he were to have some schooling, could no doubt make something of himself. As it is, he learns much from the convicts, but that is mostly of a criminal nature. His father is not a bad man, although he admits to having existed by means not entirely legal. We have become friends of sorts. He has a good mind, though untutored, and being clever in the ways of the streets, he knows how to deal with the other convicts on an equal basis, a talent which I do not possess. He looks after me in this respect, and I, in turn, attempt to teach young Cotty something of the larger world, for the lad knows little of what exists beyond the streets of London and the narrow confines of this ship. Cotty appears to take to me and, truthfully, I enjoy his company. I wonder what will become of him when we reach the new land?

*January, 1788*

I have much to record, for the past few days have been so full that I have had no opportunity to turn to my journal.

Our long voyage is finally over! After eight long months, we have arrived in New South Wales, most of us ragged and thin, but alive. Many of the female convicts arrived in a state nearing nakedness, for the few garments they had been issued were so poorly constructed that they have fallen apart. Since needles and thread were not supplied, this situation was impossible to rectify.

A week ago Friday, on January 18, as we crowded the railings to obtain a glimpse of this huge, complex harbor and our final destination, Botany Bay, murmurs could be heard amongst the officers and crew. We had heard speak of grassy meadows and fertile land, but all that met our gaze was barren and sandy. The rise in spirits which had filled us at the sight of land faded, and there was considerable confusion while the flagship, *Sirius*, carrying Captain Phillip, moved a few miles up the coast, in search of a better place to land.

The place he found, according to one of the officers, was originally called Port Jackson, so named by Captain Cook. The port was renamed Sydney Harbor by Captain Phillip in honor of Lord Sydney, after we finally disembarked on January 26. It is a fine harbor, much more inviting than Botany Bay, but the land is primitive in the extreme.

Coming in, we sailed past crumbling sandstone cliffs. Nearer to shore, the sandstone ledges dip down to the water, separating into numerous small inlets, all heavily wooded. One fact struck me as strange: the woods had the appearance of well-tended deer parks. The trees stand wide apart, with little or no underbrush. Later, I learned the reason for this. Periodically, the local natives burn off the underbrush, thus making it easier to hunt for game amid the trees.

Establishing camp that first day was a laborious and grueling task. When a sufficient number of tents had been pitched, the male convicts and the soldiers began going ashore. Twelve days later, the women followed. Although the women had been segregated

from the male convicts while on board ship, the seg-
regation ended once the women were ashore. Licen-
tiousness was the inevitable result, and the soldiers
were unable to control the debauchery and rioting,
during which Henry, Cotty and myself took to our
tent and fastened the flap as best we could.

Upon the next morning, February 7, all was again
calm, and Captain Phillip took formal possession of
the new colony. Captain David Collins, the judge
advocate, read the proclamation appointing Phillip
as captain general and governor-in-chief of New
South Wales. Afterward, Governor Phillip gave a
short speech, well spoke and to the point, promising
us justice, but warning that if we did not work, we
would not eat and, in view of the bacchanal of the
night before, advising us "to consider seriously the
holy state of matrimony."

After the ceremony, Governor Phillip invited his
officers to join him in a cold collation served in his
canvas house, which he had brought out with him
from England. We convicts and the soldiers made do
with simpler fare.

One of the things that has excited us most, officer, soldier and convict alike, is the aborigines, natives of this land, whom some call Indians. They are
very dark of color, and both men and women wear
no clothing, save for a small fillet bound round their
heads and a narrow band worn around the waists of
the men. Some of them have painted their faces and
bodies with a native whitewash made from clay, and
they present a most startling appearance. By and
large they seem to be fairly pleasant in aspect, being
lively and well-made, with eyes of an odd reddish
hazel fringed by very black lashes. Their noses are

extremely flat and wide, with nostrils often distended by the insertion of pieces of white bone.

One incident I was witness to might be considered shocking or amusing; I find that my sense of humor has roughened considerably during the voyage. When these Indian men first saw our women, their reaction was plain for all to see, and occasioned much merriment among the rougher of the convicts, of both sexes. It is difficult to know how they perceive us, although it would seem that our first meeting has gone off well enough.

Although I did not observe it myself, I am told that one of the natives put his shield into the sand, as a target, and was very surprised when a shot from an officer's pistol perforated its bark surface. It would seem that they are intelligent, for they quickly understood the power of our weapons.

Upon another evening it is said that while Captain Phillip and other officers were eating their dinners upon the beach, a group of natives approached them. Captain Phillip put his hands above his head, in a gesture of friendship, but the natives were evidently in a troublesome mood. At this point Captain Phillip drew a circle around the place where his officers were sitting, and without much difficulty made the natives understand that they were not to pass that line, which they did not. Some say that Captain Phillip owes at least a part of his influence with the natives to the fact that he is missing a front tooth, as are many of the natives. It would seem to be some mark of prestige with them.

The only really unpleasant thing about the Indians is that they rarely bathe, and their odor is abominable. This is a fact upon which all agree. It would appear to be due, at least partially, to their custom of rubbing animal fat upon their bodies, to which all manner of filth clings. In their hair, which is woolly, hang small bones and teeth; anything, in fact, that seems to catch their fancy.

Another source of amazement is the animal life here, particularly a rather large animal referred to by Captain Cook's glossary as a "kangaroo." This animal is unusual in the extreme to English eyes, looking for all the world like a huge hare, near as tall as a small man, standing upright on huge, harelike hind legs, and balancing upon a very stout and muscular tail. The forearms are very small, and appear to be nearly useless. These animals are herbivorous and appear to have no more intelligence than sheep or cows. They are marsupial, like opossums, and carry their young in pouches on their abdomens.

We, the convicts, have been set to work clearing the ground, which is very rocky. The trees, which we call "gums" because of the resinous secretions of their trunks, have trunks like iron, and there is a scarcity of adequate tools. The work is hard, and after months at sea, we are awkward.

Unfortunately, I have been assigned to a work squad under the supervision of my nemesis, the redcoat, Wilburne. Coming ashore has in no way sweetened his nature, or lessened his dislike of me, and his harassment, on top of all else that we must endure, arouses emotions in me I had thought myself too much of a gentleman to experience.

Oh, my gentle Elizabeth, it is good that you cannot see the man I am becoming; for I am indelibly marked and changed by all that I have experienced, and I can only wonder what kind of a man I shall eventually become!

# CHAPTER FOUR

IN THE YEARS TO COME, Faith would have many reasons to be grateful to Cotty Starke, but never would her gratitude be stronger than on that first night in New South Wales.

It had begun to rain just before Cotty left them at the shop of Simon Marsh, after promising to return to them before dark. Without his help, Faith and her girls would have had to spend a cold, wet and hungry night.

The shop owned by Simon Marsh was small, a two-room wattle hut. It was none too clean and smelled of damp wool. The back room was given over to the weaving shuttles, and the front room was used for customers to view the few bolts of fabric he had for sale.

The floor was packed earth, and the roof was thatched. Faith shuddered as she heard small animals scurrying around in the dry fronds overhead.

Hope, clinging to Faith's skirt, said nothing, but Charity began to cry. "Don't like it here, Momma! Hungry, Momma!"

Faith, acutely aware of Simon Marsh's gaze on her, attempted to quiet the girl, but Marsh studiously ignored Charity's cries.

"This be the shop," he said, gesturing to the narrow confines of the room. "Back in England, I was a stockin' weaver by trade. I emigrated, hopin' to better myself in a new land." He pulled a sour face. "A great lot of good it did me. Most of the sheep we brought with us are dead, and wool has been hard to come by. But your fleet has brought me wool from London, so now I shall be able to produce more goods. And that is why you are assigned to me, Mistress Blackstock."

He smiled meagerly. "You will not find me a hard taskmaster, woman. So long as you are diligent and provide me with a fair day's work, we shall get along quite well." His expression turned forbidding. "I shall expect you at the shuttle by sunrise on the morrow!"

Faith felt her heart sink. She had expected at least a day would be allowed for her to settle herself, and he had not mentioned anything about living quarters. "But I must find shelter for myself and my daughters. Do you provide such?"

Marsh shook his head. "That be your problem, woman, not mine. From me you will get food and clothin'."

"But I've been told that the government provides the food and clothing."

His gaze sharpened. "Been told that, have ye? 'Tis true, I admit, but I do not get paid for such until you actually start to work."

Faith reached out for Hope's hand. "And what shall I do with my daughters while I am working?"

"That is also your problem. Just see to it that they do not interfere with your labors." He frowned at Hope. "The older one there, mayhap she can be of some use helping you at the shuttle."

"But she is only five!"

"Soon to be six, Momma." Hope drew herself up in indignation.

Faith felt her eyes sting with tears. Hope was a daughter to be proud of, but Faith could foresee that the girl was going to have to grow up before her time. It was likely that she would never get to experience a proper childhood. Faith squeezed Charity tighter in her arms, and kissed the top of her head. Then and there she determined that she would protect little Charity from the same fate, if it was at all possible.

"This is no place for tykes," Simon Marsh said in a grumbling voice. "You should have left them behind in England."

"They are my children!" Faith cried. "I love them. Without them I would have nothing to live for."

"You should have thought of that, woman, before you committed the crime that brought you here."

Her head went back. "My crime, sir, was stealing bread to put in the mouths of my children."

"Stealin' is stealin'," he said. "We deal harshly with thievery here as well. You be caught stealin', woman, and it will be a floggin' for you." He turned away with a gesture of dismissal. "And be here at sunrise in the morn or face the prospect of a floggin' for that as well. Now, you had best get busy and see if you can find shelter for yourself before the huts are all taken."

Faith, near tears, straightened her body. "What about food? You said you would feed us."

Marsh shook his head. "And on the morrow, I will, when I receive my supplies from the ship. You may as well know that food is in short supply here. You needn't expect too much."

Faith sighed. "I heard people talking when we came ashore, but haven't you *something* for us? A bit of bread for the girls?"

Stiffening, Marsh shook his head again. "Go to the soldiers. That's all I can suggest."

Shoulders drooping, Faith motioned Hope to her side and went out into the rain. As she stepped out of the building, she saw Cotty Starke approaching, a smile upon his face. She was surprised at the relief she experienced at his appearance. Was she reduced to dependence on a mere lad of twelve?

His smile widened as he stopped before her. "I have glad tidings, Mistress Blackstock! I was fortunate enough to find an empty convict hut, and claimed it for you. It needs some work, a new thatched roof and some daubing between the palm logs, but it will have to do for tonight. I shall get busy on the morrow, and make it more livable."

Relief made Faith giddy. "You're a fine lad, Cotty. I was standing here worrying about what I was going to do for shelter tonight, and here you are. But don't you have affairs of your own to tend to?"

"Nothing that won't keep," he said with a shrug. "Here, mistress, give me your carpetbag and the wee one, and I'll take you to your hut. And put this over you, Hope. It will keep some of the rain off."

Removing his long, ragged cloak, he draped it over Hope's head, then took Charity and the carpetbag from Faith.

Cotty led the way back along Rock's Row to where a number of small huts were clustered. Even in the rain, fires were going before most of them.

As though reading Faith's thoughts, Cotty said, "No fires are allowed inside the huts, because of the thatched roofs. All cookin' has to be done outside. We have a good clay on Brickfield Hill, and brick and tile are bein' made, but so far only the gentry can afford the use of such. Mayhap in time, Mistress Blackstock, we can construct you such an abode. Here we are.''

He turned in before one hut. It was in a sad state of disrepair; half the thatched roof was gone, and chinks showed between the logs, but it seemed beautiful to Faith.

Cotty pushed open the door. A bucket of water hung on a peg within reach. With a wry smile he said, ''As you can see, there be no locks on the doors to the huts, only a length of rope looped around a wooden peg for a latch.''

''I have nothing worth stealing.''

''You may have, in time. Theft is common hereabouts. Most people hide their valuables in the thatch of the roof. You can do the same when I repair it.''

Faith followed him inside, stopping to look around. Like Simon Marsh's abode, the floor was hard-packed earth, but Faith noticed that it had been swept clean. There was only the one room, bare of furnishings, except for two hammocks slung on hooks against one wall. Rain leaked in on one side of the hut, and Faith knew that Cotty must have repaired the roof over the side where the hammocks hung, since it was dry.

''The hammocks,'' she said. ''You provided them?''

His glance slid away, and he mumbled. '' 'Tis nothing. I bartered for them. In time you may pay me back.''

"How can I ever do that? Simon Marsh will only be giving me a bare sustenance," she said bitterly.

"There are always ways to earn extra goods. I will show you. For one thing, there is a small plot of ground behind the hut. The soil is not the best, but a garden can be cultivated. It should grow more than you and your girls can use. The extra you can barter for goods. Now..." He became brisk. "We had better prepare a meal. I know you must be hungry."

"I'm famished," Faith said.

Hope piped up, "Me, too!"

Cotty laughed and tousled her hair. "We'll soon take care of that, Hopeful."

"My name is Hope!" she said indignantly.

"But you're always lookin' on the hopeful side, ain't you? I can already see that about you."

Cotty crossed to a dry corner beneath one hammock, and for the first time Faith noticed a number of items piled against the wall. Cotty picked up a roll of what seemed to be cowhide. When he had unrolled it, she saw that it was, in fact, two cowhides, laced together. He also reached for four wooden poles from where they leaned against the wall of the hut.

"Think you can help me, Hope?" Cotty indicated a small stack of wood. "Bring an armload along, and we'll start a fire."

Cotty went outside and, using the wooden poles, he stretched the cowhides over a blackened fire pit in front of the hut, placing a pole at each of the four corners. It was scanty shelter, but it provided some protection from the drizzle. By the time Hope came out dragging several sticks of wood, he was kneeling by the fire pit, which was circled with stones. Tearing some twigs and bark from the wood Hope had brought, he dug down into the wet residue of old ashes until he found dry earth. When he had made a small pile of the tinder, after laboring for a few minutes with his flint, the twigs caught from a spark. Blowing on it carefully, he got a flame going, and gently stacked the wood on the tiny flame until he had a nice fire burning.

Standing up, he said, "Watch it carefully, Hopeful, that it doesn't go out." He turned to reenter the hut.

Faith looked into his face, shaking her head ruefully. "I do believe we have found a guardian angel in you, young Cotty."

He ducked his head in embarrassment and stooped to take a package of meat from the sack of goods, along with three sharpened sticks. "The fare will be poor tonight, but 'tis the best I could manage so quickly."

"I am sure that it will be sufficient, Cotty."

"This bread..." He took a loaf of bread from the sack. "It's far from fresh, but will have to do."

He gave her the bread and went outside with the meat. Faith thought that she should help him, but she was exhausted and could not find the strength to venture out into the wet. Cradling Charity against her, she lay down gingerly in the hammock. Never having used one before, it took her a few minutes to learn to get into it without being thrown to the floor. But finally she was comfortable, and she must have dozed, for the next thing she knew, someone was shaking her gently by the shoulder.

"Food is ready, Mistress Blackstock," Cotty said.

Faith sat up, rubbing her eyes with her knuckles. She could smell the cooked meat, and her stomach spasmed in hunger.

On an upturned crate Cotty had arranged slices of meat on a battered metal plate, and had broken the stale bread into pieces. From his belt he took a tin cup. "We'll have to share this," he said, filling the cup with water.

They all sat on the hard ground around the crate and began to eat in the faint light from the fire that came through the open doorway. The meat was strong, faintly gamey, but it tasted wonderful to Faith; it was the first fresh meat they had eaten in months.

"I'm sorry there is naught but water to drink," Cotty apologized. "Wine is hard to come by. Rum is plentiful, but I thought that would hardly be fittin'."

"You did well, Cotty. This is better fare than any we've had for long months." She added wistfully. "The girls could do with some milk. They need it badly. They've had none since we left England."

"Milk cows be scarce in New South Wales. All those brought over with the First Fleet died, and most of those brought by the Second Fleet have either died or been eaten. I might be able to get you a goat. I could build a pen for it behind the hut."

"I would much appreciate it, Cotty." She gestured helplessly. "I know not how I shall ever repay you for all you are doing for us."

Again, he looked embarrassed. "Schoolin' will be pay enough."

Finally, the food gone, Faith leaned back with a sigh. "I feel better than I have for a while. What kind of meat was that?"

"Kangaroo," he said with a faint grin.

"Kangaroo?"

"Kangaroo meat is about the only fresh meat available hereabouts, and even that ain't too easy to come by. Several parties go out every day huntin', and they're havin' to range farther and farther afield."

"What's a kangroo?" Hope asked.

"Kangaroo," Cotty said with a laugh. "It's the funniest-lookin' animal you ever saw. Long back legs and short front legs, and it hops around like a hare. It's gentle and harmless like a hare, too. It's a shame they have to be killed, but people have to eat."

"And I hoped we would fare better once we arrived here," Faith said wistfully.

"If food was not in such short supply, you would. The soil around Sydney Harbor and nearby is poor, and it took all this time for the government to realize this. Now, richer soil has been found on Norfolk Island, and at Parramatta and Rose Hill; and it is predicted that the famine will soon be over. I gather then that conditions on the voyage were bad?"

"Terrible, young Cotty!" Briefly she told him of the hardships they had endured.

Cotty shook his head. "When me and my pa came over with the First Fleet, things were not so bad. Governor Phillip saw to that, I reckon. But I've heard tales from those that arrived on the Second Fleet, and they had it near as bad as you. Like with your fleet, them that was in charge was private contractors, and it didn't matter to them if their cargo got here alive or dead. In fact, some say that dead was better, because then they could sell their rations to the colony. It's a pitiful state of affairs, but they say Governor Phillip is trying to do somethin' about the situation.''

Without volition, Faith yawned widely. Cotty noticed and got to his feet. ''You had all better get some sleep. I see the rain has stopped. I brought along a pair of coverlets. They be worn, but they will help keep off the night chill. It'll likely be clear and sunny on the morrow. If it is, I'll come by and repair your roof.''

Faith also stood up. ''Won't you have to work tomorrow?''

Cotty smiled faintly. ''The sort of work I do don't require regular hours.''

''Then I wish to thank you again, young Cotty. And I wish you a good night.''

''Good night, Mistress Blackstock. And to you, too, Hope.'' He stooped and gently touched Hope's hair.

He left then, ducking out into the night.

Faith prepared the girls for bed. Charity was already asleep, and Hope could hardly keep her eyes open. Glancing out the door of the hut, Faith saw that the fire had gone out. She wondered where Cotty had gotten the water, and wished she had asked him where she could obtain more. More than likely, he had carried it from where the stream emptied into the cove.

As Faith tucked the two girls into one of the hammocks, Hope threw her arms around her mother's neck. ''Don't worry, Momma. We shall be all right.''

"Of course we shall, dear," Faith said in a choked voice.

"I am old enough to help you."

"Yes, you're my big girl. Go to sleep now."

Faith stood over the girls for a few moments, happy that Hope already seemed to be adjusting to this strange land, and at the same time envious of her ability to so accommodate herself. Faith doubted that she would ever view New South Wales as home; as difficult as life had been for them back in London, England would always be her home.

With a sigh she turned away, shivering in the chill air that came whistling through the large hole in the roof. Climbing into the other hammock, she pulled the blanket over her as the hammock rocked dangerously, and she held her breath, fearful that the thing would flip, spilling her onto the floor. But before the contraption stopped rocking, she was asleep, oblivious to the sounds of roistering that came from up the street.

COTTY STARKE ALSO HEARD the sounds from the various taverns along Rock's Row, but to him they were comfortable and familiar. Not far from the hut he had claimed for the Blackstock family, he turned into the Crown Tavern, which was one of the larger, better-regulated taverns in Sydney Town. Most of the taverns catered mainly to the soldiers and to the seamen off the ships occasionally anchoring in the bay, and their patrons were a rowdy lot; but Will and Sarah Moore were of a different stripe from the other tavern owners. Will Moore was a big, burly man who kept order in his tavern; he permitted no rowdiness, and his place was patronized by the free settlers, and even the swells from the better part of town. His wife, Sarah, baked bread, pastries and delicious mutton pies—when flour and mutton were available.

Well into middle age, they were a childless couple, and had taken Cotty in after his father died. They had been acquainted with Henry Starke back in England, and had come as free settlers with the First Fleet. The Moores looked upon Cotty as the son they never had, yet they knew that Cotty was an independent lad, and allowed him to come and go much as he pleased, for he had made it clear that if they were too restrictive, he would find other quarters. Cotty had no intention of working at odd tasks around a tavern for the rest of his life. He fully intended to own a tavern of his own before many years passed, and his ambitions extended even beyond that.

He had raided Sarah's kitchen earlier that evening for the kangaroo meat and the loaf of bread. It was a risk, since Sarah kept a close watch on her larder, food being in such short supply; but Cotty had figured it was a risk well worth taking, if it meant that he would receive some schooling from Faith Blackstock.

After all, he was accustomed to risk-taking. He grinned to himself in the darkness. If the Moores knew the chances he had been taking for some time now, they would be horrified and, most likely, quite angry with him.

Cotty had familiarized himself with every nook and cranny of Sydney, and he had become quite adept at breaking the nine o'clock curfew without getting caught. The "work" that he had told Faith Blackstock so little about involved the illegal sale of rum. True, he performed some tasks around the Crown during the day, but that was merely to recompense the Moores for his keep.

As he had mentioned briefly to Faith, rum was as valuable, if not more so, than currency, which was very scarce. Liquor of any kind could not be landed without the permission of Governor Phillip, and was, when that permission was granted, supposed to be stored in the Bonded Store on Sergeant Major's Row. The Bonded Store was shuttered and barred and under guard twenty-four hours a day.

Only people with permits could buy liquor of any kind: officers and free settlers for their private use; and innkeepers for their taverns. The permits limited the amount of purchase, even for the innkeepers. There was also a port duty, which varied from time to time, often rising astronomically to restrict the flow of spirits.

Most people of Sydney considered the liquor laws bad laws and found ways to circumvent them. There was a great hunger for rum among the populace, including the convicts, whose use of spirits was frowned upon in theory but allowed in practice. Since the convicts, both male and female, had no access to ready currency, the officers and the free settlers took advantage of this to use rum as a means of barter. They would hire the convicts to carry out personal tasks beyond their official work and pay them in rum. Under these conditions, profiteering was inevitable, and smuggling, while punishable by severe penalties, was considered well worth the risk.

As a result of this underground rum trade, Sydney Town, particularly the Rocks area, was rapidly becoming a place of all-round dissolution and brawling. In fact, it had reached the point that government soldiers—so far the only law enforcement Sydney was blessed with—would only venture into the Rocks in pairs. Cotty was astute enough to realize that this situation would only worsen as more convicts and settlers came to New South Wales, and as more and more ships anchored in the bay, their crews seeking diversion after many months at sea.

Ever alert to the main chance, Cotty had taken advantage of the opportunity offered. For more than a year he had been dealing in illicit rum. He had managed, by clever bartering, to obtain a small boat, which he kept hidden in one of the many coves near Sydney Town, and which he used to ply his trade. He found ships' crew members and officers eager to sell to smugglers, and even captains were not above the practice, since they could thus avoid the port duty.

On shore, Cotty sold to whomever had the money to buy, although he drew the line at selling directly to the convicts, since many of them were cutthroats and apt to do violence when in their cups. He never lacked for customers, since he could afford to sell at a lower price than the Bonded Store, and still make a good profit.

If he could continue his profession unscathed, he would be the possessor of a small fortune by the time he was twenty. So far, his illicit trade had gone undiscovered. After all, who would suspect a lad of the tender age of twelve of such practices?

Smiling to himself, Cotty veered past the tavern entrance and went along the side of the building toward the small lean-to room off the rear that he used for his quarters. Just as he walked past the back door of the tavern, it opened, and Sarah Moore stood framed in the candlelight from within.

"There you are, Cotty! I was fearful that you would get caught out after curfew."

Cotty stopped before her. Sarah Moore was a buxom woman, with graying hair and kind brown eyes. Her round face was smudged with flour from her baking, and rosy from the hearth's heat.

"Where have you been?" she asked with a frown.

"Just around the village," he said with a vague gesture. "I was down at the wharf when the fleet unloaded the convicts."

"I wish you wouldn't do that, lad," Sarah said with a shake of her head. "They're a rough lot. Murderers, thieves and Lord God knows what all. And after dark like this... They would slit the throat of a young lad such as yourself, if they thought you carried so much as a farthing."

Cotty shrugged. "No harm came to me. Instead, I met a nice woman, Faith Blackstock, and her two young daughters."

"She be a convict?"

"Yes."

Sarah snorted indelicately. "Then she cannot be very nice, to my way of thinkin'. But no matter..." She gestured. "I was hopin' to see you this night, Cotty. There was a thing Will and me wished to discuss with you."

Cotty was immediately wary. Had they found out about his illegal activities? "Is something amiss?"

Sarah shook her head. "Nothing like that. It's just..." She took a deep breath and looked over her shoulder. "Will should be the one to tell you, but he's busy inside. We have a good offer for the inn,

Cotty. We have been thinking for some time of returning home.''

''You're thinkin' of sellin' and leavin' Sydney Town?'' he said in astonishment.

''Aye, that we are, lad. Although we have fared better than most, we ain't been happy here. 'Tis such a primitive place, and it grows harder for Will to keep order in the tavern every day. It will only get worse. Every ship brings in more rowdies. With the money we can get for the tavern, we can open our own pub in London.''

''I had no idea you thought of leavin' New South Wales.'' Cotty was somewhat dazed by the news. ''The Crown is thrivin' better than most.''

''True, but we are homesick for London.'' Sarah Moore hesitated, fumbling for the proper words. ''And Will is ailing badly. I know he appears hale and robust, but he is often in pain. He says it feels like something is gnawing away at his innards. He wants better doctoring than he can get here, and he says if he is to die...'' Weak tears leaked from her eyes. ''He says he wishes to die on English soil.''

''I'm sorry to hear of his illness, Mistress Sarah. I had no idea.''

Sarah brushed at the tears. ''Nor did I, until a fortnight ago. But no matter.'' She became brisk. ''What we wanted to talk about, me and Will, was you, Cotty. We think dearly of you, almost as if you were one of our own. We want you to come back with us.''

''Back to London?'' Cotty said.

''Yes, we do. I know you had it hard there before, but 'twould be different now. We'll see that you be provided for, me and Will.''

Cotty's thoughts were racing. He had put the prospect of returning to England from his mind; certainly he had foreseen no way that it could ever come about. A year ago he would have leaped at the chance. At that time he could see nothing ahead for him in New South Wales but a life of hardship; but now, by his own intelligence and enterprise, he had opened up new vistas for himself.

And oddly, thoughts of the Blackstock family intruded. After an acquaintance of only a few hours, they seemed more a family to him than the Moores, as kind as they had been to him.

Sarah Moore was going on, "As I said, I know your early days in London was hard, but your prospects with us would be better. If Will and me buy a pub, some day, Cotty, it would be yours."

A pub in London, grand as it might seem to the Moores, was not what Cotty had in mind for himself. "How soon will you decide?" he asked.

"We have already decided. A man came with the Third Fleet today, a Master Robert Beller. He came to Sydney looking for just such an opportunity. He had already looked at all the taverns and decided that ours was what he wanted. What is even better, Cotty, he arrived with the money to pay! As you well know, naught in Sydney Town have the currency at hand to pay out such a sum, and promptly."

"That soon," Cotty murmured. Gazing into the woman's kind eyes, he well knew that if he gave her a flat refusal on the spot, she would be deeply hurt. Instead, he said, "I will spend the night thinkin' on it, Mistress Sarah."

She groped for his hand and pressed it fervently. "You will think hard? I have your promise on that?"

"You have my promise."

# CHAPTER FIVE

## EXCERPTS FROM THE JOURNAL OF
## PETER MYERS

### March, 1788

SLOWLY, A VILLAGE has begun to rise near the mouth of the creek in Sydney Harbor; but conditions for myself grow increasingly difficult. Although I try to make myself as unobjectionable as possible to Wilburne, he always finds some reason to badger and abuse me. Wilburne, unfortunately, was one of the few soldiers who agreed to supervise a convict work gang. After our arrival here, almost all the soldiers stubbornly maintained that their duties did not extend beyond the voyage, and refused to supervise us. Governor Phillip, consequently, was obliged to select the majority of overseers from the convicts themselves, on what basis I do not know. Most of the convict supervisors know nothing of building, but, in general, they treat those under them with more consideration than do the soldiers.

But enough of that dreadful fellow! My days are made miserable by him; I shall not allow him also to affect my nights!

Over the past few weeks we have finally evolved a building pattern. There have been many problems, not the least of which is the fact that we lack trained carpenters and knowledgeable supervisors. Most of the convicts are unwilling workers, unless forced; and there is a scarcity of proper tools. We have found that excellent sandstone abounds in the area; however, we lack mortar with which to bind it, and so are forced to use other materials for the construction of our buildings. The natives are of no help in this regard, for their shelters are little better than card houses fashioned out of slabs of bark propped one against the other.

After much experimentation, we have settled upon a method of construction that, while not elegant, is functional, and makes use of the materials we have at our disposal. The houses we construct are, in effect, little better than huts; but they have frames of timber and walls of cabbage-palm trunks, which are soft and easily cut. The spaces between are wattled with twigs, then plastered with clay. When dry, the walls are whitewashed. Floors are of packed mud, and roofs are thatched with grass or reeds.

Timber is being produced to build a hospital, barracks and warehouses; and Governor Phillip plans to have the Government House built of sandstone, when sufficient mortar has been made from the oyster shells the female convicts are collecting in the nearby coves. At the moment, most of us are still living in tents, the condition of which, when it rains, is uncomfortable in the extreme.

*April, 1788*

Two weeks ago, two male convicts escaped and vanished into the interior. Today, one has returned, emaciated and delirious; raving about his dead mate and the "black ghosts" who followed him, watching all the way.

The word is that there is no escaping this place. Thousands of miles of sea bar us on the one hand, and unknown miles of hostile and dangerous unexplored land on the other. Still, I can certainly understand the urge to escape, no matter what fate might await one. When things get too bad, the mind desires an alternative, no matter how risky.

As our little village grows, so does my discontent. Wilburne treats us unfairly and harshly, and there is much anger and complaining among the convicts, although not to Wilburne's face. Those convicts who are disobedient or difficult to handle are chained and assigned to special gangs. The work here is difficult enough without having to do it wearing thirteen pounds of leg irons and chains around one's ankles.

The few women prisoners have been allotted to officers and others of stature, and the lack of female companionship is evidencing itself. Governor Phillip has issued warnings of severe punishment to any man caught performing unnatural acts with another man; but the practice goes on, unabated, much to the disgust of those of us who are fortunate enough to still retain a veneer of civilization. However, I wonder just how thick is that veneer? I know that I have changed greatly. Much that would have shocked and pained me deeply a year ago, now I view with resignation. I dream often of my dear Elizabeth and my children, and write letters which I hope to send when the supply ships arrive.

I also dream of killing Wilburne and running free into the interior. Despite what all say of that inhospitable land, in my dreams it is green and generous, and I make my way across it, and find myself back in Mother England. A mad dream, no doubt, but comforting in its way, and no madder than the idea, put forth by some, that China exists on the other side of the range of mountains that is said to be several days' journey west of Sydney Town. These mountains have been named the Blue Mountains, because of the blue haze that covers them; and whatever may lie on the other side, I know it is not China. However, a number of Irishmen state as truth the notion that if one could only cross the Blue Mountains, one would then be in a comfortable land of friendly people. Yet, I should not mock them. We need our dreams, for often it is only our dreams that keep us from going mad or killing ourselves.

My only other comforts are this journal and the company of Henry and Cotty Starke. The boy is faring surprisingly well; but then of course he is not a convict and is allowed to run free. Although only nine years of age, he shows amazing enterprise and manages, in what fashion I can only guess, to obtain extra bits of food and other useful objects. Since, in our condition, these small amenities are greatly valued, neither his father nor I presses him for an accounting. Henry, alas, is not faring as well. He was obviously once a strong man, but now some subtle illness works in him, wasting him away. Cotty does not discuss this with me, but I can see the worry in his eyes.

There is also worry in the camp, for Lieutenant Ball, the supply officer who was sent on an expedition to Lord Howe Island where turtles have been found earlier, returned without a single ounce of turtle meat. This meat had been counted upon, for supplies are growing low.

*May, 1788*

I have seriously begun to think about attempting to escape. Since I know naught of shipbuilding or seafaring, my only hope would lie inland. I know that the interior is dangerous, but my dream keeps recurring and is beginning to obsess me. Also, there are two men in my work gang who speak of nothing else. They are strong, rough men and think themselves strong enough to face anything; anything, that is, except the life we have here. They are also fools, to some extent, in that they are without the wit to respect the adversary they have chosen. Still, I find myself talking with them often, discussing ways, means and plans. If nothing else, it is a slight antidote to our helplessness. A man needs to feel that he can do something about his situation, even if he cannot.

Henry Starke grows weaker, and I fear for his survival. I, on the other hand, have grown tough and lean, a far cry from the soft city man that I was. Could I possibly survive in the interior where others have failed? The natives seem to survive quite well in their own way. I have been observing them, whenever the chance presents itself, and have seen that although they might appear, at first glance, to be the most underprivileged of people, they not only survive but seem to do so with spirit and humor. It is obvious that they enjoy their lives, which is certainly more than we do at this moment.

*June, 1788*

The shortage of supplies is growing more desperate. Since the end of May there has been much conjecture as to when the supply ships will arrive, and many have sunk into gloom, wondering whether we shall manage to survive. Flour is very short, and the new planting of wheat has not yet sprouted. Many of the sheep we brought with us have died of disease. To combat the scurvy, some of us were sent out hunting for native plants; wild celery, spinach and parsley. We have found the hearts of the cabbage palms and fern roots to be edible, and quite tasty to a hungry man.

Despite the proximity of the sea, fish have not been plentiful, and our hunters seem to frighten away more game than they shoot. Kangaroo meat, by the way, is not unpalatable. I have also dined upon soup made from white cockatoos and crows, roasted wild duck stuffed with slices of salt beef, and opossums—which must be soaked first in water to rid the meat of the strong flavor imparted by the gum leaves upon which the animals dine. The bandicoot, a sharp-snouted, beady-eyed creature, which appears to be a member of the rat family, is very tasty when roasted, having a flavor rather like that of a suckling pig. However, with so many of us to feed, the game has become scarce, and they will not let us go into the interior to hunt, as they fear we will attempt to escape.

I should not have written of food, for now my stomach assails me. Tonight we dine on a few scraps of rancid salt pork and weevil-infested rice.

*July, 1788*

On this day, Henry Starke died. He will be sorely missed. Before he died, he gave me his knife, a good, large blade with a bone handle, which he said he wanted me to have.

Cotty is to live with Will and Sarah Moore, a free couple who were acquainted with Henry back in England. They have begun a small enterprise in the Rocks, and they hope, in time, with the coming of other ships, to establish the place as an inn. Having no children of their own, they are happy to take in young Cotty, who will no doubt be a great help to them.

On this day, also, I register my decision to attempt to escape from this hellish place and flee into the interior. I have decided that the threat of death is more desirable than the conditions under which I presently exist.

Approximately three weeks ago, one of the convicts in our hut secreted some precious scraps of food in the thatch; someone stole his food.

None would admit to the villainy, but Wilburne was eager for the opportunity to affix blame. Without any evidence against me whatsoever, he seized upon me as the culprit, and ordered me to receive one hundred lashes from the cat-o'-nine-tails. All of my protestations of innocence were ignored.

I was tied to a large tree, so tightly that my chest was forced flat against the trunk so that I could not cringe. The flogger was another convict, a man sadistic by nature, who gave every evidence of enjoying his odious task. I was flogged across the back and buttocks until I bled profusely. The blood ran down my legs and into my boots. The skin was flayed from my back in strips, and the pain was so agonizing that I was near to fainting when I was finally released, and could scarcely stand.

That night, and many nights thereafter, I could not sleep because of the pain, and I then and there decided to make good my escape, no matter what the consequences. I would much rather die than endure such a beating again!

Jones and Thomas, the other two men in my work gang who have been talking of escape, are planning to leave the day after tomorrow, and at first I thought that I would accompany them. However, we have been unable to agree upon which direction to proceed. They are determined to head west, toward the Blue Mountains. I, on the other hand, would prefer to head southwest, where, I have heard, there is a large lake. They insist that the stories of the lake are only legend.

Since none of us has been allowed to travel beyond the confines of Sydney Town, the argument would appear to be unresolvable. I have, however, seen the bones that have been brought back by those who attempted to escape west. They say that the track to Parramatta is strewn with them. Perhaps I should be better off alone, at any rate. Jones and Thomas are tough men, hardened criminals, and if things should go amiss, they might be dangerous to me. Among recaptured escapees there are tales of cannibalism and other such horrors.

I have thought long and hard about this, and have made my preparations. For days I have been secreting tidbits of food and accumulating other items that will be of use to me in the bush. I have managed to obtain a water bag in fairly good condition, a square of canvas, some rope, tinder and flint, and a measure of salt. Although Henry and I never discussed my plans for escape, I think he must have known, for when he pressed his knife into my hands he told me: "This will help you, my friend," as indeed it shall, for without it I should have no weapon of any sort; and it will also serve as a valuable tool.

A sense of excitement fills me. I may be going to my death, but at least I am doing something about my situation. Since I am already lost to my family, and have no chance of ever being reunited with them, I only risk my own life, and that, at the moment, is worth little to me. This journal will accompany me on my journey. If and when I die, perhaps someone will see that it reaches my family. Until then it is my only remaining friend, listening to my words, and never reprimanding.

I WRITE THIS as I sit in a grove of gum trees in a sheltered vale. A fortunate combination of luck and good weather helped to make my escape less difficult than I had feared. It rained heavily last night, and the bad visibility, combined with the fact that most of the guards had retired to their huts, aided my endeavor. Now I face the cruelest enemy of all, the land itself. At first glance the interior does not look unfavorable, a vista of gently swelling hills, separated by vales, which contain trees and bush; however, the look of it is misleading, for there is a scarcity of streams or springs that would exist in more gentle lands. Still, there must be water somewhere, for the aborigines survive. I have seen them following me, like dark shadows, always in the periphery of my vision, but I feel no fear. It is true that the natives have at times killed some of our men; however, I believe that they have done so only after proper provocation by these same men. And so I make no unfriendly gesture toward my shadowy entourage, for it is in my mind to try to make contact with them. It seems to me that they might help me if they could be made to feel kindly disposed toward me.

MY FOOD IS GONE, and my water is low; but as yet I have seen no sign of a lake. Since I have no compass, I fear that I may have been walking in circles. The land here looks much the same, so it is difficult to tell. Strangely, I feel no fear, not even of death.

The natives still follow me. As I grow weaker, they move closer to me. I have attempted to approach them in turn, but when I move toward them they simply vanish. I have begun to wonder if they are really there, or if I am imagining them. Last night they camped near me, and I could see their fires and smell their food cooking. Hungry and thirsty, I dared to approach them again, thinking that since they had built fires they would surely not run off and leave them; however, my way was barred by a fierce-looking fellow who motioned me away with his spear. I returned to my own dry camp, and fell into a troubled slumber in which I dreamed strange dreams. I awoke to a peculiar and unsettling sound; a deep humming or roaring that droned on without pause. It was uncanny in the extreme, and yet I slept again with this sound in my ears.

I HAVE NOW BEEN THREE DAYS without food and one day without water. This may be the last legible entry

I make, for I am feeling very faint, and my head is filled with strange thoughts and fancies.

I have decided that the natives who follow me are not going to help me, that they are merely curious, and they are simply following me to watch me die. I view this thought with a surprising lack of bitterness. I have made my attempt to find freedom, and I have failed. If I had to do it over again, I should do the same.

I am seated in the cleft of a large rock as I write this. The rock is worn almost to the configuration of a chair, or a throne. I came upon this stone this morning, and have decided that this is where I shall make my last stand, for I am too worn and weak to proceed farther. It pleases me in some way that I shall die like a king, seated upon a throne, my subjects squatting there in the bush, staring at me with dark, bright eyes. At least I shall not die alone.

# CHAPTER SIX

FAITH BLACKSTOCK, sitting in the center of the circle of children, raised her gaze from the book she held in her hand. "You try it now, Cotty."

Cotty took the worn book and haltingly began to read aloud. Faith watched him in the candlelight, a faint smile on her face. She had been instructing the lad and Hope for almost a year now, in whatever snippets of time she could spare after her long days' work for Simon Marsh; and although Hope was doing quite well, considering her tender years, it was Cotty's progress that pleased Faith the most. She had been amazed at how quickly the boy learned. He still had a bit of difficulty when asked to read aloud, but she was certain that he would soon overcome this, as well.

Looking at the boy's earnest face as he read from the page, Faith felt the warmth of gratitude. Many times over the past year she had given thanks to the Lord for the fact of their meeting. Without his help, it was very possible that she and her daughters might not have survived in this harsh land. They owed the very roof over their heads to his care and help.

Within a few days of their arrival, Cotty had managed to put the hut into a livable condition, repairing the roof and the holes in the wall and applying a new coat of whitewash. Within a week he had made them a rough table, four stools and a crude cupboard in which to store their food. The girls both adored him, and hung on his shirttails when he was around—even now they were seated close beside him. They begged him for the outrageous stories he loved to tell, and Faith had begun to think of him as a son.

As Cotty read, she glanced around the interior of the hut. It was theirs, and it felt more like home than the filthy room in which they had last lived in London. It was harsh here, yes, and alien; but in many ways London had been as bad, if not worse. Here food was always in short supply—thank the Lord for Cotty's contribution of wild game and other items to their larder—and the hours she had to work were long and hard; yet the air here was fresh, without the smoke and soot of London, and the water was pure. More important, there was some chance that things would eventually get better. Since arriving, Faith had learned that Governor Phillip was a just man, not unsympathetic to the needs of the convicts. She had learned that the convicts of the First Fleet, which Phillip had been in charge of, had fared much better than those who came with the Second and Third Fleets, of which she had been a part.

Governor Phillip had great plans for the town of Sydney, and things would surely improve. By the end of her years of servitude, she would be worn out, old before her time; but her girls were not convicts; and it was possible that by the time they were grown, Sydney would be a real town, much more civilized. Women were in short supply—especially *good* women—and they should be able to make advantageous marriages. They were both beautiful girls, and Faith intended to see that they were raised properly so that when the time came for them to wed they would have whatever advantage she could give them.

As for herself, well, she was very fortunate in that she had been assigned to a man who seemed to have no desires other than to make money. She had learned that most of the women convicts who were assigned to a private house were expected to assume the role of mistress as well as worker. No such demands had been made upon her; but because of her position in Marsh's shop, the other men automatically assumed that she belonged to him in all ways, and did not trouble her as much as they might have if they had known the truth. Still, there had been some who, intoxicated or simply not caring, approached her with propositions that made her shudder with revulsion. Her experience with her husband had not caused her to hate all men; but the hard times and suffering she had experienced since her abandonment had left her with no desire for the physical company of men.

Her thoughts were diverted when Cotty said, "I have finished, Mistress Faith."

She smiled at him. "And you did very well, too, Cotty."

Taking the book from him, she handed it to Thomas Morgan, who was sitting sullenly across from Cotty. Once word had gotten out that Faith could read and write, and that she was willing to instruct in those arts, she had accumulated a small number of students in addition to Hope and Cotty. Because of the long hours she worked at the loom, she could not teach many; yet the food and other necessities that were paid her for her service helped make her family's life a bit easier, and she did enjoy doing it.

As she gave the book to Thomas, his scowl deepened. Thomas was a hulking youth, large for his age and with little aptitude for learning; but his father was a tavern keeper and better able to pay for Faith's services than most. Also, she believed that everyone should have access to enough schooling to at least learn the basics of reading and writing, so she kept attempting to reach the boy and ignite his interest.

"It's your turn now, Thomas," she said. "Read the next few lines."

"Nah." Thomas crossed his arms over his wide chest, his features petulant and sulky. "I ain't readin' nothin'. That's for girls."

"But your parents sent you here to learn, Thomas," she said patiently. "They are paying me to instruct you."

"I don't care, I ain't goin' to!"

Cotty leaned across and seized the boy's arm in a strong grip. "You'll obey Mistress Blackstock. Now read!"

Cotty gave the boy's arm a twist, and the boy cried out.

Faith moved to intervene, then subsided. She could never bring herself to discipline children not her own. Cotty had sensed this early on, and it was he who supplied the discipline when needed.

Thomas took the book and, frowning over the letters, tried to read. He was close to a hopeless case, Faith knew, but she felt she had to try. In his anger and frustration his face twisted. Faith moved around beside him, took the book and tried to help him, using her finger to identify the letters.

Satisfied that Thomas was at least trying, Cotty settled back, watching. He was proud of Faith Blackstock for working such long, hard hours and yet finding it within herself to teach them at night. She was a good teacher, even though she was not firm enough with someone like Thomas; yet that was her nature. He would not want her to be any other way...

A small hand tugged at his sleeve. He glanced down into Hope's upturned face.

She whispered, "You were mean to Thomas."

Cotty grinned. "He needs bein' mean to now and then. Otherwise, he would be too spiteful to endure."

"If you're ever mean to me, I'll...I'll hit you back!" she whispered fiercely.

He laughed aloud. "Would you now? Well, we'll have to see, won't we?"

Faith said, "All right, children. That will be all the lessons for tonight."

Cotty waited until the others had scampered out of the hut. "Is there any chores that needs doin' tonight, mistress?"

"No, Cotty lad. It's been a long day and I'm tired. You should be, as well."

"I'll say good evenin' then." He spoke his farewells to Hope and Charity, touched Hope affectionately on the head and took his leave.

Although it was May now, and autumn in New South Wales, the night was pleasantly warm. Cotty had little inclination to return to his quarters at the Crown Tavern.

The Moores had completed their sale of the Crown to Robert Beller and departed for England four months ago. They had been disappointed that Cotty had not chosen to accompany them, and he sorely missed them. Beller was a hard taskmaster, and Cotty despised the red-faced, hard-drinking new owner and kept out of his way as much as possible.

It was only a few minutes short of the nine o'clock curfew, and Cotty knew that he should return to the tavern. His luck would not hold forever; eventually he would be caught out, and probably suffer a lashing, or at the very least some time in the stocks. But he continued toward Sergeant Major's Row. It seemed to him that each time he defied the curfew and won, it represented a small triumph.

Governor Phillip had promised that the curfew would end soon; it was his boast that he was close to controlling the rowdy element of Sydney Harbor. Cotty was dubious about this claim, yet he knew that protests were mounting against the curfew. The tavern owners were especially unhappy, since such an early closing of their establishments sorely hurt their trade.

He moved on, past the darkened marketplace, and turned right along Hospital Wharf. There was a faint moon tonight, and he could see a ship anchored a short distance from the wharf, creaking against its moorings. Cotty had been at the docks this morning, and he had received word that he could do business with that ship—the first mate had three casks of rum unaccounted for on the ship's manifest, and he wished to sell them. Tomorrow night, between midnight and dawn, Cotty would row out for the casks.

Cotty heard the thump of boots on the wooden wharf and ducked into the shadows just as a soldier marched down to the water's edge, a musket on his shoulder. He looked out over the bay, spat into the water, then turned and strode away.

Cotty decided that he was being foolish, taking the risk of being caught breaking the curfew for no good purpose.

Warily, he made his way back to the Crown, which was dark except for a flicker of candlelight from somewhere in the back. He moved quietly alongside the building and let himself into the lean-to. Closing the door, he lit a candle. The only way he could lock the door was with a piece of rawhide fastened to the inside. With the Moores he had never worried about the door being unbarred, knowing that they would never invade his privacy. But with Beller it was different; he did not trust the man.

Even as he thought this there came a pounding on the door. He went tense, starting at the movement of the wood. There was a thundering crash, and the door flew open. Beller stood framed in the doorway, in the act of lowering his foot.

He was a man in his forties, obese and panting, muddy brown eyes protruding with anger. He was not wearing his peruke, and his bald head shone like a red moon.

"So there you are, me lad," he snarled. "Finally! You be out beyond curfew again."

"I—" Cotty broke off, staring at Beller in growing outrage. "How did you know I've been breakin' curfew?"

Beller grinned cruelly. "'Cause I been checkin' your shanty here and findin' you gone most nights."

"You have no right to do that! These are my quarters!"

Beller laughed harshly. "Ain't so. The Crown and everything on the property belongs to me. I do as I like with it. And that includes you, bucko."

"That's not true!" Cotty cried. "I'm not a convict, I'm not indentured to you. I'm a free man!"

"Free man! You're nothin' but a tyke. When I bought the Crown, I was told you went with it."

"I worked for the Moores, for my food and lodgin'. Just like I do for you, Master Beller."

"Precious little work I get out of you, boy. Out sneakin' around every night. But that's goin' to change. A good lashin' will teach you who's master and who's the tavern boy."

Grinning evilly, he began to unbuckle his belt.

"No!" Cotty backed up against the wall. "You'll not lash me."

Belt out, Beller advanced. "And who's goin' to stop me, pray?"

Cotty fumbled along the wall behind him. He always kept an ax handle leaning against the wall in the event some drunken lout blundered into his lean-to; also, he often took it with him the times he rowed out to the ships for rum. His fingers closed around the ax handle.

Beller kept coming. Cotty brought the ax handle around, gripping it in both hands.

Beller skidded to a stop, gaping. "Ye wouldn't dare strike me with that!"

"Oh, but I would, Master Beller." Cotty grinned savagely, raising the ax handle high. "Suppose you try me."

Breath whistling, little eyes mirroring fear, Beller backed up a step. "I can have you publicly flogged for this."

"Not so. I do not belong to you."

"Why, you insolent young pup! How dare you talk to your betters in such a fashion?"

"Betters?" Cotty made a snorting sound. "Master Beller, you're no more my better than a rootin' pig is."

Beller took a threatening step forward, and Cotty motioned with the ax handle. Beller backed off again, his face red with rage.

"I want you off my property this night. You'll soon be beggin' to come back, and when you do, if I decide to take you back, you'll be showin' the proper respect, I'll wager."

"I'll gladly leave, and I'll never come back to you. I would starve first."

"Grand talk for a gutter tyke," Beller said with a sneer.

He turned and stomped from the lean-to. Cotty went around gathering up his few belongings. All he had were a few clothes, a number of personal items and one thing of real value—a sack of coins buried in one corner. Peering out to make sure that Beller was gone, Cotty quickly dug up the bag of coins and tucked it safely away in the bundle of clothing.

HOPE AWOKE WITH A CRY, tears drying on her cheeks. She felt bereft, deserted and alone. She tried to remember the dream that had made her feel this way, but it was gone, as tenuous and ungraspable as smoke.

She raised her head from the hammock and looked around the hut. She was not alone; her mother and Charity slept soundly, undisturbed by her outcry.

Weak daylight seeped in through the cracks in the hut. No matter how hard Cotty worked to chink them, new cracks appeared soon after. Her mother had to be to work shortly after sunrise.

Hope glanced over at her; her mother was sleeping deeply. Usually, she was up and preparing their breakfast by this time. Hope hated to waken her; she knew how weary Faith was these days. Although she rarely complained, Hope knew that her mother never got enough rest.

Still, if she was late for work, Simon Marsh would punish her severely.

Quickly, Hope hopped out of bed and, seizing the side of the hammock, shook it urgently. "Momma!"

Faith Blackstock sat up, rubbing her eyes. "What is it, child? What's amiss?"

"It's daylight, Momma."

"Well, so it is. My goodness, I don't know why I slept so late. And you, Hope." She smiled at her daughter. "What woke you?"

"I had a dream, Momma."

"A bad dream, dear?" Faith reached up to stroke Hope's sleep-tangled hair.

"Yes, Momma. Bad."

"Well, we all have bad dreams, child." Dear God, Faith thought, I certainly do! Even when she was almost dead from exhaustion, she often had dreams, nightmares of poverty and starvation.

She roused herself and became brisk. "Well, if you children are to have any breakfast, I had better get busy."

She got out of the hammock, shed her nightgown and slipped into undergarments and working clothes.

Meanwhile, Hope had dressed herself and was gazing at the hammock where Charity was still sleeping, her thumb in her mouth. Hope said, "Shall I wake Charity?"

"No, let her sleep for a bit. Take the bucket down to the stream for water while I start a fire."

Hope took the wooden pail and skipped toward the entrance to the hut. Opening the door, she started out, then stopped with a muffled scream and backed up.

Alarmed, Faith hastened to her side. "What is it, Hope?"

"Look!" Hope motioned.

Cautiously, Faith looked out. A figure was sprawled across the entrance. Thinking it was some drunken lout who had chosen their doorway to sleep off the effects of liquor, Faith looked wildly around for some weapon. Then she saw the figure sitting up.

"Cotty! What on earth . . . !"

Cotty grinned sheepishly. "Sorry if I frightened you, mistress. I have left the Crown and Master Beller. It was late and I didn't wish to waken you. I thought that I would be up and around before this." Cotty got to his feet, smoothing down his hair.

"But what are you going to do for a place to live, Cotty?"

"Well, I thought . . ." He took a deep breath. "I thought I would build a hut next to yours. If you don't mind, that is."

"Mind? I don't mind at all. I would feel much more secure with you so close at hand." Then she smiled. "And considering all the time you spend with us, it would be far handier for you, anyway." Faith hesitated, not wishing to embarrass him, yet feeling compelled to put voice to what she felt. "You know that we consider you one of the family, Cotty. You have done as much or more for us than any son and brother would have done."

Cotty, red of face, managed to look both embarrassed and pleased at the same time. He ducked his head. "Thank you, Mistress Faith. I have been glad to do it. Now I'd best be on my way, for I've business to attend to, but I'll be back this afternoon to begin work on the hut."

"Don't you want to break your fast first?"

He shook his head. "I've some bread and cheese and a bit of dried meat to do me for now, but I could probably use a meal this evenin', if the invitation is still open then."

She smiled again, longing to smooth back the hair from his thin, boyish face, but knowing that it would insult his masculine pride. "Of course, Cotty."

Cotty gave his wide grin. "Then it's settled. I'll begin this afternoon."

Sticking his hands into his pockets, he swaggered off, whistling, and Faith watched him go with a mixture of pride and sorrow, thinking that at the tender age of thirteen he was a man better than most. At the same time she wondered what was to become of him. She sensed that his "business" was not entirely of the legal sort, and she could not fault him for that; for practicality in this time and place demanded that one do what one must do to survive. The problem lay with the men he must do business with, and the atmosphere in which it was done. Despite the surface maturity, Cotty Starke was only a boy, and as such a twig still able to be shaped and bent. What would he be like, she wondered, in a few years' time?

# CHAPTER SEVEN

## *EXCERPTS FROM THE JOURNAL OF PETER MYERS*

### *Day 1*

SINCE I HAVE NO IDEA of the present date, I shall consider this the first day of my new life, and number my journal entries accordingly.

I am alive. I write these words with great surprise and wonder.

Two days ago I had given up hope of receiving help from the aborigines, had made my peace with God and resigned myself to death. I had just finished doing this when one of the older men rose from the ground where he had been squatting and approached me. I remember smiling at him widely and turning my palms upward so that he might see that I had no violent intent.

Despite my dazed condition, his appearance is graven upon the fabric of my mind. He came very close to me and stared into my eyes, while I, unable to do otherwise, stared into his. I had not been so close to one of his kind before. Beneath his heavy brow, his eyes burned with curiosity and intelligence. His dark face, striped with white, should have been frightening, but strangely I felt no fear.

He raised his callused hand and held something toward me. It was a bit of dried meat. Hesitatingly, I reached out and took the meat, stuffing it into my mouth. He watched me closely as I hurriedly chewed and swallowed, and then he handed me a bowl made from a piece of human skull, with a measure of water in the bottom. Despite the grisly aspect of the vessel, I drank thankfully.

When I had finished and returned the bowl to him, the man smiled broadly, nodded and turned away. No words had been exchanged; however, I knew that he was suggesting that I might come with him, if I so desired. Unsteadily, I rose to my feet and followed him to where the rest of his group were waiting.

My rescue had been effected!

*Day 30*

How quickly and mysteriously time passes. Without the trappings of civilization, time has little meaning. My new friends have some knowledge of the passage of time, but only in the most general way. They use shadows of trees and rocks as a primitive measure of the hours, and that seems to meet their needs. Here in the bush the days pass smoothly and seamlessly into weeks, and I neither know nor care how long I have been here; it is enough that I am away from that hellhole of Sydney Harbor, and that I am alive.

I have learned the name of my rescuer, which is Bininuwuy. He is the elder and leader, as much as anyone is the leader, of a group of perhaps thirty-five men, women and children.

Due to his protection, I have been accepted as a slightly stupid, awkward and helpless member of the tribe. I may know how to make strange marks upon paper, which they find fascinating; however, my knowledge does not approach that of the least among them as far as fending for myself and surviving in this land. But I am learning, and they are patient with my efforts.

How to describe these strange and complex people, for despite their primitivism, complex they are. In Sydney, I, like the rest, assumed that the natives were simple people with a simple culture; but now, living among them as I am, I find this is not so. They live by a system of rules and behavior that is perhaps stricter than our own. As children they are taught to obey; and those who break the rules are punished. Their life seems to be one of equality. No man seems to be considered better than another. There is the same law for everyone, and all people seem to be of equal importance.

Since I am a stranger among them, I am treated much as they would treat a child; but I am making every effort to learn as much as possible, as rapidly as possible, so that I do not incur their anger or displeasure. I find their ways endlessly fascinating, and shall note as much as possible about their culture in this journal. My supply of ink is running low; but I have found a substitute, a kind of dye made from a certain tree bark. The abundance of bird life makes the obtaining of quills a simple matter.

*Day 60*

I am making some headway with the language, and making friends with the members of the tribe. Old Bininuwuy seems to view me as something between a son and an amusing pet. So far I have managed to avoid breaking any tribal rules, and I am learning more every day. Despite the fact that the natives I saw in and near Sydney seemed to stay in one place, I have found that they are nomadic in nature. Since they are a hunting and gathering culture, it is only a matter of time before an area they are occupying is hunted out, and then they move on to another part of their territory.

Since they do move frequently, they build no lasting shelters. When the weather becomes unpleasant, they erect a simple windbreak. When the winds come up, and the winds here can be fierce, these simple shelters are constructed quickly from branches and leafy material, the holes plugged with grass or reeds. Stones are used to hold this structure in place, or sometimes the structure is merely secured to the trunk of a tree, using vines.

Last week we met another tribe, and there was considerable spear waving and shouting. From what little I know of the language, I gather there was an argument over ownership of the area. It was settled without bloodshed, but I can see how battles must occasionally occur.

The nature of the aborigines seems to be peacefully inclined for the most part; however, there are occasional fights between men, and even fights among the women, who are no less violent in their efforts than the men. I witnessed one fight between two women, where one woman inflicted considerable damage upon the other with the sharp stick they use for digging the sweet potatoes that are an important item of their diet. These sticks, which are very sharp on one end, can be almost as lethal as the spears of the men.

Their diet is varied. They eat whatever comes their way that is edible. The men hunt kangaroo, emu, opossum, koala, birds and fish when they are near water. They also eat many insects, including witchety grubs, which they consider a delicacy. The women collect the plant foods; seeds, nuts, berries, roots, tubers and palm-tree pith. Their staple is a kind of bread called damper, made from various seeds, ground and made into a paste by adding water, then cooked in ashes. I must confess that it has taken me some time to accustom myself to their diet.

Now that I am at least partially familiar with their language, I am able to understand something of the tales they tell around the camp fires at night. As near as I can gather, their religion is pantheistic and mystical, with a strong belief in good and evil spirits and magic. Our tribe has a magician, or medicine man, who tends to the needs of the people, and who always makes his camp a distance apart from the main body. He is considered to be a man of great power and as such is accorded much respect. He carries an artifact, which I have not been allowed to see, but which I have heard in the bush. It emits a roaring, thrumming sound that is frightening in the extreme; I know now that this is the sound that I heard once before. Whenever I hear it, I am made aware of the distance I have come from what I have known as civilization. I feel the urge to pray, but do not know to which god!

The natives believe in something they call "the dream time," or "dreaming," which seems to have to do with the existence of their world in the past, present and future. The dreams are very important to them. They hold certain animals and birds sacred, as well as certain trees, or even groves of trees, and certain stones. They believe that things can be dreamed into existence, including children. They are the only race I have ever heard of who do not recognize the connection between sexual congress and the conception of children. It is most amazing!

Another amazing thing is their artwork, which, although not executed in a style with which I am familiar has a peculiar, spare beauty of its own. They inscribe intricate patterned figures upon stone and bark, and also paint and carve ornamental designs upon their weapons and musical instruments.

The musical instruments consist mainly of a very long drone pipe, which emits an eerie and sonorous tone, and which is usually accompanied by percussion instruments such as two pieces of hard wood that are struck together. The people enjoy singing and dancing, and frequently arrange large celebrations or parties called *corroborees*.

They also enjoy games, of which they seem to have many. In short, while much of their time is taken up hunting for food, sufficient time remains for them to enjoy themselves with music, story telling, games, dances and artistic expression. I wish as much could be said for the lot of the common man in England!

Yesterday, we arrived at the shore of a large lake, no doubt the lake I was originally seeking. This is evidently familiar territory to the tribe, for it was as if they were returning home after a long absence. They clearly intend to remain here for some time, as they are constructing what appear to be semipermanent huts.

*Day 120*

How shocked my family and friends in London would be to see me now! Bearded, browned by the sun, my clothes worn away until I am attired in little more than the belt worn by my rescuers, I might, at a distance, be taken for one of them. My past life seems so very far away now that I seldom think of it.

I can no longer conjure the image of my wife's face, or the faces of my children.

And yet, strange as it may seem, I am not unhappy. Now that I am inured to the physical hardships of my new life, I find in it a certain peace and order. Bininuwuy has taught me the use of the spear and the spear thrower, and the odd implement that my hosts call the boomerang, a sickle-shaped piece of wood that, when thrown properly, returns to the sender if the target is not struck. He, and the other men, have helped me fashion weapons and tools, because a man must have his own. Having them, I admit, makes me feel a man of means.

In this society, you must carry all that you own; and so possessions are kept to a minimum. However, there are necessities: for a man his spear and *wommera*, or spear thrower; a mesh game bag; one or two boomerangs; a stone knife; a water bag, often fashioned from an opossum skin, or the stomach of a kangaroo; and a small dilly bag for carrying personal articles such as gum, twine, beeswax and sinew, as well as spare bone or stone spear barbs, other sharpened stones, a stone for grinding purposes, bone and feather ornaments for the hair, colored ocher for body painting, and certain magic talismans for protection and aid.

There is one practice in particular that I have found interesting and strange, and that is the practice of carrying a spear with the foot. Often, when traveling through the bush, a man must be prepared for danger or unexpected attack, while burdened with all his worldly possessions. Over his right shoulder, he may have knotted a mesh game bag, which is held in place with his left hand. This hand will also hold his shield and *wommera*. Clubs, boomerangs and a stone ax are usually tucked into his belt. A length of opossum-fur cord and his small bag of private possessions are tied to his belt. His fire stick, which is a piece of dense wood that smolders slowly for hours, and a double-bladed knife are usually carried in the headband.

The spear, then, is gripped between the big toe and its neighbor, and in this fashion is dragged along the ground, thus leaving the right hand free to grasp whatever weapon is most suitable for the emergency at hand. A certain balance is achieved when things are carried in this fashion; and although it sounds awkward, the spear can be flung in an instant into the free hand for ready use.

The men are excellent hunters and trackers, and if there is game, they will find it. I have seen some men throw their spears a distance of ninety meters, although at that distance they are not always accurate. At a distance of forty-five to fifty-five meters they are deadly, even if the target is fast moving. So far, despite the fact that I am learning to manage their weapons, they have not allowed me to hunt with them. Since all in the tribe must labor for their keep, from the young to the old, I have been relegated to the gathering chores such as are performed by the women, children and old people. I have attempted to determine why this is so, since young boys, after a certain age, are allowed to participate in the hunt, and have decided that it is because I am uninitiated. There are several young males of appropriate age awaiting this ceremony at the present time; I intend to approach Bininuwuy and ask him if, although I am greatly past the age at which it is usually performed, I may participate in this ceremony.

*Day 122*

Bininuwuy has agreed. I am to be initiated. I have been given to understand that the ceremony is secret and holy, and must be respected. Bininuwuy seems very pleased, and there is much joking and laughing around the camp fires at night, I fear at my expense. The tribe finds it very amusing that a man of my age should be going through the ceremony, but their joking is done with no malice. I await the event with anticipation and, I must admit, a certain amount of trepidation.

*Day 130*

Some days ago I went with the men into the bush. I and a number of striplings preparing for initiation had our courage and our obedience tested, and have learned the sacred rites and ceremonies of the tribe. After the final initiation ceremony, I returned to camp a full member of the tribe, and must keep the rules of secrecy, especially from women and uninitiated males. It is impossible to describe completely the feelings that fill me. A *corroboree* was held, and I danced and chanted along with the others, and felt both at peace and at one with the universe.

*Day 148*

I write this and yet cannot believe it, even seeing the words here on the page. Bininuwuy has informed me that I am to be given a native bride, and I have agreed.

It came about in an unusual way, for in the normal pattern of events marriages are arranged when a woman is but a babe in arms. At that time she is promised to a boy who is considered right for her. When they come of marriageable age, which appears to be at puberty, she is handed over to her husband. There is no courtship.

Noorina, the young woman who will be my wife, is a widow; her husband was killed some days ago when a hunting expedition was attacked by members of another tribe. The disagreement apparently was territorial. At any rate, Noorina now needs a husband, and since I am the only adult male without a woman, Bininuwuy has given her to me.

I must confess that I have felt severely the lack of a woman, and it is a sign of my acculturation that I do not find the idea of taking a native wife untenable. Noorina is young, in her twenties I should imagine, and not unattractive. She has a firm, healthy, well-proportioned body, sparkling eyes and a gentle, lovely smile. If by some miracle these pages should ever reach my family back in England, I hope they will understand and forgive me. I could not, in good conscience, omit this information, if my true story is to be told.

*Day 420*

This will be my last notation, for this is the last page of my journal. I have saved it until I had something special to say, and today that day has come.

I have a son! He was born this morning just as the sun rose, a good omen, and I have given him the name of John. Noorina, who delivered the child with little effort and apparently little pain, as opposed to English women, believes that John was conceived upon the day that I visited a magic grove and found a spirit child, whom I directed to enter her womb; but I know that he is my flesh and blood, and my heart quickens with love for him.

He is a handsome child, relatively light in color, and seems to exhibit the best physical traits of both of his parents. I look at him at his mother's breast and wonder what the world has in store for him. I hope that he stays with his people, for here he will be accepted and cared for; and I well know how cruel my own race can be to those of mixed blood. And yet, when he is old enough, I know I shall teach my son to speak the English tongue, and to read and write the English language. If this world changes, and it would seem that with the coming of my kind it surely must, perhaps this knowledge will be useful to him.

I shall now close my journal, and seal it in a bag made from a kangaroo's stomach. Thus it will be protected from the elements, and will be preserved. I have considered destroying it, but cannot bring myself to destroy the written word. Perhaps some day it will serve some historian to better understand these people, who have become my people.

Peter Myers

# PART TWO

## *July, 1800*

From distant climes o'er widespread seas we come,
Though not with much eclat or beat of drum,
True patriots all; for be it understood,
We left our country for our country's good.

(Attributed to George Barrington, infamous
pickpocket, actor, poet, transported to New South
Wales, then given his freedom by Governor Phillip
and made chief constable of Parramatta.)

# CHAPTER EIGHT

HOPE WAS ANGRY; angry at herself for weeping, and angry at Cotty for being the cause of it.

At fourteen she knew she was too old to cry, but she felt that she had received sufficient provocation.

She walked along in the remnants of the garden behind the hut, kicking petulantly at the dead corn-stalks. Now, in the middle of winter in Sydney, everything was dead in the garden, not that it had been very fruitful in any event. Every year since they had been in New South Wales, they had planted a garden; and for at least half of those years the garden had been a failure. The soil was too thin and too poor to provide proper sustenance for the plants.

Like everything else in this place, she thought bitterly; and we're as poor as the soil!

She gave her head a sharp shake. That was not wholly the truth. Oh, it was true enough that they were poor. Even with her and Charity now working alongside their mother at the looms, the pittance that Marsh paid them allowed only a small betterment of their condition. Still, there were no freezing winters like the ones she could still remember in London; and Cotty always saw to it that they had enough to eat.

Cotty! How could one person be the source of so much pleasure and pain? Sometimes she thought that she should die from loving him, and sometimes she hated him.

She kicked furiously at another hapless cornstalk and fought back another onslaught of tears. She had begged off going to the looms today, telling her mother that she was feeling too ill to work. It was not really a falsehood, she thought; for after what Cotty had told them last night, she *was* sick at heart.

As if her thoughts had summoned him, she saw Cotty coming toward her from his hut. Without moving, she watched him approach, her chest aching. She was always newly surprised at the sight of him. It was a continual wonderment to her that he had grown so tall and broad, that his narrow face had filled out smooth and brown, and that his boyish neck had thickened to a muscular column, that he had to shave the red-brown whiskers from his face— for, as he often said, much to her annoyance, he liked to keep his face smooth for the girls to kiss. Hope had always thought him handsome, even as a boy; but now it seemed that the rest of the female population of Sydney found him so as well.

Well, she had changed, too, she knew. The evidence was there for all to see in the changing contours of her body, and the unseen flux that had come—so her mother told her—to announce her impending womanhood. And yet the changes were coming much too slowly as far as Hope was concerned. Cotty still greeted her as if she were a child. A younger sister, perhaps, to be teased and joshed, but not taken seriously.

Despite herself, she admired his easy grace as he moved toward her now, smiling as if he had not a care in the world. Yet she knew that he was strong of temper and capable of violence. She had observed that firsthand. Once, over a year ago, as she and

Cotty had been strolling along Hospital Wharf, they had been accosted by a tough well in his cups. The tough had leered at Hope and made a vulgar remark. Cotty had bristled in her defense, and the tough, clearly confident that he could beat a stripling, had started a fight. It had been over in seconds. Hope had never seen anyone move so fast, so explosively, as Cotty had. He had moved easily under the tough's clumsy blows; and before Hope could fully grasp what had happened, the other man was unconscious on the wharf. Cotty was unmarked.

Hope had been both thrilled and shocked by the encounter. She hated violence of any sort, and yet the fact that Cotty had come to her defense was as exciting and romantic an occurrence as any she had read of in her mother's books. Surely, Cotty would see now that she was not a child but a woman whom a man might take an interest in. She had been quickly disabused of this notion when Cotty had muttered, ''That'll teach the drunken lout to be vulgar in front of an innocent child!''

With Hope and her family Cotty was unfailingly gentle, warm, kind and generous to a fault. Occasionally he might get piqued at her, and at Charity, but Hope was forced to admit that they usually provoked his temper. At times she could not seem to keep herself from tormenting him, and Charity was growing into a spoiled little imp. However, Hope had never once seen or heard Cotty treat Faith Blackstock with anything but the utmost respect and kindness. She could not recall Cotty ever losing his temper with her mother. But, despite her romantic fancies, the memory of his violence that day on the wharf stayed with her, like a small note inscribed in a corner of her mind.

Now Cotty stopped in front of her, smiling crookedly. "Are you going to stay out here and sulk all day, Hope?"

Her head went back. "I can if I like, Cotty Starke!"

"Of course you can, love." He rubbed a hand across his mouth. "But your mother is worried about you, being sick and all. If you really are sick, you should be in bed."

"I wanted some fresh air."

"Hope..." He gave an exasperated sigh. "It isn't as if I'm going back to England, or even a few leagues away. I'm going to move to the Rocks, only a few minutes' walk from here."

"The Rocks has become so rowdy that Momma forbids us to even enter the area. You well know that. I think you're just moving there to get away from us."

"Now, that is simply not true, Hope, and you know it. You, your sister and your mother are the only family I have."

She sniffed. "You're a man grown now. You don't need a family."

"I need a family now as much as ever." He smiled again, and reached out to touch her cheek. Hope flinched away from his touch. Feigning not to notice, he went on, "It's true that you shouldn't wander the Rocks alone. But any time any of you want to visit me at the Crown, send word, and I'll come and escort you."

"Something will happen to you over there. You'll be killed!" she said wildly.

"I can well take care of myself. You should know that."

"How could you get enough money to purchase a tavern? You're not old enough."

"A bit ago you said I was a man grown." His smile broadened. "Let's just say that I've scrimped and saved."

"All these years we've known you, and you've never once fully explained how you earn your living."

His smile died, and his blue eyes studied her intently. "That's true, I haven't."

"Well?" she said challengingly.

"And I'm not going to do so now. Mayhap when you're older I will tell you."

"I'm old enough now!"

"You may think so, but I'll be the judge of that, Hope."

Her gaze held his. "It must be something bad if you're ashamed to talk about it."

"It's not that, but . . ." He took a deep breath. "But it is illegal, in a manner of speaking, and it's better you know nothing about it. Not until you're older, at any rate."

"I think you're moving away from us because you've found a girl!"

"A girl!" He took on a startled look, then began to laugh. "Nothing like that at all. Hope, I've already tried to explain. I am the new owner of the Crown Tavern, and as such I must needs live on the premises."

"I don't believe you, and I think you're hiding something from me."

"Think what you like . . ."

But she was already striding off, head held high. Cotty stood watching her, bemused, until she vanished into the Blackstock hut.

Rack his brain as he would, he could not fathom the reason for Hope being so upset about his moving to the Rocks. He intended to see as much of the Blackstock family as time would permit; but now that he would be operating the Crown Tavern, it was simply no longer feasible for him to live here. Not only would he have better living quarters at the tavern, but he needed to be on the premises as much as possible to see that it was operating properly.

With a shrug of his shoulders, he dismissed Hope from his thoughts. Whatever was bothering her, she would get over it.

He started walking toward the Crown, looking forward with anticipation to the coming encounter with Master Beller.

Owning his own tavern had been Cotty's dream for some years. It not only would provide him with a more stable source of income, but would give him status as well. He smiled widely at the thought. It would be quite an advancement in life for an orphan lad who had had to make his way with whatever means he found at hand.

He had done very well over the past half dozen years. Although money was somewhat more plentiful in the colony nowadays, rum was still the popular medium of exchange. There was only a limited amount of cash in circulation, and what there was consisted mainly of foreign monies: guilders, johannas, guineas, mohurs, rupees, Spanish dollars and ducats, which had been left behind by visiting seamen. Mother England had yet to supply currency:

New South Wales was still considered a penal colony, and who needed cash in prison? Prices were listed in sterling, yet the only notes with real value equal to their face value were of two kinds: government bills of exchange on the British treasury, and paymasters' notes issued to the officers of the New South Wales Corps, which were bills on the regimental treasury in England. The Rum Corps notes were much preferred, often carrying premiums twenty-five percent higher than the government notes.

There had been a few changes in the rum trade over the past few years. When Captain Phillip Gidley King took office as the third governor of the colony, he stated that the country was comprised of two classes—those who sold rum and those who drank it. During the reign of Governor King's predecessor, the New South Wales Corps, under the command of Lieutenant Colonel Johnston, had gained enormous power, becoming military monopolists, and one vital part of their monopoly involved rum. In fact, the corps was commonly called the Rum Corps. Johnston had been aided by a powerful and prestigious plantation owner, one John Macarthur, whom many called the "Botany Bay Perturbator."

Governor King had begun his reign with great energy, confident that he could break the power of the military. He soon found that this was not easy. It was simple enough to forbid the military from trading in rum and to restrict the importation of spirits except through controlled channels; but the governor found himself thwarted at every turn, and soon realized that it was impossible to enforce the regulations. He often stated that he was balked "by every measure that art, cunning and fraud could suggest.''

To avoid the trading ban, the corps officers put their taverns and grog shanties in the names of their convict mistresses. They avoided the import ban by smuggling. Soon, such was the animosity between Governor King and the NSW Corps that the corps officers refused to visit Government House, even on official occasions.

The restriction on the importation of spirits had also had a bad effect on the legitimate tavern owners, since it severely limited the amount of liquor they could purchase. In fact, the situation had become so bad that a number of tavern owners had been forced out of business. One of the tavern owners adversely affected was Robert Beller, the current owner of the Crown Tavern.

Meanwhile, Cotty had flourished, continuing to smuggle his rum, selling it for several times the original price. In addition, he had opened a grog shanty of his own in the Rocks, but no one knew of his ownership, since it was registered in the name of the man he employed to operate it, one Jason Fowler.

Grog shanties were usually just that—shanties or lean-tos attached to more substantial buildings, with a large, shuttered door that could be swung up and latched open, with a makeshift bar running the length of it. Shelves of liquor lined the back wall. The customers stood at the bar and did their drinking in the street.

The grog shanties took some business from the taverns and some of the innkeepers had been forced to borrow money from time to time, usually at exorbitant rates of interest. Cotty was not interested in becoming a moneylender, yet he had kept a close check on all rumors; and when he learned that Robert Beller was in desperate straits and needed a loan, Cotty had quietly arranged it for him, through an intermediary. In exchange, Cotty had taken a mortgage against the Crown. The first loan had been made two years ago; since then Beller had borrowed money four times. He had never been able to pay on the principal, barely managing to keep the interest current. Today, the notes were due and payable. Beller had been frantically trying to renew them, but Cotty had seen to it that the man who fronted for him was unavailable.

Today, Beller was going to find out who had really loaned him the money. Cotty calculated that the money he had loaned the man constituted a fair price for the Crown. He could have probably purchased another tavern much cheaper, but he coveted the Crown. Part of the reason was nostalgia, since it had been home to him for a number of years. He had not been inside the Crown since that night nine years ago; but he knew from others, and from passing the building on the street, that Beller had let it deteriorate. Also, Cotty was willing to admit that he would receive a great amount of vengeful satisfaction in taking the Crown away from Beller. Perhaps this was unworthy of him; yet Beller had wronged him, and sorely.

He did not go directly to the Crown; he knew it would not be open for business yet. That was another thing that galled him—Beller no longer served food. He had closed the kitchen, and sold only spirits, which meant that he catered only to the riffraff.

He had, in effect, turned the Crown into a grog shanty, albeit a large one.

Cotty continued to his own grog shanty, located near the dockyard, on Sergeant Major's Row. Over the years since the Blackstocks had arrived in Sydney, the number of taverns had grown, in spite of the restrictions against spirits. They numbered over thirty at last count, and no one even estimated the number of grog shanties.

Cotty smiled at the names of some of the taverns he passed: the Mermaid, the Sheet Hulk, the Three Jolly Sisters, the Labour in Vain. Sprinkled in among the taverns were a number of gaming houses, brothels and flash houses, which provided bawdy entertainment. Thugs, thieves and cutthroats lurked at night in the narrow, dark alleys.

Cotty's own shanty resembled all the others. There was no need to make it any fancier, since he served only spirits, no food. His customers were only interested in drinking. When Cotty arrived he found it already open, and two men, well into their cups, leaned on the bar counter on their elbows. He was happy to see that they were Spanish sailors, paying in Spanish dollars.

Cotty went around to the back door of the shanty. Jason Fowler had seen him approaching and met him just outside the door, leaving it open so he could keep an eye on the bar. Fowler was a slender, grizzled man of fifty-some years. Cotty knew that the man sampled the liquor he sold, but he never drank so much that he could not do his job; and Cotty figured that the rum he drank was a part of his pay. In addition, he was reasonably honest, an excellent attribute for a man in his job.

"How goes it, Master Cotty?" Fowler asked, grinning, rubbing his enormous red nose. Watery blue eyes studied Cotty.

Another indication of how far he had come in the world, Cotty thought; being called master by a man almost three times his age.

"Everything is fine," Cotty said. "Is trade good today?"

"Not too busy this early, but it should begin to thrive afore long. Two ships from England hove to in the bay this morning." Fowler leaned closer, lowering his voice. "I got the word from the second mate a bit ago. He says he has three casks of rum for you."

Cotty nodded. "Good."

"You be wantin' me and Karl to row out for it tonight?"

Cotty thought for a moment. Karl Dietrich was a German immigrant a few years older than Cotty, who performed odd jobs for him. Cotty seldom picked up the casks of rum himself nowadays; the thrill had gone out of it for him, and he had better things with which to occupy his time. Although Governor King rarely imposed a curfew, unless he was extremely irked about something, the danger in smuggling spirits still remained. Not only did the governor's men patrol the shores of the bay when ships arrived in the harbor, but the officers of the NSW Corps also kept a sharp eye out for smugglers so they could ambush them and take the smuggled casks by force. After all, the smugglers would not dare complain to the government, since they were breaking the law.

If caught by Governor King's men, the penalty would depend upon the governor's mood—anywhere from a hundred lashes to expulsion from the colony. If captured by a member of the corps, it could mean death. Cotty knew of several smugglers who had been brutally murdered.

So far, Fowler and Dietrich had been fortunate. Cotty had taught them all he knew, and they were apt pupils. Both men were eager to do the task, since it meant extra money in their pockets—Cotty paid well.

Now, Cotty said, "Yes, Jason. But the pair of you be damned careful."

Fowler's grin widened, showing a gap between his blackened teeth. "Ain't we always?"

"Be especially vigilant tonight, Jason. I've heard rumors that some of the corps officers are desperate for rum. They'll be on the lookout for smugglers this night."

With a clap on Fowler's shoulder, Cotty left him and rounded the shanty to the street. He paused for a moment, breathing deeply the tang of the crisp salt air off the bay. The street here took a small rise, and he had a good view of the harbor.

A number of sailing ships rode at anchor, bobbing slightly in the small chop. The waters of the bay sparkled in the light of the setting sun. The streets thronged with people, and the marketplace up the way teamed with shoppers. The population of Sydney had almost doubled in the past ten years. Although much of the food in the colony was still imported from the Mother Country, it was more plentiful now than in the early days.

Cotty was happy, content with his lot. Although most people were unaware of it, he was already a man of substance; and he fully intended to become even wealthier over the next ten years.

And today was the first big step on the way!

Smiling to himself, he turned and headed toward the Crown Tavern and his confrontation with Master Beller.

It was now late afternoon, and Cotty saw with disgust that Beller had yet to open for business. Except at a distance, he had not seen Beller since the night Cotty had left the Crown. But from the rumors he had heard, Beller was sampling his own goods heavily, especially since hard times had struck; and he usually did not rise until well past midday.

Cotty found the front door of the tavern bolted, and instead of knocking, detoured around to the rear. The backyard stank of spoiled food and spilled spirits and other odors more difficult to identify. To his left, separated from the main building by the length of the courtyard, was the kitchen. Since the danger of fire was ever present, the kitchen was always isolated from the main building. It was dark, with an unused, almost deserted look.

Pushing against the back door, Cotty discovered it was unlocked. He went in and recoiled. The interior had an even ranker odor than the courtyard. It was dark inside, and he stumbled once as he made his way along the passageway running along the south wall into the barroom proper.

Cotty called out, "Master Beller?"

He waited for a bit and called again. Finally, he heard a stirring sound from the sleeping quarters in the back, beyond the long bar, and then a grumbling voice, "What's the commotion about? It's the middle of the night. Can't a weary man get his rest?"

"It's late afternoon, Master Beller," Cotty said cheerfully, "and past time for you to be up and about."

Another few minutes passed, and then Beller appeared in the doorway, carrying a flickering candle. He was still in his nightclothes. His face was bloated and unshaven, his eyes bleary and bloodshot. Bare feet slapping on the stone floor, he shambled toward Cotty, the candle held high. Long before the man reached him, Cotty could smell the stale spirit fumes, almost strong enough to get a man drunk just by inhaling them.

Close now, Beller held the candle high, letting the light wash over Cotty's face. He gasped, his eyes bulging. "You! I warned you never to enter my tavern again!"

"Things are different now," Cotty said calmly. He turned to one of the windows and began pulling back the shutters. "Light is needed in here."

"You get out of here. At once!" Beller's voice trembled with fury.

"I think not. We have business to transact." Cotty glanced around the barroom, his face registering disgust. "No wonder your patronage is gone, Beller. It looks like a pigsty in here."

"This is *my* tavern. I run it as I see fit. And you have no business with me!"

"Now, there you are wrong. Very wrong, indeed." From his pocket Cotty took some papers. He unfolded them and held them out. "Do you recognize these?"

Beller squinted at them suspiciously. Then his eyes widened, and he tried to snatch them away. Expecting just such a move, Cotty stepped nimbly back.

"Those are my notes!" Beller bleated.

"Wrong, Master Beller." Cotty grinned lazily. "They belong to me. Just like the Crown belongs to me, beginning today."

Beller scowled. "How did you come by them? Your name ain't on them!"

"That's true enough."

"Then how . . . ?"

"The CS Company. That's me, Beller. Cotty Starke. All that money you've been borrowing has come from me."

"But I got the money from a man by the name of Karl Dietrich."

"Again, true. But Karl works for me, and the money came from me."

"That's why I ain't been able to find him! I wanted to renew the notes . . ."

"But you don't have the money to pay them off, do you?"

"Not right now. But things will get better. They've always been renewed before."

"But not again. The expiration date on the notes was yesterday. That time has come and gone."

"That's not fair! What will I do?"

"Fair? Was it fair when you threw me out? For all you knew or cared, I could have starved to death."

"That was different."

"Mayhap you see it that way. I don't. I want you to pack your belongings, if you have any, and be out of here in one hour."

Beller's face became mottled, and his eyes blazed with rage. "You'll rue this day, I will see to that!"

Cotty stood easily, grinning, enjoying the man's frustration. "Is that supposed to frighten me?"

"I am not a man to trifle with!"

Cotty looked at the fat, perspiring man with contempt. He knew that he had made an enemy, but he scarcely thought there was reason to be concerned. He dismissed Beller with a gesture. "Pack your belongings and leave my premises."

He took a threatening step forward, and Beller bleated, scuttling away.

Laughing, Cotty glanced slowly around the room. It was going to be quite a task to make the barroom presentable again. The stone floor had to be scrubbed, the walls badly needed to be whitewashed—in fact, every square inch had to be gone over. And God only knew what the room where Beller had been sleeping looked like!

Cotty had already thought of some renovating plans. The building was only one story; he intended to add a second floor, where he would have his living quarters, two more bedrooms, and perhaps a private dining room for the swells. He fully intended to attract a higher class of clientele.

Now he had another confrontation, one that could be equally pleasing, if it went well. As soon as Beller had picked up and left, he would lock the Crown and attend to it.

HOPE WORKED INDUSTRIOUSLY all afternoon making the hut as clean as possible, toting water up from the Tank Stream and boiling a kettle of it over the fire outside. Fires inside the huts were still prohibited. In the winter the only heat they had was from a kettle of hot water brought in from outside, and from heated stones.

After she had swept the hard earthen floor clean and washed all the dirty dishes, she washed all their clothing, then started preparing supper—a pot of lamb stew with what few vegetables they had on hand.

She felt guilty about staying home from work today and missing a day's wages, paltry as they were. She hoped she might atone for it by cleaning and cooking. At least her mother would have an evening's rest. Faith Blackstock no longer taught children after work; she claimed that she had taught Cotty and her daughters all she had to teach, and tutoring other children was too much of a chore nowadays.

Just before sundown, Hope saw her mother and Charity coming down the street. Now almost twelve, Charity was tall and slender, her figure just beginning to show the fullness that was to come. Her dark hair was long and straight, and her eyes had a languid look. Hope knew that her sister was going to turn into a great beauty; she was also headstrong, inclined to mischief, and Faith still spoiled her. In Hope's opinion, her sister was lazy. While it was true that she had been working alongside her mother and sister in Simon Marsh's shop, she did nothing more than was required of her; and she was apt to drift off into a daydream at any given moment, sitting still as a statue, gazing into space. Often she had to be prodded into resuming her duties.

Hope's heart gave a wrench as she observed her mother. Faith walked with slow, painful steps, her head down. She was tired all the time these days, she had lost weight, and her color was bad. Once as immaculate as possible under the circumstances, she was now careless of dress and grooming; her hair hung in lank, lifeless strands, and often her clothing was soiled.

Hope knew that her mother was in her mid-thirties, but she looked at least fifteen years older. There was another six years to go on her sentence before she could hope to be free of Simon Marsh. Would she be able to survive that long? In the past few years it had become possible for convicts to purchase their freedom, their "ticket-of-leave," but it was very expensive, and how on earth could her family hope to accumulate the money necessary?

Now they turned into the yard before the hut, and Faith glanced up. Her weary face lit with a smile as she saw the kettle on the fire and smelled the stew cooking.

"Well, Hope! You must be feeling better, since you're fixing dinner."

"I've cleaned the hut, too, Momma," Hope said almost shyly.

"Did you? What brought about all this activity?" Faith touched Hope's cheek in a caress. "Are you still ailing?"

"No, Momma. I'm all right," Hope said abashedly, as her mother sank tiredly onto the bench before the fire pit. "I'm sorry about this morning. I wasn't really sick. I was... Well, it was because of..."

"Because of Cotty moving out. I know." Faith smiled gently. "But dear, you must remember that Cotty is now a man. He tells us he is going to be the owner of a tavern. Imagine! You can't expect a man of such substance to remain living in a hut here on the row."

"But we won't be seeing him anymore!" Hope fought back tears.

"Oh, I doubt that to be true. After all, Cotty is our dearest friend. Do you think he will just desert us?"

Charity said with a pout, "You mean that's the reason you stayed home today, Hope? All because of the old high-and-mighty Cotty. I had to do your work today! Simon Marsh made me!"

"Hush, child!" Faith said sharply. "Your sister is feeling badly enough, I'm sure..." She broke off, her gaze going past them, and she began to smile. "You see, he hasn't deserted us."

Hope swung around to see Cotty swinging jauntily toward them, grinning broadly.

"You're just in time for supper, young Cotty," Faith called out. A touch of the old mischief flickered in her eyes. "If you don't think your station is too far above us now."

"That will never be," Cotty said cheerfully, stooping to kiss her cheek. He dropped down beside her. "I have been busy this day."

"Are you now the proud owner of the Crown?"

"Oh, no difficulty there. But I also made another, perhaps more important, transaction today." He took some papers from his pocket and handed them almost reverently to Faith.

She took the papers and stared at them uncomprehendingly. "What is this?"

"That represents your freedom, Faith. It's your ticket-of-leave. It will have to be renewed every year until your sentence expires, but there should be no problem with that. You are a free woman, Faith!"

# CHAPTER NINE

COTTY STOOD IN THE MIDDLE of the barroom and surveyed the interior. The shutters were thrown wide, and a nice breeze circulated through the large room.

It had taken two weeks to get the place into presentable shape. He, along with Karl Dietrich and the Blackstock family, had labored from dawn to dark and often into the night, but now the floor, the tables, chairs, and the long bar glowed in the spill of light. Every inch of the interior walls had been whitewashed, and the front of the building had been bricked over.

The room Beller had used for living quarters had also been cleaned; but Cotty fancied that he could still smell the man's odious presence. No matter; he could manage until the second-story addition was completed. Construction on that was already underway.

He smiled as he remembered Faith's reaction when he presented her with her ticket-of-leave. She had been dazed with happiness, alternating between tears and laughter.

"But how will I ever repay your generosity?" she had asked.

"There is really no need. The excellent tutoring you have provided me is payment enough."

Hope, always the practical one—in most things—had exclaimed, "But how are we to live? We shall have no income!"

Cotty had smiled. "That will be taken care of. I will be adding a second story to my tavern. There will be two extra bedrooms when it is finished. You will no longer need to live in the hut."

Faith immediately began to protest—they could not live off his bounty; and it would create gossip and scandal for them to be living on the same premises with him. Cotty had responded to the first objection by saying that they could work at helping get the Crown into shape. At the second objection he had laughed. Who in Sydney would look askance at a widow woman and her daughters living with him? Half the army officers had mistresses in the Rocks area; it was accepted as commonplace. And certainly no one would consider it a scandal for a twenty-one-year-old man to be living with a woman of Faith's age, and her two daughters who were so much younger than he. He looked upon Faith as his mother, and Hope and Charity as his sisters.

Cotty remembered that Hope had scowled angrily at that, but he'd ignored her. She had been acting so strangely of late that he had found it best to simply ignore her moods. He did take notice of the fact that she had voiced no objections to living at the Crown.

Tonight was the grand opening!

Although the Crown was located in a rough neighborhood, on the very edge of the Rocks, Cotty expected a goodly turnout of the swells from above the wharf area. He had long recognized that the gentry liked to show off their superior station in life by occasionally patronizing the slum areas.

The opening of a new pub was rarely considered a grand event, since several opened every year; but he had seen to it that news of the Crown's opening had gotten around. Also, he had a large number of flyers made announcing the event and had hired several dock boys to deliver them to every house in Sydney.

His reverie was interrupted by the sound of laughter and voices from outside. The front door swung open, admitting Faith and the girls. In payment for their help in renovating the tavern, Cotty had given them enough money to purchase new clothing for that night's opening.

Regaining her freedom had given Faith a new lease on life. She appeared years younger, and she was quite fetching in a blue muslin gown made with a flowing skirt and a long-sleeved bodice, adorned by a very full kerchief tucked into the front. The ensemble was topped by a large hat of blue silk, faced with green—colors that set off Faith's pale beauty. The hat—the first real hat she had owned in years—was her pride, and she kept reaching up to touch it, as if to reassure herself that it was really there. Still, as pretty as she looked tonight, she was much too thin, and Cotty feared that her years of hard labor under Simon Marsh's thumb had ruined her health.

But despite his concern for Faith, Cotty could not help but notice that Hope was not only beautiful in her simple overgown and petticoat of gray and pink-striped chintz, with a pink gauze kerchief at the front and a plain gauze cap of the same pink, but for the first time he realized that she was on the verge of womanhood.

Even Charity, at twelve, looked almost grown-up in her dress of peach-flowered chintz and white gauze kerchief.

"Well," he said, "it would appear that the Blackstock family is growing up, almost overnight."

"It's about time you were realizing that," Hope said tartly.

"Now, Hope, you're still just a child," Faith said reprovingly.

"I am not, Momma! I'm almost fifteen!"

"Well, whatever your ages, welcome to the new Crown Tavern," Cotty said. He led them toward a corner table. "I have a table set up for all of you. You'll be out of the crowd here. Now, Faith, I know you don't drink, but do have at least a glass of ale. This *is* a special occasion."

She nodded, smiling. "I think I will."

"Good!" He glanced at the girls. "The only thing I can offer you two is goat's milk."

"Goat's milk!" Charity made a face. "We drink that all the time at home. We could at least have a small glass of wine."

"Now, Charity," Faith said, "be nice."

"Why not, Faith?" Cotty asked. "It is a special occasion, as I said. What harm can a small glass do? Why, I understand that children in France start drinking wine at meals after they are weaned from mother's milk."

"All right," Faith conceded. "Just this once, but we must see that it doesn't set a precedent. And make sure it's a small glass, young Cotty."

"Of course," Cotty said, grinning. "Oh...you'll have to wait for a minute, ladies. My first patrons are arriving."

Hope watched him stride toward the front to greet a group of six, four men and two women. The men were officers of the New South Wales Corps, resplendent in their uniforms. Hope had to wonder if the women were wives or mistresses. She was impressed by Cotty's mien as he greeted them. There was no doubt that he was at ease, in complete command of the situation.

How handsome he is, she thought.

And then the truth burst upon her—the reason she had been so depressed at the thought of his moving away from them. She was in love with him!

Her heart ached at the implication of that revelation, because it was hopeless. Cotty looked upon her as a sister, and it seemed he was unprepared to see her as anything else.

Now he was coming toward them with a tray. He set a mug of ale down before Faith and the glasses of wine before the girls. "Here you are, ladies. Enjoy yourselves. I'm going to be quite busy, but I'll join you at your table from time to time."

By the end of another hour the Crown Tavern was crowded, and Cotty felt that he could afford to relax. Not that he had really entertained any doubts about the success of the opening night; yet it was reassuring to have his judgment confirmed.

The majority of the patrons were male, which was understandable, but there were a number of women present, most of them respectable wives of the better class. Some of the women he recognized as officers' mistresses; for, although they were not invited into the homes of the better social classes, their presence was tolerated in public taverns.

He was particularly pleased to note that while the males present were predominantly from the New South Wales Corps, there were also a number of men from Government House. He knew that this was unusual, since the enmity was mounting steadily between the corps and Governor King's men. The governor was not present; however, Cotty thought it safe to assume that the men from Government House had the governor's sanction.

Shortly before nine o'clock he was sitting at a table with an officer of the corps, Lieutenant Hugh Marston. Although Cotty was adamantly opposed to the rum strictures imposed by the governor, he was also disapproving of most of the corps officers. Since the NSW Corps had grown into power over the past few years, their officers had become arrogant, overbearing and contemptuous of anyone not their own.

Hugh Marston was one of the few officers Cotty liked. Marston was in his mid-thirties, a frequenter of taverns and the flash houses, and far more interested in rum and women than he was in power or in furthering his military career. Aside from being somewhat vain of his good looks, he was amiable enough, good company and capable of intelligent conversation.

Marston was accompanied by two women, one around Marston's own age and the other not much older than Cotty. The older woman, Alice Cowan, was buxom, a little on the blowsy side.

The other one, Prudence Wilkes, was dark and slender, with thick black hair and brown eyes. She was quite attractive.

Cotty, who had had little time to spare for female companionship over the past few years, was drawn to her; and from the intensity of her eyes when their glances chanced to meet, he had the feeling that the attraction was mutual.

Why not, he thought suddenly. He had made it to the first plateau on his rise to success. He could afford to relax and enjoy himself.

On being introduced to the two women, Cotty had said jokingly, "*Two* women, Hugh?"

"My dear young friend," Marston had responded, "I like the female sex, as you well know. Are not two women far better than one?"

Alice Cowan had said hastily, "Prudence just arrived today on a ship from England. She is in way of being my ward, the daughter of an old friend in London. I couldn't very well leave her alone her first night in Sydney Town, now could I, sir?"

Cotty knew about the ship's arrival. He had received word that it had several casks of rum in its hold, and Jason Fowler and Karl Dietrich were to pick up the casks at around midnight. Cotty was courting respectability for the Crown, but he had no intention of severing his connection with the grog shanty; for that connection was the easiest way to earn quick money. In fact, he was thinking of opening yet another, putting Dietrich in charge.

Prudence Wilkes interrupted his thoughts. "I'm surprised, Master Starke, to find a pub of such refinement in a new colony."

"Well now, I don't know as to how refined it is." Cotty laughed, waving his hand around at the boisterous crowd. "This group could hardly be called that."

"Oh, but I understand that many taverns in London are much rowdier. Not that I have been in many . . ." Her soft cheeks flushed a rose color, her gaze dropping away. "But with so many seamen along the wharfs . . ."

Cotty smiled across the table at her. "That lot will rarely be seen in my place. They'll find the grog shanties and the taverns deeper into the Rocks more to their liking. I intend to have a fine place here. For instance, starting next week, I will start serving excellent food under the supervision of Faith Blackstock. As soon as the upstairs addition is finished, I will open a dining room there. I calculate that will help draw a better class of patrons. I mean to offer competition to Rosetta Stabler's Eating House."

Hugh Marston guffawed, slapping the table. "A fine ambition, my friend, but mayhap not so easy to carry out. Rosetta serves the best food in Sydney. Or anywhere in New South Wales, for that matter."

"I well know that, but there is a great need for more good dining establishments, and I intend to help fill that need." Cotty transferred his attention to Prudence. "What made you decide to come to New South Wales, Prudence? If I may be so bold as to use your first name."

"Please do, sir. I would be most honored."

"It hardly seems a fitting place for one so young, and so lovely."

"Thank you for the compliment, sir."

Alice Cowan said, "Prudence is betrothed to a young officer in the corps."

"Oh?" Cotty raised an eyebrow. "Then where might he be? Why isn't he at your side?" He leaned back, crossing one leg over the other.

"He is presently at Parramatta, so we understand," Alice said.

Prudence's gaze met Cotty's briefly. "Actually, I knew Richard back in London, but we are not really betrothed. We have an . . . understanding."

"I should think he would wish to seal that understanding quickly," Cotty said boldly. "It would be foolhardy of him to delay, with a lady of your beauty."

"We shall see."

Prudence's eyes locked with his, seemed to glow, and Cotty felt a warmth rush through him; but before he had a chance to pursue the matter, there was a commotion at the front door. Glancing that way, he saw two men just entering. They were evidently well-known, since voices were being raised in greeting.

"Oh, ho," Hugh said in a low voice. "You are indeed fortunate, my friend, to have that pair condescend to grace you with their presence."

One of the men was in the uniform of the NSW Corps, and the tall man at his side had a commanding presence, with a lean and bony face, deep-set intense eyes, a stubborn jut of jaw and a high forehead. He was well-dressed, with a high collar, a white stock and highly polished boots.

"Who are they, Hugh?" Cotty asked. "I'm afraid I don't recognize either of them."

"The man in civilian clothes is John Macarthur, down from Elizabeth Farm, near Parramatta. His own little kingdom," Hugh said with a sneer. "He has a commission in the corps, having been made paymaster of the corps by Governor Grose a few years back."

"The man they call the Botany Bay Perturbator?"

"The very same." Hugh grinned.

"Naturally, I've heard of him, but I've never had the pleasure of his acquaintance. Who is the corps officer?"

"His lackey, Major George Johnston."

"You show little respect, Hugh, for one of your own officers," Cotty said with a smile.

"Bloody bastards, the pair of them," Hugh said in a growling voice.

Cotty leaned forward. "Why do you call them that? I'm not overly fond of the corps, either, but you're an officer."

"With those two it's not military, but political. And they're infecting the entire corps with their manipulations. You know I'm not a military man at heart, Cotty. I came out here to escape a spot of trouble back in merry old England. Joining the corps seemed to me the best way to continue eating. Back then, I at least had respect for the officers.

"But no more. Macarthur has corrupted them. Not only are they rebellious, almost to the point of treason against the Crown, but they buy, smuggle, distill and sell illegal spirits. Most of the officers are whoremongers and criminals and are not loath to kill for profit. Mind you, I'm opposed to the governor's policy on spirits, but there are limits to how far I would go in opposition. That precious pair have no limits. I believe there is nothing they would not do if money and power were involved. They are the worst kind of villains! Macarthur snaps his fingers and Major Johnston rolls over like a lapdog and sticks out his tongue."

"Macarthur is a powerful man, I gather."

"Oh, yes, indeed. I would advise you not to cross him, my friend."

Cotty got to his feet. "Well, tonight they are patrons. It's only fitting that I greet them."

"We shall take our leave, then. I have no desire to share the same taproom with those two." Hugh also got up. "Come along, ladies."

Cotty took Prudence's hand and raised it to his lips. Straightening up, he stared directly into her eyes. "I was delighted to make your acquaintance, Prudence, and I sincerely hope that I shall have the opportunity to see you again."

"I would not be averse to that, sir."

Emboldened, he said, "Then I shall make a point to do so."

He stood for a few moments watching them walk away. There was a definite sway to Prudence's hips, and Cotty had to wonder if it was for his benefit.

When they had disappeared out the door, he turned away and strolled over to the table occupied by Macarthur and Major Johnston. The barmaid, Lucy Bolton, was just taking their orders.

"Welcome to the Crown, Master Macarthur, Major Johnston. I am Cotty Starke, the new proprietor. The first round of spirits is my pleasure, gentlemen."

Macarthur glanced at him, his eyes sharp and piercing. "So you are the young lad I have been hearing so much about. I'm surprised that someone of your tender years should own a tavern."

Cotty shrugged, wearing an ingenuous smile. "A result of hard work and a great deal of good fortune. I am happy to see gentlemen such as yourselves present. I hope this will not be the last time. Next month, I plan to begin serving food, under the supervision of Mistress Blackstock. I hope, sir, to welcome you and your good wife for dining some evening before long.''

"Oh, I think not, Starke. A tavern such as this is hardly the place a gentleman takes his wife.''

Cotty felt a prod of temper. Hugh Marston was right; Macarthur was a proper bastard.

"Besides,'' the man went on, "as I understand it, this Blackstock woman is a convict.''

"A *former* convict,'' Cotty said stiffly.

"No matter,'' Macarthur said with a careless shrug. "I hardly think that a convict, accustomed to poor fare, would be familiar with the proper food to serve to gentry.'' He turned his back, dismissing Cotty.

Cotty's fury rose, choking him. His hands opened and closed, and it took a great deal of willpower not to clamp his hands around the man's throat.

He finally turned on his heel, his anger still rampant. From across the room he saw Faith beckoning to him. He made his way to her table.

"It grows late, Cotty. I think we should go now.''

"All right, I'll escort you home.''

"There is no need for that. You have your duties here.''

"My duties here are not all that urgent, and 'twould not be safe for three ladies to walk the streets unescorted at this hour of the night.''

As the Blackstock family prepared to depart, Cotty turned for a final look across the room. Macarthur and the major had been served. As Cotty watched, they touched tankards in a toast and laughed together. Probably laughing at the young upstart who dared to make himself known to them, he thought; and drinking spirits that I provided free of charge!

"Cotty . . ." It was Faith. "Why are you looking so angry?"

He turned with a forced smile. "Nothing to do with you, Faith. Are you ready?"

"Yes."

The barmaid was just passing. "Lucy, I shall return shortly."

The harried Lucy said, "All right, Master Starke."

Outside in the cool night air, Cotty offered an arm to Faith and Hope. Faith took it, but Hope refused with a toss of her head. Charity, forgetting the grown-up decorum she had assumed inside, skipped on ahead.

"Are you having difficulty with your tavern, Cotty?" Faith asked before they'd gone too far. "Is that the reason you looked so angry?"

"Not really," he replied with a shrug. "I was displeased with the behavior of a pair of guests. With luck, they will not patronize the place again."

"I thought it was because your black-haired wench left so early," Hope said.

"She's hardly my wench," he said amusedly. "I just met her tonight."

"But you kissed her hand. I saw you!"

"Simple courtesy due to a lady."

"How could she be a lady and patronize a tavern?"

"Hope!" Faith snapped. "Now behave yourself. Need I remind you that *you* were just there, as well as your sister and myself?"

"That was different," Hope said with a sniff. She knew that she was being obnoxious, but she could not

seem to help herself; and Cotty's air of amused con-
descension only served to infuriate her further.

The sound of raised voices snagged her attention,
and she looked ahead. At the intersection of Rock's
Row and Surrey Lane, which they were approaching, there was some sort of melee. As they drew
nearer, Hope saw that two men in seamen's clothing
were scuffling with a near-naked aborigine. One
seaman had his arms wrapped around him from behind, while the other pummeled him on the face and
body.

Cotty said curtly, "Stay here, out of harm's way."

In a few quick steps he was on the trio. He seized
one seaman by the shoulder, half spun him around
and hit him once in the stomach; then, as the man
started to double up, Cotty hit him flush in the face
with his right fist. The seaman reeled backward, fell
to the ground and lay still.

Cotty wheeled on the second man. "Let him go!"

"Why're you buttin' in, mate? 'Tis just a boong,
for God's sake, just a bloody boong. Shouldn't be
walkin' the street with decent folk."

"You call yourself decent? Two on one?"

"But he's just a black fella! 'Sides, we wasn't goin'
to hurt him bad. Just havin' a little sport with 'im."

"You can have your sport somewhere else." Cotty's voice was savage. "Now let him go, or I'll lay
you out on the ground like your friend."

Reluctantly, the seaman let go of the aborigine and
stepped back. The native swayed and would have
fallen if Cotty had not caught him.

Cotty gestured to the man on the ground, who was
beginning to stir. "Help your friend up and the pair
of you go back to the Rocks. Anywhere but here."

In a few moments the two seamen were walking away, the one supporting the other. Hope, her mother and sister moved to where Cotty lent support to the aborigine. Up close, Hope was surprised to notice that he was quite light-skinned, and that he had distinctive Caucasian features. Clearly, he was not a full-blood native. He appeared very young.

Cotty knew a few words of the native tongue, and he tried now, in a stumbling way, to ascertain if the boy was badly hurt. There was a cut on his cheek, from which blood trickled.

To everyone's astonishment, the boy spoke in reasonably good English. "I . . . am not bad. Their blows came mostly on the body. I think nothing is broken."

"You speak English very well," Cotty said.

The lad smiled with a visible effort, teeth flashing white in his dark face. "My father, he is English. He taught me. My English name is John Myers."

Cotty stared at the youth, turning him so that his face caught the light from an open door. There was a note of excitement in Cotty's voice as he spoke. "John Myers? Was your father Peter Myers?"

The boy, wide-eyed, nodded. "Yes, Peter Myers. You knew him?"

"I most certainly did." Cotty grinned. "He was on the ship with me and my own father. He was a friend." He shook his head in wonder.

"My father is dead. He left me . . ." The boy looked around wildly. Then he spotted what he was looking for. He stooped to pick up a leather-bound book lying on the ground a few feet away. Holding it out, he said, "My father wrote in his book about his life here, and with my people."

"Mayhap you would let me read it sometime. Where have you come from, John?"

John gestured vaguely inland. "There."

"For what reason did you come to Sydney Town?"

"My mother is dead. And then my father died. I wanted to see..." Suddenly his eyes closed and he swayed.

Cotty caught him. "How long since you've eaten?"

"Two, three days," John said weakly.

"Good Heavens, John, we must feed you," Faith exclaimed.

"Of course," Cotty said, gnawing on his lower lip in thought. "Do you know anyone in Sydney, John? Do you have a place to stay?"

John shook his head. "No, no one. No place to stay."

Hope spoke up. "Your hut, Cotty. It's still empty. Why can't he stay there?"

Cotty glanced at her in surprise. "That's a thought. At least, he can stay there tonight. Later, we can figure something out."

"First," Faith said, "we must get something in the boy's belly. We can think on the rest later."

IT WAS LATE, nearing midnight, when Cotty hurried back to the Crown. He was a little concerned about being gone so long, but he had been unable to get away any sooner.

John Myers had been well fed by Faith. As he ate, he had told them about his life, and how he had come to be in Sydney. It had been a fascinating tale, and Cotty had listened, enthralled, along with the Blackstocks. But, finally, John had been bedded down in Cotty's old hut, and Cotty had taken his leave.

The crowd had diminished greatly by the time he returned to the tavern. Lucy saw him come in and hurried to meet him with a look of relief on her face.

"We were beginning to worry about you," she said, "fearing something was amiss."

"I'm sorry, Lucy. I was delayed. Is everything all right here?"

"We have been terribly busy, although people have started to leave."

"You have done a good job this night, Lucy. I'll pay you extra."

Someone called for service at a table, and Lucy rushed off. A glance across the room told Cotty that Macarthur and Major Johnston were still present; he was surprised that they had lingered so long. With full tankards before them, they were huddled together, talking in low tones.

Cotty turned with a shrug, started toward the bar, then stopped halfway there as the figure of a man lurched out of the passageway from the rear. It was Karl Dietrich.

Dietrich saw Cotty and started toward him. Cotty experienced a chill of apprehension as he saw that Dietrich was clutching his left arm. Blood seeped from between his fingers.

Reaching him, Dietrich gasped out, "Bad tidings, Master Starke! Very bad!"

"What is it, Karl?"

"Jason . . . Jason is dead!"

"What happened?"

"They were layin' in wait for us when we rowed ashore with the rum, soldiers of the corps. They shot

Jason dead, wounded me sorely, and made away with the rum casks.''

As though impelled by some primitive instinct, Cotty's head whipped around, and his gaze went to Macarthur's table. Macarthur was staring directly at him, and he wore a gloating look, as though he had been privy to the conversation. Cotty knew then why the man had lingered—he had been waiting for this moment!

# CHAPTER TEN

THE SOUND OF LOUD VOICES rudely awakened Hope from a lovely dream of Cotty; and although she attempted to cling to the pleasant fantasy, the racket grew so loud that she was forced to get up.

Raising her head, she saw that her mother was also awake. "What is it, Momma?"

"I don't know, but I suppose we should find out."

Faith got out of the hammock and began getting dressed, and Hope, still thinking of her dream, followed suit. Charity was still sleeping, undisturbed.

It was shortly after sunrise as Hope and her mother went out into the cool morning. They saw a group of people standing before Cotty's hut next door. Hope recognized most of the people as convicts from the neighborhood. As mother and daughter pushed their way through the crowd, people turned angry faces upon them and called out scathing comments. Reaching the forefront of the group, Hope saw John Myers squatting before the hut, his face impassive.

"What is happening here?" Faith demanded.

"Them that has eyes can see, Faith Blackstock," shouted a woman in the front. She had a smoldering clay pipe in her hand, and she pointed it at John. "We have a black 'un in our midst!"

"Well, Betsy Enright," Faith said, "what's amiss about that?"

"We don't want such as them livin' among us."
Betsy Enright spat on the ground.

"I fail to see how any of us are in any position to
cast aspersions."

The other woman sneered, exposing rotting teeth.
"We 'uns don't need none of your fancy talk, Faith
Blackstock! He's a black fella, and don't belong
among us!"

"The aborigines were here long before we were.
I'd say that they have a perfect right to be here, more
so than we do, in fact."

Another woman spoke up. "It's just as we was
talkin', afore you came. You be the one responsible
for him bein' here, Faith Blackstock!"

"I don't deny it. The lad was badly beaten by
toughs, he was hungry, and he needed a place to
sleep. This hut belongs to Cotty Starke, and he gave
his permission."

"Well, we demand that he leave at once!"

John got to his feet. "I will go. There is no need
for trouble."

Faith gestured in annoyance. "You will stay,
John. Don't let this rabble frighten you away."

"Now, you lookee here, Faith Blackstock." Betsy
Enright took a threatening step forward. "Just because you be a free woman now, don't mean that you
can lord it over the rest of us. We have our rights, and
we have a say in who lives amongst us and who
don't!"

Faith's face tightened with anger. "That hut belongs to Cotty, and he's the only one who says who
lives there."

"We 'uns have talked about it and decided. That
boong don't live among us, and that's final!"

The circle around Faith and Hope tightened and moved forward, the faces menacing.

Hope stepped in front of her mother and, as she did, she gave Betsy Enright a push. "You leave my mother alone!"

"Don't you be shovin' me, young missy!" Betsy Enright said in a harsh voice.

"What is going on here?" a voice demanded loudly from the back of the crowd.

Reluctantly, the mob parted, and Cotty forced his way through to stand alongside Hope.

"Oh, we're happy to see you, Cotty!" she said in relief, glad of the opportunity to seize his hand.

"What's the trouble?"

Quickly Hope explained the circumstances.

Cotty raised his voice. "There is no cause to be concerned, good people. I have given some thought to it. John will not be staying among you, so you have nothing to fear." There was a satirical twist to his voice.

Hope made a sound of dismay. "Cotty, we can't just throw him out to starve!"

Cotty looked at her with a smile. "I have no intention of doing so. He can move into my old quarters at the Crown, and he can earn his bed and board working there."

"Just bed and board? He should be paid a wage!"

Cotty was studying her with some amusement, and a new respect; Hope was maturing rapidly. "He will be paid, Hope, never fear. I disapprove of slave labor."

Glancing around, he caught John's gaze on Hope. His dark eyes held a look of worship. Oh, ho, Cotty thought, he seems to be smitten. The thought saddened him, for it could only result in the boy being hurt. Turning around again, Cotty saw that his announcement had eased the crowd's fears—they were beginning to drift away.

"I'm surprised to find you such a staunch supporter of the natives," he said, turning to look at Hope.

Her head went back. "Why should you be? It's the Christian thing to do. He hasn't done anything to harm these people."

"Oh, I didn't say I disapprove." He patted her on the head. "I'm proud of you, Hope."

"Oh!" She twisted away from him. "Sometimes, Cotty Starke, you infuriate me so!"

He stared after her in astonishment as she whirled away and stormed into the Blackstock hut. "Now what's the matter with her?"

Faith laughed. "The main thing, dear, is that Hope is caught between childhood and adulthood."

"I fail to see how that explains it," he said with a shake of his head.

"You will when you get older."

"I very much doubt it."

"Did you come by just to take John to the Crown?"

"I also came to escort you and the girls to the tavern. You're supposed to start to work putting the kitchen in order, remember? Now you have some additional help. John can help you." He paused, looking off into the distance, sighing.

"What's wrong, Cotty? You look so sad all of a sudden."

"Jason Fowler was killed last night." He had told Faith very little about his business affairs, but she did know that he owned the grog shanty; and he suspected that she knew quite a bit more about him than she ever let on.

"Oh, Cotty, I am so sorry!" she said in dismay. "How did it happen?"

He hesitated, then told her how Fowler had been killed.

"I've always been so worried that *you* would be killed while smuggling rum into Sydney. Or be arrested."

"Then you *did* know all along."

"Of course, Cotty. I may be old and tired, but I'm not stupid."

"How well I know that." He smiled at her affectionately.

"Surely, now that you own your own tavern, you'll stop all this foolishness."

"It all depends on how many restrictions the government places on the importation of spirits, Faith," he said thoughtfully. "I'll admit that in the beginning I started smuggling rum as a way to earn my living. It was the only way I could make any real money."

"But you don't have to do that now," she pointed out. "I am sure that your tavern is going to be a great success."

"I hope so, but if it's hard to get spirits for my patrons through legal means, I'll have to continue smuggling. I can't stay in business without a product to sell."

"But it's dangerous, Cotty. Jason's death must prove that to you."

"We'll see, Faith. Nothing's happened to me so far, so stop worrying." He leaned down to kiss her on the cheek. "Now you and the girls get ready to go to work."

"We have to have breakfast first. Will you join us?"

"I would be glad to."

After Faith had crossed to their hut, Cotty turned to John, still squatting by the door. "I feel that I must apologize, John, for not consulting you before making plans for you. You should have something to say about it, and if what I have suggested doesn't meet with your approval, don't hesitate to say so."

The aborigine stood in one graceful, fluid movement. His face broke into a smile. "It is all right, Master Cotty."

Cotty gestured impatiently. "Not Master, John. Just plain Cotty, please."

"Cotty," John said shyly. "I would be happy to work for you. Otherwise, I would starve."

"Well, we'll see to it that you don't starve." Cotty placed a hand on the youth's shoulder and squeezed. "Now come along and eat with us."

Cotty squatted by the coals of the hearth and nursed them into flames. He had a good fire going by the time Faith and the girls came out carrying food.

AFTER BREAKFAST, as they walked toward the Crown Tavern, Hope lagged behind. She was not sure yet how she felt about living in the same house with Cotty Starke. She was of two minds about it. She looked forward to being close to him all the time, and yet if he continued to treat her like a little sister . . . !

"Mistress..." It was John, walking up beside her. He wore a shy smile. "I wish to thank you. You stood up for me before other people. I am very grateful."

"It's all right, John. I wanted you to know that all white people aren't like those people. They're nothing but scum." In a sudden, mercurial change of mood, she called out, "Momma?"

Faith glanced back. "Yes, dear?"

"I have a student for you." She touched John on the shoulder. "You must teach John here to read and write."

"I shall be happy to," Faith said. "John, can you read or write at all?"

"I can read a little, and write a very little. My father taught me what he could."

"Well, we shall soon improve upon that. I've missed giving lessons," Faith said cheerfully.

At the tavern they went down the side of the building. Cotty paused at the lean-to he had once lived in. "Here, John, I'll show you your new quarters."

Faith and her daughters crossed the cobbled yard to the kitchen. Workers were busy on the second story of the main building—hammering, sawing and laying brick.

The cook house was constructed of stone, which was two feet thick, and which Hope knew helped keep it relatively cool in the summer; but she wrinkled her nose as she entered behind her mother. It stank of old grease and burned food. Unused for so long, everything was covered with a layer of dust, and cobwebs hung from every corner.

"Momma," Charity said in disgust, "do we have to clean *this*? It's such a mess, we'll never get it clean!"

"It's the least we can do to repay Cotty for giving us good jobs and a decent place to live. We have to have it ready for the Yule season, so patrons can enjoy festive meals for the holidays." Already she was bustling around, flinging open the shutters. "It's not so bad, and hard work never hurt anyone. And John will help us with the hardest tasks. Nothing like having a man around."

"Man!" Charity said with a sniff. "He's just a boy, and a black boy at that."

"Charity, you mind your tongue! I'll not have you saying such things!"

"But it's true. He's just a . . ."

Before Charity could finish the sentence, Faith's open hand came up and smacked her across the face. Charity backed up a step, her cheek already reddening, and tears leaked from her eyes. She stared at her mother in round-eyed shock.

Hope had watched in amazement. It was a rare occasion that Faith physically punished her youngest daughter; in fact, Hope could not remember when she had ever struck Charity.

Breathing hard, Faith said, "I'm sorry for that, Charity, but you deserved it. I've spoiled you, and you've become a willful child. And if I ever hear you saying such a thing about John again, or abusing him in any manner, your punishment will be more severe. You have my promise on that. Now," she said brusquely, "we have work to do."

AFTER COTTY HAD SHOWN John where he was to live, and had checked on the progress in the kitchen, he climbed the scaffold to the second story to see how the work was progressing.

Alex Stafford, the master carpenter in charge of the new construction, was a plump, cheerful soul, with cheeks reddened from the consumption of great quantities of rum. To Cotty's questions he replied, "It's going well, Master Starke. It should be finished before Christmas."

"Excellent, Alex!" Cotty slapped the man on the shoulder. "You are doing a fine job. I want you to know that I appreciate it."

The master carpenter shrugged. "It's grand to be appreciated, since many here in Sydney have little time for that sort of thing. All they say is hurry, hurry, get it done," the man said in a grumbling voice.

Cotty laughed and wandered across the area, trying to keep out of the way of the workers. His inspection completed, well satisfied with the results so far, he climbed down the scaffold to the ground.

At the memory of Jason Fowler's death, his momentary lift of spirits deserted him. He had to make arrangements for the man's burial; he would not see him buried in a pauper's grave. He knew that Jason had had no kin in Sydney, no one to mourn his untimely death. Jason had given his life in Cotty's service, so it was the least Cotty could do to see that the man had a decent burial.

At the bottom of his sorrow lay a deep anger that he could do nothing about Jason's death. Since Jason was his employee and had been killed in the act of smuggling, there would be serious questions raised if he complained to the governor; and, even disregarding the personal risk, complaining would accomplish little. Although the New South Wales Corps and the governor were at loggerheads, no legal action would be taken over the death of a smuggler. It did not matter that Cotty suspected that John Macarthur had knowledge of the killing; a knowing look was hardly sufficient evidence of the fact.

No, all he could do was mourn Jason, see to a proper burial, and try to put it all out of his mind. But since it appeared that Macarthur, and Major Johnston by association, knew of his involvement in the smuggling of spirits, Cotty knew that he would have to be doubly careful in the future. Of course, he could heed Faith's counsel and give up the smuggling activity. However, that might not be possible, if, as he had told Faith, the restrictions on the importation of spirits again became severe.

It was nearing the noon hour, but he was not hungry. He was tired and sleepy, for he had slept little last night after hearing the news about Jason Fowler. Until the kitchen was ready to reopen, the tavern would only be in business in the evenings. After the kitchen was again in operation, he intended to open earlier, perhaps serving the noon meal as well as dinner.

He made his way to his sleeping quarters, removed his boots and stretched out on the narrow bed, intending to sleep for an hour or so.

However, when he awoke, it was late afternoon, the sun's rays slanting in through the open shutters on the west side. The moment he sat up, the memory of Jason's violent death flooded his mind again.

He put on his boots, washed his face in cold water and let himself out through the front door. Depressed, he was in no mood for facing Faith and her daughters; he assumed they were still working in the kitchen.

Feeling at loose ends, he did not know quite what to do with himself. The grog shanty was closed, since he had no one to run it; he had to find a new man to take Jason's place.

Deep in thought, walking with his head down, he almost collided with a woman. Without looking up, he muttered an apology and started on.

A husky voice said, "Why, Master Starke, you're not even going to say hello? I consider that most impolite."

He came to a stop and raised his eyes, looking into the warm brown eyes of Prudence Wilkes. "Prudence!" he exclaimed. He glanced around for Alice Cowan, but Prudence was alone. "What on earth are you doing all alone?"

"I felt in need of a nice stroll, and Alice was otherwise occupied."

He frowned. "The Rocks is hardly a place for a woman to walk alone."

"Pooh!" she said with a careless gesture. "In broad daylight, with people all around? What can happen to me?"

"Almost anything, Prudence. They're a rough lot, the men here in the Rocks, and they have been known to molest women."

"But I walked all the way from our lodgings, a matter of some distance, and no one accosted me," she said with a pout.

"Even so, 'tis not a good idea."

"The truth of the matter is, sir, I had hoped to encounter you." Now her look was bold. "Good fortune must be mine on this day."

Staring at her silently for a moment, he felt his blood begin to race. His instincts about this woman had been correct—she had experienced the same attraction he had felt. He smiled lazily. "And how may I be of service, my dear?"

"You might offer a lady a touch of spirits."

He made a leg and said gravely, "It would be my pleasure, Prudence."

It was all he could do to keep a straight face as he gave her his arm and escorted her back to the Crown. Who would ever have dreamed that Cotty Starke would bend a knee for a lady? Of course, Faith had taught him that when she had instructed him in good manners; but even as he had learned it, he never thought a time would come when he would make use of the knowledge.

The interior of the tavern was cool, a welcome respite from the December heat outside. At the bar he said, "I have a bottle of good French wine. Would that suit?"

"That will be splendid, Cotty," she said saucily.

He got the bottle of wine and two glasses, and took them to the nearest table; but when he turned around, Prudence was still standing by the bar. "Prudence?"

"I thought you might show me your quarters."

His pulse speeded up, but he managed to keep a cool composure. "I was afraid that would be forward of me."

"Have no fear of that." She took a step toward him, her smile provocative. "Mayhap you think *I* am being forward?"

"Not at all. I am honored, Prudence." He picked up the bottle and glasses. "However, my quarters are those of a lone man, not really fitting for a lady."

"Surely more fitting than the quarters I share with Alice." She made a face. "Back in London, beggars on the streets live in better."

Privately he wondered how she could be familiar with the living conditions of beggars in London, but he merely said, "Sydney Town is not London. It may be someday, but that day is in the distant future."

Aside from the narrow bed, his room contained only a single chair, a small table and a clothes cupboard. He motioned Prudence to the one chair, and sat on the bed; somewhat uneasily, since it reminded him all too vividly of what was on his mind. Yet, why should he be bothered, if she was not? She had invited herself in. He filled the wineglasses, picked up his, and said, "What shall we drink to, Prudence?"

She arched an eyebrow. "Why, to us, of course, sir! To our acquaintance."

They touched glasses and drank. "This is good wine," she said in surprise. "I wouldn't have expected to find wine of such good quality in the colony."

Cotty grinned lazily. "You won't find many such bottles. I was fortunate to be able to buy a case of it a year ago." He did not feel it necessary to add that he had smuggled it ashore.

Prudence was studying him closely. "I'm still surprised to discover a man of your age owning a tavern such as this."

Cotty shrugged negligently. "A man tends to mature quickly in such surroundings. In fact, he must, if he is to survive."

"All of us have to do many things to survive, sir."
For a moment she looked grave, then her face broke
into a charming smile. "But let us not talk of serious
matters."

Her cheeks had become flushed, and her eyes
sparkled. Was it the wine, Cotty wondered. "How
about your young officer at Parramatta?" he asked.
"Have you seen him yet?"

It was her turn to shrug. "Oh, Richard will wait.
As I told you last night, I'm not really betrothed to
him. To be frank, he was just an excuse to visit Sydney."

Instinctively, Cotty realized that she must have
been in a spot of trouble in London, and the trip here
was probably something of an exile; perhaps per-
manent, or perhaps temporary until whatever had
happened at home had settled down. "But let's not
talk about Richard," she went on.

"Then what shall we discuss?"

She reached across the short distance between
them, and stroked her fingers lightly down his cheek.
His heart began to hammer, his mouth went dry, and
he felt heat flush through him. Cotty was not a vir-
gin; he had been introduced to sex by a convict
woman twice his age when he was sixteen. Since he
was handsome, virile and well-dressed, he had experienced no lack of female companionship whenever he had the time and was so inclined, but most of
the episodes had been with easy women. Therefore,
although he was accustomed to brazen women, there
had been none he would have placed on a plane with
Prudence, who had every appearance of being a lady.
Yet here she was, as bold as any strumpet in the
Rocks.

But why was he giving it so much thought? His earliest philosophy had been to seize the chance when it came his way. This axiom had always served him well in his business life, so why not apply it in this instance? But before the thought was fully formed, it was already purely academic.

Draining her wineglass, Prudence got up and stepped to his bed. Removing her cap, she loosened her hair and leaned down to kiss him. Her black hair fell around his face like a perfumed net, and her lips, tasting tartly of wine, were warm and soft. Involuntarily, his hands came up to grip her arms and bring her closer to him.

In a moment he moved his hands from her arms to her body, and he could feel the fullness of her breasts beneath her bodice. Desire seized him like a fever, and his kiss became insistent.

She broke free of his mouth and whispered in his ear, "I like being bedded, and I've missed it for eight long months. All the men on board the ship were rough seamen, foul-smelling and foul-mouthed. I know this may make me sound like a bawd, but I've imagined this moment since I met you last night, Cotty."

She stood back from him and began undressing without shame. Cotty sat for a few moments just watching her, still a trifle taken aback by her boldness. But again, why should he question his good fortune?

Her body was voluptuous, her flesh pink and glowing when she finally stood smiling at him, her last garment discarded.

He stood and hastily disrobed, and in a few moments they were together on the narrow bed. Prudence was a lusty lover, totally without inhibitions, and she was not loath to guide him. Cotty, well aware that his experience was limited, was happy to follow her instructions, for he calculated that it would only serve to increase his own pleasure.

When they were finally joined in passion, Prudence voiced her pleasure: "Oh, yes, love! That is what I have missed all these long months!"

She rose to meet his thrusts, writhing, and a sharp cry was wrung for her as their mutual passion broke.

After a bit Cotty escaped her embrace and lay on his back, a lassitude stealing over him, and he slipped into a deep slumber.

He awoke sometime later, disoriented for a moment, unfamiliar as it was to find a woman sleeping on his shoulder. A glance at the open window told him that the sun was almost down. It was late; it would soon be time for the tavern to open.

He touched Prudence on the cheek. "Prudence . . . you must leave. The Crown will be opening, and 'twon't do for you to be discovered coming out of my quarters. It will not do your reputation any good."

Prudence opened her eyes and smiled at him. "Love, my reputation was ruined back in London."

"But this is New South Wales. I assume you came here to start afresh. How would your young officer react if gossip reached his ears?"

He held his breath, awaiting her answer. Dalliance with her was fine, but he hoped she would not become possessive, attaching herself to him. He felt a surge of relief when she sat up in alarm, her eyes widening.

"You're right! It would never do for Richard to learn of my indiscretion. I came here hoping to marry him." She laughed at his look of relief. "Do not concern yourself, sir. I shall make no demands on you, other than what you have already satisfied." She touched her lips to his cheek. "I have no desire to wed a tavern keeper. Even if only a military officer, Richard comes from a wealthy family, and that wealth will pass on to him some day."

She scrambled out of bed and began dressing. Her chemise and stockings on, she paused to look at him. "We shall lie again. That is, if you care to."

Stepping into his breeches, Cotty had to laugh. "What about your officer?"

"Pooh! What he doesn't know won't hurt him. Besides, we're not wed yet, and unless he has changed since the London days, Richard is something of a prig. Bed to him is only a means to sire sons."

"You shall always be welcome in my bed, Prudence," he said gravely.

A short time later Cotty stepped out of his room, raking the barroom with a single glance. It appeared to be empty, and he was turning to motion Prudence out when a voice spoke his name. "Cotty?"

He spun around. Hope, silent on bare feet, her skirts rucked up above her knees, was just coming around the bar.

"Cotty, Momma wants to know..." She broke off with a gasp, her gaze going past him; and Cotty knew, without looking, that Prudence had come up behind him.

Hope went white. She looked at him with stricken eyes, then whirled and ran.

"Hell and damnation," he muttered, staring after her helplessly.

# CHAPTER ELEVEN

BY THE BEGINNING of the year 1801, the Crown Tavern, despite its location at the edge of the Rocks, was a roaring success, and by far the most popular tavern and eating place in Sydney.

The new dining room upstairs had been opened and, under Faith's supervision, the kitchen had gained a well-deserved reputation for serving excellent food. Among those who professed a knowledge of such things, the meals were considered equal to, if not better than, those served at the famous Rosetta Stabler's Eating House.

Cotty, ever alert to the way the wind was blowing, realized it would be to his advantage to become more selective in his choice of patrons.

He tried to screen out the rougher elements, even hiring a towering ex-Marine, Bart Wilson, to act as a doorman in the evenings. If people without proper credentials presented themselves at the door, they were refused admittance. Cotty's business rivals laughed at this tactic, saying that he would soon have to close his doors. For a time it appeared that their assessment was correct; even Faith openly worried. But Cotty grimly stuck with his decision, and soon it began to pay dividends. The better people of Sydney, learning that they could dine well at the Crown, unmolested by the rowdy element, began coming in droves.

Cotty knew that Faith was, in a large part, responsible for this, and he was unstinting in his praise.

Faith herself confessed to not understanding it. "For a woman who was once capable of cooking only the simplest of foods," she had told him with an embarrassed laugh, "I can't fathom it."

"You underestimate yourself, dear Faith. You are an intelligent woman. You could have done anything you wished, had you been given the opportunity."

He was more fond than ever of Faith, and not only because he thought her indispensable; she was a warm, caring person, a loyal advocate and, in a way, a silent partner in the Crown. She often said that she was happier than she had ever been, yet Cotty was concerned for her. Those years of hard convict labor had not broken her spirit, but they had taken their toll upon her body. She was thin, worn, with a constant cough. However, no matter how he remonstrated with her, she worked long hours supervising the kitchen, and was usually exhausted by the end of the day.

The second floor of the inn had been completed just before Christmas in 1800, and Faith and her daughters had moved in. Their presence was a mixed blessing to Cotty. He was delighted to have them there, but it somewhat restricted his own movements. He had a large bedroom of his own upstairs now; but since Hope had caught him with Prudence Wilkes, he did not dare invite a lady into his chambers. During his frequent trysts with Prudence, he had to use his old room downstairs, which he had turned into an office. Prudence had wed her young officer in March, yet that had little dampened her ardor for Cotty.

Not two months after her nuptials, she had appeared at the Crown, with the comment, "I was right about Richard. He cares little for the nuptial bed. He would rather spend the time with his mates in the corps."

So what could Cotty do but welcome her back? He knew there was a certain amount of risk involved, yet that risk only added spice to their meetings. However, not wishing to offend the Blackstocks, he attempted to be as discreet as possible.

And so it was that things were going well for Cotty. While he generally restricted his patronage to the gentry, he did not neglect his purpose to make as much money as possible. The port of Sydney was enjoying a great boom. Yankee ships on the way to the Orient had discovered the fine harbor, and most of them used it as a stop on the way to and from their destinations, as did ships from almost every other nation on the globe. Whaling ships also came and went with regularity. In addition, seals had been discovered in Bass Strait just last year, and the sealing industry was booming. The majority of the sealing ships used Sydney Harbor as a base. As a result of all this activity, a great many seamen were in port at any given time.

To take advantage of this, Cotty now had three grog shanties operating, and was negotiating to buy another tavern deeper in the Rocks, this one to cater strictly to the seamen.

Now that Cotty was respectable, he could generally purchase enough legal spirits to stock the Crown; but from time to time he still smuggled rum in from arriving ships. He also bought from illicit distillers, of which there were now a great number.

So far he had been able to avoid taking sides in the conflict between the government and the New South Wales Corps; but on a cool, rainy morning in June, he received a caller concerning the matter.

The Crown was not yet open, and Cotty was at his desk in the office, catching up on his bookkeeping, when he heard a loud knocking on the front door of the tavern. When no one answered the knock, he got up, annoyed at the interruption, and went to the door.

He was halfway around the bar when Hope came out of the passageway leading to the rear. Her face was rosy from heat, and he knew she had been out in the kitchen with her mother doing the day's baking.

At the sight of him she skidded to a stop, her face turning cold. She had scarcely spoken a civil word to him since that day months ago when she had seen Prudence coming out of his bedroom.

"It's all right, Hope," he said amiably. "I'll see who it is."

"I thought maybe it was your..." Her face flamed; she clapped a hand to her mouth and turned and fled back down the passageway.

With a rueful shake of his head, Cotty continued to the front door.

The caller was John Macarthur. Water dripped off his hat and cloak. Cotty realized he must be showing a look of astonishment, for Macarthur's stern face broke into a slight smile. "I would like a word with you, Master Starke."

Recovering from his surprise, Cotty backed up, motioning the man inside. Macarthur removed his greatcoat, revealing that he was not in uniform; and Cotty recalled hearing from someone that the man had had a flaming row with Governor King and had threatened to resign his commission.

Cotty remembered his manners. He did not much like this man's arrogance but, as Faith would say, that was no reason to show rudeness. "May I offer you a libation, sir?" he asked formally.

Macarthur appeared to consider the invitation deeply before replying with a nod. " 'Tis a miserable day, Master Starke. A tot of rum might be fitting." His stern visage relaxed even more. "Considering that is to be the subject of discussion."

Cotty tensed, but managed to hide his reaction as he went behind the bar to pour rum for Macarthur and an ale for himself.

Macarthur raised his glass. "To our better acquaintance, sir."

Cotty was not sure that he wished to cultivate Macarthur's acquaintance, but he saw no graceful way to refuse. He touched his tankard to Macarthur's glass.

The man took a hearty drink of the rum. "Ah! Not bad, young Starke." His eyes were keen. "Distilled, or smuggled?"

"Neither," Cotty said stiffly. "I bought it at the Bonded Store. Since I am an innkeeper, and licensed as such, I am entitled."

Macarthur nodded ponderously. "Of course you are, but you cannot purchase enough to supply both your tavern and your shanties. I am well aware of your smuggling activities, which go back a number of years."

"I am not alone in that, sir."

"You are indeed not, and I am not opposed. I hold no brief with Governor King's ridiculous position on the importation of spirits. And yes, I also knew of your man Fowler being killed during the commission of smuggling. It was an unfortunate incident, but any smuggler runs that risk. The governor's troops caught him in the act, killed him, and then denied all knowledge of the deed."

Cotty stared at the man, feeling his temper rise. He knew for a fact that the NSW Corps had been responsible for killing Jason; Karl Dietrich had been a witness. Was Macarthur a liar or simply ignorant of the true facts? "The penalty for smuggling is usually a prison term, or expulsion from the colony, not death," he said.

Macarthur looked directly at him. "A mistake was made, to be sure. Some soldier acted too hastily. Be that as it may, that is the reason I am calling on you. There is no need for such things to happen. The problem would be easily solved if Governor King would simply relax his strictures. Let the free market prevail. That is what my friends and I have been agitating for all along. But the governor is a stubborn, willful man and will not listen to reason."

"What is it you wish of me, sir?"

"Why, I am asking for your support."

"You wish me to openly defy the governor?"

"I should think you would be happy to do so," Macarthur said coolly. "After all, your business is the sale of spirits. The easier it is for you to get those spirits, the better it is for your business."

Cotty was shaking his head. "I cannot take such a stand."

"Why not, pray? Upon my honor, surely you do not approve of the governor's policy?"

"Of course not. But a large share of my patronage comes from government officials, or at least friends and associates of the governor."

Macarthur's gaze turned flinty. "The times when I have been in here, I have noticed a large number of corps officers."

"That I cannot deny. My patrons come from both sides of the disagreement. Therefore, I hardly think it wise of me to stand with either side. No matter which side I take, I stand to lose patronage."

"You are afraid then to take sides?"

"Not afraid. It just doesn't strike me as good business practice."

"There are principles in this world worth more than business considerations."

Without really thinking it through, still prodded by his temper, Cotty said, "Like killing a man for something as harmless as smuggling rum?"

"I told you, that was happenstance..." Macarthur broke off, his eyes cold as ice. "Are you accusing me of killing your man, sir?"

"Not directly, no, and probably not on your direct orders. But your influence with the corps is well-known."

"The corps was not responsible for the death of your man! The culprits were the government men."

Cotty simply stared, a tight smile on his lips.

"This is your decision then?" Macarthur demanded.

"I refuse to take sides in this quarrel, if that is your question."

"That is a decision you shall regret, Master Starke. You have my promise on that." Macarthur turned on his heel, slammed down his glass and stalked out of the tavern.

His anger still hot, Cotty stared after the man until the front door closed behind him. Then he sighed and finished his ale.

He well realized that he had made an enemy of John Macarthur, and Macarthur was a powerful man, a bad one to cross. As Macarthur had threatened, Cotty might come to regret his decision, but he figured he would have to live with that.

If he allied himself with Macarthur and his minions, he would end up having to cater to the man's whims, aside from the fact that he would lose the followers of the governor as customers. He had come too far all on his own to start fawning on powerful men. The price of keeping his pride had been high, and he would be damned if he would bend now! He had no intention of currying favor with either side.

A pox on both their houses!

With a shake of his head, he returned to his office.

HURRYING ALONG the passageway, Hope felt mortified.

She had been angry, and deeply hurt, that day she had seen that brazen woman emerging from Cotty's bedroom. She had been barely civil to him since, but she had determined that she would never mention the incident. Then, just now, in a moment of renewed anger, she had almost said too much.

Inside the kitchen Faith was supervising the two Chinese cooks who were baking bread and pastries for the evening's trade. Charity sat on a stool by the open window, pouting, staring out at the cold drizzle. Despite the coolness of the day and the fact that the window was open, the heat inside was oppressive. John Myers, dark skin glistening with sweat beads, was busy feeding wood into the huge baking ovens.

Faith turned around, wiping at her heat-flushed face with a towel. "Well?"

Hope looked at her without comprehension.

"What did Cotty say, girl?" Faith demanded. "About how many loaves he wanted baked for tonight?"

"Oh," Hope said in a meek voice. "I'm sorry, Momma. I didn't ask him."

"You didn't *ask*? Why not? That's the reason I sent you in there!"

"There was somebody knocking at the door when I went in. Cotty has a visitor."

"For heaven's sake, Hope! I fail to see why you still couldn't ask him. It's not a state secret to be kept from a visitor. I don't know what ails you of late, I honestly don't. You've been in some kind of a daze since Christmas. No, even before that." She peered closely at Hope. "Are you ill?"

"No, Momma, I'm not ill," Hope said, suddenly irritated.

"Then what *is* the matter, child?"

"There's nothing wrong, Momma. Just leave me alone!"

She spun around and started out of the kitchen.

"Hope . . . where are you going?"

"Up to my room." She flung the words over her shoulder as she went through the door.

FROM WHERE HE STOOD by the ovens, John had been watching Hope, his adoration naked in his eyes. Now, as Faith glanced at him, he ducked his head.

"That will be enough wood, John," Faith said. "Since my daughter didn't find out how many loaves of bread we'll be needing for tonight, we'll have to make do with what we have already baked." She added in a less sharp tone, "You can go now. You've done enough work for one day."

"Thank you, Mistress Blackstock," John said, grinning with a flash of white teeth. Under Faith's instruction, John's English had improved immensely.

He left the kitchen, but instead of going to his lean-to, the boy set off north, past the windmill with its clock in the tower. He walked easily, almost at a lope. Since it was cold and raining, he met few people, only an occasional person walking fast, hurrying to get in out of the weather.

Soon he was out of town, heading toward a sheltered and unpopulated inlet, his destination a grove of trees he had discovered about half a league distant. When he reached the grove, John went directly to a huge, ancient blue gum tree—his dreaming tree.

First, he looked for and found a handful of witchety grubs, which he proceeded to eat raw. He had learned to eat the food of the colonists, had even learned to like much of it, yet these grubs remained his favorite delicacy. He knew better than to eat them before any of his new friends. His ways were difficult enough for them to comprehend, and eating grubs raw, he well knew, would disturb them greatly.

The witchety grubs were also a necessity to the entering of the dream trance. Digging into the soft, wet ground underneath the tree, he obtained a handful of white clay, which he smeared upon his forehead, cheeks and chin. Then he removed his clothing and squatted on his heels near the trunk of the gum tree.

Eyes closed, rocking back and forth, John entered the dream state. When John had participated in the ceremonies that marked his acceptance as a man in the tribe, a true member, the elder had made known to him the dreams of the tribe. The dreams were the history of the tribe in oral form; they explained the past from which his people had evolved; the present in which they lived; and the future to which they were traveling.

The dream world of an individual centered around an animal or a bird, which became sacred to the dreamer as a tribal hero, a spirit who revealed to him his inheritance from the past, who acted as a protector in the present, and a forecaster of future events. John's sacred dream figure was the kangaroo.

Time passed as the boy communicated with his hero kangaroo, sinking deeper and deeper into the dream all the while. He ignored the cold rain dripping onto his face, the clay running down his cheeks like white tears.

Pictures came to him—gray as the monochrome colors of the day. He sought visions of Hope Blackstock in the dreaming but could not find her. He caught glimpses of the other one, Charity, grown to full maturity, and she appeared to be in some peril; but the dream never became clear enough to him to make out what threatened her.

Then suddenly, his dream grew darker yet. He could see a group of people gathered in a burial place, the kind the colonists used, with stone markers with the names of the dead and buried carved upon them.

He saw Hope, Charity and Cotty Starke gathered around the gravesite. The two girls were dressed in black and they were weeping. Cotty stood between them, lending support, his own handsome face somber with grief.

In the dream, John tried to call out to Hope, to offer her solace, but no matter how hard he tried to attract her attention, she did not appear to notice him.

And then John was hovering over the casket, unseen by the mourners. The lid of the coffin was folded back, and inside, lying still and pale, was Faith Blackstock, hands folded serenely over her breasts. Her face was no longer worn and haggard, but at peace.

John was jolted out of his trance by the sound of his own voice, calling Faith's name. He sat for a moment, shocked by the dream. He had never seen a dead person in one of his dreams before.

A chill swept over him, but not from the cold wind and the dripping rain. Most of the time his dreams were pleasant; never had he been frightened by one, but he was now; he was concerned for Faith, who had been very good to him.

He closed his eyes again, willing himself to reenter the dream world. Perhaps this time he could see further into the future and learn more about Faith.

It was no use. After a half hour he finally gave up. He got to his feet and, stepping out from under the partial shelter of the blue gum, he let the rain sluice the residue of the clay from his features before donning the white man's clothing. He was growing more accustomed to the clothing as time passed, yet it was good to return now and again to the natural, naked state.

There were many times when he longed for the comfort and familiarity of the tribal days. Things had been so simple then. He had known who he was and what was expected of him. There had been friends, and a woman...

Sometimes he thought of returning, even while knowing that he would not. He had come to the city of the clay faces because the things that his white father had told him and taught him had aroused in him a powerful, burning curiosity that could not be stifled. And now that he was here and had sampled some of the wonders of the white man's world, he was changed in some way that would not allow him to return to the life he had known. In some way these people, who were also, in part, his people, had stolen a part of his spirit; and at least some of that spirit had gone to the young woman, Hope. He could not seem to get it back.

As he walked toward town and the Crown Tavern, John's mind was in a turmoil. Should he tell Faith Blackstock about his dream? Or Cotty? Faith was understanding; yet if the dream was false, she might become unduly alarmed. He knew that Cotty was tolerant of tribal ways, even curious; during idle hours he had questioned John closely about the ways of the tribe. Yet John had never told him about the dreamworld and his sojourns there. He had the feeling that Cotty might think that he was crazed in the head.

By the time he had reached the Crown, John had decided that it was best to say nothing.

TWO WEEKS FOLLOWING John Macarthur's call on Cotty, Cotty was back in the cook house in midafternoon with Faith, checking out their food stores. A supply ship had arrived from England the day before, and Cotty was preparing a list of items for purchase.

After they had finished, Cotty looked at Faith with some concern. It was another cold, rainy day, and he noticed that she had been shivering, drawing a heavy shawl around her shoulders. She looked pale and drawn.

"Are you feeling all right, Faith?" he asked.

Her smile was forced. "I am fine, Cotty, just weary." She clutched the shawl tighter around her.

"You've been looking peaked of late. I'm worried about you. Mayhap you should stop working so hard. I can always find someone else to supervise the kitchen."

"I've worked hard all my life, Cotty. I wouldn't know what to do with myself. There's nothing wrong with me but old age."

"Old age? Faith, you're a young woman yet."

"In years, I'm not too old, true. But they have been hard years. Until you got me out of slavery." She placed a hand on his arm. "If I was still working as a convict, I likely would be dead by now. I can never fully express my gratitude for what you have done."

"There is no need, Faith," he said, smiling fondly. "You've more than repaid me. The reputation of your kitchen has spread all across Sydney

Town, and that has increased my business two-fold . . ."

He was interrupted by a voice calling outside, "Master Cotty!"

He recognized Karl Dietrich's voice. "In here, Karl."

Dietrich rushed in, his long face radiating excitement. "Have you heard the tidings?"

"What tidings, Karl?"

"John Macarthur, he fought a duel with his commanding officer, Lieutenant Colonel William Peterson, at Parramatta, two days ago."

"Well, I'll be damned!" Cotty said explosively. "I knew that Macarthur was a violent man."

"But that's not all," Dietrich said. "The rumor has it that Governor King is sending Macarthur back to London under arrest, to stand before a court-martial."

Cotty let his breath go with a whoosh. "Well, now! That may solve a problem or two." He nodded to Dietrich. "Thanks for bringing me the news, Karl."

When Dietrich had left, Faith said, "Why do you think this Macarthur's being sent to England will solve a problem, Cotty?"

He had not mentioned Macarthur's threat to her, but now he did so.

Faith's eyes were wide with concern when he had finished. "You think he would really have done you harm for not siding with him?"

"Macarthur is a powerful man in Sydney, Faith, as well as popular with many people. It is my feeling that he would make a vicious enemy." He gave a shrug. "In any event, I am relieved that he is being sent away. Aside from the fact that it might sidetrack any actions he may have intended to take against me, Macarthur is the core of the controversy between the corps and Governor King. With him absent, hopefully some of the tension will ease, and it will be better for all of us.''

# CHAPTER TWELVE

ON THIS MORNING, as she often did, Hope arose early, leaving Charity still asleep. Creeping past her mother's and Cotty's rooms, she went down the stairs and out into the fresh spring morning.

Now that winter had passed, and the days were warming, she enjoyed rising early and walking to the Market Place, where she could mingle with the crowd, lost in anonymity.

She loved the bustle of the Market Place. People came here early to sell and barter. Fresh produce and vegetables from outlying farms were displayed in abundance now, as were exotic fruits brought in by ship from other lands. Pausing at one stand, Hope bought a fragrant, golden banana before walking on.

She strolled among the shoppers, enjoying the good smells of fresh fruits, vegetables and spring flowers, as well as the strong odors of the imported fruits. Carcasses of fresh-killed fowl, sheep and cattle hung on hooks before many stalls, some so fresh they still dripped blood. Caged cockatoos and rosellas shrieked among the overflowing food stalls.

Also for sale were garments made by local seamstresses. Hope stopped before several stalls, fingering the dresses, shawls and ladies' caps. Faith made most of the clothing her daughters wore, although Charity was constantly carping about the drab colors her mother used.

As Hope moved reluctantly away from the dress stalls, an unsettling sight met her eyes. The stocks had been built on the edge of the Market Place, so that those being punished were in plain sight for all to observe.

There were two unfortunates in the stocks today, bent over with their hands and arms trapped cruelly in the wooden frames. A sign over one proclaimed Intoxicated and Disorderly, and the other stated, Raiding a Neighbor's Garden. As people passed to and fro, many stopped to taunt the offenders.

Hope shuddered with distaste, and hurriedly turned away, leaving the Market Place. She hesitated at the edge, debating whether to return to the Crown. It was still early, so in the end she decided to walk down to the Hospital Wharf. She liked to look at the newly arrived ships and speculate on the strange and marvelous places they might have visited on their long sea voyages.

AN EARLY RISER—all tribal members rose with the sun—John had been aware of Hope's habit of slipping out in the mornings. He had taken to following her at a discreet distance, making sure that she would not see him; for he was concerned that something might happen to her. The Market Place posed little danger, since there were always many people around; but she often ventured into the darker places of the Rocks, as well as into the wharf areas, which were mainly populated by toughs. So far, nothing untoward had occurred; yet there was always that possibility, and John wanted to be there to offer what protection he could.

On this particular morning he followed her easily enough to the Market Place, but once there she became quickly lost in the crowd. John had learned from experience that the people frowned upon an aborigine in the Market Place, so he stationed himself at the corner of Suffolk Lane and Sergeant Major's Row, from where he could watch the two main entrances.

He could also see the stocks and the two imprisoned men. John felt a rush of sympathy for them, and once again he wondered at the white man's methods of punishment. More than once he had witnessed a man being lashed, often until the man's back was lacerated and pouring blood. True, the tribal laws meted out punishment, but such punishment was usually quick and severe: banishment from the tribe for a specific time or permanently; or a quick death for the severest offenses. The settlers, on the other hand, meted out cruel punishments over a long period of time, to the point of brutal torture. True, there was an occasional hanging for the crimes like murder, but it seemed that the punishments for the lesser offenses were even worse.

John shook his head. He had determined that, on coming to Sydney, he would let the English side of his nature dominate; yet he was beginning to doubt that he would ever fully understand the white man's ways, or that he would ever entirely forget his aborigine heritage.

All of a sudden, it occurred to him that Hope had been in the Market Place an unusual length of time. He began to worry. Could she have gone out the other side?

He skirted the Market Place, looking for her, even debating venturing inside. Then he decided that she must have gone down to the wharf area. The Hospital Wharf seemed to be her favorite place. After a moment he set off in that direction at a fast pace.

Nearing the finger of the dock that jutted out into the bay, he saw a woman standing, gazing out at the ships bobbing at anchor. Even at a distance there was no mistaking the brown dress Hope was wearing, and her proud, erect carriage. Coming up behind her was a man in seaman's clothing.

John began to hurry; but long before he could reach Hope, he saw the man accost her. John saw Hope whirl around and begin to walk away. The seaman caught her by the arm.

John spotted a length of board that had been left lying on the edge of the dock. Still in full stride, he scooped it up and ran on. He knew that he could get into serious trouble for striking a white man, yet he did not hesitate. The seaman still had a firm grip on Hope's arm, holding her against him, laughing, as she struggled to pull away.

Reaching them, John swung the board against the sailor's shoulder with enough force to make him lose his grip on Hope's arm.

The seaman turned an angry face on John. "What the hell do you . . . ? A murky! How dare you strike a white man?"

John raised the board. "You are not to harm Mistress Hope, sir!"

"No black fella tells me what to do. Eh, lassie?"

With a leer the man lunged at Hope. Seizing her wrist again with his left hand, he raked the other hand down her neck. His long, jagged nails dug into her flesh, leaving bloody gashes. Hope screamed and tried to break away.

John, filled with anger and outrage, stepped closer and, raising the board again, he brought it whistling around, striking the seaman alongside the head. The board splintered and broke. The sailor grunted sharply and collapsed on the wharf.

Hope stared down at the fallen man and then at John. Quickly, she grasped his hand. "Come, John. We must get away." She started to pull him along, then stopped, looking him in the eye. "I want to thank you for coming to my rescue, but I'm sure you realize the risk you ran."

They hurried away then, John tossing the splintered board aside. Just as they reached the beginning of the wharf, Hope glanced back. The seaman still lay where he had fallen. She felt a twinge of uneasiness. Could he be dead? If he was, and John was found out, he might face a hanging. But she did not really believe the man was hurt too badly.

They hastened on. Hope glanced around as they left the dock. Insofar as she could see, the little fracas had gone unobserved. Once on a crowded street, she indicated that they should slow down, and she wrapped her throat with her kerchief to hide the bloody scratches. They then proceeded to the Crown at a more sedate pace. When they reached the tavern, Hope prayed that she would be able to slip up to her room without meeting Faith or Cotty, but that hope was in vain. As she and John walked down the side of the tavern and into the courtyard behind, Faith and Cotty were standing together outside the back door.

Faith exclaimed, "Hope! Where on earth have you been? I've been worried about you..." She broke off as she saw Hope's disheveled appearance. "What happened to you, girl?"

"I'm all right, Momma."

Hope tried to slip past them into the tavern, but Faith blocked her way, pulling Hope's hand away from her neck. "Why, you're bleeding!"

Hope had no choice then but to tell them what had occurred.

Faith paled visibly. "Hope, whatever possessed you? You could have been ravished!"

"In broad daylight, Momma?"

"Anything can happen in the Rocks," Cotty said tightly. "Those seamen are a rough lot. Since ladies aren't generally seen there, especially alone, this man probably took you for a strumpet. He thought you were inviting his attention by just being there. It was very foolish of you, Hope."

Faith turned to John. "We are in your debt, John. Without your intervention, there is no telling what might have happened to this foolish girl."

"'Twas my duty, Mistress Faith," John replied.

Cotty was pacing in short, angry steps. "I shall see to it that nothing like this occurs again. I shall pass the word. The next time any ruffian dares to accost any of you, he will have me to answer to. Without immodesty, I believe I can say that my word carries some weight in the Rocks."

"Be that as it may," Faith said angrily, "Hope, you will be severely punished if you *ever* do something like this again."

Hope scarcely heard her mother's words, so intent was she on the pacing Cotty. She had never seen him so incensed. A sense of danger came from him, so strong that Hope gave a little shiver of fright, but at the same time she was secretly pleased that he should be so upset on her behalf.

A sudden cry came from Charity. "Momma, what's wrong?"

Cotty and Hope both whirled around. Faith's face had gone chalk white, and she put a hand over her heart, moaning. She began to fall, and Cotty was just in time to catch her before she hit the ground. Kneeling, holding her cradled in his arms, Cotty said, "Faith, what is it?"

Faith groaned loudly, convulsed, then went limp in his arms.

Cotty looked up with a stricken face. "John, run and fetch Dr. Jenkins. And hurry!"

John was gone in an instant, running. Gently, Cotty picked Faith up in his arms. "I'll take her up to her room. Hope, bring a pan of cool water and a cloth."

AN HOUR LATER they were all gathered in the hall outside Faith's bedroom—Cotty, Hope, Charity and John. Charity was weeping silently, Cotty paced back and forth, and Hope stared at the closed door, trying desperately to fathom what had happened. She had known that her mother's health was not the best; the long years of sunrise-to-sunset labor at the looms had taken a dreadful toll; but even so, Faith had never had a really sick day in Hope's memory.

The door opened and Dr. Jenkins, a dour man of some fifty years, emerged, his face somber.

"Will she be all right, Doctor?" Hope asked before anyone else could say anything.

"I will not hold out false hope to you," Dr. Jenkins said. "Your mother is seriously ill, Hope."

"What's wrong with her, Doctor?" Cotty interjected.

"Her heart is very weak, very weak indeed, and her constitution is not the strongest. There is very little that I can do for her."

"Are you saying that she is dying?" Hope asked, close to tears.

"I have learned long ago never to make predictions, but I can tell you that if she has another seizure, she has little chance of surviving."

"Isn't there anything you can do for her?"

Dr. Jenkins said ponderously, "I fear not, my dear. Years of hard labor, a poor diet, and too little rest have weakened her badly. All we can do now is see that she gets plenty of bed rest, and pray to the good Lord above..."

John stood off to one side, watching and listening; he was experiencing a heavy load of guilt. He had seen Faith Blackstock in her coffin in his dream. Did that mean that she was going to die now? Would he have been able to prevent her illness if he had told someone of his dream? John knew very little of the white man's medicine; and the tribal remedies were most often useless against severe sickness—and it was obvious that Mistress Blackstock was very ill. If he had given warning the day of his dream, could anything have been done to prevent this happening? Or would they even have believed him? He felt miserable.

The doctor gave Hope and Cotty instructions on how to care for Faith, and then Cotty escorted him downstairs. John tagged along. At the front door

Cotty extended his gratitude to Dr. Jenkins and bid him farewell.

When the door had closed behind the doctor, John said, "Cotty? A word with you?"

Cotty looked at him curiously. "Of course, John. You look downcast. I know you're fond of Faith, we all are. But the end must come to all of us. Unfortunately it seems to be coming to Faith before her time."

"But perhaps I could have stopped her dying."

Cotty gave him a startled look. "How in hell's name could *you* have done that?"

John took a deep breath, and hesitantly told Cotty of his vision. Cotty listened attentively, with a grave face.

When the story was told, Cotty said, "These dreams of yours... I think I've heard something about the tribal dreaming. You've had the dreams before?"

"Many times."

"And have any of the prophecies of future events come true?"

"Oh, yes! But not of important things, not about a person dying, like Mistress Blackstock."

"John, it's nothing for you to concern yourself about. Whether or not your vision comes true, you are in no way to blame for what happens to Faith."

"But if I had told of my dream?"

Cotty shook his head. "It wouldn't have mattered. It would only have worried the girls, *and* Faith. It might even have brought the seizure on sooner." He clasped John's shoulder and squeezed reassuringly. "I'm sure that Faith would tell you the same thing."

A WEEK LATER they gathered in the small cemetery on the outskirts of town, listening to the minister speak over Faith's wooden casket. The changeable spring weather had turned, and it was a gray day with blowing rain.

Hope stood beside Cotty, her head lowered, her face hidden behind a black veil. Her thoughts were dreary, and sorrow sapped her will and strength. She paid scant heed to the minister's eulogy, although she could not have heard most of it anyway, since the driving wind snatched the words out of his mouth.

Faith had rallied for a few days after the initial seizure, and Hope had been confident that she would recover; but one morning two days ago, Hope had gone in to see what her mother wanted for breakfast and had found her on the floor, halfway between the bed and the door. She was fully dressed, evidently on her way downstairs. There had been no sign of life, and Hope had screamed for Cotty, who came running, half dressed. Dr. Jenkins had been summoned, but it was far too late—Faith had been dead for some time.

Hope's thoughts came back to the present at the sound of Charity sobbing at her side. Her sister clung to her hand, her body shaking with sobs. Hope gathered her close, pulling her head against her shoulder.

She glanced around at the group of mourners. The employees of the Crown, most of whom Faith had known and helped, had come to pay their last respects to the woman who had been unfailingly kind and generous to all who crossed her path. Even a few of the well-to-do patrons of the Crown were in attendance. Hope felt a surge of gratitude. Her mother may have arrived in this land a despised convict, but she was leaving it a respected citizen. Thanks to Cotty, she was not being buried in the convict's cemetery, which would have happened if Cotty had not arranged for her ticket-of-leave.

Hope glanced sidelong at Cotty. He was staring at the coffin, his features still. Despite her annoyance with him over the past few months, she knew how much he had loved Faith, and her heart went out to him. Cotty had been good to them, but perhaps he felt that his obligation stopped with Faith. What was going to happen to them now? There had been no time to talk about it, or even think about it; but it was going to have to be discussed, and soon.

John stood apart from the others, water streaming unheeded off his bare head. In spite of Cotty's reassurances, he was still laden with guilt. He could not help but think that if he had shared his vision with the Blackstocks, Mistress Faith might still be alive. He stood listening to these strange burial rites of the white man, and struggled with his conscience.

His glance moved to Hope, and stayed there. He noticed that while the younger daughter was weeping, Hope was dry-eyed, her face bereft of all emotion.

And then it was over. The minister spoke the last words, and the grave diggers began to lower the casket into the ground. Hope stood very still, staring straight ahead, as if totally unaware that the service was finished.

Cotty touched her arm. "Hope? We can go now; it's all over."

She gave a start, looking around vaguely. "Oh..."

Cotty extended his arm, and she moved to take it, then stopped, disengaging herself. "You and Charity go on. I'll be along directly," she said in a choked voice.

She turned toward the grave. The tears came then, as the two men shoveled dirt into the pit. It was as if her mother's death had not registered until now, not down deep where the hurt and the loss could be felt.

John stood watching her as the tears ran down her face, mingling with the cold rain; her shoulders shook. He longed to comfort her, yet he knew that he dared not.

As she finally turned away, joining Cotty and her sister, John fell in behind them, feeling Hope's pain as if it were his own.

Back at the Crown, Cotty hurried the girls inside and then turned to face them. "You'd best get into some dry clothing, and then I would like to see you both back here. I have something to say to you."

Charity looked at Hope questioningly, but Hope shook her head and led her sister away. It was going to happen now. Cotty was going to tell them what was to become of them; and the sooner it was said, the sooner they would know where they stood.

When they returned, Cotty was waiting for them with a pot of hot, fragrant tea and a plate of bread and sausage. Despite the fact that she had not yet broken her fast, Hope had no appetite and took only a mug of the hot tea, which she sweetened liberally.

Charity, however, tucked into the food as Cotty took his time about getting to the subject he wished to discuss.

Finally, when the silence had stretched to an awkward length, he cleared his throat. "Like I said, we must talk."

Charity wiped a crumb delicately from the edge of her mouth. "About what, Cotty? You sound so serious!"

"Well, it is a serious matter," he said somewhat sharply. "It concerns what is to become of you, your future."

Charity looked puzzled. "I don't understand."

"Well, with your mother dead, things must change."

"Change how?" Charity looked alarmed. "We're still going to live here, aren't we?"

Cotty's glance slid across to Hope, who refused to give him the satisfaction of showing concern. "I certainly hope so, but that will depend on a number of things. Do you *want* to continue to live here?"

"Of course we do, Cotty!" Charity said. "Where else would we live?"

Cotty was still looking at Hope. "Hope?"

"It's up to you to decide that, isn't it?" she said with all the disdain she could muster. "The Crown belongs to you."

"I certainly want you to stay. You are family to me. But I also want what's right for you two girls." He finally looked at Charity. "The thing is, Charity, we have to consider how it will look to other people, two girls of your age living with an unmarried man who is not related to them."

Hope spoke for the first time. "Who cares what other people think?" She was dismayed by her words.

Cotty leaned back, grinning lazily. "I don't really care, but you have to consider your reputations."

Charity said in a puzzled voice, "Why should living here harm our reputations?"

"Oh, be quiet, you silly girl!" Hope said crossly.

Charity assumed a wounded look and began to sulk.

"Never mind, Charity," Cotty said gently. "You'll understand when you're old enough." He glanced over at Hope. "I've been thinking hard on it, and there is only one thing to do."

"What is that?" Hope said suspiciously.

"I shall go before a magistrate and have you and Charity made my wards until you are of legal age." He beamed at her, as though proud of his acumen.

Hope's heart sank. His wards! He made it sound like she was a child. She felt rebellious, and it was only with an effort that she kept silent.

Cotty continued, "That way, you can live here with no gossip involved. No one will think the worst of us..."

# PART THREE

## *July, 1807*

In the dream I walked a narrow place
a bridge between dark and light.
Beneath the tree I hear the voices
the voices of my ancestors singing of the past.
In the mist I see the future, but
I am not there.

(From the notes of John Myers, circa 1807)

# CHAPTER THIRTEEN

IT WAS SATURDAY NIGHT, and the Crown was doing a roaring business. Hope was stationed at the bar by the cash drawer; there were two bartenders behind the bar and three barmaids working the room. The traffic to the dining room upstairs was heavy. It was Hope's duty to supervise the tavern when Cotty was absent; and since he now owned another tavern in the Rocks, he was often away from the Crown. He had named his new establishment the Blackstock Inn, in honor of Faith.

At twenty-one Hope was fully matured, a beautiful woman. Her figure was full and seductive, and she was besieged by suitors.

Cotty had remarked on the numerous proposals of marriage more than once. "I fail to understand you, Hope," he had said. "Some of the most eligible men in Sydney Town have offered to wed you, and yet you stand aloof. Most girls your age are long married."

"All in good time," she had retorted. "I haven't found any man who suits me."

"You're being awfully particular, my dear. You'd better not wait too long, or you'll soon be considered a spinster."

Of course, the reason she had not found a man to marry was simple—she was still in love with Cotty. Through all the years and the obvious hopelessness of her love for him, she could not find it in her to consider loving another man. Always in her heart burned a tiny flame of hope that he would eventually recognize her love, and come to love her in return. More than once she had thought of telling him of her feelings, but at the last moment she always lost her courage.

Living in the same dwelling with him, seeing him every day, being in such close proximity to him, knowing that he slept three doors down the hall, caused her much anguish and despair; yet she knew that the alternative, never seeing him, never being close to him, would be even more painful. Some fine day he might come to his senses and realize that all his other women were empty-headed wenches, little better than the strumpets who infested the Rocks like insects.

Looking to her left, Hope saw Charity coming down the stairs, dressed in her best gown. Now eighteen, Charity was in full flower. If she was less refined, less restrained than Hope, she was, in her own way, just as beautiful and, being flirtatious, attracted an even greater number of male admirers. Hope considered that she treated them with thoughtlessness and cruelty. Charity delighted in toying with a man's affections, leading him on until he was in love with her, then casting him aside.

Hope had attempted to make her understand the wrongness of these actions; but Charity seemed to have no conception of the fact that she was causing pain to another human being, and it had been impossible to engage her sympathies. She was as spoiled as ever, and although Hope did her best to take her mother's place as adviser to her sister, Cotty seemed to undermine her authority at every turn. Although he was usually levelheaded and clear-thinking, when it came to Charity he seemed to leave good sense behind. He took great delight in indulging her, and she, knowing he was an easy mark, took full advantage of the fact.

For a short while Hope had feared that Cotty was in love with her younger sister; but eventually she saw that this was not the case. It was obvious that Cotty looked upon Charity purely as a younger sister or a daughter, to be pampered and indulged; and it was clear that Charity had no romantic feelings toward Cotty.

Several times Hope had suggested that her sister work in the Crown, at least in the evenings when they were at their busiest; but Charity had not been interested, and Cotty would not hear of it.

"A tavern is no place for a girl of Charity's tender years and sensibilities," he had argued. "Besides, Faith would not have approved of it. Perhaps when she is older. She can work in the kitchen when you're occupied elsewhere, seeing that matters run smoothly."

And yet he had voiced no objections when she, Hope, had offered to work in the tavern; to the contrary, he had welcomed the suggestion enthusiastically. He had told her that he was pleased because he now had someone he could trust to take charge in his absence.

At first Hope had worked as a barmaid, but eventually she took over the cash drawer; and by the end of two years, she was nominally in charge of the tavern and the kitchen.

Naturally, Hope was proud of the responsibility entrusted to her, and Cotty was generous with his appreciation. But she would have been much happier to have had his love . . .

She broke off her thoughts as Charity, the focus of most male eyes in the place, strolled up to where Hope stood. A handsome young man at a nearby table eyed her boldly. Charity, taking note of his attention, sent him a saucy smile.

"Charity," Hope hissed, "stop playing the coquette with that young man!"

"Why, I don't know what you mean, dear sister," Charity said, all innocence.

"I saw you smile at him."

"What if I did! I was just being friendly. And he's a customer. Cotty wouldn't like it if I turned a cold shoulder to a customer."

"I'll tell you what Cotty would *not* like. He has told you repeatedly not to come in here during business hours, especially when he isn't here."

Charity pouted prettily. "I can't stay up in my room all the time. I shall go mad! You're always down here, I notice."

"Of course I am, you silly girl! I'm working. If you have to be down here, come around behind the bar with me."

As Charity reluctantly came around behind the bar, Hope motioned for her to sit on a stool beside her. She reached under the bar for a shawl and handed it to Charity.

"Here, drape this around your shoulders. You look shameless, no more than a brazen hussy." She stared at her sister's décolletage, so low-cut it revealed the creamy swell of her full breasts.

"But it's the latest fashion!"

"I care little if it is fashionable. At a social soiree it might be fine, but it is not fitting to be worn before a group of rowdy males. Now put the shawl around your shoulders, Charity, or you march right back upstairs!"

"Oh, all right, Miss Prim!" Charity said petulantly, and pulled the shawl around her shoulders.

"A thousand pardons, ladies, but may I introduce myself?"

Hope whirled around to stare into the darkly handsome face of the man who had been ogling Charity. His eyes were a depthless black, and piercing. He had an aquiline nose that divided his face with a strange unevenness, which only added to his somewhat sinister attractiveness. His thin lips wore a smile that Hope could only describe as supercilious.

"Sir?" Hope said coldly.

"Forgive me if I seem forward." The man bowed slightly. "I am Charles Bonney, recently arrived in Sydney. I am here as an aide to Captain William Bligh, your new governor."

"I am Hope Blackstock."

Bonney bowed again, but his gaze clung to Charity; and Hope experienced a bit of pique. She was not particularly vain about her appearance, and it was not that she would welcome his attentions—there was something faintly repellent about him—but still . . .

He was saying, "And who is your charming companion?"

Common courtesy demanded that Hope make the introduction. "This is my sister, Charity." She added quickly, "She is only eighteen."

" 'Pon my honor, a most charming eighteen. Yes, indeed."

Before Hope realized what was happening, Charity leaned across the bar, holding out her hand. As she did so, the shawl slipped off her shoulders, once again exposing her bosom.

Bonney took her hand and raised it to his lips. In spite of the awkwardness of the bar between them, he managed to make it a gallant gesture.

In one quick motion, Hope rescued the shawl, again covering Charity's exposed breasts. Bonney released Charity's hand, and for the first time he looked directly at Hope. In those dark, reptilian eyes, Hope glimpsed a mocking amusement. The message was clear—she's mine if I want her, and there is nothing you can do about it.

At that moment, Hope saw Cotty coming in the main entrance, and she was swept by a feeling of relief. As was his habit, Cotty's glance went first to her position at the bar, and she made a small motion with her head. He made his way quickly through the room, ignoring greetings on every side. Over the past few years Cotty had made some enemies in the Rocks because of his successful business tactics, yet he was respected and well liked by most of his customers.

Reaching the bar, he said, "Hope, my dear. Is everything all right?"

Charles Bonney half turned at the sound of Cotty's voice, and his narrow face grew still as he took Cotty's measure.

"I don't believe I have the pleasure of your acquaintance, sir," Cotty said evenly. "I am Cotty Starke, proprietor of the Crown."

"This is my first time in your establishment, sir. I am Charles Bonney, aide to Governor Bligh," Bonney said, with a slight inclination of his head.

"That explains it then," Cotty said. "I have not been to Government House since Captain Bligh came to New South Wales."

"The governor has been much occupied with affairs of office, but he is planning a great ball soon. I shall see that you receive an invitation, sir, provided..." He looked at Charity with his slanting smile. "Provided that the charming Mistresses Blackstock attend."

"That will be my decision," Cotty said stiffly. "They are both my wards."

"On my honor, what a fortunate man you are, sir," Bonney said with a straight face.

"I think so, yes."

"Then I certainly hope you see fit to honor the invitations." Bonney bowed slightly. "I bid you good night, ladies."

He made his way out of the tavern. Cotty watched him go, frowning. There was something about the man he did not like, but he could not quite put a name to it. Perhaps it was Bonney's air of arrogance and superiority; he most certainly seemed to have a good opinion of himself.

"Can we go, Cotty?" Charity asked eagerly. "To the governor's ball?"

"We shall see."

"I don't like that man," Hope said forcibly.

"Oh, pooh!" Charity said. "You're just jealous because he paid the most attention to me."

"Don't be ridiculous, Charity!" Hope glared at her sister. "Why should I care about that?"

Charity smiled maliciously. "Sometimes I think you don't like any men at all."

"All right, you two!" Cotty snapped. "Don't forget that you're ladies."

"You are a one to talk, Cotty Starke," Charity said with a toss of her head. "The ladies I see you with are often not ladies at all!!"

He glowered at her. "Why are you down here, Charity? I've forbidden you to come into the barroom during business hours."

"I'm old enough to decide that for myself!" she flared.

"And I say you're not. You are still my ward."

"Cotty..." Charity's manner became wheedling. "I can't stay upstairs by myself all the time. What harm can come to me here, with Hope and the bartenders on duty?"

"Well, it's best you don't come here." He scowled at Hope. "You know my wishes in this, Hope."

"She's your ward, not mine!" Hope said tartly. "She pays little heed to what *I* say. And don't forget, *I* am no longer your ward. I reached my majority two months ago. You can no longer tell me what to do."

"So long as you both live under my roof, you will obey my wishes," he said in a growling voice.

He turned away and strode toward his office, seething. Who could understand women? Especially this pair of headstrong wenches! At times like this he cursed the day he had decided to make them his wards.

He was far from the inexperienced youth he had been when he had bedded Prudence Wilkes; he had known many women intimately in the years since. In fact, he had gained something of a reputation as a womanizer, and with some reason. The affair with Prudence, which had continued for two years, until her husband had been sent back to England, had aroused a sensuality in Cotty that he had not known he possessed.

But he did resent Charity's accusation. While it was true that he occasionally dallied with some of the more comely women of the Rocks, he had not taken one for a mistress, as did so many of the corps officers. Usually he engaged in discreet affairs with the discontented wives of the corps officers, or even some of the wives of the government officials living on the hills above Sydney Harbor.

He had early learned that many men seemed to prefer their sexual adventures with the loose women infesting the Rocks, often preferring convict women, neglecting their own spouses in the process. It left their wives easy prey for a man willing to take the time to cater to their needs and treat them with at least a modicum of respect.

There had been a number of narrow escapes, but so far his liaisons had remained undiscovered. Most husbands, he had learned, were very reluctant to believe that they could be cuckolded.

There were relatively few unmarried women in the colony except, of course, for the doxies roaming the streets of the Rocks. However, Cotty generally steered clear of the few single women of good breeding. They were interested in marriage, and he had absolutely no intention of falling into that trap. His father's experience with matrimony had been a disaster, and Cotty wanted none of it.

As he sat behind his desk, his thoughts swung to the man he had just met in the barroom, Charles Bonney. In a way, Bonney represented the wave of change that had come over Sydney in the past seven years. The population of Sydney had grown by two thousand since 1800, increased by shipload after shipload of convicts and free settlers who had flocked to the colony since conditions had improved. Food was generally more plentiful now, since it had been discovered that areas such as Parramatta had fertile soil for the raising of crops. Although the seals had been somewhat depleted, the sealing industry was still thriving, as was the whaling industry, so the harbor was always crowded with ships.

All of this meant that the port was booming, which in turn meant prosperity for Cotty. Both his taverns and his grog shanties were turning a substantial profit. Of course, it also meant a number of problems, especially in the Rocks area.

Officially, the sale of spirits was banned to the convicts. But over the years it had been learned that rum was a strong inducement to make them work better; shrewd employers realized this, and the practice of giving dispensations of rum to a convict at the end of a day's work began. An appropriate amount—often twice what the employer paid for the liquor—was deducted from the convict's already low wages. Also, many convicts were allowed to hire themselves out in their spare time to other employers, thus earning enough rum to keep them happy at night.

Bonfires blazed at night along the shore, where the convicts gathered to drink and carouse, since they were forbidden to wander around the better parts of town. They also caroused in the Rocks, with the drunken seamen and other rowdies. The Rocks was now notorious for scenes of vice and debauchery. In general, no law existed there. Even Cotty, who was known and feared, had made himself proficient with pistols and took care to arm himself at all times.

The trade in rum had certainly not changed. Almost all the officers of the New South Wales Corps now engaged in the liquor trade, in one form or another. Since the government granted them land, many now owned farms; but they did not consider the income from the farms to be enough to support the style of life to which they believed they were entitled. They made up the difference by dealing in spirits. The derisive title the Rum Corps, applied to the military years earlier, was now more apt than ever.

John Macarthur had returned in triumph to New South Wales. In London he had been exonerated at his court-martial, and Governor King had been severely reprimanded for not having settled the issue himself. Not only was Macarthur exonerated, but he managed to convince a special committee of the Privy Council on Trade and Plantations that he could provide wool from his Spanish sheep for the newly invented textile machinery. His timing was fortuitous, for England was prevented from obtaining wool from the Continent by Napoléon.

Macarthur had returned to New South Wales in 1804, carrying a letter to Governor King from the colonial secretary requesting that the governor grant him, free of any charge, five thousand acres in perpetuity; the land to be used to improve his breed of sheep and the growth of his flock.

The other change that had taken place was that a new governor had succeeded Governor King—former Navy Captain William Bligh. Cotty, as well as a number of other prominent citizens of the colony, looked upon Bligh's appointment with strong misgivings.

Captain Bligh's ill fame was known throughout the civilized world. Even in a navy known for its brutal captains, Bligh was notorious for his bullying tactics, for his overbearing, arrogant manner and for the fluency of his vituperation and abuse.

However, he was best known for the incident aboard the ship *Bounty*, which he commanded on a voyage in 1787 to Tahiti. Many thought him responsible for the infamous mutiny, during which he and eighteen men were set adrift in a small open boat with only a few provisions and without a chart.

If nothing else, Bligh was a survivor. Facing incredible risks and hardships, he sailed his small craft to the Dutch island of Timor in forty-one days, a distance of some thirty-six hundred miles. Back in England, he not only was completely exonerated of all blame for the mutiny, but was promoted to commander and then to post captain, in which position he remained until he was made governor of New South Wales.

One thing definitely had not changed—the animosity between the colony's governors and Macarthur.

Of course, Cotty had concluded, it was perhaps inevitable that conflict should arise between Bligh and Macarthur, given their natures. Macarthur's arrogance certainly had not been diminished by his brief exile in England. Cotty had not seen the man since his return; but from the stories he had heard, Macarthur was more domineering than ever.

And Bligh's quarterdeck manner stayed with him. In time, the bitterness between the two antagonists became more intense than it had been between Macarthur and Governor King.

Recently, the quarrel had reached a boiling point. The story was the talk of Sydney. The Hawkesbury River had flooded, which had cost the colony most of its grain and meat supply. Prices rose steeply for what supplies were left; and for the first time Macarthur came into some disfavor with the colonists, since they were anxious to purchase food, not wool.

Macarthur, with his usual lack of tact, approached Governor Bligh with a plan to increase the size of his flock and demanded more pasture land to support the sheep.

The governor's reaction was predictable—he exploded in a fine rage. Cotty smiled as he remembered the governor's response; his words had been repeated verbatim throughout the colony.

"Damn, what have I to do with your damned sheep, sir? What do I have to do with your benighted cattle? Are you to have such flocks of sheep and herds of cattle as no man ever heard of before? No, sir, I have heard of your concerns, sir. You have five thousand acres of land, sir, in the finest area in the country, but, by God, you shan't keep it. I shall see to that!"

Thinking about the enmity between the two men, Cotty laughed aloud. But of course it might not be all that humorous; it could easily escalate into a savage physical conflict.

Well, it did not concern him, he thought; so long as he steered well clear of both Governor Bligh and John Macarthur, and did not take sides, he should be all right.

He opened his account journal on his desk, and began bringing the accounts up to date.

# CHAPTER FOURTEEN

THE CROWN WAS EMPTYING, the last customers just going out the front door, and Hope heaved a sigh of relief. It had been a busy evening, and she was weary.

"Samuel," she called down the bar to the oldest bartender, "would you see to barring the front door?"

"Of course, Mistress Hope."

Samuel Waters was a tall, middle-aged seaman, who had lost a leg to a shark and been forced to retire from the sea. Hope watched him thump across the barroom with his wooden leg. She was fond of Samuel, and she knew that she could not run the Crown without him. Despite his infirmity, he could still handle himself. He kept a belaying pin behind the bar and was an expert in its use; when a patron in his cups became belligerent, Samuel could use the belaying pin to good effect.

Now he bade the last patron good-night and threw the bolt on the door. Before he was halfway back across the room, a heavy knocking sounded. Samuel looked in question at Hope.

She hesitated, then said, "Better see who it is, Samuel. It might be important. But if it's someone wishing service, tell him we're closed for the night."

Samuel nodded and thumped back to open the door. Holding it partway open, he conversed with someone for a few minutes. Finally, he glanced over his shoulder. ''It's some'un wantin' to see Master Cotty.''

''A man?'' If it was one of Cotty's ladies, Hope was determined not to admit her.

''Yes, 'um.''

She nodded. ''Let him in.''

Samuel stepped back, letting in a man of fifty-some years, red-faced, short of breath, with a mousy-colored wig askew. He stormed toward the barroom and in a harsh voice said, ''I demand to see Cotty Starke!''

The man's belligerent manner gave Hope pause, thinking perhaps she should check with Cotty first. However, she was still piqued with him; if this man had a quarrel with Cotty, let Cotty face up to it.

''Come with me, sir.''

Hope stepped out from behind the bar, motioning, and the man followed her past the foot of the stairs to the closed door of Cotty's office. She rapped on the door.

From inside Cotty called, ''Yes? What is it?''

Hope opened the door just enough to poke her head around. ''Cotty, there is a gentleman here to see you . . .''

Before Hope could finish, the gentleman in question picked her up bodily, set her aside and bullied his way into the room.

Stunned by such rudeness, Hope stood where she was, and could not help overhearing the scene that ensued.

Cotty rose from his desk. ''Sir, you have no right to barge in . . .''

"I have every right!" the man roared. "I am Jacob Wright, and you, sir, have been cuckolding me!"

Cotty looked startled. "You must be mistaken, Master Wright."

"I am not mistaken! My own wife, Katherine, informed me just this evening. Be a man and admit your perfidy, sir!"

"I'm afraid that you have me at a loss, Master Wright. I do not even know the lady in question." Cotty was relaxed now, smiling slightly.

"My wife is not a liar!" Wright said in a choked voice.

Cotty shrugged carelessly. "Then I am a cad, no matter what I say. If I deny your charge, I name your wife a liar. If I admit it, I name her an adultress."

Wright took a quick step forward and slapped Cotty across the cheek with his open hand. In a voice trembling with outrage, he said, "I demand satisfaction, sir! You will face me at sunrise on the morrow."

Cotty stared, his hand coming up to touch his cheek. "You are challenging me to a duel? You cannot be serious!"

"I am deadly serious, sir. My honor is at stake here. I must defend it."

"And if I refuse to accept your challenge?"

"Then you shall be publicly branded a coward! The whole of Sydney will know of your cowardice. And since I hear some refer to you as the king of the Rocks..." Wright sneered in contempt. "What will they think of their king?"

For the first time Cotty showed signs of visible anger—his lips thinned to a line, and his fists clenched at his sides. "Your challenge is accepted, sir," he said quietly. "What is your choice of weapons?"

"According to the rules of dueling, the choice is yours to make."

Cotty inclined his head. "I choose pistols."

"Then pistols it shall be. I shall see you at the Meadows at sunrise."

Jacob Wright wheeled and marched past Hope without a single glance. Hope had listened to the interchange with mounting horror.

Now she came into the room. In a stricken voice she said, "Cotty, I'm sorry. If I had known what it was about, I wouldn't have shown him in."

Cotty gestured. "It doesn't matter. He's an obsessed man and would have confronted me sooner or later."

"But surely you're not going to duel with him?"

"You heard what he said." He sank down into his chair, scrubbing a hand across his face in a weary gesture. "For he's right. I do have a certain image to maintain. If I back away from this, I will become a figure of amusement, a laughingstock!"

"Let them laugh!" she said vehemently.

"My dear Hope, I cannot allow that." He gave a grim smile. "It would not be good for business."

"But dueling is against the law."

He shook his head. "That may well be, but the law is generally ignored, unless it involves an important figure, such as John Macarthur. No, Hope, it's dear of you to be concerned," he said in a softer tone. "But I have no choice."

"Was what he said true? Did you...bed his wife?"

He looked at her, faintly amused. "It doesn't really matter, does it? Master Wright is convinced it's true."

"It matters to me," she said stiffly.

"Why should it, Hope?" He turned away from her, then spoke over his shoulder. "If you see John, would you please send him in to me?"

"Men! Men and their honor!" she said with withering contempt. "Go ahead, then. Go ahead and get yourself killed, and see if I care!"

Fighting the urge to cry, she fled from the office.

Cotty turned around to stare after her for a moment, then dismissed her concerns from his mind. It was sweet of her to worry about his welfare, but he had more important matters to consider.

His thoughts moved to the morning and the duel. He smiled wryly. It would seem, after all this time, that his womanizing was about to catch up with him. The hell of it was, he had only bedded Katherine Wright the one time. She had been emotional and weepy afterward, clinging tightly to him, crying out her shame and guilt, when it had been her idea all along. That should have given him an inkling that she might run to her husband and confess. With hope, if he survived the morning, this might teach him a valuable lesson.

It would be ironic if he were killed tomorrow, after working so hard all these years to attain his goal, and finally coming so close. He smiled again, remembering Wright's comment: the king of the Rocks. Of course, he had known that he was named that in some circles, but this was the first time anyone had called him that to his face.

While some people might deride the name, it gave Cotty a certain pride and considerable satisfaction. Now he might be dethroned by a ball from the pistol of a cuckolded husband!

He was not afraid to risk his life—he had risked it on numerous occasions—but to die for such an asinine reason! Yet he knew he could not spurn the challenge, no matter how foolish Hope might consider it . . .

"Cotty?"

Cotty glanced up with a start. John stood in the open doorway, his dark face concerned.

"Mistress Hope said you wished to see me?"

"Yes, John, come in and sit."

As John perched gingerly on the edge of the chair, Cotty leaned back, arranging his thoughts. "John . . . in the morning I am fighting a duel."

"A duel?" John was clearly puzzled. "Why?"

Cotty sighed, wondering how to make him understand. "I have been called out. There was a misunderstanding. . . ."

"This misunderstanding, what is it about?"

"Master Jacob Wright considers himself a cuckold . . ." Cotty broke off. "Wright believes that I bedded his wife."

"This Master Wright would kill you because you took his woman?"

"He damned well intends to try."

"Did you—" John's stare was intent. "Did you do this thing?"

"Everybody wants to know, it seems," Cotty muttered, annoyed. Then he shrugged. "It doesn't matter, John. Jacob Wright *believes* that I did." He leaned forward. "I want you to act as my second."

"This is an honor, this second?"

Cotty nodded gravely. "Yes, John, it is an honor."

Equally grave, John said, "It is an honor that I accept, Cotty."

"Thank you, John." Cotty got up and clasped John's hand in both of his. "We must leave for the Meadows at dawn."

JOHN WAS SORELY TROUBLED as he returned to the barroom and aided Samuel Waters in tidying up the Crown for the night. John worked with his head down, deep in thought.

Should he go to the dreaming tree? Should he try to slip into the dream state to see if he could learn Cotty's fate in the morning?

Since he had envisioned the death of Faith Blackstock, John had been reluctant to court the dreams. The few times he had tried, nothing of any consequence had resulted—possibly because he *was* reluctant, because he was fearful of what he might learn.

However, there were only a few hours left until Cotty was to confront his fate; and John had rarely courted the dreams in the nighttime. Daylight was the favored time.

Often he would be in a dream trance for hours, with no means of judging the passage of time. If he went to the dreaming tree this late, it was quite possible that he might still be in the trance at dawn, and thus would fail in the duty Cotty had assigned to him as second.

Even if he succeeded in having a vision concerning Cotty's fate, it could come to naught. Cotty might not believe him, or might simply ignore any warning of a dire fate. John well knew by now that Cotty Starke was a very stubborn man; once he was set on a course that he deemed right, nothing could persuade him to change his mind.

In the end, John decided not to journey to the dreaming tree. He would accompany Cotty to the dueling ground in the morning and serve as second, sending a plea up to the gods that Cotty would emerge the victor.

HOPE WAS ALSO deeply troubled by the impending duel. It was foremost in her thoughts as she finished the count of the day's receipts and carried the cash drawer into Cotty's office. The door stood open, and he was sitting staring off into space.

"Cotty . . ."

He gave a little jump, his head swiveling around. With a wan smile he said, "Yes, Hope?"

"We had a very good day." She held out the cash drawer.

"That's good," he said absently, taking the drawer from her without even glancing into it.

"Cotty, about this foolish duel . . ."

His head came up, his eyes flashing. "Enough, Hope! There is nothing you can say that will change my mind. It is something I must do."

Tears of anger flooded her eyes and she whirled, hurrying from the room.

In her bedroom she flung herself across the bed, beating on the pillow in her anger. He was so stubborn, so strong-minded! Could he not realize how foolish the whole thing was?

How could she bear waiting to hear the outcome of this insanity? She must find a way to be present. If Cotty was to die, she would be there at his side.

SOME TIME BACK Cotty had purchased two riding horses, for occasional rides in the countryside with the girls, and for the even less frequent hunting trips with John. Although the Meadows, where the duels took place, was not much more than a half hour's walk from the Crown, Cotty deemed it more fitting to ride to the duel. Especially, he thought sardonically, if he was going to his death.

Therefore, at dawn, Cotty and John walked the short distance to where the horses were stabled, saddled them and rode out. Although mist still clung low to the ground, it showed promise of being a nice day. A nice day to die, Cotty thought.

Cotty gave his head a sharp shake in an effort to rid himself of such morbid thoughts and said briskly, "Jacob Wright will supply the dueling pistols, John. When we get there, it shall be your duty to test fire the pistol I shall be using, to make sure that it is working properly. The custom with most duels is for the seconds to do that chore the day before, but Wright is evidently eager to court death, and cannot wait." He laughed shortly.

"You will trust your life in my hands?" John asked. The aborigine had seemed edgy and withdrawn since the two men had greeted each other at the Crown.

"I will indeed, John." Cotty maneuvered his mount close enough to reach over and clap John on the shoulder. "If not you, whom can I trust such matters to? Now, after you have test fired the weapon, check the flint and pour fresh powder down the barrel.''

John was frowning, and Cotty laughed. "Don't look so worried, my friend. It's no more complicated than what you do when we go hunting."

"Hunting the kangaroo is not like hunting a man," John muttered.

"I'm not so sure about that. But in any event, do not trouble yourself unduly."

They rode out from under a grove of trees into a grassy meadow that had been named the Dueling Meadows. Normally, the glade was green, but now, well into winter, the grass was brown and shriveled.

When they rode up and dismounted, Cotty saw that Jacob Wright was already present, along with two other men. One Cotty recognized as Dr. Stanton, a relatively new arrival in Sydney. Cotty did not know the third man; he assumed that he was Wright's second.

"This is Dr. Stanton, Starke. Cotty Starke, Doctor," Wright said. "The man who has dishonored me."

The doctor shifted a wooden box he was carrying to his left hand, and Cotty shook his hand.

"And this is Ronald Newton, my second," Wright said.

Dr. Stanton said formally, "I must inquire if you both wish to continue with this duel?"

"Ask Master Wright," Cotty said with a shrug. "The whole affair is his idea."

"I do indeed wish to continue," Wright said harshly. "Where is your second, sir?"

"Right here." Cotty gestured. "John Myers."

"But he is a blackamoor, sir!" Wright said in a choked voice. "Men of honor do not use aborigines as seconds!"

"I am not all that familiar with the rules of dueling, but I don't recall ever hearing that a man's second must be of any particular race or color."

"This is an insult, sir!" Wright's face was bright red, his eyes bulging.

"So what is your wish? It is that we fight yet another duel?" Cotty asked lightly.

"This is no laughing matter!" Wright's hands were trembling visibly, and Cotty had to wonder if he was about to fall dead of apoplexy. It was then that the idea came to him.

"Shall we get on with it, gentlemen?" Dr. Stanton inquired. "Since you two are the principals, I fail to see how the seconds enter into it." He opened the box, holding it out to Cotty. "Here are the pistols, sir. Are they to your satisfaction?"

"So long as they are in working order," Cotty said carelessly. "That is the chore of our seconds, is it not, to check them out?"

John and Ronald Newton stepped up, each removing a flintlock pistol along with powder and ball from the box. Without speaking to one another, they moved a few steps away, each examining the pistol of his principal.

Cotty, noticing that Wright was still glaring at John in outrage, hid a smile behind his back. He stood at ease, while Jacob Wright strode back and forth, fuming. When his second test fired his weapon, Wright jumped, glaring around. Another shot was quickly fired, as John tested the other pistol.

John finally came to Cotty with the pistol. "It works well, Cotty, and is now ready to fire again."

"Thank you, John."

Cotty took the pistol and hefted it in his hand. Although he was unfamiliar with this particular weapon, it was the same make as his own, and had a good, solid feel to it.

"Who shall call out the paces, gentlemen?" Dr. Stanton asked.

"Since I am the challenged party," Cotty said genially, "I believe that duty should belong to my second."

Wright exploded, "No! I will not have a black fella calling the paces."

"I'm afraid I must insist," Cotty said, still smiling. "It is my privilege."

Dr. Stanton said, "And I am afraid that I must agree."

Wright spun away, striding angrily back and forth. Finally, he turned a furious look toward them. "So be it, then! Let's get it over with."

In an aside to John, Cotty said softly, "I apologize for Master Wright."

John smiled for the first time that morning. "I have learned not to take offense, Cotty."

"Well, I appreciate your doing this. Now, what you have to do is simple. We will stand back to back, then you will start calling the numbers, one to ten. At ten paces, we turn and fire."

"I wish you well." John's eyes were suddenly moist.

Cotty and Jacob Wright stood back to back. Through the material of his shirt Cotty could feel that Wright's back was rigid, and he smiled to himself.

John began the count, in a slow, measured cadence, "One, two..."

HOPE HAD ARISEN before dawn, dressed quickly and slipped out of the tavern. Since she did not wish to be recognized, she dressed in the rough clothing she wore while cleaning the tavern.

Once beyond the edge of town, she hurried toward the Dueling Meadows, reaching them shortly after dawn. The area was wreathed in fog and there was no one around. She secreted herself in the grove of trees at the perimeter of the dueling ground and settled down to wait. It was chilly where she huddled behind the trunk of a tree.

Shortly after she had arrived, three men appeared in the clearing. The only one she recognized was the angry man who had stormed into the Crown last night. The other two men stood quietly, talking, while Jacob Wright paced.

The fog dispersed, and it would soon be sunrise. She saw Wright approach his two companions and talk, waving his arms angrily, and she surmised that he was wondering if Cotty would come.

For a moment she nursed the hope that he would not; and then she saw Cotty and John Myers ride into the clearing and dismount.

She watched as the men conferred for a few moments. Then, to her consternation, she saw John and the other man prepare the flintlocks and aim them at the very tree behind which she was crouching! She made herself as small as possible behind the tree. Fortunately, the trunk was thick and wide so that it absorbed the impact of the balls.

She waited with bated breath before venturing another glance from her hiding place. She was in time to see Cotty and Jacob Wright stand back to back and then begin pacing off the steps as John called out the numbers.

At the count of ten, both men turned. Cotty stood sideways, his pistol coming up, while Wright stood face on, his feet planted wide apart, his weapon also coming up. Cotty's pistol was in firing position a second before Wright's, but he did not fire!

Hope's heart almost stopped. What was wrong with him? Why did he not fire?

COTTY MADE HIMSELF as small a target as possible. Now he waited, pistol raised, staring at the bore of Wright's weapon as it came up. Even at this distance, it looked as large as the mouth of a cannon; and he wondered, for a fleeting second, if he had made the right decision. Was the risk worth it? Had he read Wright's state of agitation correctly?

Then it was too late for further thought—Wright fired. The ball whistled past within an inch of Cotty's chest. He waited a moment longer, watching the wisp of smoke spiral up from Wright's pistol, watching the fear suddenly blossom on the other man's face.

Smiling slightly, realizing that he was weak with relief at having his judgment verified, Cotty lowered the muzzle of the pistol slightly and fired. The ball went true, striking Wright in midthigh. Wright cried out, a whinnying sound, took a step backward and fell.

Cotty walked over to him. Standing over him, he asked, "Do you calculate that your wife's questionable virtue was worth it, Master Wright?"

Face contorted with pain, Wright stared up at him with eyes darkened with hatred. "You are a terrible shot, Starke," he said in a hissing voice.

"On the contrary. I am a good shot."

"Then why didn't you kill me?"

"I didn't think that your wife's virtue was worth a man's death, even that of a bastard like you. Oh, no, I hit what I aimed for. Now, let this be an end to it." Cotty motioned. "I believe your services are required, Dr. Stanton."

He stood back as Dr. Stanton kneeled beside the wounded man, a black bag by his side, and began his examination.

A cry from behind them, and John's voice calling, "Cotty?" brought the young man's head around.

A small figure was racing across the meadow toward them, coming from the direction of the grove of trees. For a moment Cotty was at a loss, then recognition dawned. It was Hope!

Before he could react, she threw herself against him, sobbing. Automatically, his arms went around her, pulling her close. For the first time he was uncomfortably aware of her as a mature woman, as he felt her breasts, full and firm, against his chest.

Hastily, he took her by the arms and set her back from him, frowning down into her wet eyes. "You foolish girl!" he scolded. "What in hell's name are you doing out here?"

"What if you had been killed?" she said, her breath catching on a sob. "I would have gone crazy waiting for someone to bring word!"

He gestured slightly. "Well, as you can see, I am perfectly fine."

"But why did you do that? Why did you stand there and not fire until after he did?"

"I figured the odds were heavy that he would miss," he said sheepishly. "Jacob Wright was much overwrought, not only about the duel itself, but about John serving as my second. As it turned out, I was right."

"I still fail to understand why you took such a foolish risk."

"Well . . ." He scrubbed a hand across his mouth. "I figured that it would do me nothing but good, once the word gets around that I deliberately let him get in the first shot, and the word *will* be around the Rocks by nightfall, you may be sure of that."

She stared. "You mean you took a risk such as that just to enhance your reputation?"

"Well . . ." He grinned sardonically. "You know that I'm called king of the Rocks. Nothing like a legend to make a king more respected . . ."

Without warning, she flew at him in a rage, beating on his chest with her fists. Recovering from his surprise, he caught her arms and forced her back.

"Whoa, now! What's wrong with you?"

"You could have been killed, and for a stupid reason like that!" She half turned away, hiding her face.

"Well, it didn't happen, so why get so upset?" He dismissed it with a gesture. "And you still haven't really told me why you're out here, and dressed like some poor doxy from the Rocks. That rig is hardly suitable for a lady.''

She gave him a flashing look. ''So you've finally noticed?''

''Noticed what?'' he said baffled.

''That I've grown up? That I'm a lady now?''

''Grown up, yes.'' He grinned again. ''As for the lady part, I'm not so sure. Not with you dressed like that.''

Her face closed up, she glared at him furiously, and then she whirled and started off without a word.

Walking across the meadow toward the trees, her shoulders slumped, she looked so desolate that he took a step after her, opened his mouth to call her back, then closed it again. He was mystified as to what had gotten her so upset, but he was sure she would soon get over it.

# CHAPTER FIFTEEN

CHARITY STUDIED her reflection in the pier glass for the tenth time in the past hour. She had talked Cotty into buying her a new gown for the governor's ball, but he had sent Hope along to supervise the purchase; and Hope, prim as a schoolmistress, had insisted on a conservative garment. In Charity's opinion, the gown was hardly daring, far less fetching than she would have liked. The color was all right—a pale pink which set off her dark coloring to good advantage—but the décolletage was not low enough. The top of the garment hid the swell of her bosom.

Until recently, Charity had despaired of ever having a decent bosom. But during the past year her breasts had grown quite satisfactorily and were now, in her opinion, by far her best feature. So why should she hide them?

Hope was so prissy! She would be much better off if *she* dressed a little more enticingly. Perhaps then she would attract a man who pleased her. So far she had turned all suitors away, and at twenty-one she was unwed!

Of course, Charity was not yet ready to marry. She wanted to enjoy herself before she got tied down with one man. At fifteen, probably even before, she had known how attractive she was to men; and that knowledge gave her a sense of power that made her feel deliciously giddy. She fully intended to enjoy that power before she wed. Of course, she thought now as she admired herself in the glass, there was no reason she should have to relinquish that power over men *after* she was married! Was there? Of course not.

And now she was going to attend a fancy ball at the invitation of Charles Bonney! Bonney was the first man she had ever really been attracted to. Remembering those few minutes in his presence was enough to give her the shivers. He had an air of the sinister about him that only added to his attractiveness. She had no use for most of the young men of her acquaintance—all were as bland and innocuous as milch cows!

She struck a pose, one hip cocked, and fanned herself with an imaginary fan. No, it simply would not do. Judging by the gown Hope had insisted she buy, she might not have any bosom at all!

She had another dress, a pale yellow that she thought complemented her dark beauty very well. During the past half hour, she had tried on first one, then the other. Neither Hope nor Cotty knew about the second dress, which she had purchased on her own several days ago.

A glance at the clock against the wall told her that it was well after half past six; they were to leave for the ball at seven, so time was growing short.

Quickly, she divested herself of the pink gown and put on the yellow one. Standing again before the glass, she said aloud, "Yes! That's better, much better." The ivory swell of her upper breasts was revealed nicely now. She nodded to herself, setting her lips in determination. This was the one she was going to wear, no matter what Hope or Cotty said!

A light knock sounded on the door, and Hope called, "Charity, are you ready? The carriage is here."

Charity glanced around hurriedly. Her brown silk shawl was lying on the bed. She snatched it up and draped it around her shoulders, hiding the low décolletage.

"Come in, Hope."

The door opened to admit her sister. Hope was dressed in a gown of blue that set off her pale hair and delicate coloring. Charity had to admit that she looked stunning, even though the garment was hardly revealing. Thinking it might ease a potentially explosive situation, Charity said quickly, "You look lovely, sister."

"Why, thank you, Charity . . ." Hope broke off, staring at the yellow dress. "Where did you get that dress? I don't recall seeing it before."

"I bought it last week," Charity said defensively.

"Why didn't you take me with you?"

"I'm old enough to buy my own clothes, Hope!" Charity snapped.

"How did you come by the money?"

"Cotty has been paying me for supervising the kitchen, as you well know. I worked for that money, and I deserve to spend it any way I like."

"Yes, I suppose you do." Hope's eyes narrowed. "But surely you're not wearing that shawl with the dress?"

"I was just trying on several shawls."

"But why wear one at all?"

Before Charity divined her intention, Hope took two quick steps and snatched the shawl away, then fell back with a gasp. "So that's why you had the shawl on, to hide from me. You're not going to the ball like that, Charity! It's shameless!''

Charity drew herself up. ''I can wear what I like, and you cannot stop me!''

''I will not allow it, Charity!''

''You're not my mother, and I'm eighteen. And don't be so fussy, sister. This is the latest fashion.''

''I don't care a whit about the latest fashion . . .''

''What's going on, ladies?'' It was Cotty, standing in the open door. ''I heard loud voices. Are you two quarreling again?''

Hope turned, gesturing. ''Just look at what your ward wants to wear tonight. It's outrageous, Cotty!''

''It is not!'' Charity said angrily. ''Tell her that she has no right to tell me what to wear, Cotty.''

Cotty scrubbed at his mouth, shooting a glance at Hope. ''You should have *some* advice as to what clothes to wear, Charity.''

''Why should I? Most girls my age are already married, and if I'm old enough to be married, I'm old enough to select my own clothes. Hope is so prissy about such things.'' She gave Hope a withering glance.

''I may be prissy, in your estimation, but at least I exercise some decorum.''

Cotty stared at the swell of Charity's bosom, and faint color stained his cheeks. ''But Charity, don't you think that gown is a little . . . well, improper?''

''No, I do not! Other women will be wearing much the same thing tonight.''

Hope said, ''Married women, not unattached ladies.''

"That isn't true, wait and see." Charity's full mouth set in that familiar, obstinate pout. "This is the gown I intend to wear."

Cotty sighed. "I do wish the pair of you would make more of an effort to get along. You *are* sisters."

"Sometimes I wish we weren't," Charity snapped.

"All right, all right!" Cotty threw up his hands. "Do whatever you wish. You will anyway, no matter what I say." But in spite of his annoyance, he caught himself smiling fondly at Charity.

Hope, watching, barely managed to contain her anger. Damn him! He always gave in to Charity, no matter how outrageous her behavior.

THERE WERE NOT a great number of carriages in Sydney as yet, but recently an enterprising individual had started a carriage-for-hire firm. Government House was within walking distance of the Crown, but Cotty decided that they would go in style. "After all," he had said with a grin, "it's not every day that we get invited to a governor's ball. It's certainly the first time for all of us, so we will arrive like gentry."

So, shortly before seven, they were clattering along High Street in a spanking-new carriage, the team of horses stepping out smartly. Then they turned left on New Bridge Street and over the bridge spanning the Tank Stream. They could see Government House at the end, the two-story brick structure outlined in the glow of torches flickering before it.

Charity could barely contain her excitement. Hope was also excited, but managed to restrain herself, looking with pretended disdain at Charity as she squealed and leaned out the carriage window to peer ahead. On each side of the street people were walking in their finery.

Cotty, in tan breeches fitted snugly to his legs, a black coat with a white cravat and high top hat, beamed fondly at Charity.

Looking out the window, Hope commented, "I don't see any officers of the corps riding toward Government House."

"And you're not likely to, either," he said dryly. "I seriously doubt that any NSW Corps officers have received invitations to the ball tonight, not with the way Governor Bligh and the corps are at loggerheads."

"I've never really understood all the animosity. I can see why they might quarrel over the distribution of spirits, since the governor restricts their sale and the others support a much more liberal distribution, but that scarcely seems sufficient reason for such a degree of bad feeling."

Cotty was sitting across from the two girls, his long legs stretched out. "Rum is the core of it, of course, Hope. But it goes beyond that. It's basically a power struggle, with the governor, actually the government, against the corps."

"But the government has granted all corps officers land of their own. Isn't that enough for them?"

"Hardly, given the greed of man," Cotty said in the same dry voice. "Much of the land given to them is not as fertile as they would like, and developing farmland requires years of hard labor. So they figure it is their right to augment their income in other ways. And what easier way than to engage in the smuggling and sale of rum? There has always been friction since the corps was formed. It began early, back in the days of Governor Phillip, as you know.

"When Governor Grose took over, he liberalized matters. Governor Phillip believed that the trade in liquor should be subject to, in his words, 'the view and inspection of proper persons.' On the other hand, Grose had a different view as to whom the proper persons were. As soon as he took over, as you will remember, he replaced most civil magistrates with officers from the NSW Corps, even giving the senior officer at Parramatta control over the convicts there.

"Since the officers were not considered 'proper persons' by Governor Grose, they were allowed to buy all the spirits they wished. Then they banded together and used their capital to monopolize the rum trade, buying rum and other spirits from Bengal, Batavia, South America and the United States. This made it difficult for we tavern owners, since the monopolists could sell their liquor at a very good profit to the freed convicts who had acquired small farms. The convicts and free settlers alike, finding it hard to make a living farming, were willing to trade their stock and other items for rum, so they could forget their hard life for a few hours."

Cotty sighed. "And now there is Captain Bligh. He claims to despise all members of the New South Wales Corps, for their traffic in rum and their intercourse with freed convicts. He is determined to break the military's monopoly in the rum trade any way he can. He has dishonored agreements between the settlers and the government, if he judges the settlers have dealt with the military. Bligh also ignores most legal niceties, holding the view that *he* makes the laws, and damnation to those who refuse to obey them! And the rest of us, meanwhile, are caught in the middle."

"But at least under his regime, you can buy spirits freely again, and legally," Hope said.

Cotty nodded, shifting his position. "True, but who knows when it will end? The corps officers are angry and bitter, and with Macarthur agitating them, it can only grow worse. The situation has to come to a head sooner or later, even to the point of the corps rebelling against Governor Bligh and his government."

Hope's eyes widened. "Surely, it won't come to an open rebellion!"

"I would not be at all surprised. The American Revolution was started over tea." He laughed shortly. "And the people of New South Wales view rum as far more important to their existence than tea!"

Charity squirmed in her seat, squealing, "We're here! And here you two sit discussing such boring matters as politics."

Hope said severely, "Some things are more important than parties, dear sister."

Cotty laughed. "To someone her age, balls are likely far more important. Especially her first one." He leaned across to take Charity's hand in both of his, and squeezed.

Hope suppressed a stab of resentment. It was also *her* first ball, which Cotty seemed to have forgotten. Or did he simply not care?

The carriage had now stopped at the end of a line of carriages and other vehicles drawn up before

Government House. Charity could hardly wait for the few minutes it took their carriage to reach the entrance. Then a footman, smart in knee breeches and a powdered wig, opened the door with a flourish and helped the ladies out, first Charity and then Hope. In a moment Cotty stepped down, placed himself between them and gave each an arm.

"Shall we join the gentry, ladies?" Cotty said with a wry smile.

Charity giggled. "Yes!"

Hope tried to look severe, but she caught herself smiling with anticipated pleasure. "We might as well," she said.

They joined the line of splendidly dressed men and women inching their way through the entrance. Cotty noticed several disapproving looks cast his way, coming mostly from men he knew as patrons of his taverns. He nodded to each, hiding a flare of anger behind a bland smile. How dare they disapprove of his being invited here? Many of them were ex-convicts—who called themselves "Emancipists" nowadays—and the rest were no better than Cotty and his two wards.

Just inside the entranceway, a receiving line had been formed. At the head of it stood Charles Bonney, elegantly attired, his darkly handsome face smiling slightly as he performed the introductions of the arriving guests to Governor Bligh, who stood beside him.

It was the first time Cotty had seen the new governor, and he took the opportunity to study him closely. He estimated the man's age to be in the mid-fifties. Bligh had a high forehead, wide-set, piercing eyes and a small, petulant mouth. He was well dressed and had an erect, military bearing, yet there was a sloppy look about him. His clothes, although well tailored, appeared to be ill-fitting. In his left hand he held a glass, from which he imbibed from time to time, as he shook proffered hands.

Then it was their turn. Bonney's smile widened when he recognized them, and his ebony eyes took on a certain glitter. He did not remove his gaze from Charity as he made the introductions. "Governor Bligh, may I present Cotty Starke, and his two wards, Charity and Hope Blackstock."

Both girls curtsied. Cotty bowed slightly and accepted the governor's handshake. "Your Excellency, it is indeed a pleasure."

Governor Bligh's hand was soft and moist. His eyes fixed on Cotty's, he said, "Ah, yes, Master Starke, the tavern owner." His pouty lips formed a smile that could either have been one of amusement or mocking. "You are called the king of the Rocks by some, I believe."

Cotty shrugged negligently. "It means nothing, sir. Just a name that some attached to me." He smiled briefly. "I've never been sure whether it's derogatory or complimentary."

"I am sure you do yourself an injustice, Master Starke," the governor said somewhat pompously. "You have quite a reputation in Sydney Town." His eyes narrowed as he released Cotty's hand. "I heard about your duel with one Jacob Wright. 'Tis said that you allowed him to fire first. That took courage."

"Or stupidity."

Governor Bligh said sternly, "Dueling is illegal, you must know. You could be subject to punishment." Then he smiled meagerly. "However, flouting the laws seems to be a popular sport in the colony."

"Dueling laws have rarely been enforced here."

"It would seem that other laws, as well, are not enforced," Bligh said. His burning eyes took on a fanatical shine. "I fully intend to remedy that situation in the end. Just because this is a new country does not mean that it should not be civilized. For instance, the laws involving the smuggling and distillation of spirits. How do you stand on that issue, sir?"

"As the owner of two taverns and several grog shanties, I find it easier to acquire the spirits I need when the laws are observed fairly."

"Exactly." The governor nodded, his eyes shrewd. "I take it then that you do not side with this contentious bastard, Macarthur, and his minions?"

"As a tavern owner, I try not to take sides on such a touchy issue," Cotty said cautiously. "It is not good for business. My patrons come from both sides."

"There comes a time in the life of any man when he must decide where he stands. Do you not agree?"

Cotty was saved a reply by Charles Bonney, who leaned over to whisper in the governor's ear. Bligh frowned, then said, "You must pardon me, Master Starke, while I attend to my duties as a host. We shall have occasion to converse later, I am sure."

As they started to move on, Bonney took Charity's hand and bowed over it. "When my duties are over, Miss Blackstock, I shall claim a dance."

Charity dimpled, blushing. "It shall be my pleasure, sir."

As they went on into the main room, which for tonight had been turned into a ballroom, Hope said acidly, "I do not think you should encourage that man, Charity."

"Oh, pooh!" Charity said airily. "What harm can a dance do?"

"She's right, Hope," Cotty said. "What harm can a few dances do? After all, we can keep an eye on her."

Charity gave her sister a triumphant glance, and Hope, against her better instincts, curbed her tongue.

A small group of musicians was playing, and a number of people were already dancing.

Hope had to admit that she was thrilled. Everything was so elegant: the lilting music; the bright light cascading down from the row of candles in the chandeliers; the splendid clothing of both men and women; and the grace with which they danced.

Cotty escorted the two girls to the end of the room and to a long table that was laden with two huge punch bowls and platters of edibles of every description. Cotty ladled out glasses of punch for them.

After taking a sip, he said, "You'd better not imbibe too heavily. This is laced with rum."

Hope, who did not care much for spirits, followed his advice, but she noticed that Charity drank deeply. Almost at once she became flushed and gay. Hope decided to hold her tongue. If Charity drank too much and got sick, perhaps it would teach her a lesson.

The three of them stood off to one side while they drank their punch. They listened as the musicians played jigs and reels. When the orchestra struck up a minuet, Cotty turned to Hope with a dip of his head. "May I have this dance, milady?"

She smiled brilliantly and placed her hand in his. "I should be delighted, sir!" She was both pleased and flattered, since she had been sure that he would ask Charity to dance first.

They swept into the intricate maneuvers of the minuet. Cotty had employed a dancing master some time ago to teach the girls how to dance, and in the doing, had learned how himself.

He was a graceful dancer, and for a bit Hope forgot everything but Cotty and the music. When she came close to him, she could feel her heartbeat accelerate and feel the male heat emanating from him. Their proximity inflamed her senses and her imagination; it was almost as if he was her suitor, and was courting her through the dance.

All too soon the music ended, and she came slowly back to reality as he led her off the dance floor.

He left her against the wall, saying, "I'll fetch us another glass of punch. That is punishing work, and I need the refreshment."

While she waited, Hope looked around for Charity. At first she could not see her sister, and she experienced a flash of panic. Could Charity have fallen victim to some charming lecher and let herself be lured away?

And then she spotted Charity dancing a reel with a foppish young buck. Charity was flushed and laughing, clearly enjoying herself.

A young man with a face flushed from drink and wearing a powdered wig slightly askew approached Hope. He made a leg and said, "May I have the pleasure, miss?"

"I must decline, sir," she said quickly. "I have an escort."

Cotty came up in time to hear her response, as the young man turned away with a look of disappointment. Cotty took a drink of punch. "Just because I came with you, Hope, is no reason you cannot dance with the young swains. You came here to enjoy yourself, didn't you?"

"But I don't wish to dance with strangers, Cotty!"

"How else will you ever get to know any eligible men?" he said in a reasonable tone.

"I'm not interested in any eligible men," she cried. "I'd rather be with you."

He sighed. "You *should* be interested, Hope. It is past time for you to be wed."

"Oh!" She glared at him in exasperation. Why could he not see what was under his very nose? She saw the man who had asked her to dance passing by, and she said loudly, "Sir, I have changed my mind. I should be delighted to dance with you."

The young man's face lit with a bright smile. He made a knee again. "I accept with pleasure. I am Stuart Williams. And you are . . . ?"

"Hope Blackstock."

"I am most delighted to make your acquaintance, Mistress Blackstock."

He held out his arm, and Hope took it, giving Cotty a look of triumph touched with malice. Cotty sipped at the punch, shaking his head as he watched the pair dance away together. Sometimes, Hope could be exasperating, as well as baffling. Over the past few years he had thought he had come to understand women quite well, but Hope continued to mystify him.

Glancing around the room, he saw that the receiving line was finished, and Governor Bligh stood against one wall across the way, holding forth to an audience of several men. Cotty drifted across the room toward the group.

Halfway there his attention was snagged by Charity. She was now dancing with Charles Bonney. Charity wore an infatuated look, and Cotty felt a stab of apprehension. His gaze fastened on Bonney, who moved with a courtly grace, his eyes on Charity as they danced. Cotty shared Hope's antipathy for Bonney—there was something sly about the man. Cotty did not trust him with Charity, yet there was little he could do about it now without bringing on a flaming row. And what could happen to her here, in this crowd of people? He made a note to have a talk with her later.

He continued toward the governor, who had the rapt attention of his audience. As Cotty reached the fringe of the group, Bligh was saying, "I'm sure those damned mutineers thought they had seen the last of Captain Bligh when they set me adrift in the boat with no chart and few provisions. But I made fools out of all of them. Damn, but I did!"

One of the men said admiringly, "That was a heroic feat of navigation, governor."

Bligh preened. "I cut my teeth on navigation, sir. I know the stars as well as any seafaring man alive. And I was with Captain Cook when he sailed among the islands, and I knew them well." An aide handed him a cup of punch, and Governor Bligh drank deeply.

"It's too bad that more of the mutineers were not caught and given their just punishment."

"It is indeed." Bligh glowered. "But three of them *were* caught and brought back to England and justice. I saw them executed, the damned traitors." He spied Cotty on the outskirts of the group. "I view the situation here in New South Wales as corresponding to that of the *Bounty*. A seditious lot, traitors all. Would you not agree, Master Starke?"

The sudden focus of all eyes, Cotty felt himself redden, and he chose his words with care. "I would not go so far as to call them traitors, Your Excellency. It seems to me that there is always room for disagreement among men of goodwill and intelligence."

"Goodwill! Intelligence!" The governor snarled the words. "By God, sir, no man of intelligence disobeys the laws of his government. I represent the government, and my edicts are the law!"

"Hear, hear!" ran a murmur through the group of men.

"But then, who can expect obedience of the law from people who were once convicts?" Bligh trumpeted. "Look at that pair." With a sneer he indicated two enlisted men standing a short distance away. "Both ex-convicts! That a man of my position should be forced to use ex-convicts as bodyguards is a disgrace. Even worse is the fact that a governor of a British colony should have to resort to the use of bodyguards to protect his person against violence offered by his subjects!"

A man standing beside Cotty exclaimed, "Violence has been threatened against your person, Your Excellency?"

"It has indeed. By officers of the New South Wales Corps. And for what reason? Because I thwart their nefarious purposes at every turn, and mainly because I am endeavoring to put a stop to the illegal liquor trade.'' The governor's gaze once again fixed on Cotty. ''For which I should think the honest dealers in spirits in Sydney should be eternally grateful!''

There were again murmurs of agreement, and several of the men glanced at Cotty in disapproval. Although Cotty had little experience with matters of government, or with those involved in government, he recognized these men as sycophants, willing to agree to anything the governor might say, no matter how outrageous, in an effort to curry favor. Cotty managed to remain silent; he was tempted to move off, yet he knew that would simply serve to infuriate Bligh further.

''I have penned a letter to London recommending that the corps be sent home in a body,'' Bligh continued. ''At least all the rebellious officers. But I fear that before I receive a reply to my proposal, it will be too late. They grow more contemptuous of my government every day.'' His face darkened. ''Why, just the other Sunday at church some garrison officers had the effrontery to laugh openly at a dress worn by my daughter. Damn, I cannot countenance much more of this. I must act forcibly, and soon. That is the reason . . .'' His gaze found Cotty again.

HOPE, HAVING FINISHED a second dance with Stuart Williams, stopped near the group gathered around Governor Bligh. During a brief lull in the music, she was near enough to see the governor glaring at Cotty and to hear his words ring out: ''That is the reason that I hope for the support of the honest, law-abiding citizens of Sydney. Especially those merchants who have profited by my efforts on the behalf of legal spirits. In my opinion, a man who does not stand with me is against me. And I do not suffer enemies gladly. It will become you, Master Starke, to mark my words, and well!''

# CHAPTER SIXTEEN

As THEY RODE BACK to the Crown in the rented carriage, Hope said worriedly, "Cotty, I overheard the governor claiming that if you're not on his side, you're his enemy. Was that a threat?"

"It could hardly be construed as anything else," he said in a dry voice. "Of course, in that I won't be alone, since at least half the colony does not approve of Governor Bligh's conduct."

"But how can he seriously expect you to take sides? You're a businessman. If you take sides, you lose customers, no matter which side you pick."

"I fully agree, as I tried to explain to him. But Captain Bligh, in his own way, is as stubborn and opinionated as John Macarthur. I suppose, given their natures, and even without the issue of rum, they would be bitter antagonists."

"Has Master Macarthur been to see you again?"

Cotty smiled tightly. "I haven't seen the man since his triumphant return to Sydney, but I have a strong feeling that he will be around sooner or later."

"What will you tell him, if he comes?"

Cotty shrugged. "The same thing I told Governor Bligh. I intend to remain neutral."

"Cotty..." Hope placed a hand on his knee. "Take care. From what I hear of Master Macarthur, he can be a dangerous enemy."

"I'm always careful, my dear Hope, you know that."

Hope took her hand away, and said tartly, "Like you were when you fought that stupid duel? You took a terrible risk."

"But my foolhardiness served a purpose." He smiled crookedly. "The king of the Rocks gained a great deal of respect from that incident."

Hope snorted softly. "King of the Rocks, indeed! I think you're beginning to believe that nonsense."

"It doesn't matter what I believe. So long as others believe it, that's the important thing."

Charity had remained quiet during the conversation, and it struck Hope that her sister was unusually pensive. Turning to her, she said, "You're very quiet, Charity. Didn't you enjoy the governor's ball?"

With a start, Charity glanced around and gave a dreamy smile. "Oh, yes, I had a marvelous time! The best time of my life."

"I noticed that you had Charles Bonney in constant attendance. Except for the first dance, you danced every one with him."

"Charles is a marvelous dancer."

"Charles, now, is it?" Hope said sharply. "Do you think that wise, spending so much time with him? I'm sure some of the other young men are just as good at dancing."

"But why should I have danced with anyone else?" Charity said artlessly. "Charles is a perfectly charming man, and he never talks business or politics, as you and Cotty seem to have been doing all evening!"

"I have made some inquiries about this Charles Bonney, Charity," Cotty interjected. "His reputation with women is not of the best. It seems he was considered something of a rogue back in England."

Hope said, "I'm not at all surprised. There is something unsavory about the man. I thought that from the first moment I saw him."

Charity tossed her head. "You're just jealous, sister." She smiled smugly. "Anyway, he wants to see me again. He asked if he could call on me."

"That's just what I mean," Hope retorted. "He knows that you're Cotty's ward. Cotty's the one he should ask."

"Why should he? He wants to see me, not Cotty. Besides, Cotty's not my father. I've already given Charles permission to come calling," she added defiantly.

Again, Hope choked back an angry retort; she well knew that Charity thought her an interfering sister. And to say anything critical at this point would only serve to get Charity's back up.

Instead, she said, "At the ball, Stuart Williams asked permission to call upon me." Even as she spoke, Hope regretted the admission. Was she simply boasting to show Charity that men were attracted to her as well?

Charity was staring. "And what was your response?"

"Why, I told him no, of course," Hope said, flustered.

Charity made a dismissive gesture. "Then you're a fool, dear sister."

Hope's annoyance mounted, yet she contented herself with saying, "If this Charles Bonney is the rogue Cotty says he is, you would be advised to be careful. You could be badly hurt.''

''I can take care of myself with any man, thank you,'' Charity said disdainfully.

In that, she was probably right, Hope concluded; she somehow managed to act the coquette with men and yet keep them at a distance at the same time.

Hope exchanged glances with Cotty. Besides, she thought, there was little they *could* do, short of locking Charity in her room, and that they could not do indefinitely. Nevertheless, Hope felt a sense of foreboding.

COTTY HAD CLOSED the Crown for the evening, assuming that a large number of his regular customers would undoubtedly be at the governor's ball.

Now, after he had paid the carriage driver and sent him on his way, he took the latchkey from his pocket and started to unlock the door. It opened in his face, and John Myers stood there.

''John!'' he said in surprise. ''There was no need for you to wait up for us. It's late, and you should be abed.''

John's gaze was fixed on Hope, his adoration evident in his eyes. ''I do not like to sleep until I know that . . . everyone is all right.''

''Well, thank you, John.'' Cotty touched him gently on the shoulder. ''We are all fine, and we had a grand time at the ball.''

John nodded gravely. ''I will say good night then.''

As John turned away, Hope called, ''Yes, John, thank you, and good night.''

Charity went toward the stairs and her room. Cotty and Hope followed more slowly.

After John was out of hearing, Cotty said, "Poor John. You know who he was waiting up for, don't you?"

"What do you mean?"

"You know very well what I mean, Hope. He was waiting for you. John worships the ground you walk upon."

"Don't be ridiculous!" she snapped. "I'm kind to him, and he doesn't find much kindness in Sydney. He appreciates that, and that's all it is."

"You just don't see it, Hope, or refuse to admit it to yourself. You have captured his heart."

Disturbed, Hope was silent as they mounted the stairs. Were his words true? Certainly, John was always at her beck and call.

At the top of the stairs she turned to Cotty. In a troubled voice she said, "Do you think that's really true?"

"I most certainly do. I noticed it a long time ago."

"But nothing can ever come of it," she said in distress.

"I know, and that's what makes it so sad."

They were standing close together now. "Tell me, Hope, why didn't you give that young man at the ball permission to call on you?"

"Because I did not wish him to do so. Isn't that ample reason?"

"Perhaps. But other young men have shown an interest in you, and I've observed that the moment you notice them, you become cold to them. Some day you must choose."

"Some day, not now," she said with some asperity. "There is plenty of time."

"Is there?"

Cotty stepped closer, and he touched her cheek in what could have been a caress. Her heartbeat quickened and she felt that rush of feeling, the swooning of her senses, that only he could arouse in her. It was a feeling at once exquisite and painful. Her gaze was locked upon his, and it seemed as if a great current was pulling them toward one another. She sensed that he felt it as well, for his eyes had a look in them she had never seen before; and he swayed toward her until she could feel his warm breath upon her face. She knew that he was going to kiss her, and she parted her lips in joyous expectation.

Then his expression suddenly changed, and he took a step backward and said, "Good night, Hope. Sleep well."

He was gone, striding down the hall to his room, leaving her shaken and bereft. Disappointment brought the sting of tears to her eyes. If Cotty thought that John's love for *her* was sad, how did he think she felt when she was continually spurned by him?

Damn him, damn him! He was as dense as a block of wood!

She whirled away and almost ran to her room, slamming the door violently behind her.

COTTY'S WORDS concerning John Macarthur proved prophetic.

Three days after the governor's ball, Macarthur came to call. He found Cotty at work in his office.

At the knock on the door, Cotty called, "Come in," and was unsurprised at the identity of his visitor. Out of deference he got up from his desk and came forward with his hand extended.

Macarthur pointedly ignored it. His haughty face cold and forbidding, he said, "I have it on good authority that you were in attendance at the governor's ball."

"I was invited."

"Some who were invited did not attend, sir."

"I thought it would be ill-mannered of me to spurn an invitation from the governor of the colony."

"Many of us do not approve of Governor Bligh and his high-handed manner. He is causing ill will and great dissension."

As are you and your followers, Cotty thought, but did not say it. "I am well aware of that, yet he *is* the governor, appointed by the Crown."

"He may not be the governor much longer," Macarthur said in a growling voice.

"Oh?" Cotty ran a hand across his mouth. "That, I was not aware of."

"You may accept my word for it, Master Starke. We fully intend to petition the Crown to have him replaced. There is even some talk of removing him by force, if necessary, and replacing him with a man more suited to the office, one who is more willing to work in concert with the wishes of the people. I, for one, am not prepared to go to such lengths, as yet, but some of the hotbloods are. I do not know if saner heads will prevail."

"Such a move could be viewed as treason by the government in England," Cotty said carefully.

"Perhaps so, but they do not fully comprehend our problems. The reason for my calling on you, sir, is this." His stare became hard, arrogant. "Are you allying yourself with Governor Bligh?"

"I am allying myself with no one, Master Macarthur, except my customers. As I told you once before, I cannot afford to take sides. In doing so, I would lose business. I told Governor Bligh the same thing."

"We need the support of as many people as possible in our quarrel with Captain Bligh. Most especially here in the Rocks, where the sale and consumption of spirits are the highest. Since you are now known as the king of the Rocks—" Macarthur spoke with a barely concealed sneer "—although I fail to understand why, your support of either side will be heeded."

"And so will the fact that I remain neutral."

"Others may follow your lead, sir. We cannot allow that."

"Master Macarthur, I am well aware that you are a man of some standing in New South Wales and carry much influence. But you have no authority over me, sir. Neither you nor Governor Bligh has the right to tell me what to do, so long as I do not break any laws of the Crown."

"What do you think will happen to your trade should I and officers of the corps warn people not to patronize your taverns? You shall suffer, you may be sure."

Cotty stared. "You would do that?"

"I would, sir. I consider this an all-out war, and tactics must be employed that otherwise would not be considered."

"Then I shall have to take my chances," Cotty said with a shrug.

"You refuse to change your mind, and lend us your support?"

"I most certainly do. I fully intend to remain neutral."

Macarthur's face reddened; clearly he was not accustomed to being thwarted. For a moment Cotty thought the man was going to lose control of his temper, but evidently his inherent good breeding took over. He drew himself up to his full height. "I think you shall regret your decision, Master Starke." Macarthur's voice was cold.

"Mayhap. But I will have to live with that, won't I?"

Macarthur turned away. He opened the door, and then turned back. "It is indeed a decision you will have to live with. Do not expect to come pleading to me for mercy. I shall not grant it!"

JOHN HAD BEEN BUSY in the tavern when the man he knew as Macarthur came striding in looking for Cotty. He knew that the man represented a threat; he had been around the clay faces long enough now to read the signs. During the conversation between Cotty and Macarthur, John placed himself near the door and thus heard Macarthur's cold warning.

After Macarthur had stormed out of the Crown, John slipped away to his lean-to; he knew what he had to do.

In the lean-to he collected the necessities, then started walking out of town. The day was pleasant; and as the bustle of the town was left behind, John began to feel the peace that always came to him away from the distractions of civilization. It was as if the voice of the land, which spoke in many different and varied tongues, could not communicate in a place where so many people were crowded together, and where the land was changed by their presence.

When John was in the town, it was as if his senses were asleep, dulled by the many buildings; the sound of voices; the noise created by hammer, ax and saw; the hooves of horses; the creak of carts. But as soon as he was away from the town, his senses came alive again. The earth and the sky spoke to him as they had before, in the days when he had lived with the tribe. It was always a bittersweet experience, because now he felt as if he belonged to both places, and yet to neither of them. Sometimes, he felt as if he walked in a very narrow place, with dangers on both sides. He knew it would be best if he made a choice, one life or another, and yet he could not bring himself to do so.

But he had not come here to think about his own troubles. There was trouble gathering around his friend, Cotty, and it was Cotty he must think of now.

When John reached the huge blue gum tree, he was relieved to see that there was no one in sight. The clay faces did not often come here, but other aborigines did, for John was not the only one who came here to dream.

After he had prepared himself, the dream came quickly, as if it had been waiting, anxious to deliver its message. As John yielded himself to the dream-world, he first saw Hope's face, looking down at him, smiling but sad. There was pity in her eyes. He moved further into the dream and saw Charity, and there was a darkness around her that she did not see.

He tried to touch her, to warn her; but she turned away, laughing, ignoring him.

And then the dream took him to the Crown. It was night, and the tavern was dark. The front door stood agape, splintered, as though it had been broken open. Inside the tavern were strange men; they were milling around, smashing furniture. In the darkness flames leaped as one of the men set fire to a shattered table. And then there was Hope, her face white, her eyes narrow with anger, and then widened with fear. . . . But where was Cotty?

The vision vanished, and John was suddenly awake. He groaned aloud in disappointment. He had to know what followed! For another hour he remained, squatting, trying to recapture the dream, yet he knew that it was futile. From past experience he had learned that once the dream was broken, for whatever reason, it was wasted effort to try to reenter the dream state. He would have to return to the dreaming tree another time and try again.

Getting to his feet, he went down to the stream running through the meadow and washed away the clay before getting dressed. It was a clear day, and he could see all the way to the bay. Such a mass of water! It looked to be endless.

Coming from an inland tribe as he had, where water was in short supply, John found the sea both beautiful and frightening. He was continually amazed by the members of the local coastal tribe, who seemed to be as comfortable with the sea as he was with the bush. The bush was the bush—always the same. Rocks and trees stayed in one place, but the sea did not. It was ever changing, ever moving; one moment smooth and serene, the next angry and menacing. Since he had been here he had seen the storms, seen the sea swallow boats and men.

He shuddered. He had no fear of death—it came to all men—but to die that way seemed to him quite horrible. How could the tribe observe the proper ceremonies if you were swallowed by the sea?

With a shudder he turned away, starting back into the village. It was late afternoon by now, and there were several customers in the tavern when John entered by the back door. As he started toward Cotty's office, he had to pass the bar where Hope presided over the cash drawer.

Seeing him, she said rather harshly, "John, where have you been? There were some tasks that needed doing."

John lowered his eyes. "I am sorry, Mistress Hope. I had something...private to attend to. I have been derelict in my duties."

"I didn't mean to chastise you, John," she said in a softer voice. "You're certainly entitled to free time of your own. I was more worried than anything, fearing something had happened to you. I'd appreciate you letting me know whenever you plan on being away for any length of time."

John looked at her quickly, and then away. It always seemed to him that her face had a great light behind it, a light that would blind him if he looked at it too long. The memory of her face in his dream, distorted with anger and fear, tugged at him. Nothing must be allowed to hurt Hope. He must warn Cotty.

"I will try not to worry you again," he said, risking another glance at her face, "but now I must speak with Master Cotty. It is of great importance."

Going around the bar, he knocked softly on the office door. At Cotty's invitation, he opened the door and went in.

Cotty turned at his desk. "Yes, John?"

John stood for a moment, attempting to think of a way to tell Cotty what he must.

"There is something I must tell you," he finally said slowly.

At the tone of his voice, Cotty frowned. "What is it, John? Is something wrong?"

John nodded. "Yes, something is wrong, but it is difficult to tell to someone of your race. It will not be easy for you to understand."

Cotty smiled and motioned for John to be seated. "Well, I'll do my best. Are you in some kind of trouble?"

John shook his head. "No, or perhaps I should say, maybe, because anything that causes you or the mistresses trouble causes me trouble also."

Cotty looked puzzled. "Me or the girls? Just what are you getting at, John?"

John spoke slowly, thinking out his words in advance. "I have reason to believe that someone, some men, are going to break into your tavern. They will cause some damage and set the building afire. I also believe they will threaten Mistress Hope."

Cotty's face darkened. "Just who are these men, and how did you learn about this?"

"It is very difficult to explain to you. I tried once before when I dreamed of the death of Mistress Faith. My people, my mother's people, have certain...powers. We see things, we dream things, that have not yet happened.'' He leaned forward. ''But they *do* happen. Afterward.''

Cotty's frown deepened. ''Yes, I remember about Faith....''

''I know that it must sound strange to you,'' John said earnestly. ''But it is important that you believe me, and that you be prepared.''

Cotty leaned back in his chair, a faint smile touching his lips. Although he had realized at the time that it was passing strange that John had ''dreamed'' of Faith's impending death, he was still skeptical, believing it to be coincidence.

John, leaning forward, fixed Cotty with his gaze. ''It is important that you believe me.''

Seeing how serious he was, Cotty was no longer amused, but he remained highly skeptical. ''When Master Macarthur was here earlier today, didn't I see you outside my office door when he stormed out in a rage?'' he asked.

''Yes,'' John said with some hesitation.

''Then you probably heard the threats he voiced?''

''Yes.''

''It was after that that you had your dream?''

This time John simply nodded.

''John, I do not mean to scorn your dreams. I well know how important they must be to you, and your tribal fellows, but the power of suggestion is a strong thing. Do you know what I mean by the power of suggestion?''

''No, Cotty. I do not know.''

''It's when an idea, or a thought, lodges in your mind so strongly that you begin to believe it whether it's true or not. Now, I think that may have happened with you. You overheard Macarthur making threats, and so powerful was the suggestion that you dreamed of his threats coming true.''

John was silent.

Cotty sighed, rubbing his hand across his mouth. ''John, Macarthur is a bad enemy and I'm sure he will do what he can to discredit me with my customers, but he is still a gentleman. He will not stoop to the violence you dreamed of. Besides...'' He shrugged ruefully. ''What can I do to guard against it? Hire a team of men to guard the Crown? I cannot do that.''

John frowned in puzzlement. ''The expense is too much?''

''No, it isn't that, although it would be dear. But if I have men around to guard the place, it would likely frighten away many of my customers, and that would please Macarthur mightily.'' He grinned. ''I appreciate your concern, John, truly I do, but I think you worry unnecessarily.''

John leaned forward, his dark face intense. ''But the dream about Mistress Blackstock.... In that dream I saw her buried, and that came to pass. My dream was fulfilled.''

''It would seem so,'' Cotty said thoughtfully. ''But again, the thought may have been planted in your mind. Faith had obviously been in poor health for some time. Again, I'm not scoffing at your dreams, John, but even if you are correct this time, there isn't much I can do about it.''

THE EVENING BUSINESS was heavy that night, especially in the dining room upstairs. Until the dinner crowd began to thin out, Hope was too busy even to look up from her cash drawer.

Finally a lull occurred in the rush of trade. Hope had just placed an empty bottle beneath the counter when she heard a voice calling softly, "Mistress Blackstock?"

Hope glanced up into the smiling face of Stuart Williams. He was sober tonight, his round face closely shaven and powdered, and he was dressed impeccably.

"Why, Master Williams! How do you do?"

"Stuart, please. And may I have permission to call you Hope?"

Hope felt her face flush. "That is bold of you, sir, but I suppose it can do no harm."

He bowed slightly. "I would deem it a privilege." He gazed around. "This is my first time in the Crown. I am pleased to see such an establishment in Sydney. And I must compliment you on the food, since I assume it is your responsibility. The dining here equals that of the best in England."

"It is most gracious of you to say so. We have turned every effort toward making the Crown into a fine place to dine."

"Hope, at the governor's ball the other evening, I asked for the privilege of calling upon you. You spurned me. I can well understand why you might, since I was well into my cups. I beg your forgiveness for that." His gray eyes were grave. "But tonight, as you can see, I am not intoxicated in the least. So now, may I ask again if I may have the pleasure of calling upon you?"

Hope was about to give him a firm negative when she spotted Cotty standing in the doorway to his office, staring at her quizzically.

And to her astonishment, she heard herself saying, "You have my permission, Stuart."

He looked startled for a moment, then his face split wide in a grin. "My dear Hope, I am delighted! Do you like to ride?"

"I have ridden very little, Stuart. But if you do not insist on an expert horsewoman, I am willing to try."

"Then shall we say Saturday morning of this week?"

"That will be fine."

"Excellent!" He seized her hand and bowed over it. "You have made me a very happy man, milady."

He turned and made his way out. Hope's gaze followed him until he was out the front door. For the life of her she could not understand why she had agreed to let him court her; for that was exactly what he had in mind. But then, perhaps it was time she was allowing herself to be seriously courted. Had not both Charity and Cotty urged her to do so? And Stuart Williams, sober as he had been today, was certainly a proper suitor.

Behind her Cotty said, "And what was that all about? Isn't he the man who danced with you at the ball?"

She faced him. "It was. He asked permission to call."

"And what was your response?"

"I told him that he might."

For just a moment, she could have sworn that she saw an expression of dismay in his eyes, and then it was gone as he said, "You told me you refused him the night of the ball. What changed your mind?"

"I have a right to change my mind, do I not?"

"Well, yes, of course, but . . ."

"Besides, haven't both you and Charity been urging me to allow a man to court me?"

His glance slipped away, and he mumbled, "I may have mentioned it, yes."

"Then why should you object? It's what you want, isn't it?"

His gaze came back to her, and he wore a hurt expression. "But this man, after the ball you said you didn't care for him. He was intoxicated."

"In Sydney, what man isn't, from time to time? Stuart apologized for that, in a very nice way. He is a fine man, I'm sure, and he *is* one of Governor Bligh's aides."

"Stuart, is it?" he said with a faint sneer. "But you're right, Hope. The decision is yours to make." He turned on his heel and strode toward the stairs.

Cotty was angry at Hope as he went up to his room, but he failed to understand the reason for his anger. She was correct—she had every right to allow a man to call upon her.

In his room he removed his clothes and let them lie where they fell, his anger now directed at himself. Why should he care about Hope's personal life? She was over twenty-one, no longer his ward, not in a legal sense, and she was entitled to a life of her own. All the same . . .

He gave a short bark of laughter and tried to force thoughts of her out of his mind, instead thinking of the evening ahead, and another woman. He had recently made the acquaintance of a comely widow, who had welcomed him into her bed with gusty delight. Since the duel, he had been a little more careful of married women, despite the fact he usually preferred married women for dalliance, since they were not in search of a husband. For the moment, at least, Clarice Thompson was content with things as they were, but he had no doubt that in time she would start thinking of marriage; which, of course, would present little difficulty for her, since there were still twice as many men in Sydney as women. It was only when she started thinking of *him* as a possible spouse that he would back away. He had no intention of marrying, not after what had happened to his father....

With a rueful shake of his head, he broke off that train of thought.

A few minutes later, again fully dressed, he left his room and went downstairs. It was late now, near to closing time, and the tavern was almost empty of customers.

He paused at the bar to speak to Hope. "I have some business to attend to, Hope," he said brusquely. "Be sure that everything is locked up tight before you retire."

She looked at him skeptically. "What possible business could take you out so close to midnight? Or isn't it any of my affair?"

"You're right. It isn't any of your affair."

SOME ALIEN SOUND brought Hope out of a deep sleep. She sat up, listening intently. She had had no difficulty going to sleep, troubled as she was over her hasty decision to allow Stuart Williams to call on her. Also, she had been angry and upset about Cotty's "business." She knew very well what that business was—he had a late-night rendezvous with some woman. Probably another married woman. Soon, another outraged husband would seek him out and challenge him to a duel. . . .

There! The strange sound came again, louder this time. She pushed the covers back, reaching down to the foot of the bed for her robe, and froze as a crashing noise sounded from downstairs.

Without another thought for her robe, she was up and running, in her bare feet and nightgown. Outside her room, she sped toward the stairs. Charity, now in their mother's old room, was probably undisturbed; it took something well out of the ordinary to waken her from a sound sleep. And Hope doubted that Cotty had returned as yet. Just as she reached the top of the stairs, she heard another crash from below; it sounded like the splintering of furniture.

She hurried down the stairs so fast she almost tripped and fell, only regaining her balance at the last moment.

At the bottom of the stairs, she saw a flare of yellow light from the barroom. Rounding the bar, she skidded to a stop at the sight that greeted her.

Three men, in rough clothing, with kerchiefs over their faces, were gathered around a table they had broken up and piled in the middle of the floor. Flames were licking greedily at the wood.

Her fear forgotten, Hope ran at them, screaming in outrage at this sacrilege. One of the men glanced up and saw her. He caught the attention of the other two, and all three started toward her, spreading out in a menacing half circle.

Belatedly realizing her danger, Hope turned to flee, but she was too late. One of the men seized her arm in an iron grip and held her fast.

''Well, lookee what we have here, mates! A little added spice to our game. Ain't she the juicy wench now?''

# CHAPTER SEVENTEEN

WITH THE MEMORY OF THE DREAM still vivid in his mind, John did not sleep well. He was dozing when the first unusual sound from the tavern brought him fully awake.

Accustomed to the dark, he did not bother to light a candle, but slipped into his breeches and shirt and picked up the loaded musket from where he kept it beside his pallet.

Barefoot, carrying the musket in one hand, he hurried from the lean-to and around to the back door just as the second splintering crash sounded from inside. In his haste, John had to fumble for a few moments before he could insert the brass key into the lock. Finally, the door yielded to his frantic efforts, and he stepped inside. As he did so, he heard a woman scream.

Running down the passageway, he threw open the door to the main room, exposing a tableau that matched what he had seen in the dream. Flames arose from a pile of broken furniture, and three rough-looking men were silhouetted in the dancing orange light. One of them held Hope in a tight grip.

John leveled the musket and shouted, "Let her go!"

Three pairs of eyes swiveled in his direction. The man holding Hope said in a jeering voice, "Well, lookee here, mates! A boong tellin' us what to do."

One of the other men said harshly, "We don't take orders from murkies. You'd better just go back to where you came from, boy."

John raised the musket and said tightly, "If you do not let her go, I will fire. I am a good shot."

"A black fella shootin' a white man? You don't dare! You'll hang sure as hell is hot. 'Sides, you have only one shot, you can only get one o' us."

"I am sworn to protect Mistress Hope. I will shoot."

"I think he means it, mates," said the man holding Hope. He released her, holding his hands high. "We'd better do as he says."

Hope was in instant flight. Running behind the bar, she snatched up the loaded pistol that was always kept there. Resting her arms on the bar, she pointed it at the three men. "I can also shoot well. So now we can kill two of you. Are you willing to risk that?"

The man who had seized Hope held up his hands again, backing a step. "Now mum, don't be hasty. Me and my mates are goin'."

At the door one turned back, glaring at John. "You be regrettin' this, boy. We ain't about to forget it. No black fella points a musket at a white man in Sydney Town!"

Hope raised the pistol. "You're in no position to make threats. Go before I shoot!"

Hastily, the three men scrambled for the doorway. In other circumstances it might have been amusing—three men fighting to get through the door together—but Hope was in no mood to see the humor in it.

As the men disappeared, she sighed in relief and lowered the pistol. Her tension had been such that the muscles in her arms ached.

"Mistress Hope?"

With a start she glanced around. "Oh, John! I'll be forever grateful to you for saving me from those louts. There's no telling what they would have done to me."

Even as she spoke, she rounded the bar and threw her arms around him. John went rigid, arms at his sides, but Hope did not notice.

She was trembling badly. "I did not have time to be frightened before, but now I realize how much peril I was in. Thank you again, John."

Realizing what she was doing, she stepped back with a shaky laugh. She did not look into his face, but instead glanced around the room. Had she looked at him, she would have seen the pain and longing in his eyes.

"We'd better dump a pail or two of water onto the flames," she said. "The table is ruined, but at least we can be thankful that the floor is stone, else the whole tavern might have burned to the ground."

John quickly got two pails from behind the bar and hurried out to the barrels of water kept by the back door for just such an emergency. Hastening inside, he dumped the water onto the flames. The fire had died down considerably, but there was a strong stench of burned wood in the barroom.

"AH, SWEET COTTY!" Clarice Thompson said as she rose and clung to him in the final tremors of ecstasy. "You are so good for me!"

The widow Thompson was voluptuous, with lustrous brown hair, a round, pouty face and white skin. She was also very active in bed.

While she still writhed beneath him, Cotty attained his own moment of release and collapsed beside her, his heart thudding, his breath coming fast. He lay on his back, sated and content.

"Ah, Cotty!" Clarice ran fluttery fingers across his chest, then let her hand fall away. Looking over, Cotty saw that her eyes were closed; her generous breasts rose and fell with her uneven breathing. From past episodes, he knew that she would be fast asleep within moments.

Cotty lay staring at the ceiling. Despite the pleasure of the moment and his physical contentment, his mind was active. He recalled John's telling of his dream, and Macarthur's implied threat; and worry gnawed at him. It was ridiculous, of course, to place any credence in the dreamings of an aborigine, and yet the worry refused to go away.

With a soft sigh he slipped out of the bed and began dressing as quietly as he could. But when he sat down to put on his boots, Clarice stirred and reached across the bed for him.

When she could not find him, she sat up, squinting in the dimness. "Cotty? Where are you?"

"Here, love." Boots on, he stood up. "I'm sorry, but I must take my leave."

"But why can't you stay the night?"

"Not tonight, love." He stooped to kiss her on the forehead. "I have pressing business."

"But Cotty . . ."

"Shh, go back to sleep." He pressed a finger over her lips. "I shall be back, depend on it."

He let himself out of the house and started the short walk to the Crown. As he walked, his worry increased and his step quickened. By the time the Crown came in sight, he was almost running. And when he came close enough to see the front door standing wide, he broke into a frantic lope.

Bursting into the tavern, he saw Hope and John dousing a fire in the center of the room with pails of water. "What happened here?" he demanded.

"Oh, Cotty!" Hope turned a wan face to him. "Three ruffians broke in the front door and set fire to one of the tables. I came charging down when I heard the noise and I . . ." Her voice choked off for a moment. "They caught me, and I don't know what would have happened if John hadn't come in just in time, with a musket."

For the first time, Cotty noticed that she was wearing only a nightgown, which clung to the contours of her figure with a disturbing effect.

Distracted, Cotty looked quickly away, staring at John.

"I suppose I owe you an apology, John. There was some substance to your dream, after all."

Hope said quickly, "Dream? What dream?"

Cotty related what John had told him about his dream trance.

Hope glanced at John with curiosity. "These dreams you have, they foretell the future?"

"Sometimes," John said reluctantly.

Cotty added, "He dreamed about your mother's death as well. When he told me, I scoffed at the idea. You can be sure that I won't be inclined to scoff again, John."

"Cotty, do you think Macarthur was actually the instigator behind what happened here tonight?"

Cotty gave the idea some thought, then shook his head slowly. "I very much doubt it. He is a ruthless man, but he wouldn't stoop to such tactics."

"But then who *is* responsible?"

"Oh, he was probably indirectly responsible. He no doubt made his displeasure known, and word got around the Rocks that Cotty Starke would not kowtow to Master Macarthur, so some toughs thought they would curry favor by doing damage to the Crown. If they had succeeded in burning the place to the ground, I'm sure that Macarthur would have laughed heartily in private."

She looked worried. "But won't they try again?"

He nodded. "It's quite possible."

"What can we do about it?"

"Not very much, I am afraid. Be more vigilant, of course. And I'll hire some men to stand guard at the Crown and the other places I own. It will cost me dear, and may lose my trade, but it seems necessary." He sighed and looked at Hope more closely. "Now, my dear Hope, I think you should retire. The way you are attired, it would be unseemly of you to be seen like that should anyone chance by."

Hope looked startled, glanced down at herself and then turned a fiery red. She crossed her arms over her breasts and, turning, hurried upstairs. Cotty looked after her with a musing smile. She was indeed grown up and had become a very attractive woman in the process. Why was it that he had not really noticed this before?

"You'd better retire, too, John. It grows late. And I want you to know how much I appreciate your coming to Hope's rescue. After your warning, if something had happened to her, I would never have forgiven myself for not heeding you.''

John smiled. "It was a privilege, Cotty."

STUART WILLIAMS, dashing in riding clothes, with boots polished to a mirror shine, easily controlled his prancing black stallion. He had brought along a brown mare for Hope to ride.

As Hope eyed the mare dubiously, Stuart smiled. "There is nothing to fear, Hope. Feather is as gentle as her name." Dismounting, he gave Hope a hand up onto the side saddle, then again mounted his stallion.

"I thought we would ride out of town a ways. It is a nice day for riding, don't you agree?"

Hope simply nodded, busy clinging to anything she could find to hold on to, fearful she would tumble off the horse and disgrace herself. She was perversely disappointed that Cotty was not around to see her ride off with Stuart.

It was indeed a nice day; it was late morning and the sun was warm. Soon, they were out of town, and the landscape became wild but exquisite as they rode through ancient eucalypti. Hope was startled as a green cloud of budgerigars rose above them, and she almost lost her balance. A moment later, several white cockatoos flapped overhead, shrieking as they flew from tree to tree.

Stuart said very little as they rode, which was just as well as far as Hope was concerned. She was too busy trying to hang on to the horse to engage in conversation. However, after a bit she became more at ease and took time to look around. Through the trees occasional glimpses of the bay could be seen, sunlight glinting off the water with blinding flashes of light.

As they emerged into a glade, Hope saw movement under a huge gum tree some distance to the right. She saw that a naked aborigine, painted with stripes of white, was squatting under the tree. It was too far to be certain, but the man looked like John Myers. Could it be? If it was John, should she ride over and speak to him?

Stuart laughed suddenly. "An aborigine in his dream trance. I suppose you've heard about the boongs and their dreams?"

Hope had reined in her mount, still staring at the tree and the squatting man. If it was John, he would not be likely to welcome being interrupted. To Stuart she said, "Yes, I've heard of their dreaming."

He grunted. "They say they can see the past and foretell the future. Superstitious nonsense!"

"We all have our dreams, Stuart."

"But that is a different matter, my dear Hope, a different matter entirely. Mind you, I am not scoffing at the black fellas. They have their place in the scheme of things, but they will never become civilized until they rid themselves of their superstitions."

Hope was inclined to be mulish and debate the issue with him, but decided to hold her tongue for the present.

Stuart gestured, smiling suddenly. "But why spoil our outing with such a subject? It is certainly nothing to occupy the mind of such a pretty lady as yourself."

He clucked to his horse, and they rode on. Shortly, John and his dreaming tree were behind them, and soon they rode up to the grassy banks of a small stream trickling down toward the bay.

Stuart reined in his mount. "I brought along a repast for us. Cold fowl and a bottle of good wine. It is near nooning, and this strikes me as a good spot." He dismounted and came around to help Hope down.

She stood, trying to work the stiffness, caused by the ride, out of her limbs as Stuart unlashed his saddlebags. It was indeed a nice spot. New spring grass coated the bank thickly, and it was quiet here. Then a small worry edged into her mind—perhaps it was *too* quiet and lonely, not another soul in sight. She darted a sidelong look at Stuart, her uneasiness growing. Although unfamiliar with men on a personal basis, the ones she did know, including Cotty, were as randy as goats. Had Stuart taken her out to this lonely spot with an ulterior motive? Normally, she was confident of her ability to defend herself, yet she had never been in this situation before.

JOHN HAD SEEN and recognized Hope when she and the young man with her stopped their horses a distance away. He had been trying without success to go into his dream trance, and the sound of hoofbeats had broken his thin concentration. His first impulse, on opening his eyes and seeing Mistress Hope, had been to rise and greet her; but then he knew that would never do—a naked aborigine approaching her. So he had remained where he was, utterly still, hoping that she would ride on.

Mistress Hope was actually the reason for his being under the dreaming tree today. He had been plagued by apprehension for her, yet his feeling had no substance, no source; and he had hoped that a dream would define it for him.

To his relief, through squinted eyes, he saw Mistress Hope and the young man ride on. For just a moment, a dangerous moment, he allowed himself to dwell wistfully on how it would feel if he were riding with her, instead of the other young man.

He shook his head, forcing such thoughts out of his mind, and closed his eyes, trying to make his mind a desert, empty of everything, as he courted the dream.

After some time, he sighed and opened his eyes. Today, the dream eluded him. Again fully dressed, he stood looking in the direction in which the pair had ridden. There was no sign of them.

The same feeling of uneasiness weighed upon him, and John debated with himself for a few moments. Should he follow the tracks of the horses, staying out of sight until he was certain she was all right?

But if he did, and if she should perchance spot him, she would most likely be very angry. What gave him the right to intrude upon her privacy? The feeling of apprehension for her safety was, more than likely, the result of the three bullies who had broken into the Crown and threatened her. If she was truly in danger, would it not have come to him in a dream?

In the end, he shrugged helplessly and turned the other way, heading toward the village, and the Crown.

# CHAPTER EIGHTEEN

STUART REMOVED the bottle of wine from the stream where he had placed it to cool. Pouring the spirit into two cups, he handed one to Hope, then sat beside her on the grassy bank. Cold chicken and bread had been laid out on a small cloth.

Stuart raised his cup in a toast. "Here's to you, Hope, and to the evening I met you. I believe that shall be a most fateful day in my life."

Hope raised the cup to her lips to hide her discomfiture. She was seated across the cloth from him, and intended to remain so.

" 'Tis a poor repast, I know, but the best I could find after raiding the kitchen at Government House."

"Everything is fine, Stuart." She looked at him intently. "How long have you been in Sydney?"

"Not long. I came over with Captain Bligh when he was appointed governor. He wanted to bring a few people with him from England to serve as his aides."

"What sort of a man is he? I've heard conflicting stories."

"And all probably true," Stuart said with a grin. "He is a contradiction, our Captain Bligh. A martinet in many ways, but a good administrator. He has done some good things here and will do more, if given the chance, I am sure."

"Yet many people, such as the officers of the corps, dislike him."

He shrugged. "Unfortunately, the governor is a bristly man, accustomed to having his own way, and he does not brook disobedience. He believes there is one way to do things, and that is his way. Such an attitude does not make him popular."

"What did you do in England?"

"I was a clerk in the government, a mere functionary. I seized the opportunity to come to New South Wales, hoping to better myself."

"You sound bitter."

"I hate it here. It's an uncivilized country, and my chances of bettering myself are small. I shall serve out my time, until the end of Governor Bligh's term, and then hie myself back to England." He gave her a measuring look. "Do you ever think of going home to England, Hope?"

She made a startled sound, then said thoughtfully, "To be truthful, no."

"But surely a lady of your refinement could not be happy in such a backward country."

She had to smile. "I appreciate your compliment, sir, but any refinement I may have is due to my mother." She looked at him defiantly. "My mother was a convict, you know."

"No, I didn't know. But it matters little. After all, the majority of the people here are convicts, or were when they were transported."

Her head went back. "I feel no shame. I am very proud of my mother. She made the most of a terrible situation, and in the doing raised my sister and myself. As for returning to England, I doubt I would be so inclined if I had the opportunity. I found it terrible here when we arrived, but our condition has improved greatly, and Cotty says that within the next few years we should become quite civilized. Also, my memories of England are not kind. Our life there, as I remember it, was not much better than life here in the early days.''

Stuart laughed shortly. ''I doubt that this land will ever be civilized.'' His gaze grew still. ''This Cotty, he owns the Crown?''

''Yes. Charity and I were young when my mother died. He made us his wards and took good care of us.'' She added defiantly, ''Cotty Starke is a fine man!''

''I mean nothing derogatory, Hope.'' He held up his hands defensively. ''I'm sure he is a fine man.''

To bridge the brief moment of embarrassment, Stuart poured the rest of the wine into the cups.

Hope took a sip and said, ''Do you know Charles Bonney?''

''Charles?'' he said reflectively. ''Yes, I know Charles.''

''What kind of a man is he?''

He hesitated, then said slowly, ''He's a very good administrator. He has the full confidence of Governor Bligh, and the governor relies on him heavily.''

''I have the feeling you're being evasive, Stuart.'' She looked at him steadily. ''What kind of a man is he personally?''

''He's utterly charming, well-spoken, and he's arrogant and accustomed to having his own way.'' He met her gaze and sighed. ''Very well, Hope. Back in England he had a rather bad reputation. He has a degree in the law, you know, and apparently had a promising future as a barrister before him. But he has a rather . . .''

He coughed, looking away. ''Well, to put it delicately, he has a weakness for the opposite sex and became involved in a rather messy affair with the wife of a man high in the government. I am sure you would recognize the man's name, should I mention it. I gather it was a scandal in certain circles, and Charles apparently deemed it wise to leave England for a time. Fortunately for him, the opportunity to serve as Captain Bligh's aide came his way, and he took advantage of it.'' Stuart's gaze sharpened. ''Surely you are not involved with the man, are you, Hope?''

She made a startled sound. ''Oh, my heavens, no! I've scarcely spoken to him; but I'm afraid my sister has taken something of a fancy to him.''

''Then you should advise her to turn her fancy to someone else.''

''That's not so easy to do. Charity is strong-willed, and not given to taking advice from me.''

''Of course, there is always the possibility that Charles learned his lesson back in England.'' He got to his feet abruptly. ''It grows late, Hope. We should be starting back.''

Hope rose and helped him return the cloth and cups to his saddlebags. As he turned to give her a hand up, they necessarily stood very close. For a brief moment, time seemed to stop as they stood unmoving, staring deep into each other's eyes.

He is a personable man, Hope thought distractedly. He was perhaps thirty, slender, well-muscled, and graceful of movement. His eyes glowed warmly, and his hands reached out to her. For a dizzy moment she was sure that he was going to take her into his arms and kiss her. She had never felt a man's lips on hers, but she had often wondered how it would feel, how she would react.

The thought wrung a small cry from her. Of protest, or in acquiescence? She was not to learn at this particular time, for the small cry broke the spell; and time began to move again as Stuart stepped back slightly and stooped to boost her up onto the mare.

COTTY WAS CONCERNED about Hope's whereabouts. He had had business in his other tavern that had taken up most of the morning, and when he returned to the Crown just past the noon hour, Hope was not to be found. With a shrug, Charity had told him that she had no idea where her sister was. He could not find John, either. Had they gone off somewhere together? It did not seem very likely.

By two o'clock, about the time the Crown opened for trade, Hope was still missing. Angry and fretting, Cotty retired to his office, but found that he could accomplish little, since his thoughts kept straying to Hope.

A knock sounded on the door, and he felt a rush of relief. She was back! He called out, "Come in!"

When the door opened he was surprised to see Hugh Marston and two other men he recognized as tavern owners in the Rocks. One was Robert Beller, who, over the years since losing the Crown, had managed to recoup his finances enough to buy another tavern—a small, mean place deep in the Rocks, little better than a grog shanty. A thought quickly crossed Cotty's mind; could Beller have been one of the masked men who had broken into the Crown and accosted Hope? The man was certainly mean enough.

Cotty got to his feet. "Hugh! I'm delighted to see you."

Hugh Marston had left the NSW Corps a couple of years earlier and had opened a flash house in the Rocks. The entertainment there was not to Cotty's liking, and he had seen little of the man recently. Marston had a sleek, well-fed look, as plump as a pouter pigeon, and heavy drinking had given him a permanently flushed complexion.

Hugh turned to the two men with him. "Cotty, these gentlemen are George Palmer and Robert Beller. Perhaps you know them. Both are innkeepers in the Rocks."

"Gentlemen. I have never met Master Palmer, but Robert Beller I do know." He held out his hand to George Palmer, a middle-aged man with a paunch and a full beard that was beginning to gray, and Palmer took it; but Beller pointedly ignored the extended hand.

With a shrug, Cotty motioned. "Please be seated, gentlemen. To what do I owe the pleasure? Not that you're not always welcome." He grinned faintly. "I am always happy to meet my competitors."

"We heard about what happened here, Cotty," Marston began.

Cotty glanced at Beller, but the man merely glared back balefully. Cotty said, "No great harm done. The ruffians were routed in time."

"But they could easily have burned your tavern to the ground."

"But they didn't, Hugh." Cotty frowned. "What's your point?"

Hugh drew a deep breath. "Surely, you realize this wasn't just random violence?"

"I had reached that conclusion, yes. I have received veiled threats, from one John Macarthur." He looked from face to face. "Although I also concluded that he would not stoop so low. Have you gentlemen received such threats?"

"Not directly, no," Hugh said. "But the word is out in the Rocks. Choose sides, the *right* side, or suffer the consequences."

"You think Macarthur put the word out?"

"Who else? He's the leader. However, I agree with you. He wouldn't dirty his own hands with acts of violence, but he agitates, and other people prone to acts of vandalism or violence are stirred up."

Once more, Cotty looked at Robert Beller, and found the man grinning nastily. He was fairly sure now that Beller had been one of the three, and he longed to smash his fist into the man's face. Forcing his temper down, he said, "I still haven't been informed as to your purpose here today, gentlemen."

Hugh hesitated, then said slowly, "We represent the TOA."

Cotty stared. "The TOA? What the devil is that?"

"The Tavern Owners Association."

Cotty shook his head. "I've never heard of it."

"We have just recently organized."

"And to what purpose?"

"The purpose is to get all the tavern owners to band together and agree on a course of action." Hugh leaned forward. "We have to stick together, my young friend, or we may all go up in smoke."

Cotty scrubbed a hand across his mouth. "I see. At least, I think I see." He said shrewdly, "I have a feeling that you're trying to get all the innkeepers to support Macarthur. Am I right?"

Hugh nodded. "That is correct."

Cotty laughed shortly. "Who was it who told me some years back that he totally disapproved of Macarthur? As I recall, you said he was a disgrace to the corps. Or words to that effect."

Hugh had the grace to look sheepish, a look that quickly turned belligerent. "I know I said that, Cotty, and I still detest the man and all he stands for, but he controls a large part of the supply of rum in Sydney. We tavern owners are forced to deal with his minions from time to time."

Cotty was grinning. "Haven't you ever heard, Hugh? If you lie down with the devil, you're likely to get up with fleas."

Hugh retorted, "And there are times when, if you don't lie down with the devil, you risk a pitchfork in the arse!"

"A large part of my custom comes from people from Government House, or from the gentry who look favorably upon Governor Bligh. If I side with Macarthur, I stand to lose their trade."

"How about the Blackstock Inn, your other tavern in the Rocks? None of your precious gentry patronizes that one, nor your grog shanties." Hugh leaned forward again. "This is a power struggle here and, in my view, Macarthur will come out on top in the end. The situation grows more volatile daily, and could explode at any time. If that happens and you're on the losing side, you may be driven out of business."

Exasperated, Cotty said, "I'm not on *any* side, Hugh! Nobody seems to understand that."

"You'd better join in with us, you young whelp," Beller said in a snarling voice, "or you'll rue the day!"

"And who will see to that?" Cotty said in measured tones. "*You*, Master Beller?"

"No need for harsh words, gentlemen." Hugh waved a hand. "But you have become arrogant, Cotty. I think you're beginning to believe that you're king of the Rocks."

"I cannot account for what some call me," Cotty snapped. "And I am not arrogant, but I am my own man."

Hugh stared at him intently. "That is your final word?"

"It is, Hugh. I appreciate what you're trying to do," Cotty said in a more temperate tone. "But I have made up my mind to remain neutral. That way, when it's all over, I hope I shall have a few friends left on both sides of the issue."

"For God's sake, Cotty, it's not going to just fade away! This conflict has been going on for years, and it will not subside until something drastic happens. I think you are being very foolish, my young friend, but it is your decision." Hugh got to his feet. "We may as well take our leave, gentlemen. It seems we are wasting our time here."

Cotty also got up. "I am sorry, Hugh. I hope this doesn't affect our friendship."

"Our friendship!" Hugh snorted softly. "I don't know if it'll even be safe to be seen talking to you. But you are my friend, Cotty. Nothing can change that."

He held out his hand, and Cotty took it, gripping it firmly.

Hugh dipped his head. "I bid you good day, and good fortune. I believe you will be needing it."

Cotty grinned. "If I come to a bad end, you may have the privilege of telling me you told me so."

Hugh grunted. "It's a privilege I can do without."

There were a few customers in the barroom now. One bartender was on duty, and Bess Iverson, the daytime barmaid, was busy serving the patrons. But Hope was still absent. Cotty felt his annoyance return, but at the same time worry gnawed at him. Where the devil was she?

He escorted the three men to the front door and, opening it for them, he saw two horses before the tavern. A man Cotty vaguely recognized was helping Hope down from one of them.

As Marston and the other tavern owners departed, Cotty stood framed in the doorway, staring angrily at Hope. She caught his glance and flushed.

Then she turned defiantly to the man. "Farewell, Stuart. And thank you for a nice day."

The man bowed over her hand, gave Cotty a flashing glance, then mounted and rode away, leading the second horse.

"Thank you for a nice day," Cotty mimicked savagely. "Where have you been all this time?"

"Why? Have you been worried about me?" she said, somewhat archly.

"Well, of course I was worried about you! No one knew where you were!"

"I went for a ride in the countryside with Stuart," she said composedly. "And I did have a very nice day. There was nothing for you to be concerned about. Stuart is a perfect gentleman."

"A perfect gentleman, is he?" Cotty growled. "How can you be so sure about that, Hope? You've had little experience with men."

"Do you think I can't tell, that I'm just a silly little fool?"

"No, of course I don't think that . . ."

She plunged ahead, angry now. "As both you and Charity have told me repeatedly, it's time I let a man court me. Well, that's what I am doing!"

"You could at least have told me about this," he said.

"For one thing, you weren't here this morning when I left, so how could I?"

"But you must have known beforehand."

"I am over twenty-one, Cotty Starke! I don't have to account to you for my private life."

"That's right, you don't, but I do care what happens to you."

"Do you?" she said challengingly. "You have a poor way of showing it."

He stared. "Now what does that mean? Haven't I taken good care of both you and Charity?"

"What I have gotten lately, I have earned. That's probably what worried you the most, that I wasn't here when the tavern opened for business."

"Now that is unfair, Hope."

"Is it?" She swept past him into the tavern, knowing that he was right—that she was being unfair. But in her annoyance she cared little.

Cotty stood looking after her in frustration and anger. It was an anger he could not fully understand. Hope worked hard and faithfully, and he really did not know what he would do without her. So why was he so upset? She was her own woman, and had a right to see a man if she so desired. Of course he knew nothing about this Stuart Williams. What kind of a man was he? What if he was a rakehell? Hope deserved a fine, decent man. Cotty decided to make a few discreet inquiries about Williams.

HOPE WENT UPSTAIRS to her room. Charity's door was closed, and she hesitated for just a moment, wondering if she should confide in her sister. She finally decided against it. Charity was never interested in things that did not directly involve or concern herself. Hope doubted very much that her sister would be at all interested in discussing Stuart Williams, or Cotty's angry reaction.

She went into her room and quickly changed into her working clothes. She did feel some guilt about staying out so late. It was late afternoon, and the tavern, she had noticed on her way through, was filling up.

Leaving her room, she noticed that Charity's door was open slightly, and she saw her sister peering at her. The door closed quickly. Curious, she rapped on the door. "Charity? Let me in."

The only sound she heard was a metallic rattle, which she identified as a key being inserted into the lock. She twisted the doorknob and pushed against the door with her shoulder. The door flew open, and Hope half fell into the room. She saw Charity backing up, her eyes wide in alarm.

"Why are you trying to lock me out?" Hope demanded.

"This is my room!" Charity wailed. "I have a right to my privacy!"

Then Hope noticed that her sister was dressed in a pink silk gown, with a low-cut bodice, and had a lacy cap on her head. "Where did you get that dress? I certainly haven't seen it before."

"I bought it with my own money."

Hope's eyes narrowed. "But why are you dressed like that? Surely, you're not going downstairs into the barroom in such attire?"

Charity drew herself up defiantly. "I am enjoying the company of a gentleman this evening."

"The company of a gentleman? I knew nothing of this."

"You're not my mother, Hope. I don't need your permission to be escorted out."

"Does Cotty know?" Hope asked.

"Of course not. Why should I tell him?"

"You're his ward, for one thing."

"If I'm old enough to earn my keep working around a tavern, I'm old enough to decide for myself what man I see."

In a way, Hope supposed, Charity was right; certainly most girls her age in Sydney were already married. Still, Charity *was* her sister, and she felt a certain responsibility. With a sigh she said, "And I suppose the man you intend to see is Charles Bonney?"

Charity tossed her head. "Yes! Charles is a fine man!"

"That's not what I hear, Charity. Just today, I was told that Charles Bonney has a terrible reputation back in England. In fact, the reason he came here was to escape the consequences of a shoddy affair."

"Gossip, nothing but gossip!" Charity snapped. "Charles warned me that lies would be told about him."

"I'll just wager he did," Hope said dryly. "Well, young lady, you're not going anywhere tonight."

"You can't stop me!"

"Oh, yes, I can. And when I tell Cotty, he'll see to it that you don't go. I have to go down to my duties now. You are to remain here in your room. If I see you outside this room tonight, I will lock you in."

"You wouldn't dare!"

"Try me and see."

Hope turned away and went out, closing the door behind her. Downstairs, she knocked on the office door, intending to tell Cotty about Charity's plans for the evening. When there was no answer, she opened the door and glanced in. The room was empty. And when she took up her place behind the bar, she could not see Cotty anywhere in the main room.

Naturally, he was not around when he was needed, she thought with a burn of anger; he had probably gone calling on one of his strumpets!

For the next two hours Hope was extremely busy. From where she was stationed at the cash drawer she could not see the stairs without craning her neck, which she did from time to time; but when she did not see Charity after nearly an hour, she relaxed her vigilance somewhat.

It was Lucy's chore to escort the dinner guests upstairs to the dining room. Hope pulled her aside just before she made a trip up. "Lucy, Charity is in one of her snits. Keep a sharp eye on the stairs. If you spot her trying to sneak out, alert me at once."

At the end of the two hours, the parade of diners began to slack off, and Hope started to feel a bit guilty about her sister. True, Charity was willful and headstrong, used to having her own way, and needed to be spoken to harshly on occasion; yet she had not had her supper. She should be over her disappointment by now, and in need of food.

Hope summoned Lucy to preside over the cash drawer for a few minutes, while she went upstairs.

She rapped on the door to Charity's room. There was no answer, so she knocked again. Still no answer.

Feeling a spurt of alarm, she turned the knob and pushed the door open. A quick glance around the room told her that it was empty.

Charity was gone!

# CHAPTER NINETEEN

CHARITY WAS IN A QUANDARY. She had promised to meet Charles Bonney outside the Crown at seven sharp, and according to the ticking clock in the corner of her room, it was now six-thirty.

How was she going to slip out of the tavern without being seen by Hope or Cotty? Despite the defiance she usually displayed toward Hope, she was intimidated by her older sister; and she knew that Hope was fully capable of keeping her promise to lock her in her room, if she was pushed far enough. And while Cotty could usually be wheedled into letting her have her way, there were times when he set his foot down. She suspected that this was one of those times. Tempted as she was to just march downstairs past them and out of the tavern, she could not quite work up enough courage to actually do so.

Nervously, she paced back and forth. There *had* to be a way! If she did not meet Charles and he left without seeing her, it was quite possible that he would not make another assignation with her. She had never known a man like Charles, and she likely never would again; not in this barbaric place.

She opened the door a crack and peered out. From here she could see people coming and going into the dining room down the hallway. It was then that an idea came to her. Hurrying to her clothes cupboard, she found an old cloak that she had not worn for some time. It was an all-weather cloak with a hood that pulled up over her head. She put it on and resumed her vigil at the door.

Now and then she glanced at the clock; the hands moved toward and then past seven. Charity was so frustrated that she felt like weeping.

Then she saw what she had been waiting for. A group of six people, three men and three women, were leaving the upstairs dining room. Pulling the hood around her face, Charity hurried down the hall and caught up with the group just as they started downstairs. They were members of the gentry, splendidly dressed, laughing and chatting among themselves.

Charity forced her way into the center of the group, ignoring dark looks and murmurs of disapproval. When they reached the bottom of the stairs, she remained in the center. She sneaked a glance out of the corner of her eye and breathed a sigh of relief when she saw that Hope, who was standing behind the bar, had her head down, and Cotty and Lucy were not in sight.

Her heart pounding in anticipation of discovery, she and her group of unknowing conspirators reached the door. She was free. Breaking away from the group, she looked wildly around for Charles, half expecting him to be already gone.

Then she saw him standing near the corner of the building. He was handsomely dressed, wearing a short-waisted coat of plum-colored silk with pearl buttons and nankeen breeches. On his head was a high-crowned felt hat. He leaned indolently on a pearl-handled walking stick, his stockinged legs crossed.

Filled with relief and excitement, she hurried toward him. At the sound of her footsteps he turned, and her heart almost stopped. He was so handsome, so assured! How fortunate she was to have such a man interested in her!

Then she saw with dismay that he was scowling darkly. "I am sorry, Charles," she said breathlessly. "I thought I was never going to be able to slip away!"

"I am not accustomed to lurking about, like some lackey at the back door. This is demeaning."

"I know, and I am sorry. But as I told you, my sister and Cotty think I'm still a child and do not approve of me seeing a man yet. If you had come calling for me in the proper way, there would have been a big fuss. Hope even threatened to lock me in my room."

He smiled then, the uneven slant of his face lending him a dangerous look, and she shivered with delight.

"Your sister, I can perhaps understand, but your guardian, this Cotty Starke, must be blind. You are in no way a child, my dear Charity. Or perhaps..." His smile died, and those depthless black eyes sent a chill through her. "Perhaps that is why he does not wish you to be courted, because you *are* a lovely creature. Perhaps he has plans of his own for you."

"Cotty?" she said incredulously, then giggled. "Oh, no, not Cotty! He's more like a father to me."

"I would say he is a little young for that."

"Well, my brother then. He would never think of me in that way."

''Methinks you *are* young in many ways. But then let us not concern ourselves with Cotty Starke. We have pleasanter things to think on.''

He extended his arm, and Charity took it. The feel of firm muscles under the cloth, and the nearness of him, excited her, but she tried to keep her feelings from showing. She instinctively knew that her usual high-handed tactics would not work with this man, but she also knew it would be unwise to let him know how much he interested her. For the first time in her experience, she felt that a man had the advantage of her, and the knowledge both intrigued and frightened her. She had already given too much away when she had greeted him so effusively.

''Where are we going this evening?'' she asked.

''I thought Hugh Marston's flash house.'' His dark eyes, faintly mocking, stared down into hers. ''Have you ever been inside a flash house?''

Would he think her naive if she told him the truth? She very much wanted to appear sophisticated in his eyes, but perhaps in this instance the truth was best. She had already admitted to having been sheltered; she could play the princess, not knowing certain things because of this protection.

''No, never,'' she said calmly, ''but I have heard about them.''

''Then it is time you were having the experience. We shall dine there before the entertainment. The food may not be as good as that served at the Crown, but it will be adequate.''

They began walking toward the Rocks. If Hope and Cotty knew she was visiting a flash house, they would be livid; yet the lure of the forbidden sent a thrill through Charity. She was sure that it was to be an evening she would never forget.

She had never been deep into the Rocks at night; the only times she had been there had been in daylight and with Cotty escorting her. The streets thronged with men in rough clothing, and they eyed her boldly. The only women she saw were obviously doxies—laughing raucously, as bold as brass with the men, and dressed to show their wares. She supposed they were what men called a "flash piece of mutton," or, if diseased, "a queer mott."

She also supposed they were to be pitied, but what she felt for them, for the most part, was horror and contempt. How could any woman who had any self-respect allow herself to sink so low? It would never happen to her, she thought fiercely, never!

And for the first time she thought of marriage; the best way to assure that she would never become like these women was to wed a man, a man of some position. A man like Charles....

The thought startled her. Why was she thinking of marriage now, at this particular time? Was it because she was suddenly fearful of the future? Or was it because of these depraved women surrounding her?

She sneaked a look at Charles—so in command of himself and his environment—and she was proud to be with him. Cotty and Hope were wrong about his character....

Her thoughts were interrupted as a pair of drunken men staggered toward them. They stopped directly in the path; and as Charles started to maneuver Charity around them, they moved to block him.

One of the men said jeeringly, "Well, what have we here? One of the swells out for a stroll with his doxie?"

In a cold voice Bonney said, "You would be well-advised to step aside, my man."

"My man, is it?" The man nudged his companion. "Did you hear that, mate? And just what do you aim to do 'bout it if'n we don't step aside?"

"This, my good fellow." Bonney raised the cane, there was a clicking sound, and a slim blade snicked out, glittering in the faint light. "If you do not give way, you will soon regret it."

"Now, wait, guv'nor!" The man who had been doing the talking backed up, raising his hands, his face turning chalky with fear. "We meant no harm. Just havin' a little sport."

"Then be off with you," Bonney said in that cold voice.

The two men scuttled around him and vanished into the darkness. Bonney calmly resheathed the blade and extended his arm to Charity. "Shall we continue, my dear?"

She took it with a shiver. "You were marvelous, Charles! I was frightened."

"No need to be, my dear Charity. Those men are scum, and dare not offer violence to anyone who faces them down."

A few doors down, Bonney turned in. The building was unprepossessing, with a front of dirty brick and a small sign over the door reading Marston's.

Bonney rapped on the door. "An elegant establishment," he said sarcastically. "Admittance is by invitation only. To be truthful, to members only. To attend entertainments here, one must be a member of a club. Not an exclusive club, by any means, but what else is one to do for amusement in this primitive place?''

In a moment a peephole was opened in the door, and Charity could see a single eye peering out.

Then the door swung open, and a burly man bowed them in. ''Master Bonney! You are welcome, as always. You and your lady.''

''Thank you, Jackson,'' Bonney said regally. ''Is our alcove ready?''

''Yes, sir. Right this way, sir.''

The man led them to the left toward a stairway obscured by dimness. As they mounted the stairs, Charity craned her neck to peer into the lower floor of the club. The room was murky with smoke, loud with boisterous laughter, and smelled of perspiration, perfume and tobacco smoke.

Bonney held her arm all the way up the dim stairwell. At the top they emerged into a corridor running the length of the front of the building, with a wall on their right, and velvet, floor-length curtains on their left. Halfway along the corridor the man named Jackson paused and swept aside a curtain, then bowed them into a roomy alcove. There were two chairs, a table and a plush settee. There was also a pair of curtains on the other side of the alcove.

''Do you wish the curtains open, sir?'' Jackson inquired.

''If you please.''

The man drew back the drapes, and Charity stepped to the waist-high railing. The room below was crowded, all the tables filled, and dimly lit by three chandeliers dangling from the ceiling. At the far end of the room was a small stage, empty at the moment. An almost animal heat rose from the packed room, and Charity experienced a flash of apprehension. What had she let herself in for?

Then Charles Bonney touched her elbow, and her reservations vanished. In his deep voice he said, "The evening's amusement doesn't start for another hour. We have ample time to dine at our leisure."

With his hand under her elbow, he turned her toward the table. As he seated her and moved around to his own side, a waiter parted the curtains and entered with a bottle of wine. He poured a glass for Bonney to taste, and after Charles had nodded his approval, the waiter filled Charity's glass, then Bonney's.

"I have already given our food order."

"Yes, sir," the waiter said respectfully, and left the alcove.

Bonney raised his glass. "To you, my dear Charity."

They touched glasses and Charity drank, feeling deliciously wicked. Even at eighteen, she rarely drank anything alcoholic; Hope and Cotty said she was too young. Oh, what would they think if they could see her now!

Before she could set her glass down, Bonney raised his again. "Another toast.... To us!"

Before supper was served, Charity was already feeling the effects of the wine; she was warm, flushed and giggly. Dimly, she realized that she should not drink any more, but Bonney kept filling her glass; and when the first bottle was gone, he ordered another.

By that time, Charity was quite giddy, her mind empty of all thought save of the man across the table.

When she asked him why he had come to New South Wales, he shrugged. "Life in England had become boring, and I looked upon this as a relief from tedium."

"And you have found it so, Charles?"

"Not really." He grimaced. "This is a primitive place, inhabited by fools and drunkards and the vilest kind of criminal..."

Charity made a small sound, thinking to voice a protest. Her mother had been a convict. Did not Charles know that? Perhaps he did not. If she were to tell him, he might spurn her. She subsided, saying nothing.

Bonney, evidently not noticing her stir of protest, was going on, "I thought there would be opportunities here for a man of intelligence and experience, but there is nothing worthy of me. Except..." He hesitated briefly, his expression revealing a naked hunger. "There is one possibility always in my mind. From what I have learned here, governors do not last overlong. There is the possibility that, if I do well as Governor Bligh's aide, I stand a chance of being appointed in his place when he is removed. And if I am any judge of the events occurring here, that may be quite soon."

Charity leaned forward. "I think you would make a fine governor, Charles!"

Eyes glittering, he nodded complacently. "I agree with you, my dear. To rule this ungodly place takes a firm resolve, an iron hand, a will that brooks no sedition. For that is what exists here!" He slammed the palm of his hand down on the tabletop. "The damned military needs to be whipped back into obedience to Government House!"

He talked on, but Charity scarcely listened. What if he did become governor, and she became his wife? Delightful vistas opened before her, and she dreamed as he talked.

And then something began to happen that was inexplicable. As Bonney talked, and as she watched him intently, Charity slowly started to sense a tension growing between them. It flowed across the table like an invisible charge of energy. It made her uneasy, but at the same time it was pleasurable. She seemed to be caught in a bubble of colors and dark undercurrents, and nothing existed for her but the flow of his rich, warm voice and the sense of his nearness.

Gradually, she became aware of what it was—he wanted her! Could such a feeling actually be felt without them touching? If she had been more introspective, she might have tried to analyze her own feelings, because she knew that she was responding to him. She longed to reach across the table and touch him in some way.

At that moment the waiter came with their food, breaking the spell, but only for a brief time. When they began to eat, she was caught up in it again. They were served a leg of mutton with accompanying side dishes, and she ate without really tasting the food.

She noticed that Bonney ate with unabashed appetite, almost greedily, which struck her as strange for such an ordinarily fastidious man. She was not repulsed, but found it fascinating. Dimly, she sensed that here was a man with enormous physical appetites, and a man who was not reluctant to state them without regard for the niceties.

While they were eating their sweet, a juicy berry tart, a drumroll sounded from the room below. Glancing down, Charity saw a tall man in a buffoon's costume on the small stage. As the drumroll ended and the hubbub died down, the buffoon raised a lady's open parasol over his head, twirling it.

"Just perchance it might rain. In Sydney Town, who ever knows!"

The buffoon's sally was greeted by laughter and catcalls as he marched back and forth on the stage.

"As the parson said to the recently bereaved widow, as he paid her a visit with his breeches undone, I always come prepared. But I know, gentlemen and, uh, ladies, that you're not here tonight to hear my humor, as hilarious as it might be. We have singing and dancing and quips galore. If our dancing girls don't stir your ardor, gentlemen, you have one foot in the grave. Our chief attraction this evening is a lady straight from Liverpool, newly arrived this week. She is the flower of Sydney now, Liverpool Lilly! But first, let's bring on the dancing wenches! Sit back and enjoy yourselves!"

Off to the right a man sat down at a pianoforte and struck up a lively tune.

"Shall we move over to the railing where we can observe better?" Bonney asked.

Without waiting for her answer, Bonney got up, came around to help her, and then carried both chairs over to the railing. After he had seated Charity, he went back to the table and filled their wineglasses. Charity realized that she had already drunk too much, but, her attention fastened on the stage below, she accepted the glass automatically.

Four buxom women were now on stage, dancing wildly to the tinkling music. They did not look a great deal different from the women Charity had seen on the street outside; younger perhaps, but they all had the same shopworn, debauched look. Their dresses were shorter than fashionable, striking them halfway between the knee and the ankle, and all had full bosoms almost bursting free of their confinement. As they gamboled, they flipped their dresses up high, exposing plump legs and thighs.

The buffoon skipped in and out among the dancing women, now and then running the folded parasol under their dresses and flipping them high, showing pink drawers. Once, when one woman had her back to the audience, he flipped her dress all the way up over her head, turning his face to leer out at the crowd. The woman, instead of pulling her dress down, half bent over and wiggled her bottom. Roars of male approval erupted from the audience.

Charity, blushing, darted a sidelong glance at Bonney. He was engrossed in the performance, his narrow face intent. She looked back at the stage, taking a sip of wine.

The entertainment went on in much the same vein for some time—the girls performing numerous lewd dances, to the great approval of the crowd, and the buffoon telling vulgar jokes in between each dance. Charity watched in morbid fascination, in much the same way she might observe the mating dance of strange, exotic creatures.

Bonney kept her wineglass filled, and she drank steadily, now beyond the point of caution. Sometime during the performance he had moved his chair next to hers and placed an arm around her shoulders, his long fingers caressing her bare shoulder and upper bosom. Charity thought of protesting; but the touch of his stroking fingers was exceedingly pleasant, and she sat in a warm daze of pleasure.

Quiet suddenly fell on the room below, and with an effort, Charity focused her gaze on the stage, which was now empty except for the buffoon.

"Now comes the main event of our evening's entertainment. I bring you Liverpool Lilly!" He half turned, flourishing the parasol.

From the wings came a woman much younger than the dancers. She had curly auburn hair falling in ringlets to her shoulders. She was dressed far more decorously than the other women on view this evening, and her face had a demure, innocent look.

Charity leaned forward, squinting to see better. Why, she looks like an angel, she thought in astonishment. Could it be that they were going to be witness to some refined entertainment? Charity concentrated as much as possible considering her intoxicated condition, determined to listen carefully.

Liverpool Lilly, as the pianoforte began to play, opened her ruby lips and began to sing in pure, lilting tones:

"I am a lass that's young and free,
I've traveled the country round, do ye see,
Because I'm a female of that kind,
That will have a workman on my mind.
All tradesmen I have had at will,
And tried their various ways and skill,
And all that I have had, ere long,
I'll quickly tell you in my song."

As the singer continued, the verses grew more and more vulgar; and Charity felt her face burn. She wanted to cover her ears, but was afraid that Charles would think her a prude. There were words in the song she did not know the meaning of, yet she knew instinctively that they were not only naughty, but obscene. And if she had not guessed their meaning, she knew she was right; for the crowd's raucous reaction told her so. As Liverpool Lilly finished the song and, still decorous, bowed off the stage, the men in the room below stood and loudly cheered her.

Before the bedlam below had fully ceased, Bonney was on his feet. Charity watched, vaguely puzzled, as he quickly pulled the curtains closed.

Then he turned to her, holding his hand out. She took it, and he pulled her to her feet and led her toward the settee. His arms went around her, and his mouth descended on hers. She was too startled, too dazed from the wine, to resist. His breath scorched, and the touch of his lips was like fire.

Her blood pounded in her ears, and she clutched at him frantically as exquisite sensations rolled over her in wave after wave. All the while, he was moving her inexorably to the settee. Then she was on it, her skirts pushed up above her waist. His mouth still fastened to hers, he fumbled with her undergarments.

Finally, with an inarticulate snarl, he began tearing at them. She made a small sound of protest, which was smothered by his hard mouth. Awash with sensation and sodden from too much wine, she had no thought of fighting him off; and she vaguely realized that any resistance would have been futile in any case.

Her undergarments were discarded and she felt a rush of cool air on her upper thighs. A fever raged through her at his touch; and then he mounted her with rough urgency, and she felt a sharp pain.

# CHAPTER TWENTY

HOPE WAS FRANTIC with worry. After finding Charity missing, she had sent John in search of Cotty; and she waited tensely for his arrival.

He did not show up for almost two hours, and when he finally came in with John, she flew at him in a rage. "Where in heaven's name have you been? I thought you would never come!"

"Wait, wait!" He held his hands up before his face. "I'm sorry, Hope, but I had some business to attend to, and John had trouble finding me. What's wrong?"

"We'd better go back to your office, where it's private." She turned to John, saying, "Thank you. Don't go too far away; we may need you again."

"Never mind privacy, Hope," Cotty said impatiently. "There must be something badly amiss if you'd send John looking all over Sydney for me. Now, what is it?"

She glanced around at the few patrons still present and lowered her voice. "Charity is gone."

He blinked. "What do you mean, gone?"

"Just that. I went up to her room and found her gone. That was when I sent John in search of you..."

He brushed past her and ran up the stairs. Hope waited patiently where she was. In a few minutes he came back, face as black as a thundercloud. "She *is* gone! Where could she be?"

"I told you she was gone. Why would I—"

Cotty batted a hand at her. "Never mind. I had to see for myself. Something must have happened. Did you two have another of your quarrels?"

Unaccountably, tears sprang to her eyes. "Why must I always have to shoulder the blame when Charity does something like this?"

"Hope..." His expression softened and he touched her cheek gently. "I am not blaming you. But something must have happened. Tell me!"

Dashing away the tears, she told him about the scene with Charity. "And I had to forbid her to see Charles Bonney! You would have done the same."

He nodded. "You're right, I would have. But how could she have left the Crown unseen?"

"We were very busy tonight, and I never dreamed she would try to slip away. She must have chosen a moment when my attention was diverted."

"Well..." Cotty sighed, rubbing his knuckles across his mouth. "I suppose she went somewhere with Bonney, but where is a good question." He glanced at John. "Do you have any ideas?"

"No, Cotty, I do not," John said gravely.

Cotty shook his head. "I hardly know where to start, but we have to look for her. Come with me, John..."

Hope interrupted. "There she is!"

Cotty turned around. Charity was just coming in the front door. As she came toward them, Cotty saw that she wore a bemused look and that her hair was in disarray. She staggered slightly and had to catch at a table to keep her balance.

As she reached them, Hope sniffed audibly. "Why, you have been drinking. You stink of wine!"

Charity grinned a little foolishly. "So what if I have? When a lady is out with a gentleman, it is perfectly proper to take wine with supper."

"You hardly look like a proper lady at the moment." Hope surveyed her sister closely. "And if you were with Charles Bonney tonight, you were hardly in the company of a gentleman."

"That just shows how much you know about gentlemen, sister," Charity said impudently. "He has mentioned marriage to me."

Taken by surprise, Hope said, "He has?"

"He has indeed, but I do not know if I will accept. I asked for time to consider his proposal. And now, good night, dear sister and Cotty."

Gathering herself, Charity swept past them and started up the stairs, stumbling on the first step, then righting herself.

Hope and Cotty stared at one another. Hope said, "Could we be wrong about Charles Bonney?"

Cotty's glance went to the stairs. "I suppose even a rogue can change, and I suppose we shall just have to wait and see."

"I hope he isn't just leading her astray." Hope sighed. "I must confess that I would be much easier in mind if she was wed. I just wish it was to someone else. I still don't trust that man."

CHARITY LET HERSELF into her room, bolted the door, kicked off her slippers and fell across the bed. She giggled at the remembered look on their faces when she had made her announcement.

Then she sobered. Of course, Charles had made no proposal of marriage. Very little, in fact, had been said after the consummation on the settee. But he *was* a gentleman, and the only honorable thing for a gentleman to do after what had happened was to offer to wed the woman involved. Charles was a busy man, with many things on his mind; he probably just assumed that it was understood that they would be wed eventually.

Charity's thoughts strayed back to those few minutes on the settee, in Charles's rough embrace. She had often wondered what it would be like to be intimate with a man. Now she knew. Or did she?

She tried to assess what she was feeling. She was a little disappointed, she had to admit; it had been over so quickly and, she also had to admit, she had been too befuddled by the wine to really observe what went on. However, she had enjoyed the sensations his mouth, hands and body had aroused in her, and she had responded as best she could, considering her besotted condition and the haste in which the act had been performed. She decided that she had received enough pleasure so that she wished to do it again.

She felt heat rush to her face at the thought. *Would* there be a next time? Certainly, Charles seemed to think so; for he had asked to see her again when he left her at the door of the Crown.

Only one thing really bothered her about the evening: she was keenly disappointed that she had not been more in control. She had always thought that the beauty of her face and body, and the fact of her sex, were enough to enable her to control a man in such situations.

With Charles Bonney, it would appear that she was mistaken; he was not a man to be so easily manipulated. Certainly, she could not have him at her beck and call as she did the other young men who came around her. For an instant she experienced a thrill of fear. Was she getting involved in something she could not handle?

No, she refused to believe that. She was confident that she could eventually have Charles in thrall to her. She certainly had no intention of refusing to see him again.


OVER THE NEXT FEW WEEKS a sort of uneasy truce existed between the two sisters. Charles Bonney continued to call for Charity, once or twice a week, but he came to the tavern now to fetch her. His behavior was always proper, if somewhat arrogant, when he came calling, and Hope held her tongue. She still did not like the man; but if he had mentioned marriage to Charity, perhaps she was misjudging him.

As for Charity, she was enjoying herself thoroughly. Bonney took her for rides in the countryside, to the best restaurants Sydney had to offer, twice to the small theater that had recently opened, and twice more to the flash house.

She never mentioned the flash house to either Hope or Cotty, but she did talk at length of the good times she had with Charles at the theater and the restaurants.

Charles made love to her on those occasions when they rode out of town and when they visited Marston's flash house. Their lovemaking was better for Charity now, consummated more slowly, giving her more satisfaction. Also, she had learned to exact a measure of control over their couplings. She could entice, tease and torment Charles to a certain point; and he not only suffered it, but seemed to enjoy it. Yet, beyond that point she dared not go; she could only withhold her favors so long before he became darkly angry and rough with her. Several times she had taunted him until he seized her, throwing her to the ground and taking her violently. In those instances, she glimpsed an explosive violence that frightened her, yet at the same time made their lovemaking more intense, more satisfying.

He had yet to mention marriage, but she fully intended to bring the subject up herself. So far, she had not been able to muster sufficient courage.

MEANWHILE, STUART WILLIAMS'S courtship of Hope continued apace, although her duties at the Crown restricted her nighttime activities. Heretofore, she had worked seven nights a week, but now she demanded at least one night off. Cotty bowed to her wishes without protest, and she and Stuart dined out once a week. Except for the theater, there was little else to do at night. Of course, nightlife boiled and seethed in the Rocks, but it was unthinkable that they should venture there.

During their days together, they rode out into the countryside, or went sailing in the cove in a small craft that Stuart owned. In the process Hope learned to be a fine horsewoman and a good sailor.

Stuart was never anything less than proper, always courtly and solicitous of her. Not once did he make untoward advances. Hope was perceptive enough to know that he was in love with her, but she was ambivalent about her own feelings. She enjoyed his company very much. They had good times together, and she had grown quite fond of him; but she was not in love with him, certainly not in the way she had been in love with Cotty for all these years. And yet, she reasoned, perhaps that was all she could expect—a fondness and a deep respect.

Her feeling for Cotty might be nothing more than infatuation, something that would pass in time. In any event, it had long been clear to her that her feelings were not reciprocated, and she could not spend her life pining for him. Perhaps it was time she put him out of her heart and mind, and accepted a comfortable relationship with a man like Stuart Williams. But would it not be wrong of her to accept a devotion she could not return in full measure?

COTTY, FROM A SAFE DISTANCE, watched the activities of his two wards with mixed feelings—amusement, some mystification, and occasional dismay, since he finally had to face the fact that he might lose both of them.

He did not care for either suitor. The more he saw of Charles Bonney, the more reason he found to dislike the man; yet he had to admit that he had no real cause for his feeling of antipathy toward Stuart Williams. Williams was always perfectly proper, and showed respect for Hope and Cotty. He was handsome, easygoing, and from the reports Cotty had received, a valued aide to Governor Bligh. In short, a perfect suitor.

So why, Cotty wondered, do my hackles rise whenever he comes courting Hope? It was an aggravating mystery, and one he was no nearer to solving as the weeks passed.

But Cotty had learned his lesson with both girls— to complain to either of them about their choice of suitors would only bring their wrath down upon his head; and God forbid that he should order them to stop seeing the young men!

So he gritted his teeth and endured. Actually, he had little time to spare to brood about the two sisters. He devoted most of his time to overseeing the operations of his taverns and grog shanties. Since Hugh Marston's visit, and the vandalism of the three ruffians who had broken into the Crown, Cotty had become more vigilant, going from the Crown to the Blackstock Inn and back again, with visits in between to the grog shanties.

He had hired several ex-Marines to stand guard on the taverns around the clock, but it was not really worth the extra expense to do so with the shanties. He was so busy that he had time for little else; even his love life suffered. Strangely enough, he found that this lack did not bother him overmuch.

So far, there had been no overt action against him. This could well be because John Macarthur was occupied with his feud with Governor Bligh. Since the governor had refused to grant him more land, Macarthur had instigated several court actions against Governor Bligh; but they were little more than harassing actions, attempts to diminish the governor's authority, and had come to nothing. In retaliation, the governor had Macarthur arrested on a trivial charge in December, but Macarthur was shortly released. In a rage, Bligh seized some of Macarthur's property without a warrant, and then began to demolish the dwellings of those who had offended him on the pretext that they were unsuitably placed, or that they caused obstruction. Among the buildings destroyed were some on Macarthur's own property.

In addition, the governor had once again lowered the legal price of imported spirits to the point where it was no longer profitable for the ships to unload their cargoes through port channels, which naturally resulted in a marked increase in smuggling and further incensed the rum monopolists.

Cotty could sense that the feud was quickly coming to a climax, possibly a bloody one; but he still refused to take sides. True to Hugh's prediction, trade at the Blackstock Inn was suffering; it had fallen off so badly that Cotty was losing money, yet he was grimly determined not to close. Since his ownership of the grog shanties was not general knowledge, their trade had not suffered; and the Crown, catering as it did to the gentry, had lost very little business. Cotty was grimly determined not to change his neutral position. Let the two bitter, bullheaded antagonists fight it out! He could only hope that he would still be in business when it was all over.

ALTHOUGH IT WAS SUMMER NOW, much of December had been rainy and cold, and not good weather for riding. Finally there was a change for the better the week of Christmas. The rain stopped, and warm, clear days returned.

On the second nice day, Stuart Williams came to fetch Hope, and they rode out of town to their favorite picnicking spot on the bank of the stream.

After their repast was laid out on the cloth, Stuart lay back, propped on his elbow.

At his deep sigh, Hope glanced over at him. "What's wrong, Stuart?"

"It's this weather." He waved a hand around. "Sunshine and hot weather. It's not normal. Back in London, during the Christmas season, it would be crisp and cold, with snow on the ground."

She laughed. "All I can recall of England in the winter is bitter cold, and the snow was usually black with soot."

"Well, I miss it." He sighed again. "This will be my second Christmas in New South Wales. I miss England most at this time of the year." He smiled in reminiscence. "Sledding in the snow, roaring fires, mulled wine and the company of good friends and family."

"I'm afraid my memories of England are not so pleasant," she said wryly.

He turned to her. "But it doesn't have to be that way, my dear. I know from what you have told me how hard life was for your mother, and for you, in England. But life there can be quite pleasant, under the proper circumstances."

"And just what circumstances are those, Stuart?"

He was silent for a bit, gazing off. Then he turned to her again, his eyes intent. "You know that I love you, Hope. Don't you?"

She made a startled gesture. "Why, I . . ." She swallowed, dismayed at the turn the conversation had taken. "I suppose I haven't really given it that much thought . . ."

He was shaking his head. "You must know. I've certainly made no secret of my feelings. But no matter. I do love you, deeply."

"I wish you wouldn't speak so, Stuart," she said in distress.

He brushed her protest away with a sweep of his hand and leaned toward her. "Marry me, Hope, and go with me back to England."

Stricken dumb, she could only stare at him.

Eyes glowing, he continued, "I promise you that the life I can give you there will be nothing like that which you knew as a child. My father has a comfortable estate north of London. He is growing old now and has been in poor health for the past two years. He has written me requesting that I return home and take over my responsibilities. Truthfully, I am not averse to doing so." He grimaced. "I have had just about enough of 'adventuring,' and if I could have you by my side, I know I would be content. Please say yes, Hope!"

Hope looked down at her hands, clasped in her lap. Panic filled her. It was too soon to be asked to make such a decision; and yet, to be the wife of a gentleman, to have all the comforts and privileges such a union would provide . . . how such a marriage would have pleased her mother! But how would Stuart's family react?

"What about your family, Stuart? What would they think of you taking to wife the daughter of a convict?" As the words came, she realized that she was talking as if she was seriously considering his proposal. Was she?

"I am the only child left in my family. I had a sister, who drowned in a pond on the estate when she was six. My mother and father, especially Mother, often talked wistfully of having another daughter, but she could never have any more children. And *you* are not a convict, Hope. You are a free woman. Once my mother met you, she would love you, I know she would. And although they may be gentry, my parents have few of the usual snobbish prejudices. In fact, my father heartily disapproves of sending convicts to New South Wales. He believes it to be a barbaric practice."

Hope shook her head. "Being against the practice, and having the daughter of a convict in his own household, are two different things."

"You're wrong, Hope. They will welcome you gladly."

Before she could divine his intention, he was on his knees before her. He took her right hand in both of his. "Marry me, dear one. I will make you happy; I shall devote my life to making you happy!"

"Stuart, I don't...I don't know if I love you enough."

"Perhaps not now. But you could if you let yourself. And I have enough love for both of us."

He drew her into the circle of his arms and kissed her, for the first time. His hands on her shoulders were gentle, his lips soft and warm; and despite herself, Hope felt a stir of response. Perhaps she did love him. Or if not, she could come to love him in time. She could not deny to herself that she had long yearned for devotion such as he offered. She had never received it from Cotty, and from all indications, never would....

She forced thoughts of Cotty Starke from her mind. By thinking of him at a moment like this, she felt that she was somehow betraying Stuart.

He took his mouth from hers, and said passionately, "Just think about it, my dearest. I know this is sudden. But promise to consider it seriously. That is all I ask.''

Hope heard herself saying, ''I promise, Stuart. I will think about it.''

# CHAPTER TWENTY-ONE

CHRISTMAS DAY, business was always slow at the Crown, since most of the customers who frequented the place had families and therefore preferred to spend the day at home. Cotty, realizing this, decided to close the tavern to the public and have a Christmas dinner with Hope and Charity and the employees. He had even given the sisters permission to invite their suitors.

Stuart Williams showed up promptly at four, the agreed-upon time, carrying a small wrapped package. He bowed to Cotty, who had opened the door for him. "I must extend my gratitude for your kind invitation, sir. With no one near and dear by one's side, Yuletide can be most melancholy."

"It was Hope's invitation, not mine," Cotty said in a dry voice. "But you are most welcome, Master Williams. Do please come in. Hope and Charity are still upstairs dressing."

He led Stuart to the center of the barroom where a large table covered with a white linen cloth was set with good china and silverware. The rich smell of roast goose and pastries came from the serving pantry, and Stuart inhaled appreciatively. "It smells wonderful!"

In that moment Hope came down the stairs, dressed in a red silk dress. Her face broke into a smile at the sight of the two men. "Welcome, Stuart!

We did the best we could, but we cannot provide snow, and it is too warm for a Yule log.''

"This will be more than sufficient, my dear.'' Stuart took her hand and bowed over it, then handed her the small package. "Happy Christmas, Hope.''

Blushing, Hope said, "Why, thank you! You didn't have to..." She broke off, her glance going to Cotty. "May I open it now?''

"Why not?'' Cotty said casually, feeling a stab of jealousy at the happy look on her face.

Hope quickly unwrapped the package and opened the small box it contained. Inside was a small heart-shaped locket and chain. There was a brief note enclosed that read, "My heart, Stuart.'' She hastily closed the box and smiled at Stuart. "Thank you, Stuart. It's lovely.''

"Aren't you going to show it to us, Hope?'' Cotty asked.

Cotty had given both sisters identical fringed shawls for Christmas; nice enough gifts, but nothing to compare to the locket. For a moment she was sorely tempted to flaunt it before him, but some instinct told her it would not be wise. She was saved a reply by the parade of their employees coming in from the serving pantry, carrying the food. John was carrying a golden-roasted goose on a large platter. The two bartenders and the barmaids bore trays of side dishes. None of their employees had any family in Sydney and Hope knew that they really appreciated this Christmas dinner. For a short time, at least, they would all be one happy family.

Cotty began introducing them one by one to Stuart, watching closely to gauge how the man reacted to having to eat and socialize with not only the employees, but an aborigine as well. Insofar as Cotty could tell, Stuart displayed no snobbery. If he felt any reluctance, he hid it well, shaking hands with everyone and greeting them pleasantly enough.

Hope was also watching covertly, with the same thought in mind. She was pleased and proud of Stuart when he began chatting with one or the other, as Cotty distributed drinks around the table.

"Take your seats, everyone!" Cotty glanced at Hope. "I see that Charity is tardy as usual."

"I'll fetch her." Hope turned and hurried upstairs.

Cotty took his place at the head of the table. He picked up the tankard of rum. "Shall we drink to Christmas in New South Wales?"

Everyone around the table drank to the toast, except for John, who never touched spirits. As he had told Cotty on several occasions, he was disgusted by the many aborigines he had seen drunk and stumbling around the streets of Sydney.

Setting his tankard down, Stuart said, "I drank to your toast, sir, but I am not happy about it. Oh, how I long for England, and home, this night!"

"Then I gather you are not delighted to be in Sydney, Master Williams?"

"Indeed not, and at this time of the year, even less than usual."

"Of course, to most of us here, this is about the only home we have ever known," Cotty said musingly. "But I can readily see how a newcomer to our shores would feel homesickness. Do you have plans for returning soon to England?"

Stuart nodded. "I do indeed, sir."

His gaze went past Cotty, and Cotty faced around to see Hope coming down the stairs with her sister. A disturbing question crossed his mind. Did Williams's return to England depend on Hope? More to the point, did he intend to take her with him?

The men got to their feet as the sisters approached. When they were seated, Cotty picked up a carving knife. ''As host, I suppose the carving duties fall to me. Carving is not one of my better skills, but I shall endeavor to do my best.''

After he had served everyone and they began to eat, Cotty glanced at Charity, who was seated on his immediate right. She was merely picking at her food, and she looked desperately unhappy.

He could not resist a jibe. ''And where is your swain, Charity? Didn't you invite Charles Bonney?''

''Yes,'' she said petulantly.

''Then why isn't he here?'' He glanced pointedly around the table. ''He appears to be the only invited guest missing.''

She looked up, eyes flashing, then shot a contemptuous glance down the table. ''Charles said he would come if he could, but he also said that he might be busy. Charles is an important man at Government House. He is not a tavern employee.''

Cotty suppressed his irritation and kept his voice low. ''These people, Charity, are our friends, even if they are tavern employees. Besides, Stuart Williams also works at Government House.''

His glance went to the other end of the table, where Stuart and Hope sat together. Stuart had his face close to Hope's, whispering in her ear. Cotty tore his gaze away.

"Stuart is just an aide," Charity said loftily. "Charles is indispensable to the governor. He says the governor would be lost without him."

"He says that, does he? Master Bonney seems to have a rather high opinion of himself."

Charity tossed her head. "He is only telling the truth!"

"At least you seem to think so," Cotty muttered, and dropped the subject.


By eight o'clock all the guests had gone home. The girls were upstairs in their rooms, John had retired, and Cotty sat alone in the taproom having a nightcap. Occasionally, he could hear the heavy footsteps of the guard patrolling outside.

For the first time in his life, Cotty was feeling sorry for himself. During his early days in Sydney, he had never realized that he missed having a family; but when Faith and the girls came along, they had filled an emptiness he had not known was there. Now Faith was gone, and it seemed that Hope and Charity would soon be leaving to start families of their own. Then he would be alone again. It might have been better, he reflected, if he had never known them!

He shook his head in disgust at himself. Why should he feel self-pity? He had everything he had ever wanted. More than he had ever thought possible. As for Hope and Charity, he was not sorry for having known them; they had brought much happiness into his life. They were people, not possessions, and had a right to a life of their own. Still, he knew he would miss them terribly, especially Hope....

With another shake of his head, he got to his feet and climbed the stairs. At the door to his room, he paused with his hand on the knob, head cocked to one side, listening.

Some unusual sound broke the silence of the hallway, the sound of muffled weeping. Was Charity crying because Charles Bonney had not put in an appearance tonight?

Quietly, he moved along the hall to her room, and bent his head to the door. The sound did not appear to be coming from her room. Could it be Hope? What could cause her to weep? Hope rarely wept.

He moved closer to her door. Yes, the sound of crying was definitely coming from within the room. After a moment's hesitation he knocked softly.

A silence fell, and then Hope said in a choked voice, "Who is it?"

"It's Cotty, Hope. Come to the door."

"No! Go away!"

"No, Hope. Open the door," he said firmly. "I can stand out here all night if need be."

After a few moments he heard soft footsteps, and then the door opened. Hope's tearstained face was framed in the crack.

"Why are you crying, Hope? I could hear you out in the hall."

"It doesn't concern you. Just go away."

"I'm not going away until you tell me what's wrong. Anything that concerns you concerns me. I can't remember when I've seen you cry."

"All right then, come in if you must."

She stepped back, opening the door, allowing Cotty to enter. Except for her shoes, she still wore the clothes she had been wearing at supper. Her eyes were swollen and red; even as he watched, a single hiccupping sob shook her.

Cotty closed the door softly, not wishing to waken Charity; he was certain that Hope did not want her sister to know about whatever ailed her.

Cotty took Hope's hand, led her to the bed and sat her down. He pulled up a straight-back chair, took her hand again and said gently, "Now tell me about it, Hope."

She gazed off for a moment, then spoke, looking down at their hands. "Stuart has asked me to marry him and return with him to England."

Cotty's heart sank, but he kept his voice light. "And that's something to weep about?"

Her head came up. "I don't love him, Cotty! He's a good man; I feel great affection for him, but I don't love him."

A wave of fierce relief swept over Cotty, leaving him almost giddy; but he heard himself say calmly, "Perhaps you don't know what love really is, my dear."

The words came out of his mouth seemingly without volition. What on earth was the matter with him? He had never felt so emotionally confused. He did not want her to go, and yet he seemed to be arguing in favor of it.

As these thoughts sped through his mind, Hope said something that he did not catch. He tried to pull himself together. "What did you say?"

She raised her hand to wipe away her tears. "I said, yes, I *do* know what love really is."

He stared at her in shock. Was there some other man that he did not know about? Had she been seeing someone else without his knowledge? "But how can you?"

Hope slowly raised her eyes to his. Cotty felt his chest constrict. Even with her eyes red and swollen from weeping, she was lovely, and he wanted her. He always had. Why had he not realized this before? Anxiously, he waited for her reply.

She spoke in a very soft voice. "I know what love really is, Cotty, because I love *you.* I've loved you ever since I can remember."

He could not take his eyes from her face. The truth of her statement was there, in her eyes; and yet he felt compelled to protest, "You don't know what you're saying!"

Gazing into his eyes, her lips moved in a small, rather sad smile. "Oh, but I do know what I'm saying," she said softly.

And without his really knowing how it happened, he was on the bed, and she was cradled in his arms, her head on his shoulder. "I love you, too, Hope. I suppose I have for a long time, without realizing it."

She raised a radiant face, and he felt that he had never seen anything so beautiful. "Oh, how I have ached to hear those words from you!"

He kissed her. Her lips tasted of the salt of her tears. Her arms went around him, urging him closer, and he could feel the supple firmness of her body yielding to him. He could take her now; there was no doubt of that in his mind. And he did want her; he had long wanted to make her his. How stupid he had been not to have realized that!

But it would not be right. This was Hope, a woman who had lived under his roof for years, a woman he had cherished and loved without knowing it. She was not a woman to make free and easy with. Yet the feel and the taste of her lips and the suppleness of her body fired his senses and aroused a passion so powerful that he was trembling on the verge of sweeping aside all reservations.

Then she took her mouth away to say, "All my dreams are coming true, darling! I am happy beyond belief. Now we can be married! We shall be man and wife, and I will bear you children...."

"No!" he said violently. He tore himself out of her embrace and jumped up.

"I don't understand..." She stared up at him dazedly. "You just said that you love me."

"And I do, Hope, I do!" He swung around, forced to look away from the fading radiance of her face. "But I will never marry."

"I don't understand," she said in bafflement. "Why not? All men get married sooner or later."

"Not all men. Certainly not me."

"You must have a reason."

"I have a reason, a very good reason," he said grimly. He began to pace back and forth, not looking at her now.

Hope leaned forward. "Tell me! I have a right to know."

Finally, he faced her. With a sigh, he said, "Yes, I suppose you do."

He took the straight-back chair, moving it back from the bed a little way. "My mother was gay, Hope," he said bluntly.

"Gay?" She looked blank.

"A woman of the streets, a lady of the night. A whore!" He said it brutally.

"Ah, I'm sorry, Cotty. That must have been terrible for you." She reached out a hand to him, then withdrew it as he flinched away. "But I thought you said you came to New South Wales with your father?"

"I did, and that is the truth." And then he began to tell her the story, the first time he had ever told anyone.

"My mother wasn't always a whore. Certainly, she wasn't when she married my father. He was a carpenter, and a good one, I understand, much in demand. He earned a decent living. He was a good provider. Then I was born. Some of what I will tell you came from my father. Apparently, she didn't want children. She was such an unnatural mother she didn't even *like* children. So, when I was three years old, she left, just walked away one day when my father was at work."

Hope was deeply moved. "Then you didn't even know your mother. You probably can't even remember what she looked like."

"Oh, I saw her when I was older. I think I was about six or seven." His face was set and hard, his eyes like flint. "After she left us, my father began to drink heavily, but not so much that he neglected me. He continued to work enough to keep us sheltered, fed and clothed, but the life had gone out of him. Then one evening..." He paused to take a deep breath. Hope was sure that he no longer even saw her; he was deep into the past.

"We were out for a stroll, my father and I. For some reason, which is not clear in my mind, we wandered off the beaten path and wound up walking past Christ Church's Itchy Park, so-called because that was where many of the drabs slept on summer nights, to save the price of a bed.

"As we passed along, a woman's voice spoke from the shadows, 'How about a poke, luv? Only fourpence.' My father drew me close against him, and the woman laughed coarsely. 'Don't mind the lad, luv. He can watch for free. Let him learn.' Then the woman stepped out of the shadows into the light, and my father gasped. At first I thought it was because of the way the drab looked. Her clothes were soiled and tattered, her hair a bird's nest, and her face was ravaged and bloated, probably from some disease."

Cotty paused for a moment, still lost in the past, then continued in a bitter voice. "Then she moved even closer, looking right into my father's face. She began to laugh. 'Well now, it's Henry! My dearly beloved spouse! And that's the brat I bore you, I'd hazard.' She threw back her head, laughing even harder, and I could see the blackened stumps of her teeth. Up close, she reeked of gin.

"So far, my father hadn't said a word, but I could see that his face was white with shock. Now, holding me tight against him, he started to move around her, but she put a handlike claw on his arm. 'We can still have a poke, dearie. Remember, you used to enjoy it more than a little. Just one for old times' sake, luv.' Her voice was wheedling. 'I'll do it for just enough for a tot of gin.'

"Most men, I'm sure, would have knocked her down. But my father was not a violent man. He plucked her hand from his sleeve, like he would a piece of offal. And then he was hurrying me up the street. Behind us came her cackle of laughter. 'Next time, come without the brat, Henry. Mayhap you won't be so loath all alone?' "

A shudder shook Cotty, and he blinked, looking at Hope for the first time since he had begun his explanation. In a dull voice he said, "After that, my father started drinking heavily. Soon, no one would hire him. We lost our lodgings and had to sleep wherever we could. He began to steal, for money for food and gin. Then he was caught, and we were transported."

"Darling, how horrible for you! Having to live with that memory all your life," she said, her voice soft with compassion.

"For a long time I had nightmares about that meeting with my mother. And hardly a day passes that I don't think about it still."

"I can well understand how something like that would haunt you. But Cotty, all women aren't like that. There are bad men in the world, too, but that doesn't mean that I think all men are bad."

Cotty thought of the married women he had seduced, but he remained silent.

"And because of what your mother was, is certainly no reason for you to forswear marriage."

He gestured sharply. "It's enough reason for me."

"But you're not being logical!" she cried.

"Perhaps not, but it's the way I feel."

"Surely you don't think I am like that?"

He squirmed uncomfortably. "I . . . No, not now you're not, Hope, but how do I know what will happen in the future?"

"A few minutes ago you said you loved me."

"I do, Hope. At least I think I do."

"Also, a bit ago, when I told you about Stuart's proposal, you said that I may not know what love is." Her voice hardened. "It seems to me that applies to you as well. If you truly loved me, you would marry me.''

"I like my life the way it is. I have no intention of complicating it by getting married.''

"What about me?" she said angrily.

"What about you? Your life here is fine. Why not let it continue as it has been?''

"And I suppose you would not expect me to share your bed?''

"I would like that very much, but I would never demand it of you. And if you are concerned about other women, you need have no fear.''

She was shaking her head, fighting back fresh tears. "Can't you see, Cotty? If I did that, without being your wife, I would be little better than your mother, or other such women here in Sydney.''

"That's not true. It is common here for men to take mistresses.''

"I will not be your mistress, Cotty Starke!''

"If you love me, as you say you do . . .''

"I love you too much to degrade myself in such a manner. And if I consented, you would lose all respect for me.''

"That is simply not true. I swear that I would never . . .''

"You say that now, but in time you would come to despise me. How many times have I seen that happen with the mistresses of other men? If we are to know love together, you must marry me.''

"Then it seems we've said all there is to say." He started to turn away.

"Then you leave me no choice. I shall marry Stuart and return to England with him!''

He stopped in midstride, going rigid, and her heart leaped with hope. Then he plunged on, striding through the door and slamming it shut behind him.

Hope fell across the bed, letting the tears come once more.

"I HAVE DECIDED," Hope told Stuart Williams when he came to call three days later. "If you will still have me, I will marry you."

He looked stunned for an instant. Then his face lit with a smile, and he whooped with delight. "Will I have you! Oh, my darling Hope, you have just made me the happiest man in the world!"

He seized her in his arms and danced her around the empty barroom. When he finally stopped to catch his breath, he held her away from him, beaming. "I shall tell Governor Bligh this very day that I am leaving his service. Since matters are tense at the moment, he may ask that I stay for a few weeks. But I promise you that we shall be married within a month. We shall be married the day we set sail for England, and home. I shall make you happy, dearest Hope. You have my solemn promise on that!"

# CHAPTER TWENTY-TWO

WHEN CHARITY LEARNED that Hope had agreed to marry Stuart Williams, it was all she could do to contain her jealousy and frustration. Charles had yet to openly propose, although Charity was certain that he would when the opportunity arose.

The opportunity came at Marston's flash house several days after she learned of Hope's pending marriage. Although Charles plied her with wine, she drank relatively little, determined to keep a clear head.

Liverpool Lilly was no longer performing at Marston's. Her replacement was older, coarser, her songs were bawdier, and she lacked Liverpool Lilly's special appeal.

Even Charles, Charity noted, appeared disappointed; but if so, his disappointment did nothing to dampen his ardor. He did not even wait until the end of the woman's performance before drawing the curtains closed and leading Charity to the settee.

They had established a routine for their lovemaking. Bonney no longer pushed her down onto her back and shoved her skirts up. He sat back on the settee and watched her undress; he liked to watch her remove her garments one at a time.

Charity had learned to draw it out, taking her time, turning her back to him, before turning around to reveal a little more of herself each time. Charles sat without moving, his burning gaze intent upon her. By the time she was down to the last garment, he was breathing hard, his eyes glazed over with lust.

When she was undressed, Charity stretched out on the settee, and Charles almost tore his own clothing off in his haste to join her. As he lay beside her on the settee, his hot mouth seeking hers, Charity turned her face slightly aside. She caressed his cheek and murmured, "Charles, did you know that Hope is to be wed?"

"What?" he said in a thick voice.

"My sister, she is marrying Stuart Williams."

He grunted. "That milksop! Why in hell's name did she agree to marry him?"

"Why, I suppose they are in love," she said artlessly. "Just like we are. You *do* love me, don't you, Charles?"

"Certainly, my dear Charity. Would I be with you like this if I didn't?"

"And we are going to be married?"

He raised his head to stare down at her, and for just a moment, something dark and dangerous moved in his eyes. Then he grinned, a mere baring of his teeth. "But of course," he said smoothly.

He bent to her mouth again, but she still held him off. "But when, Charles? Can't we set a date?"

"Soon, Charity, very soon."

"I have your promise?"

"You have my promise," he muttered against her throat.

Charity relaxed then, content, and let him take her.

WHEN THEY EMERGED from the flash house an hour later, Charity held onto Bonney's arm, laughing, chatting gaily. She failed to notice John Myers standing in the shadows, across the street.

John, who rarely invaded the Rocks at night, was on his way to deliver a message from Cotty to the man who was left in charge of the Blackstock Inn when Cotty was not on the premises.

In passing, John glanced across the street just in time to see Charity and Bonney come out of the flash house. He paused, shrinking into the shadows as they continued up the street.

John recognized Bonney as the man who had been squiring Mistress Charity of late. He had no liking for the man, since Bonney did not bother to hide the fact that he considered John beneath him. Once, Bonney had spoken roughly to him when John happened to be in his path, asking him why he did not know enough to give way to a white man.

Lowering his gaze to hide a blaze of anger, John had stepped aside.

After that day, he had made it a point to stay out of Bonney's way.

Now here Bonney was taking Charity to a flash house! Cotty and Mistress Hope, if they knew, would be furious. John looked upon Charity as a spoiled, petulant child, and he certainly did not feel as protective toward her as he did toward Hope. Still, was it not his duty to report this to Cotty? Aware of how accustomed Charity was to having her own way, he well knew that if he told Cotty and Hope, a bitter quarrel would ensue, which could last for days, disrupting the household. And in the end, Charity would do as she pleased anyway.

John was already greatly disturbed by the announcement of Hope's betrothal to Stuart Williams. He had known, of course, that nothing could ever come of his love for Mistress Hope; but the news that she was marrying, and leaving them forever to go to England with her husband, had come as a great shock. Since he had learned of it, John had been seriously considering leaving Sydney for good, and returning to the bush and his tribal brothers.

With a heavy sigh, he continued on his way to perform the errand for Cotty.

SINCE HIS BITTER SCENE with Hope, Cotty had felt depressed and out of sorts; and he, too, had been devastated when he learned of her plans to wed Stuart Williams.

In an attempt to alleviate his anguish, he plunged into an affair with another married woman, but it did little to ease his suffering. After each rendezvous he had felt soiled, dissatisfied and disgusted with himself. He had even turned to drink, falling into bed at night in a stupor, but that had not helped, either; it only resulted in his feeling sullen and remorseful the next morning. He had always despised anyone who used drink to forget his problems; and on this morning as he walked down the streets of the Rocks, he resolved to stop the drinking. His head throbbed, his belly roiled, and he certainly was in no mood to talk to Hugh Marston; but Hugh was standing before his flash house as Cotty walked down the other side of the street.

Spotting Cotty, he hurried across to him. "Cotty, did you hear the news?"

Reluctantly, Cotty stopped. "What news is that?"

"Governor Bligh had Macarthur arrested this morning," Hugh said excitedly.

Cotty's interest quickened. "Again? What was the reason this time?"

"Well, as you probably already know, some time ago a convict escaped on Macarthur's ship, the *Parramatta*. Governor Bligh demanded a nine-hundred-pound bond because of this. Macarthur, in retaliation, refused to provision his ship, and this forced the sailors to come ashore or starve, and this is an illegal act. Bligh then demanded forfeiture of the bond. When Macarthur refused, Bligh ordered the ship seized, then summoned Macarthur to appear before him. Evidently relishing the chance to force a showdown, Macarthur did not obey the summons. The governor had him arrested, charging him with sedition."

"Do you think this will resolve the conflict, Hugh? If Macarthur is found guilty and sent to prison, that should break the back of the rebellion."

Hugh snorted. "My dear young friend, do you think for a minute that Macarthur will be convicted?"

"Well, he did perform illegal acts."

"Do you know who will be sitting in judgment on him? Bligh has already appointed a panel of corps officers to try him. Do you think there is any way *they* will find Macarthur guilty?"

"It would seem, then, that the governor erred in selecting corps officers. Why not civilians, since Macarthur is no longer with the military?"

"I suppose, in his usual arrogance, Bligh calculated that even corps officers would not dare go against his wishes openly. And of course a guilty verdict handed down by a panel of corps officers would look much better back in England than a verdict by a group of civilians.''

Privately, Cotty was inclined to agree, but he said, ''Remember, Macarthur is no longer with the corps. He resigned some time ago.''

''I know, but that matters little. Major Johnston and Macarthur are still the best of friends, and Macarthur tells the major what to do. Major Johnston is presently the senior military officer in Sydney, and the officers sitting in judgment will most certainly respect the wishes of their commanding officer. Mark my words, the trial will be a farce.''

''Then what do you think will happen?''

''It probably depends on what action the governor takes next. If he acts too rashly, I would not be at all surprised to see the corps march on Government House.''

''You think they would go that far?''

''In my opinion, yes, they would.''

''If they do, that will mean that Macarthur will likely emerge as the most powerful man in Sydney.''

''At least for a time, until word gets back to London. His Majesty's government will not likely sanction such an action, but it would take many months, mayhap as much as two years, for word to reach England and for any reaction to take effect here. Meanwhile, it will be chaos. And who do you think will suffer the most?''

''I should think everyone would suffer, in such a state of uncertainty.''

''But if Macarthur, or somebody under his thumb, takes over, things will be rough for the tavern owners, especially those who defied him.''

"Of which I am one," Cotty said glumly.

"Exactly. You will find spirits hard to obtain, and what you *can* buy, you will pay dearly for. If my judgment of the rum monopolists is correct, they will make all of us suffer, some more than others."

"At least I don't see you gloating, Hugh. I want you to know that I appreciate that."

"Why should I gloat at your misfortune, if that should come about? You are my friend." He placed a hand on Cotty's shoulder. "Besides, as I said, it likely will not be an easy time for any of us. But then, let's wait and see what actually happens. Will you attend the trial with me, Cotty? It should provide us with much amusement."

Cotty shook his head. "I think not, Hugh. I've refused to take sides thus far. If I attend, no matter who wins, the loser will think I came to gloat."

"As you wish." Hugh shrugged. "Methinks there will be such a crowd that the presence of any one person will go unnoticed. As for me..." He grinned hugely. "I wouldn't miss it. It should be more amusing than my flash-house buffoon!"

DESPITE COTTY'S RESOLUTION, curiosity finally drew him to the trial. It was conceivable that his fate, as well as that of a great many others, hung on the outcome. Besides, anything would be better than having to listen to Hope and Charity chattering on about their wedding preparations, loftily ignoring him.

But the trial was already over when he finally decided to attend. People milled around the building, some cheering, others shouting angrily. As Cotty approached the seething crowd, several men came through the open doors with John Macarthur hoisted on their shoulders. Grinning broadly, he clasped his hands together over his head as a large cheer went up from the crowd. There were also a number of jeers.

Clearly, Macarthur had been found innocent of the charges, and opinion seemed to be equally divided for and against the verdict.

A few feet away from where Cotty stood, Macarthur was set on his feet. As he passed Cotty, the man gave him a look of pure malice, but strode past without speaking. A portion of the crowd fell in behind him. A number of corps officers surrounded Macarthur, as though guarding him, and Major Johnston walked beside him.

A voice said in Cotty's ear, "So you couldn't keep away, after all."

Cotty turned to see Hugh Marston. He grinned sourly. "You're right, I couldn't."

"That was a right mean look Master Macarthur gave you, my friend."

"Clearly, the trial is over, and Macarthur escaped unscathed."

"It's all over. For now, at any rate. The whole affair was a complete farce, as I predicted. Macarthur claimed that the magistrate was not competent to sit in judgment on him, and the corps officers on the panel concurred. The governor raged at them, and finally declared that they were no court, so Macarthur was allowed to go free. Actually, it was no trial at all."

Cotty scrubbed his knuckles across his mouth. "I suppose this is not the last of it?"

"You can place a wager on that. Governor Bligh worked himself up into a frothing rage, and he is certainly not finished with Macarthur."

"What do you suppose his next move will be?"

Hugh spread his hands. "Who can foretell? But whatever he decides to do, it will not be long in coming. Of that, you can be sure."

Cotty gazed after the departing Macarthur and his entourage. "He certainly has enough corps officers around him. Are those the ones Governor Bligh selected to sit in judgment?"

Hugh nodded. "Yes."

"They appear to be his personal platoon of guards."

"Oh, they are. Inside, I heard Major Johnston give the order. From now on members of the corps will stand guard over Master Macarthur. Well . . ." Hugh stretched, grinning. "After all the excitement, I could stand a tot or two of rum. Would you care to join me, my friend?"

"An excellent suggestion." They began walking toward the Rocks. "But are you sure it's safe to be seen drinking with me, Hugh?"

"I will risk it. Perhaps Master Macarthur will be magnanimous in victory."

Cotty grunted. "From what I know of the man, I'm inclined to doubt that very much."

JOHN WENT to the dreaming tree in the early afternoon of the day following Macarthur's farcical trial. Since seeing Bonney and Charity coming out of the flash house, he had gone to the tree twice, but his dreams had revealed little of import. He was hoping to dream something of either Hope or Charity. The only thing that had come to him was a glimpse of Hope in a wedding gown, but there had been nothing beyond that. He knew that she had already purchased a wedding dress; undoubtedly she had tried it on a few times.

As John passed through the town, he noticed there were more men than usual on the streets. They appeared agitated as they gathered in little knots, talking heatedly and gesticulating. He paid them little heed; he was long accustomed to the strange antics of the clay faces.

At the dreaming tree, he went through his usual ritual, then squatted on his haunches. Eyes closed, he endeavored to make his mind a blank, rocking back and forth on his heels.

After an interminable time, he found himself hovering over a building, a structure he recognized from the steeple on top as one of the places where the clay faces worshiped their God. He moved inside and he saw Hope standing at the altar in her wedding dress and veil. A man stood by her side.

Try as he would, John could not see the man's face. Another man in a black suit was standing before them, intoning the words of the wedding ceremony. As the last words were spoken—words that John could not quite make out—the man beside Hope turned, and she lifted her veil, turning a radiant face up to him. . . .

The dream was gone, and John was jarred awake. He groaned in frustration. Why had he awakened before he could see the face of Hope's husband? He was plunged into gloom. But why was the identity of the man important?

John once again courted the dreaming, although usually after his concentration had been broken it was futile to try again. However, this time proved an exception, and shortly he was in a dream.

It was very confusing. Many men, most of them in the red coats of the white soldiers, moved in a mass toward an unknown destination. Cannons were drawn up, aiming at something John could not see. A few random shots were fired.

Then the dream changed with bewildering rapidity. John saw Charity struggling in the grasp of a faceless man. Then John saw that she was being pulled forcibly, and that the man was . . . yes, it was Charles Bonney!

Now another woman entered the dream—Hope! She was trying to get Bonney to free her sister. Bonney pulled a pistol and clubbed Charity with it. He threw Charity over his shoulder and forced Hope before him with the pistol in her back.

The next bit of the dream was unclear, a confusion of milling men and movement. Then, with jarring suddenness, Bonney and the sisters were in a boat, rowing across an expanse of water toward a ship. There was so much water in every direction that John felt dizzy; he felt as if he were going under, water above and under and all around him. He was drowning!

Then the dream was gone, and John jumped up with a shout of fright. He was weak and trembling, drenched in perspiration.

For a few moments he leaned against the trunk of the blue gum. His heart was pounding madly, and he could scarcely force air into his lungs.

Slowly, the import of the dreaming sank in, and he was filled with a sense of urgency. Both Hope and Charity were in grave danger!

He hurriedly washed off the clay, got dressed and started toward town at a run, realizing that he had spent much more time than usual under the tree. It was now late afternoon, and as he entered the outskirts of Sydney, he noticed that the streets were almost eerily empty.

When he burst into the Crown, he was surprised to see that there were no customers.

"John, where have you been!" Hope, who was at the bar, cried out when she saw him. "I've been frantic with worry! Both Cotty and Charity are gone!"

Breathing hard from his run, John gasped out, "Where is Mistress Charity?"

"That's just it. I don't really know. That's the reason I'm so worried. Something is happening at Government House, some kind of trouble. It's been going on all day. When Cotty heard, he left, telling us not to open for business until he came back. He hasn't returned."

"But Mistress Charity?"

"You know how she is, John. About thirty minutes ago she was standing in the doorway, looking out, when some men came rushing past. She called out to them, and one man stopped long enough to tell her that something was afoot at Government House. I got to the door just as she started off in that direction. I told her not to leave, but she shouted back that she was going to Charles Bonney, to warn him. I didn't know what to do. Foolish girl! I hope she comes to no harm."

"Mistress Hope, I have been for most of the day at the dreaming tree."

She stared at him, her breath quickening. "More dreams? Of what is to happen?"

He nodded.

"Something dire?"

"I fear so."

"Then tell me!"

As quickly as possible, John told her of the dreaming.

Hope put her hand to her cheek, her eyes wide. "Then Charity *is* in danger!"

"Yes," he said gravely.

"In the dream you saw soldiers, other men and guns, and Charles Bonney struggling with Charity?"

He simply nodded.

"I must go to her at once. I must warn her, get her away from Bonney."

"I shall come with you."

She hesitated, then shook her head. "I think it better that you don't, John. If tempers are aroused and you are seen with me, you might come to harm. No, I must go alone."

"But I also saw you being threatened, Mistress Hope. It will not be safe for you," he said in alarm.

"I'll be all right, John. If I can find Charity, I'll get her away, if I have to drag her. Your dreamings . . . I don't doubt their accuracy, John. But they must only forecast what *can* happen, not what actually will. If Cotty had heeded your warning about those ruffians coming here, and had mounted guards, it would not have happened. Now that I have been warned, I shall be careful."

"Mistress Hope..." John could not contain his agitation. "I think this would be very foolish of you."

"Perhaps. But I have little choice." She snatched up a shawl from behind the bar and wrapped it around her. "As foolish as Charity is, she *is* my sister, and I must do what I can. You see if you can find Cotty, and tell him everything. Tell him I went to Government House in search of Charity."

She was already out the door. John stared after her, feeling despair well up in him. For a moment he thought of following her, but he knew that she was right; if the clay faces were in a bad temper, they would welcome an excuse to vent their anger on a black man in their midst.

He hastened from the tavern in search of Cotty.

# CHAPTER TWENTY-THREE

CHARITY DID NOT UNDERSTAND what was happening around her as she hurried toward Government House. She knew only that a great many other people were moving in the same direction.

Someone in the crowd shouted an obscenity at Governor Bligh, and Charity frowned, trying to remember something she had once heard. She normally paid scant heed to current events, but since Charles worked for Bligh, she had developed a slight interest in what was going on at Government House. Finally she remembered there was a quarrel brewing between Governor Bligh and the NSW Corps. Something to do with rum. Could that be the cause of this growing crowd? she wondered. Surely not. There was an ominous air about the men she saw striding down the street. They were grim of face, and many were drunk and cursing. Some were carrying muskets and pistols. Whatever was behind all this, it could only mean danger for Charles. She must find and warn him!

The crowd thickened as she turned off High Street onto New Bridge Street, and she had to push her way through the throng. When she reached Government House, Charity was dismayed to see soldiers massed before the building, with bayonets fixed. She also noticed two cannons aimed at the building facade. A large crowd was gathered behind the soldiers, some jeering at them, while others shouted encouragement.

There was a scattering of other women among the civilians, and no one paid any notice to Charity as she began to force her way around the edge of the mob. She knew where Charles was quartered, for once on a Sunday afternoon, when the day had been wet and unpleasant so they could not go riding, Charles had escorted her to his rooms, where they had made love.

Reaching the front of the crowd, Charity made her way around to a side door, which she was relieved to find remained unlocked. As she slipped into the building, she could hear the shouts outside growing louder. A sense of urgency seized her. It was late now, not long before sunset, and she hoped that Charles was not dining with the governor and the other aides.

At the door she knocked softly. A voice called out, "Who is it?"

"It's me, Charles. Charity," she said in a low voice.

She heard a curse and heavy footsteps. The door was thrown open, and Charles snarled, "What in the devil's name are *you* doing here? 'Pon my honor, this is hardly the time to come calling!"

"I came to warn you. You could be in trouble, Charles. There is an angry mob outside, along with a large number of soldiers."

"You think me a fool and deaf as well? I know that." He stepped back, letting her in, then poked his head out the door to look both ways. He closed the door and turned to her. "Did anyone see you come in here?"

"Not that I noticed, Charles."

"Does anyone know you're here?"

"Only my sister." Charity's gaze was drawn to a chest of drawers against the wall. On it was a satchel, already half full, and beside it items of clothing and other personal objects were laid out ready to be packed. Her eyes widened, and she exclaimed, "You're packing, Charles! Why?"

"Why do you think? I'm getting out of here. That fool Bligh has made mistake after mistake with these military traitors. He should have dealt harshly with them. Now it's too damned late. They're going to force their way in here at any minute, and I want to be gone when they do. Bligh is finished, and so is everyone else in Government House. I warned him repeatedly that something like this might happen, but he kept saying that he knew what he was doing. Damn, why couldn't I have seen that he's too weak to be governor of this infernal colony?"

"But where will you go, Charles?"

"Back to England, where else? There is a British ship in the harbor. I shall commandeer it, demand that it sail at once." He bared his teeth in a savage smile. "The ship's master knows me as Bligh's chief aide. If I can get to his ship before he learns of Bligh's downfall, he'll up anchor and sail."

"You were just going to leave without me?" Charity asked in a wounded voice.

He stared at her blankly. "Why shouldn't I leave without you?"

"You promised to marry me!"

"Did I?" His smile was cruel, and he shrugged carelessly. "A man is likely to promise a wench anything in the grip of passion."

"You lied to me! Hope is right! You're nothing but a..." She swung her open hand toward his face.

He caught it easily, holding her arm in a brutal grip. "You dare to hit me?" he demanded. "No one dares that, man *or* woman." He stared at her with hard eyes. "Why in hell's name should I marry you? No man in his right senses marries a wench as empty-headed and as easy to bed as you."

She began to struggle, and his grip tightened painfully on her arm. Then he froze as a shot rang out outside. He looked at her in calculation, then slowly smiled. "But it might not be a bad idea that you should accompany me. A comely wench might be good protection against some hotblood, should I be seen and recognized."

Charity stared at him in disbelief. "You would use me as a shield?"

"I would, without the least hesitation."

"Then you are a despicable cad!"

She started to struggle again, but her strength was no match for his. Holding her easily with one hand, he dragged her over to the chest of drawers. Using his free hand, he stuffed the rest of his belongings into the satchel and closed it, leaving only a pistol. He rammed the pistol into the top of his breeches and picked up the bag.

"Now we go, my dear. If you scream when we get outside, I may just lay my pistol alongside your silly head. And remember, with all the noise and confusion, I doubt you would be heard."

He shoved her toward the door. "Open it!"

Crying now, Charity opened the door. Bonney doubled her arm up behind her back and propelled her ahead of him into the hallway. It was empty, shattering any hope she might have had of rescue.

At the side door he twisted her arm harder. "Now open the door, and remember, if you raise any fuss, I'll make you sorry!"

The pain was severe. "You're hurting me, Charles!" she whimpered.

"That's the idea; now open the door so that I can be quit of this place."

There was no one at the side of the house, again dashing Charity's hopes.

"Before we reach the corner of the house, we'll veer off to the right and make our way down Government Street, and head for the harbor," Bonney directed. "That way, we won't have to brace that motley mob in front."

At that moment, Hope came careening around the corner. She skidded to a stop, her eyes flaring wide. "Charity!"

"'Pon my honor, 'tis the other Blackstock wench," Bonney said in a jeering voice. "How fortunate can one man be?"

Hope advanced, eyes flashing. "You let my sister go, sir!"

"Oh, I think not."

"Be careful, Hope, he has a pistol!" Charity said in a choked voice.

"I have indeed," Bonney said, grinning. He let Charity go and plucked the pistol from his waistband. "And I will not hesitate to use it."

Charity cried, "I'm sorry, Hope. I should have listened to you and Cotty. Charles is every bit the blackguard you both claimed he was."

Ignoring her, Bonney dropped his satchel onto the ground and motioned with the pistol. "Come closer, sister."

Hesitantly, Hope approached closer, her heart pounding with fear.

"Now what am I going to do with the pair of you?" Bonney said musingly. "Ah, I know! This way will be even better."

In one quick motion he raised his arm and slammed Charity alongside the head with the pistol. She cried out and began to fall. Bonney caught her and slung her over his shoulder like a sack of grain.

"You've hurt her!" Hope exclaimed. "You may have killed her!"

"I doubt that very much," he said genially. "Anyone as empty of thought as your sister has a particularly hard head. She will be fine. You will both be fine if you do exactly what I tell you. Pick up my satchel and walk in front of me. If someone sees us and is curious, you will tell them that your sister has been taken suddenly ill, and we are hurrying her to the doctor. That should satisfy any curiosity. Do you understand all that?"

"Yes, but . . ."

"No buts, Mistress Blackstock!" With shocking suddenness, he rammed the pistol into her side. "It's true that I only have the one shot without reloading, but that one shot will kill you, wench. I am in a desperate situation here, and I will not be balked! Is that clearly understood?"

"Yes," Hope said hastily and she began to walk. Ahead, she could see the sun just setting across the cove, and behind her the voices of the mob rose in volume.

She trudged on, always aware of Bonney's pistol in her back. She fought the rise of despair. What was going to happen to her and Charity? Would Bonney let them live? She had seen enough of the ruthless side of him in the past few minutes to realize that he was fully capable of killing them both.

Where was Cotty? Would he come to their rescue? But how could he, since he had no inkling of what was happening?

WHEN COTTY HEARD the rumor that John Macarthur had been arrested once again on Governor Bligh's orders, he left the Crown, admonishing Hope and Charity to stay inside the tavern until his return, and to keep it closed to business. Then he went in search of Hugh Marston. Hugh, who appeared to always be privy to the latest news, seemed his best source of information.

Since it was early, Marston's flash house was closed. Repeated hammering on the door finally brought the scowling doorman. He opened the door and frowned out at Cotty. "We ain't open yet."

"I know that, damn it," Cotty said impatiently. "Is Hugh in? Tell him that Cotty Starke is here to see him."

"Wait here."

The door was slammed and bolted in his face. Cotty looked up and down the streets. The Rocks, which was normally a fairly quiet spot this early in the day, was alive with activity. Men were gathered on street corners, drinking from bottles and talking together excitedly. Clearly, the word of Macarthur's arrest had spread quickly.

He heard the door opening and turned. Hugh Marston was grinning at him from the doorway. "Well, I would hazard that you have heard the news!"

"All I heard is that Macarthur was arrested again."

"Oh, that's only the linchpin of the whole affair." Hugh opened the door wider. "Come in, my friend, and I shall bring you up to date."

Inside, Hugh walked toward the right, motioning for Cotty to follow. Cotty trailed him across the front of the building to an open door leading into Hugh's cluttered office. Once inside, Hugh closed the door, and both men took seats.

"Why on earth would Bligh have Macarthur arrested again, after yesterday's farce?" Cotty asked. "And on what grounds?"

"This morning, the governor sent two constables to arrest friend Macarthur, on the pretext that no trial was really held and that Macarthur jumped bail. To add fuel to the flames, our tactful governor had the judge advocate issue a memorial to the effect that the officers attempting to shield Macarthur have usurped the powers of the government, and that they encouraged rebellion and treason in the colony."

Cotty whistled softly. "My God, that must have raised a few hackles!"

Enjoying himself, Hugh said, "That, my young friend, is putting it mildly. He might as well have poked a stick into a hornet's nest."

"And that is where matters stand at the moment?"

"Damn, no! At Macarthur's instigation, and I have this on good authority, a petition has been drawn up and signed by both civilians and NSW officers and presented to Major Johnston. The petition says, and I quote: 'We implore you to place Governor Bligh under arrest, and to assume command of the colony.' ''

''And is the major going to act upon it?''

''Does honey draw bees?'' Hugh snorted. ''The major has been waiting for just such an opportunity. The word is that he has already named himself lieutenant governor of New South Wales, and has issued a warrant for Macarthur's release from jail.''

Cotty said in disbelief, ''But the colony already has a lieutenant governor, Lieutenant Colonel Peterson.''

''Ah, but . . .'' Hugh held up an admonishing finger. ''Colonel Peterson is well out of harm's way, being in Tasmania. By the time word reaches him, it will all be over.''

''Major Johnston plans to march on Government House then?''

Hugh nodded. ''Oh, yes. But it will take some time to gather troops, and I have the feeling that much rum will flow, among officers and soldiers alike, before the proper courage can be mustered. Even considering Bligh's unpopularity, arresting a duly appointed governor of the Crown is a drastic step.''

''I don't suppose the governor can do much in the way of resisting.''

''Not bloody likely, not with the military under the control of Johnston and his manipulator, Macarthur. Bligh has only a handful of constables at his command, and I'd hazard they have lit out for the bush by this time. Besides, if I have gauged the governor correctly, he is going blithely about his duties, certain in his arrogance that no one would *dare* do anything to him.''

"So it has come to pass, just as you said it would," Cotty said glumly. ''I cringe to think what will happen if Major Johnston and Macarthur take over the government.''

"Cheer up, my young friend." Hugh clapped him on the shoulder. ''The optimistic view would be that if that happens, the whole colony will be in such chaos for some time that no reprisals will be taken. With hope, in time, forces will be set in motion in England to set things aright again.''

"When that happens, I hope they will send a reasonable man to govern, one who will end this rum mess once and for all.''

"I share your hopes, Cotty. Now..." Hugh looked at the clock on the wall behind him. ''The day is waning. If my calculations are correct, the major and his troops will take action about sundown. They should be full of false courage by then. Speaking of which, how about a libation or two? And then shall we stroll over to Government House for the final act?''

"A libation would be nice, but won't we chance being late if we linger too long?''

Hugh gave a shrug. ''As I said, the usurpers will have to work up sufficient courage first. Besides, I sent a man over to keep watch. If matters are about to come to a head, he will alert us.''

BY THE TIME they set out for Government House, the streets were totally deserted, and the shutters on all the buildings were tightly closed. The sun was low in the sky.

Hugh laughed. "The curious and the vengeful are already gathered, no doubt, like vultures waiting for the kill, and the cowards are hiding in their abodes."

Before they had progressed very far, the sound of drum and fife could be heard, growing louder behind them. They turned to see troops approaching, marching in battle array, with colors flying and bayonets fixed.

Cotty and Hugh stepped out of the way. "You see, we are just in time, my friend," Hugh said softly. The band played louder, and Hugh grinned. "They are really doing it right! Recognize the tune? 'The British Grenadiers'!"

"And they aren't taking any chances," Cotty commented. "I'd guess at least two hundred soldiers."

"More likely three hundred."

"The three officers marching in front of the column . . . I recognize Major Johnston, of course. But who are the other two?"

"Captain Kemp and Lieutenant Lawson," Hugh replied.

It was a colorful sight—red coats bright in the setting sun, bayonets glittering, the men marching in cadence—and might have been stirring except for the circumstances.

Cotty and Hugh fell in at the end of the column. When the soldiers marched across the bridge and were within sight of Government House, a cheer, mixed with a few jeers, went up. Cotty noticed that some soldiers were already stationed there, and others manned cannon aimed at the building.

In a low voice he said, "It strikes me this is like using a hammer to smash a gnat. Certainly, this many soldiers aren't needed."

"Don't want to take any chances, I would surmise," Hugh said dryly. "Actually, I agree. It would have been much more humiliating if only a few men were here to take Bligh."

As the officers arranged the soldiers in ranks, with muskets aimed at Government House, a few civilians fired pistols into the air. Cotty and Hugh made their way through the crowd to a location from which they could see the entrance to Government House, which remained closed.

Now Major Johnston and the two officers accompanying him stationed themselves on both sides of the main entrance, and motioned a half dozen soldiers forward. One of the soldiers raised his musket and thumped the butt loudly against the door. After a few moments the door opened, and a woman stood framed there.

"Who is the woman, Hugh?"

"That's Bligh's recently widowed daughter, Mary Putland."

"I thought she looked familiar."

The woman waved her arms agitatedly, talking fast, but Cotty was too far away to hear what she was saying. The soldiers began to push past her, and she screamed piercingly. Then she turned and fled into the house, the soldiers on her heels. With the woman's scream, the crowd fell silent and seemed to be holding its collective breath.

"Maybe the governor has already made good his escape," Cotty said. "Since a crowd has evidently been gathering out here for hours, he must have realized that something was up.''

"It's not uncommon for citizens to gather outside Government House in protest of something or other. Bligh has always ignored them. I would wager that he's doing the same this time.''

They stopped talking, waiting in silence with the rest of the crowd for the next development. There was no sound from inside Government House. After about fifteen minutes, a soldier appeared in the doorway and conferred with Major Johnston for a moment, then the major entered the house.

Another few minutes passed. Finally Major Johnston reappeared, and two soldiers came out behind him, holding a red-faced, struggling Governor Bligh. A great roar went up from the crowd. Grinning widely, Major Johnston let the roar continue unabated for a bit, and then he raised his hands, motioning for quiet. Gradually, the crowd grew silent.

"Good people, it is all over. The tyrant, William Bligh, has been deposed and placed under arrest,'' the major said in ringing tones. "Following the will of the good people of Sydney, I will become lieutenant governor of New South Wales until such time as my position shall be officially confirmed by His Majesty's government. And John Macarthur shall be appointed by me to be secretary. And there shall be free rum for everybody on this glorious night!''

Another roar erupted from the crowd. As it subsided a little, Hugh said to Cotty, "Secretary! You know what that means, don't you, my young friend? In effect, Macarthur will be chief administrator. In other words, he will be running things, the power behind the throne.'' He sighed heavily. ''Bad tidings, indeed.'' Then he laughed shortly. ''Do you realize that today, January 26, 1808, is the twentieth anniversary of the founding of the colony?''

Cotty, his attention on the entrance to Government House, did not answer, and he noticed more soldiers coming out, herding several men at bayonet point. ''Apparently, they have also arrested several of the governor's aides.''

The crowd began to break up and drift away, and the soldiers were being mustered in preparation for marching off. Then Cotty saw Stuart Williams coming out of the building. He was alone, and it appeared that he was not under restraint. Cotty took Hugh's arm and urged him toward the entrance.

''Stuart!'' Cotty called, waving. ''Over here!''

Stuart saw him and came toward him. His expression was angry and troubled.

''I saw several of the governor's aides under arrest,'' Cotty said. ''How did you escape?''

''I had to use the convenience out back,'' Stuart replied, ''and had left the dinner table momentarily. By the time I came back, it was about all over. No one seemed to recognize me as an aide.'' He smiled wryly. ''Naturally, I didn't introduce myself.''

''What exactly happened in there?'' Hugh asked.

''Why didn't the governor slip away?'' Cotty questioned. ''He must have known that something was up that boded him no good.''

''Part of it I know firsthand, the rest I only just heard from one of the servants. We had all warned Governor Bligh that he was in danger, but he refused to listen. He said it was just an uproar over nothing and would die down. He said that no one would dare enter Government House uninvited, and calmly went on eating."

"You were at dinner?" Cotty said incredulously.

"Oh, yes. The governor said we should conduct ourselves as if nothing were happening."

"At least he has courage," Cotty observed.

"Courage? *Courage!*" Stuart said in utter disgust. He turned his head and spat. "I shall tell you about the governor's courage. When Mrs. Putland answered the door and screamed, the governor finally realized what was happening. He ran like a frightened rat! You know where the soldiers found him? Under the bed; he was hiding under his bed! I knew that the governor had his faults, but like you, I assumed he was a man of honor and courage. This is a day of shame, and I am shamed for it to be known that I was in his service."

Hugh laughed heartily. "Now that is a scene I would have loved to have observed. The great William Bligh, cowering under his bed!"

"I see very little humor in it, sir," Stuart said stiffly.

"I beg your pardon, Master Williams. I can easily see why you might feel that way."

"What happened to Charles Bonney?" Cotty asked. "He wasn't one of the aides arrested. Is he still inside?"

Stuart looked startled. "I really don't know. Now that I think back, he wasn't at the dinner table. But then, I am not too surprised. Charles has an uncanny instinct for survival," he said caustically.

Cotty heard his name being called, and he glanced around to see John Myers hurrying toward them.

Except for a few stragglers, everyone had left the area around Government House.

John skidded to a stop before him. "Cotty, I have been searching all over Sydney for you!"

Cotty experienced a twinge of alarm. "What is it, John? Has something happened?"

"Have you seen Mistresses Hope and Charity?"

"Of course not," Cotty said. "Why should I have seen them?"

"Mistress Charity heard of the trouble here and came to warn the man Bonney. Then I..." He glanced at the other two men. "I had been to the dreaming tree and saw Mistress Hope and Mistress Charity in danger from the man Bonney. When I told Mistress Hope, she hastened here, telling me to search for you."

"What is this nonsense about the dreaming tree?" Stuart asked sharply.

"Later, Stuart," Cotty said, motioning him quiet, his gaze never leaving John. "How long ago was this?"

"About an hour. I looked for you, and finally realized you must be here."

"Did you stop at the Crown on your way?"

John nodded. Anticipating Cotty's next question, he said, "And they were not there."

Cotty glanced around the deserted area. "Of course, there have been so many people here, I'm not surprised we didn't see them. But where are they *now*?"

Stuart demanded, "Hope is in danger? Hope is *here*?"

"It would seem so. We must look for her, and for Bonney."

"We must indeed."

"You know the premises, Stuart. You lead the way."

As they entered Government House, Cotty stayed John with a hand on his arm. "Stuart, you and Hugh go ahead and look for them. I want a quick word with John here." As the other two men hurried off, Cotty said, "Now tell me about your dreaming, John."

John quickly told him about what he had seen in the dreaming.

At the finish, Cotty scrubbed a hand across his mouth in thought. "You saw them in a boat, rowing to a ship?"

"That is what I saw."

"It has to be the harbor, of course. Bonney is trying to leave on one of the ships anchored in the bay, and he is holding Charity and Hope hostage to make good his escape." Anxiety gnawed at him. "Damn him to hell and gone! I knew that man was a blackguard through and through. Why didn't I heed my instincts? Not that it probably would have done much good as far as Charity is concerned..."

Stuart and Hugh came hurrying back. Stuart was pale with worry. "There is no sign of them, and it is apparent that Charles has packed in haste."

Cotty nodded. "From what John has told me, I didn't expect you to find them here."

Stuart glared, taking a threatening step toward John. "What does he know? What does he have to do with this?"

Cotty barred his way. "Gently, Stuart, gently. John is on our side, and without his help we may never find them. And don't ask me to explain. You wouldn't believe me, anyway."

Stuart looked baffled. "I can understand why Charles might have fled, but why Hope and Charity?"

"Our esteemed Master Bonney has taken them hostage to insure his escape."

"Then we must find them at once!"

"You are no more anxious than I, and I am fully intending to see that Master Bonney pays dearly for this outrage," Cotty said darkly.

"But where do we look?"

"Bonney has taken them on board one of the ships in the harbor. We can only pray that they haven't sailed as yet."

Stuart looked even more mystified. "How do you know that's where they are?"

"John just told me. No more explanations. Let's hurry."

Darkness had fallen as the group set off. Before they had gotten too far, Cotty pulled Hugh aside. "Hugh, this isn't your problem. You have a business to tend to."

"I'll tag along. You may need me. Besides..." Hugh grinned faintly. "You heard the major. Free rum tonight for all. No innkeeper will be doing any business this night."

As they hurried toward the harbor, they passed a number of bonfires, and saw many others blazing in the distance. Both men and women were dancing and singing around the fires, already well into their cups.

They reached the docks and paused, looking out at the harbor. Lights could be seen from at least two dozen ships bobbing at anchor.

"Now which ship did you see, John?" Cotty asked. "Which one was Bonney heading for?"

"I do not know, Cotty."

"You don't know!" Cotty said in dismay. "All those vessels out there, and you don't know which one?"

"All I saw was the small boat with the man Bonney and the women rowing. All that water. I am frightened of water, Cotty!" John said wretchedly. "In my fright the dreaming was broken, and I could see no more."

Frustration gripped Cotty as his gaze raked the harbor. It would take them all night to row from ship to ship, and even then they might be too late. Meanwhile, Hope was out there somewhere, and God only knew what was happening to her!

# CHAPTER TWENTY-FOUR

By THE TIME Bonney found an empty dory moored to a small dock, it had grown quite dark; and Hope was sure that no one would see them and come to their rescue. Charity had revived, but she was extremely groggy; and when Bonney dumped her roughly into the dory, Hope protested. "Please! If you have any decency.... She's hurt!"

Bonney motioned Hope into the boat with his pistol. "Keep your mouth shut, woman, or you'll get the same. Now get her onto the seat. You will both have to row."

"Row! How can she row in such condition?"

"She looks fine to me; mayhap a little addled, but she doesn't need her wits about her to row."

"You are a monster, sir!"

Bonney grinned cruelly. "Most wenches don't think so. Certainly your sister did not." He leaned forward, his crooked face dark and threatening. "Now pick up the oars and row, both of you!" He aimed the pistol at them. "I still have need of you, but I will kill the both of you without compunction if you do not obey me."

Charity obeyed docilely, her face slack. Hope took the other oar, and they began rowing in the direction that Bonney indicated, toward a merchant vessel anchored several hundred yards out in the harbor. Its lighted lanterns hung both fore and aft.

Charity was simply too weak to match Hope's strokes, and the small boat began to veer off course. Bonney chafed and swore at them, and finally ordered Hope to take over. Hope's arms and shoulders were already aching and she soon felt blisters forming on her hands.

"Pick up the pace," Bonney said savagely. "A snail could make better progress."

"I'm doing the best that I can!" Hope argued.

"If you don't row faster, your sister will feel the barrel of my pistol again, and this time the few wits she has will be permanently scrambled."

Hope, fearing for Charity, put all her remaining strength into the oar. They drew near the ship, and at last the curved side of the vessel rose before them, smelling of tar and salt.

"Halloo, the ship!" Bonney called up.

In a moment a lantern appeared at the railing. "Who is hailing the *Saragossa*?"

"Tell your captain it is Charles Bonney, Governor Bligh's chief aide. I ask permission to come aboard."

The light vanished. Shortly, it reappeared, and a Jacob's ladder slithered down the side of the ship.

In a tense whisper Bonney said, "Now, if I hear one word from either of you, no matter what I say to the captain it will go badly for you. But if you follow my lead, I shall let you live."

Hope put her arms around Charity, who was slumped in uncharacteristic silence. "You wouldn't dare harm us in front of the ship's captain and his men!"

"Are you willing to risk that? I am a desperate man." He bared his teeth in that savage grin. "If I am caught here and sent back to England under arrest, whatever hopes I have for a distinguished career will be shattered forever. But if I return of my own free will, there will be no stigma attached to my name. This Captain Bostwick and his men are little better than pirates. His livelihood comes from smuggling rum, and he cannot risk exposure or even a ruckus."

"You think I am a fool?" Hope said angrily. "You're not going to just let us go!"

Bonney smiled again, his features faintly illuminated by the aft lantern. "If you behave yourselves, no harm will come to you. When Captain Bostwick is ready to sail, you and your sister will be placed in this dory, and you can row ashore."

Hope was certain that he was lying. "Then why not let us go now?"

"Because I need you as hostages until we sail, in case any corps officers come out to the *Saragossa* looking for me. Now enough talk!" he snapped. "Up the ladder before me!"

She hesitated, torn. Should she make a stand here and now?

Bonney's head darted forward. "Now!" he hissed. He seized Charity by the shoulders and pulled her against him, raising the pistol. "Or I club her and throw her into the water."

"All right," Hope said submissively. She took Charity's hands and placed them on a rung of the ladder, realizing that her sister had not spoken a word since she had recovered consciousness. "Come, Charity, we have to climb the ladder to the ship," she said gently.

As the dory rocked and bumped against the side of the ship, Charity hesitantly grasped the ladder. Bending over, Hope raised Charity's right foot and placed it upon the bottom rung. "You must climb, Charity. Please!"

Slowly, her sister began to climb. Hope followed her, her head back so she could be alert should Charity falter. It was difficult and awkward work, but they reached the railing without incident. A seaman gave them a hand over the railing, where they stepped into a pool of light. A man with a full black beard stood nearby, scowling darkly.

The instant Bonney reached the deck behind them, the man said harshly, "What is the meaning of this, Master Bonney?"

Bonney said, "Master Bostwick, I am here under orders from Governor Bligh. I am to sail to England with you."

Captain Bostwick laughed. "You take me for a fool, sir? Your Captain Bligh is no longer governor of the colony."

"And that is precisely why he is sending me to England with all haste," Bonney said smoothly. "His Majesty's government must be notified as soon as possible as to what has transpired here." He took the captain by the elbow and moved him away, all the while talking animatedly but in a low voice, so that Hope could not overhear.

Charity mumbled something and slumped. Hope put an arm around her sister, supporting her, and turned her attention again to Bonney and the captain. She thought of speaking up, of exposing Bonney; but what assurance did she have that the captain would believe her? And if he was the villain Bonney said he was, would the man care? If Charity was functioning properly, Hope could have taken a chance and jumped overboard with her; but her sister was certainly in no condition to take such a risk. Hope decided to wait until Charity was herself again, and then seize the first chance to escape.

She saw Captain Bostwick staring at them as he said something to Bonney. Bonney said something in turn, and Hope caught two words, "my betrothed...."

After a few minutes, the captain threw up his hands, turning away. Bonney came toward them then, smiling blandly. He picked up his satchel from where he had left it by the railing.

"It is all settled, Mistress Blackstock. I am to sail with the ship. But Captain Bostwick refuses to sail until the tide, and that does not happen for two hours yet. Meanwhile, there is an empty cabin where you may rest."

"Why don't you let us leave now?"

His smile vanished. "I have already told you, not until just before we sail. Besides..." He smiled again, craftily. "Your sister looks like she could use a lie down. She is in no condition to handle an oar right now. So come along, my dear, and have a nice rest. You'll be the better for it."

Filled with misgivings, Hope followed Bonney's directions, helping Charity below deck. In a dimly lit passageway, Bonney stopped before a cabin door, opened it and stood back, motioning them in.

"I'll be back to fetch you just before the ship is to sail," Bonney said, closing the door quickly.

Hope heard the snick of a bolt being thrown, and with a sickening feeling she realized he was locking them in! Just then, Charity moaned, and Hope turned all her attention to her sister, helping her to the bunk. The cabin was tiny, and Hope noticed that the one porthole was clamped shut, making it very hot and stuffy.

Charity blinked up at her, her eyes seeming to focus for the first time. "Hope? Where are we?"

"We're on board a ship, the *Saragossa*. Bonney forced us to come here. Don't you remember?"

Charity shook her head and cried out in pain, her hand going to the back of her head. "My head, it hurts. I remember seeing you, and then there was this terrible pain. Everything seems so vague." She buried her face in her hands.

On a washstand against the bulkhead was a pitcher of water, a basin and a cloth. Hope poured water into the basin; and sitting beside her sister, she wet the cloth and gently applied it to the swelling on the back of her head. Charity flinched, then set her teeth and endured.

After a moment, she groped for Hope's hand and squeezed. She said wretchedly, "I'm sorry, Hope. I have been such a little fool! I should have listened to you and Cotty."

Hope thought that this was hardly the time or the place for a reprimand, so she merely said, "It's all right, dear."

"No, it's not all right, and when this is over, I will make it up to you." A look of alarm crossed her face, and she clutched Hope's hand more tightly. "What is Charles going to do with us?"

"He says he is holding us hostage until the ship sails, then he will let us go."

"How can we believe him?" Charity cried. "He is a liar and a blackguard. How can we believe him now?"

"We just have to pray that he has some decency."

"He has no decency!" Charity broke off, biting her lip. Then her face brightened. "But maybe Cotty will come for us. He must be wondering where we are by this time. He will, won't he, Hope?" She gave Hope a pleading look. "Please tell me that he will. Cotty has always taken care of us. He won't let anything bad happen to us."

Hope experienced a surge of annoyance. Charity was acting like a child again, expecting Cotty to appear, like a white knight, to fight off the dragons. Of course, *she* also hoped that Cotty would appear, yet she realized that it was simply wishful thinking. However, she said reassuringly, "Of course, Charity, Cotty will come."

"When he does, when everything is all right again, I promise that I shall always take his advice." Charity added hastily, "And yours, too, Hope."

"There, there." Hope cradled her sister's head on her shoulder, caressing her hair, mouthing words of reassurance as she would to a frightened child. Charity's eyes fluttered closed, and she slipped into sleep.

Hope was thinking of stretching out on the bunk next to her sister when noises overhead caused her to stiffen. She heard muffled voices giving orders, masts creaking as sails were unfurled, and then the clank of the anchor chain as it was being drawn up.

Bonney had lied to her! The captain was not waiting for the tide; he was preparing to sail now!

As Hope moved, Charity's eyes flew open, and she paled at the look of alarm on her sister's face. "What is it, Hope? What's wrong?"

"Bonney lied! The ship is readying to sail *now*!" She jumped up and ran to the door, screaming, "Let us out!"

Even as she screamed, even as she beat upon the door with her fists, Hope knew that it was hopeless. If anyone heard, they would simply ignore her.

Whatever Bonney had in mind for them, it did not involve letting them go.

"I'M REASONABLY CERTAIN that Bonney will use a ship bound for England," Cotty told the other three men as they hurried toward the harbormaster's office. "At least, I pray that I am right," he added grimly. "If we can find out which ships are sailing for England, it will eliminate a goodly number of vessels."

When they consulted with the harbormaster Cotty found, much to his relief, that of the ships in the harbor, only five were due to sail for England. Of that five, two had only recently arrived and had yet to unload their cargoes.

"Only three vessels to check," Cotty said. "I only hope that my surmise about Bonney is correct."

"Then let's get started," Stuart said urgently.

"How about placing the matter in the hands of the authorities?" Hugh asked.

"*What* authority?" Cotty said. "We're not even sure at this time where the real authority lies."

"You're right, Cotty, we don't know," Hugh said with a faint smile.

Using the harbormaster's longboat, they began their search, checking the first vessel on the list. As they rowed close to it, Cotty turned to John Myers. "John, does this one look familiar?"

"I do not know, Cotty," John said with a helpless shrug. "My dreaming was broken before I could see the ship clearly."

"What *is* all this about dreaming?" Stuart demanded.

"Never mind," Cotty said. "It's far too complicated to explain right now. After we get Hope and Charity out of the clutches of Bonney, I'll try to explain."

The first ship yielded no information about Bonney and the Blackstock sisters. Time was passing quickly, and Cotty felt despair rising in him. They might already be too late.

Then, as they rowed up to the second ship, Cotty felt his hopes rise. A dory was tied against the hull. He could just make out the name of the ship in the dim light; it was the *Saragossa*, and it was making preparations to get under way!

As the longboat bumped against the side of the ship, Cotty cupped his hands around his mouth and shouted up, "Ahoy, the ship!"

After a moment, a man's head adorned with a seaman's cap appeared in a circle of lantern light at the rail. "Who hails the *Saragossa*?"

Cotty nudged Stuart. In a low voice, he said, "I think this is the one, Stuart. You take over."

Stuart stood up in the rocking boat. "I am Stuart Williams, aide to Governor Bligh. I wish to come aboard. Inform your captain, if you please."

After an interminable wait a bearded face appeared at the railing. "I am Captain Bostwick, master of the *Saragossa*. We are about to get under way. What is it you wish, sir?"

"As I told your crew member, I am the governor's aide, Stuart Williams."

The captain threw back his head with a bellow of laughter. "We are indeed blessed. We have another of the governor's aides on board."

Stuart's voice quickened with excitement. "Charles Bonney?"

"That is the fellow, sir."

"And he has two ladies with him?"

A voice shouted angrily from behind the captain, and the man turned away for a moment. Then he reappeared. "I don't know about them being ladies, but Master Bonney has two wenches with him, yes."

"Charles Bonney has taken the women against their will. We demand to come aboard," Stuart said strongly.

"On what authority, sir? I am not ignorant of what has transpired in Sydney. William Bligh is deposed."

"On the grounds of common decency, sir. Charles Bonney is nothing but a criminal and must be punished for what he has done."

The captain was silent for a moment, then he shrugged his massive shoulders. "Very well, sir." He bellowed, "Lower the anchor again, men, and let down the ladder!"

The anchor chain began to clank as it was lowered, and the rope ladder snaked down the side of the ship.

Cotty placed a hand on John's shoulder. "John, you had better stay in the boat. I'm sure you understand the reason."

John nodded. In the dim light his face was concerned. "You will rescue Mistress Hope?"

"You can depend on it."

Stuart was already scrambling up the ladder. Hugh was next, and Cotty went up last.

As Cotty stepped onto the deck alongside Stuart and Hugh, he found their way barred by the hulking figure of the bearded captain.

"What is this about?" Bostwick demanded. "Bonney said that he brought the women along for their own protection, that one is his betrothed and the other her sister."

Cotty rested his hand on the pistol in his belt and stepped forward, his gaze raking the deck. All he could see were several sailors bustling about. "The man is a liar, captain, as well as a blackguard. He took the women as hostage against the rebel soldiers. We demand that you give him over to us, as well as the ladies."

"Demand, is it?" Captain Bostwick growled. "I am not accustomed to obeying demands on my own ship, sir!" Then he raised and lowered his shoulders. "But damn, if it be the truth you're telling me, I'll wash my hands of it. If Bonney is what you say he is, I'll not be standing in your way."

"Where are the ladies?" Cotty asked.

"Resting in a cabin belowdeck."

"And Bonney?"

"Why, he is . . ." The captain turned, looking around. "He was here, not five minutes ago, making *his* demands that I deny permission for you to come aboard.''

HOPE HAD POUNDED on the cabin door until her hands were bruised, and had screamed until she was hoarse. Then she stopped with her head cocked, listening to a noise from the deck above. It sounded like the anchor was being dropped. Her heart began to beat wildly with hope, and she spun around. ''Charity, they're letting out the anchor again!''

Charity jumped up. ''They're going to let us go!''

''It's possible . . .''

She whirled back to the door as she heard the bolt being drawn back. It opened, and a fiendishly grinning Bonney stood there, his pistol aimed at her. He motioned with it.

''Out of the cabin, bitch!''

''You're letting us go?'' She half turned to Charity. ''Come, Charity.''

''Not her,'' Bonney snapped. ''Just you.''

Hope stared at him in bewilderment. ''But I don't understand . . .''

''Out!'' He motioned again with the pistol.

As Hope reluctantly left the cabin, Bonney gave her a shove, sending her staggering along the passageway. She heard the bolt slam home. Knocking against the bulkhead, she looked back. ''You can't just leave my sister in there.''

''I can and I will.'' He was close to her, taking her arm in a firm grip and turning her around. She felt the muzzle of the pistol against the small of her back. ''Everything has gone to hell. That damned captain wants to give me over to them. But they don't have me yet, goddamn them! You, wench, will be my ticket off this ship!"

"Give you over to them? Who are they?"

"Stuart Williams and Cotty Starke!"

Hope's heart leaped with gladness. Cotty had come for her! And for the first time she realized that she had not once thought of Stuart since this nightmare began. When she had thought of being rescued, it was Cotty who had been her savior.

"But if you're thinking that that precious pair will help you, disabuse yourself of the notion." The pistol prodded. "I'm going to march you right past them and down the Jacob's ladder to the dory. If they so much as twitch an eyebrow, you are a dead woman!"

COTTY, STUART AND HUGH had started in a rush for the steps leading belowdeck, and had almost reached them when Hope's head and shoulders emerged.

"Hope!" Cotty exclaimed. "Thank God you're all right..."

"Don't come any closer, Cotty!" she cried. "He'll shoot."

Cotty had already come to a stop when he saw Bonney behind her.

"She's right, Master Starke," Bonney said in a voice high and shrill with hysteria. "I have a pistol at her back, and she goes off the ship with me. One move from either of you, and she dies!"

"Now Charles," Stuart said in a soothing voice. "There is no need for this. The rebellion is over. The worst you face is some time in jail."

"You're lying!" Bonney said, his voice climbing even higher. "I overheard the corps officers talking.

They intend to hang Bligh and his aides as traitors.''

"If you heard that, Charles, it was the rum talking. They would not dare do that, and they have no such intentions, I assure you.''

"Even if what you say is true, I'll face the lash or imprisonment for taking the two women. Nobody lashes Charles Bonney!'' All the while he talked, Bonney was edging along the railing toward the Jacob's ladder, with Hope always a shield between him and the others. "The woman stays with me until I am safely away from Sydney. Now, I'm going down the ladder first, with Mistress Blackstock climbing down after me. My pistol will always be on her, and she will die if she makes a wrong move, or if one of you is foolish enough to rush me.''

He reached the spot where the ladder was hooked over the railing, darted a quick glance to the boat below and then searched for the first rung of the ladder with his foot. "Now, we go over, Mistress Blackstock. I shall be only one rung below you, so we shall be in a lover's embrace.'' His harsh laughter jarred Hope. "And my pistol shall always be at your back, in the event your friends try anything rash.''

Hope's heart was pounding so hard she felt giddy. Backing down the swaying ladder, she was certain she would fall. She went down step by step, feeling blindly for each rung with her feet. Bonney was only a foot below her, and she shuddered in revulsion at his nearness. Just before her eyes were below the level of the deck, Hope sent a last despairing glance to Cotty.

As Hope's head disappeared below the deck, Cotty and Stuart hurried as quickly as possible to the railing to peer down.

Stuart whispered in Cotty's ear, "You realize he's not going to let her live."

Cotty was silent, knowing that Stuart was right, and knowing that if he lost Hope, all that he had—the money, the inns, the power—meant nothing. He *must* save her.

"What are you going to do?" Stuart asked.

"What do you suggest?"

"We can't just let him row off with her. When they reach the boat, I'm going to dive in next to it."

"That won't do, Stuart," Cotty said firmly. "He'd kill her before you could reach her. We'll have to let them get away from the ship, then take the other boat and follow them, hoping for some kind of a chance at Bonney."

JOHN HAD WAITED in fear for Hope, always acutely aware of the dark, foreboding water stretching away from him on all sides. When he saw Hope start down the ladder, his spirits soared. She was safe! Then he realized that something was wrong. The man coming down ahead of her was not Cotty or Stuart Williams.

John shrank into the shadow of the ship's hull and waited, scarcely breathing. And then, when they were halfway down the ladder, he recognized the man—Charles Bonney!

In a quandary, he waited a few moments longer. Unless Bonney turned his head and looked at him—and there was no reason for him to do so since all his attention was focused on Hope—John did not think the man would see him. Then he saw that Bonney held something in his left hand, a pistol, which was against Hope's back.

Very carefully, John got to his feet, staying crouched in the shadows, just a step away from where Bonney would step when he reached the end of the ladder. He waited until Bonney stepped into the longboat, which started to rock; and then John moved, wrapping his arms around Bonney from behind, knocking the pistol aside and down with his right hand. The pistol discharged, Bonney yelled, and John felt the pistol ball strike his foot. The pain was excruciating, and he knew that he would not be able to fight Bonney on equal terms with the injured foot.

There was only one alternative, and he took it without hesitation. With his arms tight around Bonney, he jumped into the sea. The last thing he heard as they went under was Hope screaming his name.

Laden with the weight of their clothing, the two men went under at once. As the water closed over him, terror seized John like a ravenous animal, and panic threatened to overwhelm him. He wanted desperately to let go his grip on Bonney and try to reach the surface; but he grimly hung on to the man, who was struggling wildly, kicking at John's feet and legs, his hands reaching over his head in a frantic effort to grasp handfuls of John's hair. One flailing boot heel struck John's injured foot, and the pain was such that John's grip was broken momentarily.

Taking advantage of the opportunity, Bonney spun around in the water and started to propel himself toward the surface. In a desperate lunge, moving in a slow motion against the heaviness of the water, John had Bonney again, his hands closing this time around the other man's throat. Bonney tore at the hands, but John held fast. Bonney used his knees, striking John in the stomach and the groin. When that failed, he searched for John's eyes with his thumbs. John held on.

Dimly, through the pain, John could feel that they were in the grip of a powerful current now, which was carrying them rapidly away from the ship.

Bright lights flashed before his eyes, and his lungs burned for lack of air; yet his hands continued to tighten, putting more pressure on Bonney's throat. John realized that his strength was beginning to fail, but there was only room in his mind for one single thought: this man must not be allowed to hurt Hope again. Exultation rose in him as he felt Bonney's struggles growing weaker. He well knew that his own death was near, yet his fear was gone. Bonney gave a convulsive shudder and went limp. John still held on, as a strange peace filled him.

His mouth opened, gulping for air, and the water rushed in. John's last thought was of Hope.

Locked together in death's embrace, the two men spun slowly, as the current carried them out and down.

AT THAT MOMENT Cotty clambered down the ladder with so much haste that he fell, rocking the longboat dangerously. He was on his feet instantly, and Hope fell into his arms, sobbing.

"Are you all right, my love?" he asked, caressing her hair. "If anything had happened to you...! I've been such a fool, and I..."

Hope sobbed in exasperation. Cotty was finally saying the words she had wanted so much to hear, but it was not the time or the place. "I'm all right," she said, "but John has gone overboard with Bonney. Oh, Cotty! He can't swim!"

"My God, you're right!" Cotty squinted into the darkness. The water was smooth and unbroken, and neither John nor Charles Bonney could be seen. He heard Stuart join them in the longboat. Cotty was already tearing at his clothes. "I don't know whether I can find him in the dark, but I must try." Down to his drawers, he dived into the water and began to swim.

Hope's glance went to Stuart, who was staring at her intently. "You love Cotty, don't you?" It was more of a statement than a question.

"There's no time for that now," she said impatiently. "John must be found or he'll drown. And I must see if Charity is all right."

"John?" he said blankly. "You mean the black fella?"

"He risked his life to save me. Didn't you hear what we said? John can't swim!"

"Oh . . . of course, I'll do what I can."

Quickly, Stuart removed his shoes and coat, and then went into the water after Cotty.

The boat rocked as a weight came down on it, and Hope glanced around to see Hugh Marston.

"Miss Blackstock." He inclined his head. "What has taken place? Where are Cotty and Stuart Williams?"

Briefly, she told him what had happened.

He gazed over the expanse of black water. "I very much doubt they will find the men. I would join in their search, but I, like your friend John, cannot swim.''

For a time Hope and Hugh listened to the voices of Cotty and Stuart as they called out, and to the splashing sounds as they swam and dived. After about twenty minutes, Cotty swam back to the boat. He hung on to the side, his chest heaving. "I don't think we're going to find him, Hope," he said. His teeth chattered. "It's so dark."

"You're not going to give up, are you?"

"No, not yet." He turned and swam away.

Hope stared after him for a moment, then made a decision. "I'm going up on deck, Master Marston." She climbed the ladder and asked to see Captain Bostwick.

When he finally appeared, scowling and grumpy, she demanded he lower boats and have his men look for John.

"This John, he's a black fella, ain't he?" Bostwick asked.

"What does that have to do with it? He's a human being, and he risked his life for me, knowing he can't swim!"

The captain shrugged carelessly. "I have no men to spare for such a search. All this commotion has disrupted my ship enough as it is. Besides, it would do no good. After all this time, the two men are dead, you can depend on that, Mistress Blackstock."

"Then would it be too much to ask for the loan of some blankets?" she asked quietly.

He shrugged again. "I'll have my cabin boy find some for you."

"Thank you, captain, for your generosity," she said with contempt. "While he does that, I will go below and fetch my sister."

When Hope opened the cabin door, Charity flew at her in a temper. "Why have you left me down here all this time alone? What is happening?"

Hope looked at her sister critically; she seemed to be fully recovered now. "A lot has happened, Charity, and I haven't had time to come for you. You were safer here." Once again, she related what had taken place.

"Then Charles is dead?"

"It would appear so, and John as well. You'd best come with me now."

On deck, by the ladder, Hope found two ratty blankets. Picking them up, she climbed into the longboat with Charity right behind her. As Hope stepped down, Cotty swam up. Hugh stretched an arm down and gave him a hand into the boat. Cotty was shivering, water dripping off him.

"It's hopeless. There is no sign of either man. We have to assume that both are dead. Certainly John, since he couldn't swim, and I'm sure he took Bonney to the bottom with him."

Hope handed him one of the blankets, and he began to dry himself as best he could. Stuart appeared at the side of the boat. "Find anything?" Cotty asked him.

"Not a sign of either one."

"Come aboard and get yourself dry, Stuart. We've done all we can."

As Stuart clambered into the longboat, accepting the other blanket from Hope, she stared off into the darkness, feeling immeasurably sad, her eyes hot with unshed tears. John was dead; there was no longer any doubt. In all the years he had been with them, she had come to take his presence for granted, and she knew now that she had never fully appreciated him. She had grown very fond of him, but of course had never dared tell him so, since she knew that his feelings for her were much stronger.

"We might as well row in," Cotty decided. "The bodies will be found eventually, washed up on the shore somewhere."

DAWN WAS JUST BREAKING as they rowed up to Hospital Wharf. On the way, Cotty and Hugh had told Hope of the events that had taken place at Government House, and that the rebel NSW Corps had taken over the government of the colony. Smoke from the bonfires that had burned all night still hung over the town, and even from the wharf Hope could see several men and women lying where they had fallen in drunken sprawls.

She stood quietly beside Cotty after he helped her out of the boat. The streets were empty of people, except for those in drunken slumber. Appalled, Hope said, "You said no shots were fired in anger, and no one was killed, yet the whole village looks devastated, as if the entire population had been massacred."

Hugh laughed softly. "The population has been devastated by free rum."

"And it's all for nothing," Hope said dully. "All that has happened is that we have exchanged one tyrant for another."

Hugh glanced at her with respect. "You are indeed correct, my dear, except that some of us will have to suffer for that change."

"I disagree," Cotty said unexpectedly. "Something *has* been accomplished. Oh, I do agree that tavern owners such as myself will likely feel the sting of Macarthur's wrath. But I think this uprising will be the beginning of a change for the better in the attitude of the Crown toward us when the news reaches London."

"In what way will it change, Cotty?" Hugh asked skeptically.

"Heretofore, New South Wales was looked upon as nothing but a penal colony. Few were concerned with how it was governed. I believe this will shock them greatly, and well could be the turning point in our relations with the Crown. Remember, they lost the colonies in North America not too long ago through a bloody revolution. Although this was bloodless, I think it will force the governing powers in England to pay closer attention to affairs here, lest our next revolution be fought for freedom from the Mother Country and not over rum."

"You may well be right. I sincerely hope so, my young friend." Grinning, Hugh clapped him on the shoulder. "And now, I think I should check to see if my establishment is still standing. I bid you good day, Cotty, Master Williams." He dipped his head at Hope and Charity. "And ladies."

Stuart spoke for the first time since they had left the longboat. "Hope?"

She looked at him and said gently, "I'm sorry, Stuart."

With a melancholy look he said gruffly, "I thought as much. I'm sorry, too, Hope. Goodbye." He started away.

Charity made a startled sound, staring at her sister. "Does that mean what I think it means?"

"I suppose it does, Charity."

Charity was already in motion, calling, "Stuart, wait for me!"

When Stuart halted, turning back, she slowed to a walk, that provocative walk she had perfected of recent years. She smiled up at Stuart, linking arms with him, and they walked off together, Charity's face turned up as she talked animatedly.

Staring after them, Hope laughed. "Last night, she promised me faithfully that she would change." She shook her head ruefully. "I should have known better. She will never change."

"I may be a little dense this morning..." Cotty rubbed a hand across his mouth. "But I'm not sure that I understand what that was all about."

She looked at him with a grave face. "Yes, you do, Cotty Starke."

His glance skipped away and he mumbled, "I don't know what you mean."

"Cotty!"

He finally looked at her. "If you're referring to what I said earlier..."

"Cotty!"

"All right." He placed his hands on her shoulders and gazed down into her eyes. "Will you marry me, Hope Blackstock?"

"I will marry you, Cotty Starke," she said with the same grave face. And then her face lit with an incandescent smile, and she threw her arms around him. "Oh, yes, my love!"

Their mouths met in an ardent kiss. His lips were rough, demanding, and Hope responded in kind, pressing against him. When he took his mouth away, she was breathless, with relief and pleasure.

"This is hardly the place for this," Cotty said huskily. "Let's go home where we can have some privacy."

He put a protective arm around her shoulders, and they started home. The Rocks was usually astir with people at that time, but on this morning, it was deserted. Hope did not know if the events of last night meant a new beginning for the colony, as Cotty had prophesied; but she knew, in her heart of hearts, that it meant the beginning of a new life for her. She snuggled closer to Cotty and was content.

# EPILOGUE

By 1810 A NEW GOVERNOR, Lachlan Macquarie, a just and fair man, ruled the colony of New South Wales. Major Johnston was court-martialed and cashiered, and John Macarthur was temporarily exiled to England to testify at Johnston's trial. The Rum Corps was disbanded, and the grip of the rum monopolists was broken. William Bligh demanded harsh reprisals against all the rebels, but his demands were ignored. In the end, he returned to England, where he lived out his life in relative obscurity.

And Cotty and Hope Starke had a boy child they named John.

*Dear Friends and Readers:*

Of all the natural treasures of our world, precious gems are perhaps the most fascinating. Beyond their value and rarity, we are drawn by their beauty and by a quality difficult to name, an almost mystic power.

It is this special world, the world of great gems, that I chose for the background of my next novel, *Sapphire*.

The story begins in the West End of London, in the autumn of 1880. It is shortly before dawn, and a middle-aged woman named Adelaide Paxton is hurrying homeward from her job as a charwoman at Slostrums, the famous gem dealers, when she hears the sound of a baby crying from the recesses of a fog-shrouded alleyway. On inspection, Adelaide finds a baby girl hidden in a carpetbag. This is how the young woman who will become Regina Paxton is introduced to the world.

As she grows into womanhood, Regina becomes fascinated by the gems she sees at her adopted mother's place of employment, particularly a large star sapphire, and despite Adelaide's advice, she becomes determined to make a place for herself in the man's world of the jewelry trade.

This determination gains Regina a lowly place at Slostrums, where she begins as a gemstone cleaner and sorter. But she will not be kept down, and her intelligence and drive soon start her on the first step of her journey to prominence and success in the jewelry trade.

Her search for her dream and its symbol, the star sapphire, takes her from the lovely and primitive Vale of Kashmir to the sophisticated world of New York City, and from the arms of Brian MacBride, the wild and improvident Irish gem hunter, to those of William Logan, a sensitive and understanding gem buyer for Tiffany's.

I hope that you will all join me in visiting the special world of gemstones and Regina Paxton in September 1989, when *Sapphire* is published by Worldwide Library.

Affectionately,

*Patricia Matthews*